RIVALS
in the
TUDOR
COURT

Books by D. L. Bogdan

SECRETS OF THE TUDOR COURT

RIVALS IN THE TUDOR COURT

Published by Kensington Publishing Corporation

RIVALS
in the
TUDOR
COURT

D. L. BOGDAN

KENSINGTON BOOKS
www.kensingtonbooks.com

KENSINGTON BOOKS are published by

Kensington Publishing Corp.
119 West 40th Street
New York, NY 10018

ISBN-13: 978-0-7582-4200-6
ISBN-10: 0-7582-4200-X

First Kensington Trade Paperback Printing: May 2011
10 9 8 7 6 5 4 3 2 1

Printed in the United States of America

For my sailor

Acknowledgments

I want to thank first and foremost my wonderful agent, Elizabeth Pomada, who has tirelessly lent her time, wisdom, patience, and encouragement throughout this journey. I also want to thank my editor, John Scognamiglio, of Kensington Publishing, and his wonderful team, all of whom have helped me improve my work, always taking time to answer my questions and guide me when I feared losing my way. I want to thank my favorite panel of critics, including my mother, Cindy Bogdan, along with Cathy Renner and Candy Baer, who always see my work before I get brave enough to send it out! I ride on your confidence in me, girls! I also want to thank the libraries, namely McMillan Memorial Library of Wisconsin Rapids, Wisconsin, and the Marshfield Public Library, where I always found a place of solace for working and conducting research. Again, this novel could not have been possible without consulting the work of Dr. David M. Head, whose wonderful biography of Thomas Howard, *The Ebbs and Flows of Fortune: The Life of Thomas Howard, Third Duke of Norfolk,* provided so much documentation and other resources to authenticate the historical accuracy of this book. In addition, I want to thank the readers, bloggers, reviewers, and fellow authors who have encouraged me along the way and helped me promote my debut novel *Secrets of the Tudor Court* (Kensington)—you know who you are! You have all taught me so much about how to handle this new adventure and I value you more than I can say. Not least of all, I must thank my wonderful husband, Kim, my number one fan, my encourager, my supporter, my forever sailor. I couldn't do it without you, Chief! Finally, I want to thank my children, Quinn, Cody, Ashley, and Kristina, for allowing me the space and time I need to work. You are the best! I thank all of you from the bottom of my heart and pray you all enjoy my work.

BOOK ONE

Thomas

The Tower of London

Thomas Howard, January 1547

Two bitches, a bewildered dolt, and a hothead have condemned me to this wretched place. The first wench would be my lovely wife, Elizabeth, whose list of virtues is far too extensive to catalogue. The second is my mistress, Bess Holland, who found it expedient to trade her lover for jewels and lands. The dolt is my daughter Mary, whose endless capacity for ineptness exempts her from being entirely to blame. But the hothead! The hothead is my own son Henry, Earl of Surrey, that talented boy I put such store in. My Surrey. Surrey, who claims to loathe upstarts with all his being yet decides to become one himself, quartering his arms with that of Edward the Confessor (a right reserved for kings alone!), bragging about what we Howards would achieve while ruling through Prince Edward when he comes to power, even plotting the kidnapping of His little Highness. . . . Oh, I cannot think of it! Fools!

It is cold in the Tower. Dampness seeps through the bare stone walls, rats scamper about, eager to feast upon my flesh should my soul decide to vacate it.

"You will have to wait," I tell them.

I lie on my bed and scowl at the ceiling. This will not do. I have written Henry VIII. I have groveled and sniveled and humiliated myself to the fullest extent. But why would he break with tradition to spare me? What am I saying? It is thinking like this that will kill me. I have never entertained such notions before. I have always survived. I have always pressed on.

I am Thomas Howard.

Armor

"It was a vulgar display!" cries my grandfather, Baron John Howard, slamming his fist on the dining table, regarding my father, Sir Thomas, with hard black eyes. "Children, Thomas! Five-year-old brats—my God, it's like handing a dukedom to that one there!" He waves an impatient hand at me. I wish I could crawl under the table to sit with my dog, but the last time I did that the baron pulled me up by the arm so hard that it ached for days. "That daft king would rather see two children wed than honor me with what is due," he goes on. "*I* am the rightful Duke of Norfolk! Mowbray was my cousin, after all! It is fitting that I should have been named heir instead of his sniveling, drooling girl-child!"

Sir Thomas purses his lips, annoyed, though whether it is with my grandfather or the situation, I cannot discern. He shifts on the bench, his thick hands toying with a piece of bread. "It was most unfair, my lord," he says. "We can thank God, however, that the king had the grace to knight me at the wedding ceremony."

"Oh, yes, thank God for that," spits the baron, but I have the distinct feeling he is not thankful at all.

I look under the table at my favorite dog, a gray mongrel named Rain, offering him a reassuring smile.

"What are you thinking over there?" barks the baron.

It takes a moment to realize he is addressing me. I right myself. "Nothing, my lord," I tell him.

"Don't lie to me, boy," the baron hisses. His face is crimson; a thick vein pulsates in his neck. "You find this amusing, do you? Something to laugh at?"

I shake my head, my cheeks burning. A lump swells in my throat. I reach down to lay a hand on my dog's head, reassuring myself with the soft fur. Soon I can get away from this tirade and run outside with Rain, loyal Rain. I shall lay my head upon his warm side and find shapes in the clouds with my brother Neddy.

"Do enlighten us with your anecdotes, child," says the baron, leaning back, gripping the edge of the table with slim-fingered hands.

I don't even know what an anecdote is. I begin to tremble. "I was—I was—"

" 'You were'? 'You were'?" The baron's voice has risen an octave in mockery.

My lip quivers.

The old man's hand springs across the table to grip my collar, pulling me halfway across platters of food. My breeches are ruined. Rain is barking somewhere in the background. My knee is digging into something, the corner of a tray perhaps, but I am too terrified to look down. I can only stare into the dark face of the baron in horror.

His breath reeks of spirits. I cough.

"Do not mock me, boy," he seethes.

"I wasn't mocking you!" I cry, my mind scrambling to recall my exact offense.

"Thomas, best rein in your brat," cries my grandfather as he brings me across his knee before the hall of family and servants and liveried guards. His hand, when he brings it across my bared bottom, hurts indeed, but the eyes of the hall bearing witness to my shame is a pain far greater. "You will be taught to respect your betters, lad!"

At this moment my dog launches himself at the baron, tearing into his ankle with a strangled growl.

Grandfather unleashes a howl, pushing me from his knee to the floor. I reach out in terror, trying to pull Rain off the old man, but the baron has reached him first. In one swift move he grabs the creature by the scruff of the neck, pulling him up onto his hind legs while retrieving his dagger.

"No!" I scream, hot tears streaming down my cheeks.

The baron does not look at me once. He slashes Rain's throat, discarding the animal on the floor and returning to his seat. He takes in a deep breath, wipes his hands on his linen, and commences to eat his mutton.

I crawl toward my slain dog. Steaming blood oozes from his silvery throat. I do not know what to do. I start trying to push it back inside him. I press my hand to his throat.

I regard the baron, whose back is to me, hoping to project as much hatred into my eyes as is possible, but it does not matter. He does not see me. He is eating his supper, complaining of King Edward IV, who has wronged him so.

I am glad, I think to myself, that he was denied his grand title. Indeed, I hope every misery possible is heaped upon the man until he draws his dying breath.

"Tom!"

My grandmother's voice is stern.

I turn toward her, blinking back tears. Rain's blood is slick against my hand.

"Take that thing out of here and bury it," she orders.

As I gather my pet in my arms, I hear her tell the baron, "Really, my lord, you should have commenced with that unpleasantness elsewhere. It has positively ruined my appetite."

I take Rain outside, laying him in the snow; I have no idea where to bury him. I will not think of it now. I cannot. Icy tears slide down my cheeks as I remove my shirt and wind it about his throat, then, shivering, rest my head on his side, raising my eyes to the heavens, seeking out the clouds.

One of them looks like a dagger.

Three years later my grandfather announces the death of little Anne Mowbray, King Edward IV's eight-year-old daughter-in-law and heiress to the dukedom of Norfolk.

"I have lost all to a child-prince. Richard has won the day," he laments.

We are in the "war room," a large chamber devoted to maps and a store for the family's finest suits of armor. The baron is standing over the large mahogany table, tracing the unattainable Mowbray lands with his index finger.

My father shrugs. He is not as afraid of the baron as the rest of the family is. They are a bit alike, though my father, Sir Thomas, is more subtle in his approach, favoring locking someone away in a chamber without food for a few days as opposed to wasting his energy on the administration of beatings.

I am certain to keep my face void of expression during their exchange. After the countless lashings I have endured, I know anything—a blink, a dreamy smile, a twitch—can set Grandfather off. I stay still. Calm. I have practiced in the glass, this look of impassivity. Many an hour has been devoted to learning the art of self-control. I will not speak against him; I will not cry out.

Perhaps this frustrates him the most. The others cry when he beats them and indeed they should not, as they are not beaten half as much as I. I do not cry. It is what he waits for, I think; he longs for my tears, for me to beg him to stop.

But I will never beg him for a thing, not ever.

And so in this vein we shall continue, until one of us outlives the other.

Sir Thomas turns to me with a slight smile. "But we shall remain the king's loyal servants, shall we not?" he asks in light tones. "Edward is a mortal man, God bless him. His reign cannot last forever." How easily he speaks treason! "Meanwhile, we shall serve him and elevate ourselves the old-fashioned way."

I wonder what the old-fashioned way is but do not dare ask. I am wondering why Sir Thomas has summoned me to this little conference to begin with.

"Here, my boy," says Sir Thomas, extending his arm to me. "A gift for you." With a dramatic gesture, he pulls a large bolt of velvet aside to reveal in the corner a suit of armor. "Happy Christmas, lad."

My very first suit of armor!

"I am big enough now?" I ask, smiling in spite of myself.

Sir Thomas nods.

"I wouldn't say that," pipes in the baron, "but we cannot wait forever. You are already a year behind the other boys; most everyone receives their armor at seven. He's a little mite, Thomas."

"Size is irrelevant," says Sir Thomas in firm tones. It is the first time I have ever heard him address the baron such. To me he says, "It is about intelligence, Little Tom." He taps my temple with his fingertip. "Battles are won up here before they are ever won on the field. Learn the art of strategy and you will make an incomparable knight. Now. Have a look."

I inch forward, ignoring the baron's insult regarding my diminutive stature as I reach out to touch my new armor.

How grand it is! I run a hand along the shining breastplate, imagining myself a strong, tall man of twenty or so, lance poised at my hip as I forge ahead on my charger—a black charger—ready to oust my opponent. It will be easy. I will be the greatest warrior in the land; everyone will admire me. Even girls; they will throw their tokens at me and I will flash them my winning smile. I will not mind their attentions because supposedly men that age actually *like* the gentle sex.

"What do you think of it, lad?" asks my father. He is smiling down at me. I raise my eyes to him, another great warrior, and smile.

"It is the most wonderful thing I've ever seen," I breathe in awe.

"Be worthy of it," says the baron, his gravelly voice hard.

I turn to face him, meeting his gaze, hoping my hatred reflects in my uncompromising black eyes. "Let there be no doubt that I shall."

I have usurped the hayloft as my own personal hideaway. It is far more peaceful than the manor, and up here I have created my own little world. No one knows about it, not even Neddy or Edmund. It is my place. I carve and paint toy soldiers and set up elaborate battlefields where the general—I, of course—always wins the day. Sometimes I draw pictures, maps mostly, planning out my battles. My toy soldiers take to slaying dragons, conquering kingdoms, and even rescuing dumb girls.

It is a wonderful place, a place no one can take away from me.

Or so I thought until the day the baron took the dairy maid in a bed of straw and manure. I peek over the ledge when I hear the familiar voice. I want to look away but cannot. He is telling her to hush, covering her mouth as he proceeds to do something I didn't know was possible. Yet I had seen animals do it, so I suppose people must, too. I just didn't know it happened like this.

The girl is in a frenzy, wriggling against the baron, tears streaming down her cheeks. "Please, my good lord, stop!" she cries. "Please, let me go!"

In response the baron slaps her.

It is then that the girl's wide blue eyes find me.

I cannot move. I cannot shrink back. I would make noise and he would know and do . . . I cannot think of what he would do.

The girl holds my gaze as the baron commences with his strange act. Her eyes are alight with horror and sadness and defeated submission. I long to reach out to her. I find myself wishing in vain that my toy soldiers would come to life and rescue her, slaying the baron in the process.

But such wishes are for children and I cannot think myself a child after today.

When the baron finishes, he pushes her aside. "Go now. Off with you."

The girl gathers her torn skirts about her and struggles to her feet, rushing out without a backward glance.

The baron collects himself. He stares straight ahead of him.

"We Howards take what we want," he says without looking toward my hiding spot. "To get anywhere in life, you have to take what you want."

He quits the stables.

I lie in the straw and vomit.

He knew . . . he knew I was there, watching.

And he did it anyway.

I never go to the hayloft again. The soldiers I give to my little brothers, encouraging them to play with them as I cannot. I cannot play again. Instead I will learn how to become a real knight, a chivalrous knight. No lady will have need to fear me.

When not forced into study, something that while it comes easily to me is not my passion, I devote myself to learning the sword, riding, archery, anything physical. Anything that will enable me to become the greatest soldier in the land. Anything that will inspire the bards to sing my praises. I shall be the unforgettable Thomas Howard. The hero Thomas Howard.

I, and not the baron, shall make the Howard name great.

I still do not grow very much, to my eternal dismay, as my brothers have already surpassed me and they are much younger. But I will not be daunted. We shall see who will prove their mettle when on the battlefield.

Sir Thomas and the baron are too busy to notice my development; they are occupied with missions of their own and are not much seen at Ashwelthorpe. It is just as well. With them gone I can sing and laugh and play with my brothers with no one to tell me otherwise.

We pass a happy spring and in May, Mother is delivered of a baby girl. When I am permitted to see her I bound into her chambers, eager to meet my new sister.

Mother lies abed, her brown hair cascading about her shoulders like a maiden, and as the sunlight filters through the window, it catches threads of auburn and gold. I have a strange urge to reach out and touch it but refrain as I approach the cradle. The baby is a tiny black-haired cherub. She sleeps with her little fists curled by her face.

"Oh, my lady," I breathe. "She's beautiful."

Mother stares at me a moment, her expression vacant, before averting her head.

"What do you call her?" I ask.

"It has yet to be decided."

I think this is quite odd. "But she is three days old. What are you waiting for?" I ask.

"Oh, Tom." She rolls onto her side, her back to me. "You know so little about this life. . . ." She draws in a shuddering breath. "This cursed life."

I am moved to pity for this thin, defeated woman whose beautiful baby lies so near her. She seems so unhappy in her role. I furrow my brow in confusion as my eyes shift from mother to daughter. I thought this was what all women yearned for, that it was something as natural for them as longing for a sword is for men.

I approach the bed, daring to touch her shoulder. "Mum," I say in soft tones, "shouldn't you name her? She shall be christened soon and it wouldn't do for her not to have a name."

Mother throws an arm over her eyes. "Yes, yes, I shall name her. Do not worry. It's just . . ." She sits up, hugging her knees. Tears light her brown eyes. "It's just, Little Tom, to name a child is to give it meaning. To attach yourself to it. And He waits for you to become attached."

"Who?"

"God." Mother casts wild eyes about the room, as though God might leap out of the wardrobe any moment and smite her. I am caught up in her panic and find myself doing the same thing. Years later I would have laughed at my young self and assured him that of all the things holy and unholy to lie in wait for him, God would never be one of them.

Mother returns her gaze to me. "You see, He takes them then, Tom. The moment you open your heart, He takes them. Three of them are gone now; you are too young to remember. But I remember. They are in the cemetery. Their headstones have names."

I am unsettled by her. She does not appear altogether well and I wonder if it would be prudent to fetch the midwife. I turn to the cradle once more. "This one seems strong and splendid to me, my lady," I tell her. "I expect she shall be with us a good long while."

At this the baby awakes and begins to fuss. I scoop her up in my arms, holding her to my chest. She is so warm and soft I do not want to let her go. I smile down at her crimson face as she howls her displeasure.

"Listen to that set of lungs!" I cry. "She shall be a force to be reckoned with, my lady, you shall see."

Mother has covered her ears. "Fetch the wet nurse, Tom. See that she is fed."

I take the baby to the buxom maid, who I must say seems quite perfect for her profession, and she is happy to relieve me of my little burden.

"Has the missus decided on a name yet, milord?" she asks me in her grating country accent.

I shake my head, heart sinking.

The nurse sits in one of the chairs, baring her breast without a thought. "I suppose it's in God's hands."

God. I shiver. Wasn't I just looking for Him a moment ago?

The baby is eventually named by Sir Thomas, who settles on Alyss. I admit to feeling a special tenderness for her. As she grows, cooing and laughing and forming short sentences, I teach her to say my name. "Say Tom," I tell her over and over.

"Tom," she repeats, her round blue eyes filled with the unbridled adoration only a baby or a dog is capable of projecting. "My Tom," she says again.

"Yes," I say, picking her up and twirling her about. "I shall always be your Tom. I shall be your brave knight and protect you from all harm."

But I cannot protect her from God. He takes her from me in 1483 when she is but two. A fever, a terrible scorching fire of the humors, consumes the soul of my little Alyss and she perishes.

Everyone moves on. Mother is with child once more. The baron curses my tears—babies are lost all the time, he tells me, and are replaced easily enough. Sir Thomas does not address the issue at all. So I have found a dual purpose for my helmet. Not only does it serve to protect me from blows to the head in practice, but I can also put it on and cry to my heart's content. When wearing my helmet, no one sees my tears. No one knows I cry.

The night my little lady is interred, I keep vigil by her headstone, her headstone that bears her name.

I wear my armor. I wear my helmet.

Two Bonny Lads

My Alyss is not to journey to the Lord alone. She is accompanied by our king, Edward IV. The baron carries his banner during the funeral procession and keeps vigil over his body that night, shedding tears and mourning with such conviction, one would have thought he had never spoken ill of him and that they were bosom mates.

This leaves the crown to twelve-year-old Edward V. His uncle Richard Plantagenet, Duke of Gloucester, is to serve as regent until the lad reaches his majority.

However, it is not a smooth transition and on the way to the coronation, Gloucester descends upon the party and arrests Anthony Woodeville, Earl Rivers, along with several others for their supposed conspiracy to assassinate the young king. For their protection, King Edward V and his brother Prince Richard are taken to the Tower of London to be supervised by my grandfather, Constable of the Tower.

On 25 June, Gloucester names himself king of England—he is to be styled as Richard III now and installs himself at Westminster. My grandfather stood at his right as acting earl marshal. The baron's heirs will be named earls marshal by heredity, which means someday I will hold the title. Then came the honor my grandfather had yearned for as long as memory served. He is named Duke of Norfolk at last. My father is created Earl of Surrey. We are given many of the Mowbray lands along with properties that once belonged to Earl Rivers, who had met with the executioner's axe.

I wonder at this and decide to question the newly created duke about it on one of his brief visits home (I admit with delight that since the accession of Richard III, my grandfather's calls are few and far between).

"How can you be styled the Duke of Norfolk when Prince Richard already holds the title?" I ask, referring to one of the princes in the Tower.

Grandfather seizes my shoulders, shaking me till my teeth chatter. "Never mention that name to me again, do you hear me? Never!"

True to my nature, I cannot let it go. "But if they are in the Tower for their protection, they will be let out soon, won't they?" I ask in subdued tones. "When the danger passes? Why has he been stripped of his title?"

Grandfather averts his head a moment. He works his jaw several times before returning his deep black eyes to me. He draws in a breath. His voice is surprisingly calm. "You must not think of them anymore, Tom. They are . . . they are to be forgotten."

"Why?"

He pauses. "There is a new regime now."

I feel a rising sense of panic. Something terrible has occurred, something dark and evil that I should not pry into. But I want to know. I *have* to know.

"What happened to them, Grandfather?" I whisper in horror. "What happened to the princes in the Tower?"

Grandfather releases my shoulders. He regards his hands a moment, turning them palm up. They are trembling. "In life, Tom, there is a time when it is expedient to do things . . ." He shudders. His voice is a gruff whisper. "Terrible things . . . in order to survive. Survival, Tom; that is what it is all about. The Howards are to be allied to the Crown, no matter whose head it rests upon. We are climbing out of the ashes and will be great. But we cannot hesitate. We carry out our orders without question. We demonstrate our loyalty. We crawl on our bellies and sing their praises; we cavort with demons—whatever it takes. We will rise up to be the greatest family in the land. Play it right and not only will we be able to claim a royal past, but we may see one of our own sit the throne in the future. Do you see?"

I don't see at all. He evaded my question by launching into some abstract philosophical discussion of our rise to power through justifiable treachery and shameless flattery.

He leaves it thus and my curiosity is unsatisfied.

Perhaps it is better I do not know the part Grandfather may have played in this particular instance.

For the princes are never seen again.

A New Allegiance

In October my father and grandfather quell Henry Stafford, Duke of Buckingham's rebellion, which had arisen to support the Earl of Richmond, Henry Tudor, and resulted in the duke's beheading. As a reward we are given more lands, and Grandfather and Sir Thomas are steeped in favor and royal responsibilities.

On 22 August 1485, our brief interlude with peace is interrupted when Henry Tudor lands in Wales to launch another attack, resulting in the death of Richard III during the Battle of Bosworth. We learn Grandfather is also slain (I grudgingly seek the Lord's forgiveness for not mourning him) and a wounded Sir Thomas has been taken prisoner in the dreaded Tower of London. We fall at the speed with which we had risen. Our lands, all except Mother's Ashwelthorpe, are seized. Sir Thomas is referred to as the attainted Earl of Surrey. The dukedom of Norfolk is no longer in Howard hands.

And yet the new King Henry VII is merciful. Neddy and I are styled lords and called to court to wait upon him as pages. Not only this, I am to be betrothed to the king's future sister-in-law Lady Anne Plantagenet, daughter of the late King Edward IV. The white rose of York and red rose of Lancaster will be united through the king's marriage to Elizabeth, and I will be his own brother-in-law. I, Thomas Howard, brother-in-law to a king! It makes the thought of dealing with a female much easier. What is most important is that this new connection may one day free my father and restore the Howards to glory.

"Be warned, Thomas," Mother whispers before we depart. "The king holds you as favored prisoners; if your father does not continually demonstrate loyalty even from the Tower, you shall be snuffed out without a second thought."

I shudder at the thought, recalling the poor little princes in the Tower, other innocents snuffed out in the name of ambition. Neddy and I are of no great consequence to anyone and yet still find ourselves pawns. How much greater is the risk to our lives should Sir Thomas offend His Grace further?

I must serve the king, impress him with my loyalty and devotion. I must prove myself indispensable. For love of me, the king may spare my father. Grandfather, despite his own questionable character, did say that we are to ally ourselves to whoever is in power in order to survive. I believe I can see the logic in this with a little more clarity now. With me near, His Grace will see that we Howards are loyal, the most loyal servants he can come by. My heart swells with hope. Yes, that is what I will do. I will prove to this new king, this King Henry VII, that he can trust the Howards as he can his own God.

The court is maddening—wonderful, dizzying. I am caught up and loving every moment. I sleep in the dormitory with the other pages and spend my days on errand for His Grace. I am Lord Thomas Howard, fancy that! It rolls quite nicely off the tongue.

There is always something going on, always work to keep me occupied. Henry VII is not the most personable of men, but I am not here to be petted. I am here to learn, and learn I shall. Henry VII is not a frivolous king. His wish is to keep a firm hold on his throne and oust any pretenders. He is a master of government, installing a King's Council, increasing taxes among rich and poor, and shipbuilding to strengthen the Royal Navy. He keeps a select number of Privy Councillors for his Court of Star Chamber in which he can deal with delicate matters of justice in a swift and efficient manner. His isn't a court of endless parties and needless expenditures. He is too set on rebuilding the royal exchequer. He is determined to make himself great and in this I am in sympathy with him.

The hardest lessons are learned in the dormitory. Pages are a rough group of lads and as I have remained quite small, an endless source of consternation, I find myself in many a quandary that only a combination of quick thinking, agility, and fisticuffs can rescue me from.

My energy is devoted to the dagger I have taken to carrying with me at all times. From every position conceivable I practice retrieving it, ensuring that I will be able to rely on the sleek blade no matter the circumstances. I weave it about, practicing that steady, certain upward motion that is the dagger's deadliest move.

I'll not let anyone get the best of me.

Of course they do try. I'd be a fool to think they would not. I am small and an easy target, but I meet them as a snarling badger would an unsuspecting rabbit and soon my reputation as a fierce and uncompromising opponent precedes me. There is no longer a doubt in my mind that I can be a competent and able soldier, that in hand-to-hand combat I can run a man through without faltering. It is a matter of us or them, after all.

"Aren't you afraid of *anything?*" asks Neddy one day.

I laugh. "And what is there to fear? God's body, Neddy, I've no time for that nonsense." I shrug. "Fear stops you from everything. I've never heard of a coward rising to power. They remain a nobody."

"But we're nobodies," says my little brother.

I seize his arm. "No, we're not. We are the Howards. Our family's known success before and we will know it again!"

"You sound like Grandfather." Neddy laughs.

I release his arm, stepping back, the fear I so condemn surging through me.

I do not want to sound like Grandfather.

I first see Anne Plantagenet at the king's wedding to her sister Elizabeth on 18 January 1486. We are to formally plight our troth this day and I have a little ring for her that was given to me by my father, who still passes his miserable existence in the Tower.

The ring bears no coat of arms, but I was able to scrape enough together to have an *H* and *P* interwoven in it to remind her that this is a union of the houses of Howard and Plantagenet.

I steal glimpses of her throughout the grand ceremony that is held at Westminster. She is looking at her sister and new brother-in-law, however, and does not glance at me once.

"She's beautiful, Tom," says Neddy in dreamy tones.

I flush and look away, casting my eyes to the ring I am wearing on my middle finger. I hope it fits her. I hope she doesn't laugh at me and think it a cheap token. Were I in a better financial situation, I would have a beautiful signet ring designed, but such is not my present fate. She will have to settle for this.

At the wedding feast, we are presented to one another for the first time. My heart sinks when I note that she is taller than I, though the long tapering limbs that make up her arms and undoubtedly her legs suddenly take on a new appeal I hadn't thought to appreciate when first learning of our betrothal.

She is beautiful with her rose-gold hair and soft green eyes that bespeak nothing but gentleness. Her cheekbones are high and well sculpted, her nose long but not unattractive. Her mouth, though not full, gives itself over to a wide, eager smile, revealing a row of straight white teeth.

The king and his new queen-consort oversee the formalities themselves, the queen ever doting to her sister, rubbing her back as she introduces us.

I cannot look the girl directly in the face as I pull at the ring that has decided to make its home on my middle finger. My slim fingers seem as though they have expanded to three times their size in the last two minutes, and my hand trembles as it works at the stubborn piece of jewelry. At last it gives and I offer a grunt of surprise.

The princess laughs.

I keep my head bowed, holding out the ring. "Here," I say, unceremoniously. "I plight my troth."

"Lord Thomas," remonstrates the queen in good-natured tones, "aren't you going to place the ring on her finger yourself?"

I look at the princess through my lashes. My heart is racing. Truly I believe facing an army of Scots would be easier than making physical contact with this one maid.

Lady Anne offers me a delicate hand. I cannot help but admire the daintiness of the long slim fingers as I slide the ring on.

"You have perfect fingers for the virginals," I find myself saying.

I look up at her then. My nervousness recedes like the tide; calm surges through me as warm as wine. Everything about me fades, obscured by the light of her face, that sweet, beautiful face. I do not think that I am fourteen, with fickle fourteen-year-old passions. I think of her.

And love her. Just like that.

And just like that, with our hands joined here at Westminster among a bustling court before a jubilant king and his bride, I know she loves me, too.

My father is pardoned and released in 1489, returning home a different man from the one who entered the Tower three years ago. He is harder, darker, proving with his short temper and ruthless management of his household that he is indeed his father's son.

He is styled the Earl of Surrey and allowed to keep the lands in his wife's inheritance but none from his father's or the Mowbrays.

He is certain to unleash his bitterness at being withheld the title he covets with as much longing as his predecessor, that of the Duke of Norfolk. I, for one, think he should be grateful to be alive, but I suppose he isn't dwelling on that now. I imagine that he figures since he is alive he should receive what he considers his due.

The king tests his loyalty by sending him to Yorkshire to quell a rising there. Lord Surrey wins the day. As a reward, His Grace grants him the Howard lands he had still retained.

All of this I take in with interest, being that my father's elevation is equivalent to my own. However, there is more to interest the lads at court than advancement and soldiering. The fair sex has entered our awareness. We watch them, these gentle daughters of Venus with their curves and long, lustrous hair, their soft voices, their perfume, their graceful, fluid movements as they dance . . . and are seized by fever. Suddenly, there are not enough whores to be visited, not enough maidenheads to deflower. I join in, always one to participate in sport of any kind. Besides, I am to be married soon. I must know what to do. And so I learn.

No sooner do I become a student in the art of love than I become enslaved by it. The gangly girl I met when plighting my troth has returned to the court of her sister a beautiful woman, and my love for her is rejuvenated the moment our eyes lock. When not engaged in my duties I court her with all vigor. Together we stroll in the gardens. She plays for me upon the lute and the virginals, lifting her sweet voice in song, and I close my eyes, trying to emblazon in my mind and heart every note, every sound, every nuance that is this girl, this girl I have come to adore and love with every fiber of my soul. The strength of this emotion terrifies and excites me; like wine I drink it in but remain insatiable. All about me is the growing need for Lady Anne, my princess, my forever love.

To impress her I try my hand at poetry and fail miserably. She laughs that soft laugh that resembles the gurgling of a stream—how the sound intoxicates me!—and strokes my cheek, assuring me I need not impress her with flowery words.

"All I need," she tells me, grasping my hands, "all I could ever want, is you, Lord Howard."

On 4 February 1495, I stand in Westminster Abbey; she has me. Hands entwined with my bride, my princess, we stand before the Archbishop of Canterbury and are wed.

She is still taller than I, almost too tall for what is comely, but it is a trait I will excuse. I make up for my own lack of height in muscle and after we are led to our wedding chambers that night by giggling courtiers who see us to our bed with all manner of crude jokes befitting the occasion, the princess seems duly impressed.

Our settlement is the most pathetic thing a bride and groom of our illustrious station have ever seen and I cannot contain a sigh of dismay when I learn that the princess and I will be living on nothing but the charity of our relatives. We are penniless and it is seen to that we will remain so until my grandmother, the Dowager Duchess of Norfolk, passes on. With my luck the cantankerous old bird will live forever.

The queen provides for her sister in the manner she sees fit, and my princess is given a household of two ladies, a maid, her own gentlemen and yeomen, along with three grooms. She is also given twenty shillings a week for food and a promise that the proper gowns will be provided.

My father allows us use of his residences at Lambeth and Stoke in Suffolk and when I ask my princess where the best place to start our family would be, she blinks back tears.

"Stoke, my lord," she tells me in her soft, husky voice. "The country. Far away from court."

"Then we shall remove to Stoke," I tell her, taking her dainty hands in mine. "And there I will be your goodly and devoted knight and will love you till I die."

This passionate display sends her into a deep flush and she bows her head. My God, she is a beauty! I cannot believe she is mine.

I find I am relieved to depart from court as well. I am not a born courtier. I am as yet unskilled in the art of empty flattery. I know my calling and that is to arms; should the king need my service, he is assured that I am ready to prove my worth as his loyal and able defender.

We set up our meager household and I find it isn't altogether bad to be poor (though I will seize every opportunity to reverse my fortune—I'm not an idiot, after all). My princess is quite competent and demonstrates a keen ability for frugality. She is formal; I imagine being raised at court has instilled this in her and as a result she is not given to initiating demonstrations of affection.

She does not talk much; she is a dreamer. One could never accuse her of being silly or frivolous. Often I find her staring out the window or seated in the gardens, her expression soft with melancholy whimsy.

"What are you thinking about?" I ask her one day when I find her seated beside the duck pond. She holds an old loaf of bread but is not breaking any off to feed the ducks that are gathered about in anticipation.

To my surprise, tears light her eyes. She averts her head.

"Princess?" I call her nothing else; to utter her sacred name would be sacrilege. So she is Princess, my forever princess, and her tears twist my gut with pain. There is nothing I long for more than to bring her comfort. I kneel beside her, taking her chin between my fingers, turning her head toward me. "What is it, my love?"

She blinks rapidly. "I cannot help it, my lord," she tells me in tones that ring with desperation. "I cannot stop thinking of them. I try to will away the thoughts . . . I pray to the Lord for guidance, that He will help me banish them from my mind—"

"Who, my lady?"

She buries her face in her pretty hands. "My brothers . . . the princes . . . the princes in the Tower."

"Oh, Princess!" I cry, gathering her in my arms, rocking back and forth. What can I say to this? Never once had I thought of how the event affected her. Truly she must have had to disguise her grief well at the courts of her uncle Richard III and now her brother-in-law Henry VII.

"I suppose we'll never know what happened, will we?" she asks, her eyes lit with an innocence I long to preserve.

I shake my head. If Grandfather alluded to anything the day we discussed the ill-fated princes, I will never share it with this poor girl. What purpose would it serve except to further her grief and drive a wedge between us?

"We must press on," I tell her, stroking her cheek. "Pray for their souls, my love, and press on. We have so much to look forward to."

She offers a little half smile. "Yes," she acquiesces. "Do you suppose they are in the faery country?"

This was the last thing I would suppose, but what can I say? I shrug, offering a smile of my own. "You are truly English, I think—one moment speaking of God and the next of the fey. Only a true Englishman can seamlessly marry the two."

The princess covers her mouth with a hand. "Do you think it blasphemy?"

I wave a hand in dismissal; I want to say I don't believe in blasphemy any more than I do the faery folk. "Of course not."

I take her in my arms again, daring to kiss the lips I crave, daring to distract her the best way I know how.

She is a peculiar girl, this princess of mine, but her peculiarities are so endearing that I am beside myself with love for her. She leaves gifts for the faery folk, strange little gifts. A sweetmeat, a piece of string, a thimble, rose petals. In the oddest places—windowsills, the hearth of the fireplaces, my chair in my study, pressed between the pages in one of my ledgers. She writes them little notes, then burns them. The messages will be sent to the faeries in the ashes, she tells me.

When I ask her what she communicates to her faery folk, she answers in all seriousness, "To bid them safeguard of my brothers."

Often she is seen in the garden, twirling about in her gauzy gown, her little voice lifted in song. I watch her when she thinks she is alone.

It is a beautiful sight.

A year into our marriage the princess approaches me in my study. She wears a dreamy smile as she climbs onto my lap and snuggles against my shoulder. As such a show is so opposite of her character, I wrap my arms about her, reveling in her closeness and warmth. I cover the soft cheek and neck in gentle kisses.

"My love, my love," I murmur against her rose-gold hair. "How now, dearest?"

She pulls away, roses blooming on her cheeks. She reaches for my hand and places it on her belly.

It takes a moment to realize what this gesture portends. When at last understanding dawns on me, I begin to tremble.

"Truly?" I ask her.

She nods. "Truly."

"Dearest little mother!" I cry, taking her in my arms once more.

"We shall know such happiness! Never will our children question or wonder whether or not *we* love them. Never will they be afraid of us."

The princess pulls away, cocking her head. She places a velvet hand on my cheek. "As you were?"

I blink, averting my head.

She does not pry. Instead she leans against my shoulder once more.

I hold my princess for a very long time.

Family Man

I watch my wife's pregnancy advance in a state of awe. I chase the dark thoughts from my mind, cold stabbing fears of losing my princess and the baby, memories of my mother and the six siblings that succumbed to one childhood ailment or another.

My princess does not grow plump in any area other than her belly and I love watching her waddle about, cradling the curve wherein rests the life I planted. At night I hold her in my arms as she guides my hand to where it kicks and stretches. I tremble and laugh as I feel the little feet and hands jutting out.

"A regular knight we have, and so eager for combat!" I cry, rubbing her belly in delight.

She does not say much. She never says much, but now and then I catch her humming, rubbing her belly with that ethereal smile on her face, a smile she shares with her faeries and her fancies. I take pleasure in the sight of her; I drink in her radiance.

And then in the spring of 1497, the call to arms I had been waiting for arrives. I am to help subdue a rebellious lot of Cornishmen.

My princess gazes at me from her bed, her soft blue eyes lit with pain. "But the baby is to arrive any day now," she says, her voice taut with anxiety. "If you leave, you will miss it and what if something—what if something goes wrong?"

My heart lurches. "I cannot disobey the king, my lady," I tell her in soothing tones. "If I am successful, I may be given the favor of more royal assignments and you know what that would mean for the family. You must see that."

She furrows her brow in confusion, cupping her belly with a protective hand. "Then you must go," she says, her voice weary. "I know well that one must not refuse royal service."

I lean down to kiss her, but she averts her head.

I suppose I understand her grief, though what can I do? I can't very well stay home to pamper a child when the king calls for me! This may be the first of many chances to serve him or it may be the last—in any event I will not forfeit the opportunity.

I leave my princess with a kiss and the promise of my return. She says nothing. Her blue eyes stare past me, through to that world I am never quite able to enter.

I ride away. I will not look back. I will forget the tears sparkling off the cheeks where roses once bloomed.

A man remembers his first kill. Mine is made at the Battle of Blackheath on 17 June when I run my sword through the body of a bulging-eyed Cornishman. It is a very strange sensation, holding the knowledge that someone's very existence is in my hands. But I snuff it out without hesitation; indeed, to hesitate would be tantamount to my own demise. No, this is no time to lose control and yield oneself to philosophy. I am a soldier and that is that.

The sound of sword splitting through chain mail, sliding through soft flesh is like no other in the fact that it is eerily gentle, like that of permeating wet sand with a stick. I look into his eyes, big blue bulging eyes, watching them widen in surprise. He tries to grip my hilt in a vain effort to deflect the inevitable but in his shock miscalculates and grips the blade itself, slicing his palms through to the backs of his hands. Blood begins spewing from his mouth then, a mouth that had previous ownership of the ability to scream but is now gurgling and gulping the steaming red liquid of life instead. I ease him to the ground, placing a foot on his chest in order to extricate the sword from his failing body. It is difficult, far more so than running him through.

His face drains of color; the life ebbs out of him like the receding tide and as it does, it is as though what I have taken from him is now surging through me. I am tingling, pulsating. My heart pounds in my ears. I begin to feel the creepings of philosophy, the urge to ponder my situation: Have I done right? Am I normal?

Did I enjoy it?

What makes combat odd is the closeness. I wonder what it would be like to kill a man from far away; many kings have that ability. They sit on a hill and watch the battles commence below yet, by giving the orders, have as much a part in the killing as the knights. It must be easier for a king on a hill. They are not quite so close; they do not have to look into those eyes, those bulging blue eyes. They do not smell the steel and the blood. Nor, do I imagine with that strange surge of life flowing through me, do they ever appreciate the full taste of glory on the battlefield.

I gaze at the bloodied blade a long moment. This is blood I spilt. I killed. I killed for my king and my country.

I am a soldier.

Of course I only have a moment to review this fact as I am accosted by more rebels. They are easier to take than my first man. I do not think as hard. I have not the time for such an indulgence; there is only kill or be killed.

And I will kill.

I return to my princess victorious, and my biggest reward for my efforts is in holding my son. He is the most beautiful baby I have ever seen. And I should know: I have seen dozens of babies and most of them are horrific, red-faced howling things.

He does not howl or fuss much; he is robust, with my wife's almond-shaped green eyes and a tuft of rose-gold hair that I cannot stop petting.

"What do we call this little lad?" I ask my princess as I sit beside her on her bed.

She offers her gentle smile.

"I call him Thomas, my lord," she tells me in her soft voice. "If that pleases you?"

I reach out to stroke her cheek. "Of course it does. There can never be too many Thomas Howards about." I laugh.

The baby begins to mew a bit and I hand him to her. "Would you like me to fetch the wet nurse?"

"I nurse him myself," she tells me. "I like nursing him."

I screw up my face in confusion. "It isn't done, my lady. It is not good for you. A country wench suited for that type of life would be far better. But you are a dear for trying. I shall send for a proper nurse." I rise, patting her head. "And that way we can commence with the happy task of giving Thomas here a brother or sister."

The princess cradles the baby to her heart. I note the plea in her eyes. I cannot help but yield to her desires. She is so fair. . . . I nod, her helpless servant. She unfastens her nightdress and allows him to suckle, a smile of gratitude lighting her face.

I turn to quit the chambers but, as I do, am reminded of another birth, that of my sister Alyss so many years ago. How my mother would not take to her, how she thrust the little lamb into the hands of the wet nurse as soon as she was able to prevent any chance of becoming too attached before death claimed her.

I turn toward the princess. I want to say something; I want to warn her.

But I don't know how. Nor do I understand the nature of the warning.

And they are so lovely, sitting there like that. Almost holy.

I will not part them.

The king and queen have sent gifts for the baby, a lovely baptismal gown and fine garments sewn by the queen's own hands. They have been blessed with a flock of their own children these past years, including two bonny princes, Arthur and Henry. I wonder how often my Thomas will interact with the boys. It would be wonderful if they grew up together to become best mates. I am still in a state of awe that my Thomas is first cousins with the Crown Prince!

That summer, Neddy and I are sent north with our father, who is now lord lieutenant of the army defending the homeland against Scottish invasion. With him we will do our best to keep the barbarians where they belong. They had been making a show of support for Perkin Warbeck, a Yorkist pretender, which gave Henry VII plenty of reason to be annoyed.

I tell myself it is just in a day's honored service, burning villages, setting the thatched roofs of these little humble huts aflame while tuning out the screams of the families perishing inside. But this is a different kind of warfare, far different from hand-to-hand combat against men born and bred to kill.

I have to do it, though. It is for the country, for the king who is rescuing me from obscurity.

This is how life is, my reasoning continues. People live and people die. Everyone's time comes. One day it will be mine and if it is by the sword, I will not blame my slayer for doing his duty.

I tell myself this at night when the dreams come, when I hear the screams, the pleas, the vain cries to God for mercy. I tell myself this as I imagine the situation reversed and it is Stoke up in flames, my wife and baby inside, surrounded by merciless barbarians.

No, I cannot think of that. I must never think of that.

We prove successful and by September, King James IV of Scotland makes a truce with Henry VII. For our role, Neddy and I are knighted by our father at Ayton Castle.

I am now Sir Thomas Howard.

By Epiphany my princess announces in her subtle way that she is again with child, by setting an egg on my desk. It takes me a moment to realize this is not one of her odd gifts to the faery folk but her wordless communication to me about her condition.

I laugh, enchanted by my lady's newest antics.

She carries this precious cargo in the same manner she did Thomas, all in front. Never is a sight more beautiful to me than my princess with child. I cannot believe my good fortune, to be blessed with a fertile bride and a flourishing career. I am not about to dwell on what I do not have; that is a fool's hobby. I focus on what is to come, what is to be achieved and gained. It is this thinking that earned me my knighthood and, hopefully, further advancements, advancements that will benefit my growing family.

I must say I think it was easier fighting off the Cornishmen than standing outside the princess's birthing chamber the day she labors with our second child. As I had missed Thomas's birth, this is a new and altogether uncomfortable experience for me. I am wrought with anxiety, pacing back and forth outside the door, starting at every sound that comes from within. My mother had always screamed in childbed and I was expecting the same from my wife. My princess's silence is more disconcerting than my mother's agonizing cries ever were, and I am beset with fear as I imagine any number of terrible scenarios.

"She's a strong one, is your lady," says Tsura Goodman the midwife in her strange accent when she comes out to report on my princess's progress. "She doesn't make a sound." She cocks her head, searching my face for something I am unsure of. She is a peculiar woman, this midwife, said to have descended from the wandering Gypsy folk. Her ancestry reflects in her dark skin and penetrating gray eyes. Her black hair is wound atop her head in a knot; loose tendrils escape to frame her olive-skinned face, and her dark beauty is as alluring as it is haunting.

The woman takes my sword hand. "Beautiful," she says as she admires it, turning it palm up. "Beautiful and dangerous." She raises her eyes to mine. I shudder. I have never been keen on what some call the dark arts; indeed, my wife's attachment to her faery folk is unsettling enough. Looking at the woman before me confirms that she is in possession of something otherworldly. "Take care of its power, my good lord," she tells me in an eerie tone suggesting that she speaks not by choice but at the command of some higher being with which I have never become familiar.

"What are you about?" I snap, trying to quell my trembling.

She is unaffected, unafraid. Her full, claret-colored lips curve into a slow smile. "There is always a chance for redemption; no fate is ever certain," she hisses in urgency, and the incongruity of her seductive expression and harsh tone causes me to start.

"Attend your charge at once, woman!" I cry, snatching my hand from hers and backing away, stifling the urge to make the sign of the cross and run in terror.

Tsura the Gypsy dips into a curtsy, then returns to my wife's bedside.

I stand outside the chambers, studying my hand a long moment. I clench it into a fist.

Take care of its power indeed.

It is a boy! Another bonny boy! We call him Henry after the king and his son. He is a delight, so blond and rosy. His eyes are lighter than his brother's; their silvery blue gaze penetrates the soul as he studies me, his little face earnest as a judge's. I find myself particularly attached to this wee mite, perhaps because I was here when he was born, and I love holding him, caring for him. It touches me to feel his tiny hand curling about my thumb and I marvel at his perfect small feet, an example of God's attention to the finest details.

I never knew I could love like this.

The princess and I spend many an hour in the gardens with the children. She laughs more now. Our toddling Little Thomas brings her delight as he discovers his world; he is everywhere at once and it takes a great deal of energy to keep up with him, but it is energy we are happy to spare.

When Thomas is out of his swaddling bands and put into short pants, assembling words into short sentences, following me about wherever I permit him to go, my princess tells me I should begin considering names for our third child.

I stare at her in wonder. How is it a man can be this happy?

The princess is eight months gone with child when the nurse tells her our baby, our Henry, was found dead in his cradle one spring morning.

I have never heard my princess raise her voice, but now she is screaming. The sound rips from her throat, raw and terrifying. She sinks to her knees before our lamb's little cradle, thrusting her long arms skyward, bidding the Lord to answer for His decision. When at last she has collected herself, she turns to me, staring, large green eyes filled with questions I cannot begin to answer.

Tears stream down my cheeks unchecked as I approach the cradle. He does not look dead at all, his tiny head lolled to one side, eyes closed, fists curled by his chin. He is so still. I reach out to touch him, then draw back in horror. The warmth I had treasured when cradling him so close is gone. He is cold; the breath of life has departed.

I sob, great gasping, gulping sobs of despair.

There is no reason. There is no good reason.

I turn to the nurse, hot anger replacing the tears that I now wipe away in disgust. "Why was he not attended to?" I seethe.

The woman backs away in horror. "But he was—he was as he is every night, my lord. We checked on him right good, sir."

"If that were so, he would be here with us!" I cry. "You are dismissed! This whole nursery staff is to leave this instant and I do not care where you go! May God rot your souls for your negligence!"

The woman retreats with the two rockers and nursery maids. I hear them fleeing, their voices raised in panic.

"Pray you make it out of here before I reach the door!" I shout.

I turn once more to the cradle. What do I do now?

"He was perfect," I tell the princess in softer tones, shaking my head in agonized wonder. "I do not understand. . . . He was perfect. How can he be here one day and gone the next?"

The princess shakes her head, then sinks to the floor, rocking back and forth, inconsolable.

He did not have many effects. He did not live long enough. But I did save his first pair of little shoes, tucking them into a drawer in my desk, a strange reminder of lost perfection. I will not look at them . . . often.

We bury him at Stoke. He is too small to be traversed to the family chapel at Lambeth, so I do not bother. We receive sympathy from the royal family along with the Howards—indeed, everyone is well acquainted with loss. My mother had passed that same year and if anyone could have offered me counsel on the subject, it was she. But she is gone and the earl has remarried. Somehow his marrying within months of her death does not make his grief altogether convincing.

As it is, I do not care about anyone's shared grief or stories of their own losses. All I can think of is my own, of the princess's face as she asks me wordlessly, *Why?*

How in God's blood am I supposed to know?

I fear for the princess, for the faraway look in her eyes. She no longer laughs. We do not speak to each other very much.

We await the birth of our next child, neither of us filled with the hopeful anticipation we harbored for the first two.

Yet when she brings forth another little boy, the knot in my chest eases a bit. He takes after me with his dark hair and skin, but is long like his mother. He seems healthy. I want to love him. I want to enjoy him. I don't want to grieve anymore.

We call him William, Wills for short.

As he grows I find myself relaxing a bit. When he reaches nine months, the age our Henry was when he was taken from us, tension grips me. I awake in the night, crying out in terror. Sometimes I sit by his cradle all night to make sure his soul is not stolen from me.

But he lives.

It seems God will let us keep our sturdy little Wills.

In 1503 I am blessed with two other events. The first is the birth of a daughter, my own little girl to pet. We name her Margaret after our niece, Princess Margaret Tudor, which leads me to the second event. We are to accompany Princess Margaret to Scotland with my father and the rest of the family to witness her marriage to King James IV. I am thrilled about the journey for so many reasons, not only because of the royal exposure but because I will be with my entire family again. It will be a wonderful opportunity to acquaint myself with my father's new bride, Agnes Tilney, and an excellent chance for the children to get to know their Howard relations.

"Perhaps I should stay home with the children," my princess tells me before we depart. "I should not feel comfortable leaving them with a nurse, and bringing them does not seem prudent either. They could catch a chill, what with the nasty Scottish winds."

I offer a dismissive laugh. "Father said the whole family is to go.

I want to bring the children, treat them to a spectacle. We didn't get to collect Princess Catherine from Aragon when she came to wed Prince Arthur, after all."

My princess rests a slim hand on her heart. "God rest his poor soul," she murmurs of the late prince. "He was so young and frail. . . ." She casts her eyes to our son, little Wills, who cannot be described such. He is as robust as Princess Catherine's new betrothed, young Prince Henry. She is not thinking of the late prince, however, or of the new Crown Prince. She is thinking of our boy, our Henry, and fearing the others perishing of the Scottish wind.

I clear my throat. "No use dwelling on all that," I tell her, hating the awkwardness that has arisen between us since the baby's death. "We are going to have a wonderful journey, my sweet, you will see. The children are going to love it. And they should be there to attend their royal cousin."

My princess offers a sad nod of acquiescence and I find myself balling my fists in frustration, wishing just once that I could see a grin of joyous abandon cross that beautiful melancholy face.

Our Maggie is too young to appreciate anything, but she points her chubby little finger at her beautiful cousin Margaret Tudor, saying "red" in reference to the princess's lustrous red mane, which seems to be a Tudor trait.

Thomas and Wills are beside themselves with pleasure as we progress north to Edinburgh and I tell them about all the famous battles that have occurred in this town or that.

No one looks at me the way they do; no one admires me as much. I am brought to tears by their flagrant adoration; as I had never admired many growing up, I didn't realize children were capable of it themselves.

"When they are given love, it is returned," says my princess when I comment on this as we sit in Holyrood Abbey, watching Princess Margaret become the Queen of Scots. She squeezes my hand. "No one will ever love you like a child," she adds.

I press her hand in turn. A lump swells my throat. I wonder who our Maggie will marry; it seems odd to think the thought of it affects me far more than marrying off the boys. I suppose all fathers feel that way about their little girls.

I wonder how the king feels. Is it easy giving one's children up to faraway kingdoms for political expedience?

King Henry is a practical man, however. I would be surprised if he gave himself over to such fancies. Indeed, I should take care that I don't become some kind of blithering idiot, crying at weddings like an old grandmother.

I am fortunate that I do not have to think about alliances just yet; I have years before my Maggie is marriageable.

She will be at my side a good long time.

We return to Stoke to pass a happy autumn. The children are looking forward to Christmastide. Maggie is running everywhere and is far too smart for her own good, and Thomas is itching to have a suit of armor of his own. I tell him he must wait a year but am pleased to practice archery with him. He is a fine boy, full of potential and enthusiasm. He will be an asset to any king's court.

These are happy days. My princess's smile is brought on a little easier now. I have stopped waking up at night to check on the children. I enjoy living the life of a country knight.

My grandmother passes away that year and I admit little grief as her death was the stipulation in allowing the princess and me to live in more comfort. Besides, she was one of the few who lived to a ripe and proper age, so there is no use mourning a full life.

I save the mourning for the young and there are plenty of young to mourn for.

That winter Wills takes ill with a fever. He writhes and twists in his little bed, his black eyes wild as they make helpless appeals to the princess and me. We do not know what to do aside from calling the physician, who can only bleed him.

I hate watching the leeches attach to my little boy's back; I cry when the butcher of a doctor makes little slits in the tender skin to allow escape of the bad blood that has corrupted my son's humors.

It is all to no avail. Wills dies in his mother's arms. The princess does not scream this time. She bows her head, allowing her tears to mingle with the sweat on our child's brow.

I cannot watch this.

The only thing I can think of to do is chase the inept physician off my property with a horse whip.

"You did nothing!" I cry as he leaps onto his horse, his eyes wide in terror. "You killed him! You and your leeches killed my son!"

The physician rides away without looking back and I throw myself in the dust of the road, sobbing. There is nothing to be done. I look at the horse whip in my hand and in a moment of sheer madness bring it across my own neck. It curls about it and strikes my back. There is something strangely satisfying in the sting of this blow and as I watch the blood pour down my neck onto my shirt, I start to laugh at the insanity of it all. I strike myself again and again until my arm is too weak and my throat is too raw from the laughter that has converted to screaming, racking, useless sobs.

Thomas does not understand what has happened. He does not understand death. He asks about Wills daily, so much so that I have to extract myself from him. I take long walks and longer rides. I swim, immersing my body in the coolness of our pond. Sometimes I wish I would drown.

One day the princess finds me there, floating on my back, staring at the sky. I do not think of anything but the gray sky, gray as the Gypsy woman's eyes, and the water that envelops me and comforts my broken soul.

"Come back to me, my lord," she pleads in her soft voice.

She stares at me pointedly, then walks away.

In that moment, tears of gratitude replace those of sorrow. I rise.

Indeed, no one on this earth is wiser than my princess, for there is nothing that can be done but to press on. I cannot abandon the children who are here, looking to me for guidance. I cannot teach them that it is permissible to wallow in selfish grief while life surges on about me.

With new determination I dress and go into the house. To my children. To my princess. To the life I still have.

* * *

It is a vain goal, trying to seize something that is not mine to have, trying to hold in this hand, this hand that is said to be so powerful, the thread of life that binds my children to this world.

In early 1508 my daughter, my precious little Maggie, succumbs to an imbalance of the humors of the bowels. She doubles over in pain one evening at supper and we allow her to take rest in the nursery. I had thought she was trying to avoid eating the eels; she never had a robust appetite and hated trying anything new.

"You're a manipulative little creature," I tell the six-year-old, my voice stern. "Feigning a stomach ache to get out of eating supper. Well, you shall have nothing to eat, not one thing, for the rest of the evening, and I don't care how much you cry or beg. You have to learn that you cannot always have what you want."

How was I to know those would be the last words of mine she would ever hear?

The nurse fetches us moments later, her eyes wide with fear. "The little one has taken ill, my lord," she whispers, crossing herself. "She is in such terrible pain . . ." She bows her head. "Such terrible pain."

The princess and I rush to the side of the writhing child, her face flushed with fever, her black hair matted to her fair forehead with sweat.

I take her in my arms, rocking back and forth. She is clutching her little belly, her head lolling about from side to side in restlessness. There is no outlet for her pain. She reaches out for my face, seizing it between her tiny hands.

"It hurts, it hurts," she cries. "Make it go away . . . please, make it go away!"

There is no physician to call. He would have done nothing but bleed her, anyway, and I could not have suffered it. I hold the little girl to my breast as she slips into delirium. She drops her hands. Her face relaxes, the black eyes glaze over, her small body goes limp.

And she is gone. In less than twenty-four hours she went from a healthy, jolly girl to this. Gone.

I stare at my princess in horror, but she cannot abide to be in the same room with death this time. She runs from the sight as though demons surround us, holding her hands to her ears to blot out my cries.

I hold my Maggie in my arms, rocking back and forth. I cannot let her go like this. She was just here. Maybe she isn't dead. Maybe she will get better. I have heard strange tales in which people appeared dead only to have a resurgence of life moments later. Yes, this can happen for my Maggie. I must hold her a while, will my strength into her so when she wakes up she won't be afraid.

I talk to her, I tell her she will get better, she is just sick. I apologize for scolding her about supper. I tell her she can eat whatever she wants whenever she wants if she'll just come back to me. I tell her she must return so she can become a great lady and serve in the queen's chambers someday. I tell her I am going to arrange a marriage for her with a strong, handsome knight.

I tell her she cannot leave because no one loves her like I do.

She does not move.

No matter, she just isn't awake yet. She just isn't awake yet, yes, that is it.

The princess enters collected and composed late that evening with two gentlemen servants.

"You must let her go now, my lord," she tells me. "She must be interred soon."

I shake my head. "I have heard of things . . . of miracles. . . . She might not be dead. She may be in that deep sleep some people go into and it takes them months or years to wake up. . . . What if we bury her and she is merely asleep?"

The princess's eyes mist over with a pity I loathe. I avert my head. Why doesn't anyone understand? Why do they all look at me this way?

"She isn't coming back, Thomas," she says.

It is the first time in our thirteen years of marriage she has ever called me by my first name.

She steps forward. "You must give her over now."

"No!" I cry, clutching the child to my breast. "You cannot take her!" I kiss my daughter's cool forehead, stroking her cheek. "I won't let them take you from me, Maggie, not ever. I will be here when you wake up. I will always be here when you wake up."

The princess nods to the servants. Some understanding passes between them and at once my arms are seized. The princess has taken Maggie in her arms and is carrying her away from me. I struggle against the men, crying for Maggie, cursing my wife.

I am too weak to break free, however. Perhaps some part of me knows I can no longer follow where she goes. I go limp, ceasing my struggling.

It is over. It is all over.

I press my face against Maggie's pillow. It still smells of her, of lavender and roses and little girl.

I do not attend her interment.

My son Thomas isn't the same after the echo of Maggie's laughter can no longer be heard ringing throughout our house. He takes to his bed with severe headaches and requires possets to alleviate the pain. My wife attends him, sitting by his side, singing softly, stroking his brow and massaging his throbbing temples.

With me he discusses the other children; we talk about Heaven.

"You don't feel any pain there, do you?" he asks me one day as I sit beside him while he clutches his head, tears streaming down his cheeks. "There is no pain in Heaven?"

"No pain," I whisper, taking his hand. I swab his head with a cool cloth.

"And I will see my brothers and Maggie again?" he asks me, his eyes filled with hope.

I nod, swallowing the lump in my throat. "When it is your time, when God calls you to Him. But that will not be for many, many years."

Thomas shakes his head. "No," he tells me. "The angel who visited me last night said I will be coming home soon."

I draw away from him in horror. "You are just sick with grief, Tommy," I tell him. "We all are. Sometimes when we are agitated, we take on peculiar fancies. That is what has happened. One doesn't really see angels or anything of that nature."

"Mummy sees them," says Thomas. "Only she calls them faeries."

"Mummy sees nothing," I say with a little more harshness than intended.

"What about the people in the Bible?" Thomas asks. "They saw angels all the time."

I had never really read the Bible. I want to say I always intended to, but it isn't true. I can't bring myself to pick it up. I shrug. "Times were different then" is the best thing I can think of to say. "Do not worry, Thomas. We will get through this. You will feel better. We have no other choice." I recall my grandfather's words, words that seemed so cold but were the best he could come up with. "We are Howards."

Perhaps it is better clinging to this abstract idea of a name and the greatness that can be associated with it than to the realness of people, people who are bound to leave in one way or another.

I rise, leaving his bedside. In the hall I encounter the princess, who has brought a basket of sweet-smelling herbs to the room along with some embroidery.

I seize her upper arm. Her eyes widen in surprise.

"What are you thinking, passing your fancies on to our son?" I seethe. "Aren't we in trouble enough as it is without his having to believe in such drivel? There is nothing that can come of it. Shroud him with illusions and the world will be all the more cruel to him when reality sets in."

"Reality has set in," returns the princess. "And I can think of no better way to ease his pain and sorrow than with these 'fancies' of mine. What else have we to cling to but our faith in the unknown, our faith in something bigger and better waiting for us on the other side? If we have not that, we have nothing."

I release her arm, half pushing her from me. "It is all nonsense. I'm sick and tired of it."

Her face is a mingling of sweetness and pity. "Of course you are. But it isn't that you're tired of; it's the death and the pain and the grief. You want something to blame, so you will blame anything to make sense of it all. I do not seek to make sense of it. There is no rational explanation that could ever justify what has happened. So let me keep my nonsense. I will lose my mind without it."

"Perhaps, madam, your mind is long since gone," I say before turning on my heel and quitting her presence.

Everything is so simple to her. I want to accept things as she does, but I cannot. I cannot throw myself into some fantasy world while reality stalks me with the relentlessness of a falcon.

I have never realized to this day how different the princess and I really are from each other.

The angel of Thomas's vision claims him in August, four months after the death of his sister. His is a peaceful passing. He complained of a headache, something the princess and I had come to grow used to, and closed his eyes. That was it. He was gone.

Six servants hold me down to force a sleeping posset down my throat after I have screamed my throat bloody and raw for four hours straight. The princess takes her grief out of doors and sits swaying on a garden bench, singing to herself.

I am alone when I awake; my children are still gone. No amount of screaming against the fates or God or whatever force of divinity that decides these things will return them to me. I am silenced. I require no comfort. It is over, all over. My dynasty has collapsed.

As my heir and namesake, he is interred at the family chapel of Lambeth, and the occasion is celebrated with the property dignity.

Some of my siblings attend the funeral and we are approached by my sister Elizabeth and her husband, the ambitious and untalented Thomas Boleyn.

My sister wraps her arms about my princess in an impulsive embrace that she does not know how to respond to. She is rigid and almost frightened of the show.

I reach out, resting a hand on my sister's shoulder. "Thank you for coming," I murmur.

Elizabeth turns a tearstained face to me. "I don't know what we would do if our situations were reversed," she whispers, reaching up to touch my cheek with a long-fingered hand. "My God, brother, I'm sorry."

I swallow the ever-present lump in my throat. "There's nothing that can be done," I say in husky tones. "They are gone. All gone."

"There may be more," says Elizabeth, her voice taut with desperate hope. When I respond with a cold laugh, she adds, "Oh, Tom . . . I don't know if this is the proper time, but we would like to ask Lady Anne to stand as godmother to our new baby. We—we named her for her."

"That is most kind. She will be honored, I am certain." I turn to the princess. "Won't you be honored to be godmother to your little namesake?"

The princess nods, her expression vacant.

I disengage from the group, allowing the Boleyns to discuss their children, sweet baby Anne and the promising little George, along with the rest of the family.

I want to be alone. I want to stand by my son's tomb and recall when I first held him in my arms, how I stroked his hair, how I would coo at him and laugh with him. How he held his bow with such promise. How he laughed and sang and told his childish jokes that caused my sides to ache in genuine mirth because he was so convinced of their humor. I think of his eyes, so like his mother's, alive with intelligence and mischief. I think of his sensitivity and gentleness. I think of his little clothes and shoes and the new armor I planned to have made for him this year. I think of the great knight that will never be, the grandchildren I will never see, the future we all have been denied.

I think of another child God has claimed for no good reason.

A silky hand slips into my own and I turn toward my princess.

"They know no more suffering," she tells me. "At least now they are all together."

"Yes," I say, my tone oozing with bitterness. "Let us thank God for that."

We cannot seem to speak to each other, the princess and I, and we take to our grief separately. I throw myself into the running of Stoke. I hunt. I read without grasping the words. I attend Mass, managing to separate the comforting monotony of sacred ritual from the God who I now find too callous to worship in private.

The princess keeps to the gardens. She leaves no more offerings to her faery folk.

We do not go to each other as husband and wife anymore. I want to. I want to reach to her, but something stops me, something in her, something in me. She has drifted further into her world and I am held back as well. I am not so ready to chase her; everything requires too much effort, and what comfort can we offer each other really? Empty words, useless embraces?

Nothing will bring them back.

We attend the christening of my niece and I do not allow myself the luxury of sentimental tears as I hold the child in my arms. She is not my baby. She is someone else's pet.

My princess can neither hold nor look at the baby. Indeed, I almost find it cruel that she has been named godmother at all in the wake of her tragedy.

I look down into the black eyes of this child; she could easily pass for mine. I stroke her downy soft hair and offer a bitter sigh. "May fate be kinder to you, little Anne Boleyn," I say to the trusting baby's face.

I pass her to my stepmother, grateful to be rid of her.

I do not want to hold her.

I do not want to hold any baby but the ones that are gone, the ones I can never get back.

The Passing of a Crown

After a long battle with illness and severe pain, King Henry VII passes into the next world, joining his wife, who died in childbirth in 1503.

"Another family reunited," says my princess, and I swear her tone rings with envy. "I suppose they have charge over our children now," she adds as she helps dress me into the black velvet livery I have been issued as I am to be a lord attendant at the funeral.

I say nothing. This talk, as with anything abstract and impractical, frustrates me to no end and I extricate myself with haste.

I attend my king's funeral but am far from being lost in grief. My thoughts are dominated by the new King Henry, styled His Majesty rather than His Grace, so magnanimous is his presence, and the favor I hope he bestows upon me. The Howards are in the ascendant. I cannot help but feel a thrill of excitement as my eyes are drawn to the strong young king, who even at the tender age of eighteen bears an aura of pure energy and power.

I have a feeling serving this Henry VIII will be the adventure of a lifetime.

The king marries Catherine of Aragon, freeing her from her years of sparse living and enforced patience while the old king was hemming and hawing about whether or not he saw political advantage in a union with Spain. This is the first thing this feisty young king does, with special dispensation from the Pope granting permission to wed his brother's widow on the grounds that their marriage was not consummated.

The June coronation is a grand affair. It seems this young king has a taste for extravagance. There is feasting, dancing, and masquing. I have entered the lists along with my brothers Neddy and Edmund for the jousts that are held in the king's honor, and I take the prize for most skilled combatant on the first day, along with Sir John Carre. What a thrill to have proven my worth even on this small scale! I shall stand out among these pretty boys and show the king who will serve him best when battle really comes calling.

I doubt he is thinking of any of that now, however. Now is a time for celebration, for frivolity and fun, something this lusty Tudor indulges in without hesitation. This is going to be a far different court from that of his stoic, cautious father, but then, this Henry does not understand what it is like to have to struggle for his crown. His was given to him as God intends, with the passing of a monarch, not with bloodshed and battle. Sheltered and protected his entire life from the harshness of reality, this robust and rosy Henry thinks nothing of the sacrifices that brought him to his glorious apex. He thinks of his parties, of the culture he is set on bringing to England, of his bride.

It would be hard not to think of her. Queen Catherine of Aragon is at the peak of her beauty, though six years her husband's senior. I admit it is difficult to tear my eyes from her as she sits in her box, where entwined are *C*'s and *H*'s on the royal canopy along with her symbol, the pomegranate, and Henry's red and white Tudor rose.

She is an unusual Spaniard with her deep auburn hair and gentle blue eyes. Her skin is fair and I would never have guessed her to be the daughter of Isabella and Ferdinand.

I have the privilege of dancing with her at one of the masques. She is elegant and formal, keeping the proper distance between us, much like my own princess.

"We are compelled to offer our sympathies, Lord Howard, for

the losses of your children," she tells me in her softly accented voice.

I flinch at the mention of them and the queen squeezes my hand. Her eyes are lit with tears.

"I thank you, Your Grace," I say. Knowing her to be a pious woman, I add for good measure, "But I suppose it is the will of God."

"Yes," she says with a nod.

We both know I do not believe it, but she is too gracious to call attention to it.

My princess does not dance much that evening, though she does accept a twirl about the floor with her irresistible nephew the king, while I am paired off with one of the queen's young maids, the young daughter of the third Duke of Buckingham.

All I remember about that family was that the grandfather, the second Duke of Buckingham, was executed during the reign of Richard III for supporting Henry VII. It is that of which I am thinking when dancing with this child, who is young enough to be my own.

She examines me with fierce blue eyes. Indeed, they draw me from my reverie and make me call attention to her face, a determined little face with a set jawline. Everything about her is a paradox: delicacy and strength, angularity and softness. Her chestnut hair falls in thick curls to her waist and I find myself wondering rather stupidly if she sets it in rags or if the attractive asset is natural.

"You are Lord Howard," she tells me.

I nod.

"I saw you in the jousts today," she says. She cocks her head, her arresting eyes squinting as though they are searching for my soul. It is so disconcerting I have to avert my face a moment.

"And who were you hoping would take the day?" I ask her.

She shrugs. "I suppose you want me to say you," she says and I cannot help but laugh at her candor.

"No, you may say what you like," I assure her.

She smiles. "I should have liked Charles Brandon to win," she says of the king's boon companion, the handsome courtier who follows him like a lovesick pup. Noting my expression at the thought of the doe-eyed boy, she laughs. "No, in truth I am not so fond of Brandon. I just wanted to see what you'd do."

"You are an instigator, Lady—"

"Elizabeth," she says. "Elizabeth Stafford." Her lips curve into a sarcastic little smile as her eyes take me in from boots to hat. "And you are the very devil."

"How old are you, Lady Elizabeth?" I ask her, amused.

"I am twelve, sir," she says proudly.

Twelve. The age my Thomas would be. I close my eyes a moment. Would I have chosen her for his bride? It would have been a good arrangement, the daughter of a duke for my handsome boy. But those are thoughts for the past and the past is gone.

The young girl standing before me will make someone else's son a fine wife.

"Lord Howard?" Her low voice cuts through my reflection and I start. She offers a perfect little curtsy. "Thank you for the dance, Lord Howard." She leans up to whisper conspiratorially, "And everyone wanted you to win, even the queen."

I laugh as I watch her bound through the crowd. It catches in my throat as I find myself wondering when life will find it prudent to dole out its first cruel blow to her.

I shudder, longing for one day of not being assaulted by dark, bitter thoughts.

I return to the side of my princess and ask her to favor me with a dance.

She shakes her head, tears lighting her eyes.

"I do not think I can bring myself to it, my lord," she says. "I am so tired."

She coughs into a small handkerchief and upon pulling it away attempts to hide it in the pocket of her dress. It is too late. I have seen the flecks of blood on the cloth, bright as a cardinal's feather in the snow.

We stare at each other in mutual horror.

BOOK TWO

Elizabeth

Kenninghall

Elizabeth Stafford Howard, January 1547

Every time I think of my husband, I want to dance the fleet, light steps of a maiden. Of course this urge to avail myself to such joyous abandon is only due to the fact that he is now keeping company with his like, the rats of the Tower of London.

In truth my mood is far from celebratory. One can be triumphant and unhappy at the same time; my husband is a prime example of that.

God gives and God takes. He gives me the peace I crave, but my son is made sacrifice for it, my son Henry, who also sits in the Tower awaiting his fate. No doubt he is blaming everyone but himself for the arrogant and impulsive actions that led him to that dark and evil place—he learned that from his father.

I imagine I will not attend the execution. Thomas made certain to turn my little boy against me years ago. I mourned his loss long before an Act of Attainder was passed against him.

I sift through a casket of sentiments. No one would believe me to be in possession of such a thing; indeed, I rarely look at it save for when they die. Now, faced with more death, I open it again to find the poems written by Henry when he was a child and could barely make his letters. Pictures Mary, guileless girl that she is, drew of our "happy family" when she was too young to know otherwise. My daughter Catherine's wedding ring. A dried flower my son Thomas gave me when he was five.

A miniature of the third Duke of Norfolk.

He had given it to me years ago; indeed, I think he passed them out to half the kingdom in case anyone should be overcome with the urge to admire him.

I stare at it now. How grave and proud he looks, holding his staffs of office in those elegant hands! His face is an impervious mask; it is a perfect rendering.

I must stop crying. Where have tears ever gotten me?

I clutch the miniature to my heart a long moment before casting it across the room. Good God, would Thomas be seen crying over a portrait of me?

He may never have cried for me, but there was a time . . . oh, yes, there was a time. . . .

A Little Maid

I am installed as one of Catherine of Aragon's ladies-in-waiting in the spring of 1509 at the great age of twelve, when the golden and glorious King Henry VIII ascends the throne of England. She is so beautiful, this unique Spanish woman with her charming accent and her silky auburn hair. She is pious and kind; her gracious sweetness warms me like the sun and I adore her.

She was first married to Prince Arthur. How we pitied her when he died, leaving her to live in a wretched castle with a meager household and dwindling funds for six years while surly King Henry VII tried to figure out what to do with her. Once he even pondered marrying her himself after the death of his wife, the gentle Queen Elizabeth, but then decided against it in favor of a union with his son. He could never bring himself to carry it out, however. I think he enjoyed holding the King of Spain's daughter hostage just as much as King Ferdinand liked dickering over the dowry agreement. It was a frustrating situation.

But Henry VIII set it right. He swept in, like a great glorious knight of old, and married the radiant princess. England could not be blessed with a nobler nor gentler queen.

They have a joint coronation ceremony and I am able to attend everything: the jousts, the parties, the fine banquets, everything. I stay up late and gossip with the other girls in the maidens' chambers and we are beside ourselves with excitement. It is far better than home, where there was nothing to do and no one visited save old boring people who discussed the tedious things that old people relish, like their failing health and war and death. Oh, what a dreadful place!

But here! Oh, it is grand! At the joust celebrating the coronation, we pick our favorite champions; some of the girls give tokens, but the queen says I am too young so must settle on waving instead.

Many girls give their tokens to Charles Brandon, the king's dearest friend, and the handsome Howard brothers, Edward and Edmund. As fetching as they are, my eyes are drawn to the oldest Howard, Thomas, uncle of the king through his wife, Anne of York. He is a compact man but rippling with lean muscle, and something about him makes me shudder with a mingling of fear and peculiar delight. His dark face is set with determination and he does not offer the easy smiles his brothers do. Curling hair black as pitch reaches his jawline and his long-lashed obsidian eyes seem distracted, as though not really as caught up in the spirit of the events as the rest of us are.

I watch fair Lady Anne tuck her token in Lord Howard's armor. He kisses her cheek and she flushes furiously.

"Those poor souls," whispers the queen's maid of honor, Maria de Salinas, a woman so devoted to the queen that she opted to stay and suffer with her through her years of deprivation rather than return to the land of sunshine and oranges.

I arch a brow. "What happened?" I ask, eager for any court gossip.

"You don't know? They had a houseful of children, three boys and a precious little *niña*. Lost them all."

"Oh, how dreadful," I breathe. This is not the variety of court gossip I enjoy. "Do you expect they'll have more children?"

"Would you?"

I shake my head. I would never risk bringing another child into the world after such heartbreak; loving something that seemed destined to be taken away was rather an invitation for more pain.

We watch the jousting tourney, where Lord Howard takes the

day. His victory is met with the briefest of smiles and a curt nod of gratitude but he is not as demonstratively ecstatic as his rivals are jealous. I find myself pleased that he has won some sort of recognition—not that it will make anything right for him by any standard, but it is nice to be favored once in a while.

That evening at the entertainments, I am paired off with Lord Howard for a dance. It is strange. He isn't a big man at all but there is something so powerful in him, an energy that flows through his elegant hand into my own. We talk of nonsensical things, the joust and Charles Brandon. I tease him a bit to bring a smile to his face. It is not easy, but I find at this moment it is what I wish for most.

When I am rewarded with a slow, almost nervous smile, I offer my most charming in return. He is an older man, old enough to be my own father, but I have no designs on him. He is married to a fine lady, after all.

I just want to see him smile.

The next day a miniature deer park and castle are set up in the tiltyard and there is a spectacular show in honor of Diana, goddess of the hunt. It is quite the display, with the lads slaying the stags and hanging their bloody carcasses from poles for the delight of the ladies.

I cannot say that I am particularly delighted. I have never been keen on the idea of blood and gore, and from what I can tell, neither is Her Grace. She offers a tight-lipped smile as though trying to swallow a gag and waves at the gentlemen who are trying so hard to win her favor.

Charles Brandon is there along with all the Howards. They are quite handsome, even Brandon, who I love to tease about because nearly everyone has taken a fancy to him. I haven't. Despite his pretty face, it is easy to see he will soon take to fat.

Lord Thomas Howard takes part in the festivities with his grim face set in determination. He draws back his bowstring with skilled perfection, hitting every intended mark. There are moments when his expression softens as he gazes at his bow, but they do not last long. Whatever emotions he allows to creep into his heart this day, he manages to keep at bay.

"Pray for him," the queen urges when she finds my eyes have rested upon him. I flush in embarrassment. "There are only two ways a man can go in the wake of such tragedy."

I offer a grave nod, then bow my head and murmur a quick prayer for the poor wretched Howards.

I am relieved when the hunt is over and we are allowed to take some rest. I never thought there could be such a thing as too much celebrating, but when I lay head to feathers that night, I drift into the blissful sleep of the overtired, dreaming of all the happy things I have been pleased to bear witness to.

Long forgotten is the Howards' tragic lot. All I can think of are the conduits of London running red with wine in celebration of our glorious king and queen.

On 29 June, the king's grandmother Margaret Beaufort passes on. The bells toll for six days in her memory and I admit I am more saddened that our celebrations have been cut short than over the passing of that old curmudgeon.

Still, she was the king's grandmother, which means she was the queen's relation by marriage, too, so I give the proper deference and pray for her obstinate old soul.

When the period of mourning passes, the king takes to ruling his realm and everything is made merry again. Into the kingdom drift minds of more intelligence than I could ever possess and they bring to us their Greek and Latin plays and books, their ideas about religion and art and music, their passion, their energy, and novelty.

King Henry relishes his merrymaking. Everything is cause for celebration: feast days, holidays, anniversaries of this event and that. There is always jousting and masquing. The king loves leaping out at us in disguise and scaring the queen, who offers her sweet giggle and adoring eyes to the strong and bonny prince. Watching them, I am beset with fantasies about marriage and new love.

Love is all around at court. Not a day goes by when some letter or poem or token isn't delivered to this lady or that from one handsome courtier or another. Even though the queen runs a devout and chaste household, it is far too easy to get swept up in dreams of romance.

"I think that you are awaiting the day when you, too, receive these love-gifts," says Fra Diego Fernandez, the queen's confessor, one afternoon when he finds me sighing in the gardens.

I offer the handsome Spaniard a bright smile. "Oh, no, sir, I do not think about such things."

He laughs. "Of course you do! You would not be human otherwise!" He leans toward me, nudging my shoulder with his upper arm. "And besides, I won't tell a soul—remember, I am a confessor."

His nature is so jovial and inviting I cannot help but warm to him. Fra Diego covers my hand with his. "And you being such a fair child will no doubt have the suitors circling."

Something about his physical familiarity alarms me. I withdraw my hand. "I am a chaste and virtuous maid," I tell him in case he may be testing me for my fitness in the royal household.

He only tilts back his dark head to laugh. "Such a treasure!" he exclaims. He snaps off a rose from one of the nearby bushes, twirling it a moment between thumb and forefinger before giving it to me. "Here: your first token," he says in a whisper before rising from the bench and making long confident strides toward another group of ladies, who are making sheep's eyes at him.

I study the rose a long moment, confused and delighted.

So absorbed am I in reliving my moment with the handsome Spaniard that I do not notice the pair of feet rooted in place before me. My eyes travel up the well-turned legs to the trunk, which is swathed in fine livery, at last resting on the stern countenance of Lord Thomas Howard.

He snatches the rose from me and crumbles the petals in one fine hand before casting it to the ground. "Don't be seen dallying with that," he says in dark tones. "He is a knave and a scoundrel. Who is attending you? You should not wander by yourself."

"And you should mind your own affairs, sir!" I tell him in haughty tones.

He laughs at this, but his is a peculiar laugh, lacking in real mirth. "*My* affairs?" He runs a hand through his curling black hair and sits beside me. I try to ignore the flutter in my belly at his nearness. "I recommend that you mind your own. Take care around the Spaniard. The 'pious and devout' friar who has you so caught up in his charms will bed anything that moves, my little lady. Everyone knows it."

"My lord!" I cry, scandalized at his language. "Retract that statement at once! The queen would never trust her soul to a degenerate!"

Lord Thomas's smile is filled with mockery. " 'Retract my statement'?" He laughs, that odd half laugh. "Am I in the presence of a little lawyer?" The smile fades to a grim line. "I cannot retract a truth. Her Grace is a trusting woman and stubborn at that. Anyone who can last six years in a dreary castle awaiting her fate is not faint of heart. People have warned her against her friar—even old Henry VII—but all to no avail. She will retain him despite his reputation because she does not believe it. She sees what she wants to see in those she loves—a most dangerous trait." He regards me with penetrating black eyes.

Annoyed, I avert my face. "Well, I suppose he can't help being a knave, he being so handsome and delightful, unlike some," I add pointedly. "Besides, he was probably forced to become a friar by his family. He may not even want to be one."

"You are a silly little creature," says Lord Thomas. "And one of poor judgment."

I turn toward him to glare.

"I may not be delightful," admits Lord Thomas as he rises, "but I am exceedingly handsome." He chucks my cheek.

"I suppose so," I say with a slight smile as he retreats. "For an old man!"

"Take heed my warning!" he returns.

When I can no longer hear the footfalls and soft laughter of the arrogant knight, I stoop down to gather up the petals of my first love token, cursing Lord Thomas for spoiling my fun and alerting me to the darker side of life at court.

Of Princes . . .

Thomas Howard, 1511

I have reaped many a reward serving our new king, this boisterous Henry VIII. Not only have I been elected into the elite ranks of the Order of the Garter but I have been given more lands than I know what to do with.

My princess is not as enthused about our triumphs.

"What will we do with it all?" she asks in her soft voice as we prepare to take to London to await the birth of the king's first heir. "Who will we pass it down to?"

I shake my head. "We can't pass it down to anyone if we . . . if we don't . . ." I can't say it. We have not coupled in three years; neither of us can bring ourselves to risk the agony that our unions seem to breed. Instead we watch with heavy hearts as everyone around us celebrates the births of their children. My brothers and sisters have given me a slew of nieces and nephews. Indeed, my own father has proven as fruitful with his second wife as his first, and I have so many new half brothers and sisters I cannot even remember some of their names. I do recall, with a measure of annoyed amusement, that he named another one of the brats Thomas, which strikes me as wholly unoriginal, but I suppose that is his matter.

It is hardest on the princess. When confronted with these rounded bellies and lusty little baby cries, I see her hand stray to her own flat stomach wherein lies a vacant womb too scathed by sorrow to bear fruit.

The queen's pregnancy is the most difficult to bear, something that sends me into a rage of guilt. Queen Catherine delivered a stillborn daughter the year previous and I can well empathize with the anxiety she must be suffering while anticipating the birth of this child. Despite that I wish her nothing but the best, my heart still contracts in pain whenever my eyes travel to Her Grace's belly.

The joy of the realm is a constant assault to our grief. The princess begs to be left at home for the duration of the celebrations that will follow the birth, but I stand firm.

"How would that look to our sovereign?" I ask her. "You have to go. We can't be seen hiding like petulant children. The queen is a gentle woman and can identify with you, at least somewhat. I imagine she will take into consideration your loss and not try to draw attention to . . . things when you are in her presence."

"How can that be avoided?" the princess demands, tears streaming down her cheeks. She begins to cough as she does whenever she becomes excited. Breathless, she collapses onto her chaise.

I sit beside her, checking the handkerchief that she so tries to hide. I don't know why she bothers. I am well aware of the blood that stains it.

"You must stop upsetting yourself like this," I tell her in gentler tones. I stroke her clammy cheek. "Their triumph is our triumph. We must celebrate with them just as they would with us should we ever . . ." There is no use saying that. We both know there will be no such celebrations for us.

But the princess seems just as content to pretend as I do and she nuzzles against my upper arm. "Yes, of course. Do pardon my foolishness." She wipes her eyes with a slender hand. "I want everyone to be happy—you know that, don't you? Oh, of course you do." She offers a defeated sigh. "We must remove to London directly to share the joy."

I stroke her hair and kiss the top of her head, wondering if we shall ever savor joy again.

*   *   *

The Prince of Wales is born at Richmond Palace on New Year's Day, another bonny little Henry. How can I begrudge anyone this kind of joy when I see the queen's face, so tender as she beholds her newborn son? Was not my own princess the owner of that same dreamy expression, was not her sweet face once filled with a love so overwhelming, none but a parent can appreciate it? No, now is not a time for resentment or envy. The princess and I give ourselves over to the contagious atmosphere of celebration that cloaks the kingdom.

My father is named one of the infant's godparents, another mark of the king's favor, and the earl's eyes shine with triumph at the honor.

The king makes a pilgrimage of gratitude to the Priory of Our Lady of Walsingham in Norfolk, making the mile progress barefoot from Slipper Chapel to the shrine to light a candle and offer an expensive necklace. Bernard Flower, the Royal Glazier, is commissioned to create stained-glass windows for the chapel as another sign of his appreciation.

I think it's a lot of showy superstition but hold my peace, for when the king returns, I am required to attend festivities the like of which I have never witnessed. The queen is churched and ready to commemorate the birth of her son with her husband and once the baby is installed at Richmond, they meet the rest of the court at Westminster, where the first of the jousts and banquets begin.

On 1 February, I tilt against the king, Charles Brandon, Edward Neville, and my brother Neddy with the lords Essex, Dorset, and Devon. Even mock battle sends that satisfying surge of heat through my limbs. Everything is so certain—you either win or lose. I savor the rawness of it all, the lusty battle cries, the clank of lance against armor, the pounding of the horse's hooves against the field, the sweat, the breathlessness.

I look to the stands, to the queen sitting in her box, so merry and exultant, to my princess, so wistful and pained. I expect her thoughts have traveled down that wicked path, the path I catch myself wandering. All the what-ifs, all the wondering. Would our children have participated in the festivities today? No doubt

Thomas and our Henry would have been betrothed by now and probably serving the king as pages. Wills and Maggie would have been too young to partake; they would have remained at home. We would have been choosing a tutor for them. . . . I have to stop this.

I concentrate on the sport, on the simple feat of ousting my opponents, which I am incomparably successful at, though I would never show up His Majesty. No one is foolish enough to do that.

The rigors of play work at our appetites and we are treated to banquets laden with more food than I have ever seen. Venison, hare, mutton, beef, stuffed capons, eels, fish, cheese, breads, sauces rich and savory on the tongue, puddings, tarts, comfits, wines that warm the blood and bring a tingle to the cheeks. My appetite has changed and I cannot consume as much as in years past, nor have I ever been a drinking man, but in a place where everything is a contest, I am compelled to take in as much of both as possible. I am so sick the next day that it is all I can do to keep my eyes open against the blinding sun.

It is no bother. I am so caught up in it all that I live in splendid excess throughout the whole of the festivities.

By mid February, the celebrating takes such a turn that I am just as happy not to participate in the grandest tourney of all, in which the lads are dressed in such foppery that my princess must remind me to keep my mocking laughter to myself. The king, styled as Sir Loyal Heart, challenges his costumed knights in a spectacle that thrills the ladies and gives the gentlemen spectators something to drink to.

That night, after Henry has taken Brandon twice on the field, there is a pageant entitled *The Garden of Pleasure* in which the king, as Sir Loyal Heart, is dressed in such a stunning costume of purple satin with gold *C*'s and *H*'s dangling from it that even I am rendered breathless. Few believe the array of jewels hanging from his person are real, including the Spanish ambassador, and as we dance, His Majesty, in his endless display of jocularity, orders him to have a yank at one of them to see for himself.

This innocent gesture causes the crowd of onlookers to break into pandemonium. Apparently, they are under the impression that the court jewels are theirs for the taking. No one is safe. The king, who does not seem to be the least bit uncomfortable being manhandled, is stripped to his hose and doublet.

Contact with this rabble does not please me in the slightest and I do not hesitate to swat the offenders away with a closed fist. The most amusing aspect of the evening thus far is that my brother-in-law Thomas Knyvet is stripped to his skin and has to climb a pillar to avoid having anything else yanked at. Even the princess laughs when she sees Knyvet's skinny white arse on display in the torch-light for the whole of the court.

When the assault closes in on the ladies, guards and gentlemen sweep in to push them off.

"Lord Howard! Help!" a shrill voice cries, and my attention is called to little Elizabeth Stafford. I turn to see a couple tearing off the sleeves of her Tudor green and white gown. The child's blue eyes are wide with terror.

I force myself through the throng, taking her by the shoulders and pulling her away from a crude old woman and her toothless husband, whose hands were so busy in their task, they did not see me coming. It is all I can do to refrain from breaking the king's peace and running them both through. Had she been my own daughter, I know I would not have hesitated and would sit out a spell in detainment somewhere as a result.

"What madness is this?" I seethe. "Get you out of here, hag!"

Startled, the couple begins to back away. "No offense, milord," says the man. "We was just joining in the fun."

" 'Tis not your fun to be had!" I shout, moving toward them as if to strike. "Now be gone!"

"And take the bloody sleeves!" Elizabeth adds, finishing the job herself, throwing the sleeves at her assailants. "May they feed you for a month!"

She stands, a tiny pillar of indignation, shivering in the February air, hugging her little arms across her stomacher. I kneel before her and take to vigorously rubbing her upper arms. "Are you hurt?" I ask her.

She shakes her head. Her eyes are bright, fueled with the same fire I imagine to be in mine when engaging in battle.

"Everyone is removing within doors," I tell her. "We shall have a splendid banquet where you will be left quite intact for the rest of the evening."

"Oh, how very disappointing," she says, her mouth curving into that odd little smile, which is both sarcastic and disarming at once. Noting my expression of mock disapproval, she adds, "Thank you for rescuing me, Thomas Howard."

"You are most welcome, Lady Elizabeth," I say in turn as I lead her to the rest of the ladies.

When I encounter my princess again, I take her hand. "You were not hurt?"

She shakes her head. Her cheeks are rosy with a mixture of mirth and fever. "The little girl is all right?"

"Quite," I say. I remove my hat, running my hand through my sweaty hair. "Perhaps it is best we do not have a daughter at court. I could not bear to watch her assaulted so."

My princess's face is stricken and I know I have said the wrong thing. I did not mean it, not that way, but the words are out and as she disengages her hand from mine, I note a new depth to the sadness already lighting her eyes.

There is no use apologizing. What is said cannot be unsaid.

Nine days after the closing festivities, in which I had the honor of carrying the king's helmet, the bells begin to toll. The little prince is dead.

My princess and I exchange a look of horror as we receive the queen's messenger at our home in Lambeth. I do not understand why the queen has sent a messenger, unless it is to seek out my wife so that she may comfort Her Grace in her grief. The princess knows well the meaning of loss, and her gentle presence would console even the most hardened heart.

But it is not my princess who is sought. It is I. I am called by Her Grace with no other explanation and so, dressed in the black livery of mourning, arrive at the palace to learn what is required of me.

I am received in the presence chamber where Her Grace sits under her canopy of state, her face grave and aged. One would not recognize the gay young woman who sat in her box watching the knights joust in honor of her newborn son just a few weeks ago.

I bow, removing my hat. "Your Grace."

She offers a brief nod. "We are pleased to ask you to ride in the Prince of Wales's funeral procession as one of the six mourners."

I am shaken. "Thank you for bestowing such an honor upon me," I say at last. It is awkward to be honored by such a sad undertaking, but it is a practical task and the queen and I are of like mind in practicality, it seems.

She averts her eyes a moment. "I have had two miscarriages," she goes on, dropping the royal "we," and I raise my head, startled as much by the familiarity as by the confession. Queen Catherine is never one to break with proprieties. "I thought that was suffering. But nothing compares to this. I have lost my first child, the first child to be successfully carried to term. He was so special, a gift I felt was hard earned and much anticipated not only for me but for the whole kingdom. A prince at last." Her face adopts a dreamy expression. "There is something about one's first child. . . . He will never be replaced. Even when we have another, this little Henry will always be considered my first." Her voice catches on the last word. She turns grief-stricken eyes to me, her face arranged in an appeal. "How do you bear it, my good sir?"

"Dear lady," I say, at a loss. "I—words cannot express . . ." Searching her honest, open face, I am struck by the thought that she is hoping I have some divine answer that will explain her tragedy away. I draw in a wavering breath. "I can say much about grief, but in the end, to someone whose pain is still fresh, all of my words would sound commonplace, empty, and as pointless to you as all the well-intended sympathizers did to me when I lost my children. So the only thing I will tell you about managing grief is this: Press on." I swallow hard. "Find comfort in what you may, Your Grace." I bow my head, then add in soft tones, "I appreciate your grief more than is in your estimation. You could not have chosen a more appropriate person to fulfill the obligation of mourner than I."

The queen leans forward, resting a bejeweled hand on my shoulder. For a moment we are locked in each other's gaze. Her eyes are wide with a mingling of fear and confusion. She bows her head, slowly removing her hand.

"We thank you for your service, Sir Thomas," she says, still avoiding my eyes. "You are dismissed."

I quit the chambers, unsettled and awkward and pitying another mother's loss.

. . . and Pirates

I ride in the procession, sitting numb on my mount, keeping vigil over yet another dead child. The spectacle of a kingdom in mourning is too much to take in. I begin to tune it out: the sound of the church bells, the tears of the crowd, the queen's anguished face.

The little prince is interred, grief is set aside for state business, and we forge ahead. The king recovers in time to go a-Maying, ordering the festivities to commence as usual. There is feasting and masquing and tourneys, of which my brother and I take part. We oust our opponents in typical Howard style and the king claps my brother Neddy on the back, thrilled by the display. He is far more familiar with him than with me. I tell myself it is my age that prevents me from having a closer relationship with His Majesty, but in truth, Neddy isn't much younger than myself. Rather, Neddy possesses charm and flamboyancy, attracting everyone to him without effort. He enjoys people where, as a whole, I am bothered by them. He is open and cheerful and converses for enjoyment, whereas if something isn't being gained by the conversation, I have little use for the art. What's more, he is ever ready to partake in any festive situation, bringing his own merry element, which itself proves endearing, else why would the king retain the useless Charles Brandon? I am not of the same nature as Neddy and Brandon so have not commanded the king's personal attentions as much.

But what I cannot be as a courtier, I can make up for as a soldier. All the prowess demonstrated in the jousts and tourneys has proven worthwhile. We have impressed the king sufficiently so that he sees fit for Ned and me to take on Sir Andrew Barton, the pirate who has been terrorizing our trade routes by capturing English ships under the pretext that they are in possession of Portuguese goods. Barton's case is peculiar. His motives are based on an old family grudge: His father, John Barton, was captured by a Portuguese ship, and the King of Portugal never made amends. Thus the King of Scots permitted him to take any Portuguese ship that crossed his path, along with their goods. In truth I do not think he was permitted to take Portuguese goods off ships that weren't from Portugal and this is certainly something that could have been smoothed over had Henry VIII only asked James IV. But my father is so eager to dissuade the king from supporting favored councillor Thomas Wolsey's encouragement of a French campaign that he urges His Majesty to engage Barton in the hopes of rousing a war with Scotland. Hence the Scottish king is not consulted.

I am not about to make suggestions. If the king is prompted by my father, so be it. My father's interests are my own; his gain is my gain. If the king asks me to take Barton, I take Barton.

And so in August, I trade land for sea and, from the very first, know that I was born to it—the rolling waves, the salty spray, the eternal motion of the ship, all this coupled with the anticipation of impending battle.

We encounter Barton's ships, the *Lion* and the *Jenny Pirwin*, on the Downs, that narrow roadstead off the eastern coast of Kent where warships patrol the gateway to the North Sea.

"Raise the willow wand!" I cry, indicating the symbol of merchant ships, so that we might lure him in. The *Lion*, which is being guided by a captain whose ship they looted the day before, comes about.

I stand on deck, gripping the ledge. I am tingling; power surges through my arms straight to my fingertips. My knuckles are white.

The wind whips against my cheeks. I lick my salty lips. We lurch into a wave; the spray splashes me and I laugh out loud. There is nothing like this, not the love of a woman or the cry of a newborn guaranteed to be stolen away—no, this kind of satisfaction is not given by another human being; it is achieved from within and I savor every moment.

The *Lion* is gaining. She is ready to take us. I stand firm, making certain that Barton sees the man who is fated to kill him.

"Cut the flags!" I order.

The flags are cut and we reveal ourselves to be the Enemy.

"Fire a volley—hit her broadside!" I shout. I am trembling as I watch the other ship closing in. We hit her with the cannons; the damage is not extensive but enough to rock her off balance and send the crew scrambling.

Barton is on deck, a formidable figure in his fine armor. About his neck is a golden whistle. He is shouting orders, indicating the strange apparatus his ship is outfitted with: weights suspended on large beams. They are peculiar and I imagine in the right circumstances quite effective. When someone climbs up the masts to release the lines on which the weights are connected, they can drop onto other ships. This is a machination I cannot help but admire, but only for a moment, as I realize Barton is hoping to utilize them against us.

I look to my archer, a Yorkshire man called Hustler. "Kill any who try to go aloft," I tell him.

He offers a nervous nod, readying his bow. He aims. My body tenses, but there is even a thrill in the anxiety as I watch the arrow cut through the air to hit its mark, a young crewman attempting to scuttle up the mast, in the shoulder. He falls to the deck to be immediately replaced by another brave sailor attempting the same thing.

"Get him!" I cry.

Hustler draws back his next arrow and releases, again hitting his target.

After this is reduced to a monotony of death, Barton himself begins to climb the mast.

"Kill him," I tell Hustler.

Hustler's glance is unsure as he returns his eyes to the pirate.

"Kill him or die," I say with urgency.

Hustler flinches. "I've but two arrows. . . ."

"Use them well," I urge.

Hustler draws. The first assault bounces off Barton's armor like a twig against a stone wall. Trembling, Hustler reaches for his last arrow.

"Do it, man!" I command.

Hustler pulls back. Barton reaches up to assure himself better grip on the mast.

"Now!" I shout.

Hustler releases. The arrow slices through the air. I can hear it even over the shouts of the men. It pierces through Barton's armpit, that soft bit of flesh left vulnerable to attack.

He falls; it seems too slow to be real. I watch him hit deck. Crewmen rush to his side.

"Fight on!" he orders in his brogue, loud enough for me to hear. "I am a little wounded but not slain. I will but rest a while and then rise and fight once more. Meantime, stand fast by St. Andrew's Cross!" He raises his eyes to the Scots' flag.

I shake my head in admiration. As my eyes travel to the sailors on board the *Lion*, I note how stricken they are. He is not only a good commander, he is also loved; it is not an easy combination to attain.

When Barton can no longer shout orders, he resorts to blowing his golden whistle.

And then the whistle is heard no more.

Barton is dead.

We bring in the *Lion*, where it is added to the royal fleet, and we are toasted as heroes.

I have won!

Elizabeth Stafford, Spring 1512

King Henry has joined the Holy League in an allegiance against France's King Louis, who was hoping to conquer Italy. Everyone is drunk with war; even the masques and pageants all feature weapons and armor, and the themes are not at all as pleasant as they used to be. I must say, I blame the Howards. They are so hungry for conquest, any kind of conquest, that they started the whole thing with the slaying of the pirate Barton, giving the king his first taste of victory. If Lord Thomas Howard is any indication, once a man tastes victory, there is created in him an insatiable thirst for more. When the king sent him off with the Marquess of Dorset to engage the French army near Bayonne in early June, I thought the stern-faced man would break into a jig of excitement.

Now it is the king who is parched. He does not want to send others to fight his battles; he needs to be a part of them. He wants to be a warrior-king like his father before him and drink in a long draught of Tudor triumph.

Ralph Neville, a young courtier newly arrived, is quick to correct me as we walk in the gardens of Greenwich in late June. "The Howards are all about the Scots," he tells me. "It is Wolsey who prompts action against the French, to reclaim our lost holdings there for the glory of King Henry!"

Whenever Ralph speaks to me, I am far too beside myself to think of war or anything disagreeable. Ralph will be the fourth Earl of Westmorland and was made a ward of my father in 1510. He was the lankiest, gawkiest, and most thoroughly awkward lad I had ever seen back then. But now! Now he is the handsomest man at court, tall and lean and self-assured, with honey blond hair and clear blue eyes that are so light they are almost silver. His smile is easy and he is quick to laugh. He has sought me out a number of times now for walks in the gardens and I relish every encounter.

"I don't care who prompts what," I tell him. "Whether it's the Earl of Surrey or Wolsey or whoever; I just don't want a war."

"You're not even the least bit excited to see the knights leave? It's going to be quite a spectacle. I think the king will even make war an entertainment," he adds with a laugh.

"It's all a pretty spectacle till they return fewer in numbers," I say in haughty tones. I lower my eyes, swallowing a painful lump in my throat. "My father is accompanying the king, you know."

Humbled, Ralph reaches for my hand. It is our first touch. We are fifteen years old, two trembling youths wondering what lies be-yond this brief contact of skin against skin. His eyes seek mine. They are soft and calm as the afternoon sky.

"If I offended you, I am sorry," he says in sweet tones.

"I am not offended," I respond, trying to keep my voice steady. "I just—I just agree with Father Colet. Don't you remember his Good Friday sermon? He said 'an unquiet peace is preferable to a just war.' "

"You must learn this now, Lady Elizabeth," says Ralph, stroking my thumb. "That an unquiet peace can be more miserable than a decisive battle. One can live a whole lifetime in a state of unquiet peace."

I do not know how to respond. I do not like being challenged this way. I would just like someone to see things as I do. I expel a heavy sigh of frustration.

"Your father will return, my lady," he assures me. He bows his head. "Oh, I do wish I could be among them! But, alas, I must re-main behind." He casts a shy glance my way and I shiver in de-light.

"I hope you can find ways to pass the time while everyone is harvesting their fruits of fortune on the battlefield," I say with a smile.

He reaches up, tracing my jawline with a velvet fingertip. "I'm sure I can find something. . . ."

He leans forward, pressing his lips to mine. They are soft and moist, warm, filled with sweet eagerness. Only loyalty to my good queen's virtues gives me the will to pull away and stare into his face in bewildered joy.

"Ralph . . ." I murmur, just for the sake of saying his name.

He kisses my forehead. "I have longed for you, Elizabeth," he says. "Say you are mine."

The courtly language is not the least bit original but as it is ad-dressed to me, I cannot help but offer a giddy little nod and say, "Yes!"

"When your father returns, we will seek his permission to be married," he continues, his eyes wide with excitement.

I cannot say I really know Ralph altogether well, but he is so handsome and charming that the thought of being his wife has me nodding my assent, caught up in his enthusiasm. I am already imagining what our children will look like. They'll have our blue eyes, no doubt. I begin to tingle.

"Oh, Ralph, do go away so I can find someone to confide our news to!" I cry, shooing him off.

Ralph laughs, rising from the garden bench and dipping into an extravagant bow. "Fare thee well, my wife," he whispers.

My face flushes bright crimson. I lower my eyes, watching Ralph's boots as they plod off.

All thoughts of battle and bloodshed are abated, replaced with fantasies of a grand wedding.

I shall be Elizabeth Neville!

The king departs with great fanfare. My father accompanies him with an entourage of six hundred archers, three hundred household servants, musicians—even the choir of the Chapel Royal! No one is left out of this campaign. Wolsey leaves, Bishop Foxe leaves—everyone. They are all dressed in the Tudor livery of green and white. It is a splendid farewell.

The queen rules as regent from Greenwich Palace and it is very quiet without His Majesty. In the company of Her Grace I help sew banners and badges and standards for our soldiers. As my fingers work the needle, I feel I am a part of something great, that somewhere in France someone will be carrying a standard or wearing a badge that I, Elizabeth Stafford, have sewn with all of my love and good wishes.

We follow the war from our safe vantage, learning that on 16 August the king and Emperor Maximilian I routed the French at what became known as the Battle of the Spurs, taking the town of Therouanne.

But the triumphs are accompanied by tragedies. We learn of the casualties. Thomas Knyvet, the shy courtier who amused us all by climbing naked up a pillar when the rabble stole his clothes at the festivities celebrating the late prince's birth, died at sea off Brest when fighting the French. There are so many others, all young merry men eager for such useless enterprise.

With heavy hearts we mourn our soldiers. Soon there are no more banners to sew, no more standards to bear. The queen's household grows smaller and smaller.

I am sent home to Thornbury that autumn, but to my delight, Ralph Neville, as my father's ward, is there as well. As much as I am devoted to Her Grace, I am relieved to be away for a while. The household was so tense waiting for news of the king's success that my gut was constantly churning and lurching in anxiety.

Now I have but to await the return of the king and his army in a more peaceful place with my betrothed at my side.

Change Winds

It is a thoroughly disgusting affair. No one has come through for me, not the kings of England or Spain. I am short supplies, horses, everything needed for any successful endeavor of war. I write Wolsey, that ridiculous upstart, appealing for some sort of objective in all this. After our success at Bayonne, I am left with little or no direction. Should we try for Aquitaine? No one knows and they're certainly not inclined to inform me.

Meantime I am beset with sick men, bad weather, and worse morale. Wolsey is blamed for it all, to my good fortune, and it is not long before I decide it prudent to wash my hands of the whole affair.

I hire ships to take us home. The king is in a Tudor temper, but there is nothing else to be done. I am not going to remain so that we might be obliterated by dejection, inactivity, and Spanish food.

And so I leave Spain behind. I have not failed. I cannot help if no one cooperated with me and I was given no aid or support. This affair could not have been handled more ineffectively. It is Wolsey's fault, not mine. Yes, that is it. Someday the king will see that, hopefully sooner than later.

I will not think on it anymore. There will be other wars and other victories. For now I am content to go home to my princess and rest.

*   *   *

She is at Lambeth with my stepmother, Agnes, and her increasing brood. When I arrive, Agnes greets me with a sad shake of her head.

"She cannot rise from her bed," she tells me in her gruff voice. "She's in a bad way, my lord. I am sorry."

I rush to her chambers, panic gripping my heart. It is thudding wildly in my chest; I hear it pounding in my ears. I slow my steps upon entering her sanctuary. Everything about her suggests the need for quiet and tranquility.

She lies abed. Her rose-gold hair is plaited and worn over her shoulder. Her skin is so pale it is almost translucent, pearly and ethereal as a seraph. She is so much thinner than when last I saw her. Once so tall and fine of figure, she is now all bones. Upon seeing me, she offers a weak smile. Her lips are blue.

"My lord . . ."

I have not cried in a long while, not since the death of my Thomas. I had thought to be through with tears forever, but now they come easily enough, flowing icily down my cheeks unchecked as I approach the bed. I am as tentative as the child I was when I approached my mother's bed after she bore my Alyss, another life fated to be stolen from me.

I sit beside my wife, reaching out to stroke her fevered brow. I remove her nightcap. "This is making you hotter," I say uselessly. Then in a strangled voice I add, "I do not understand. You were not this bad when I left. . . ."

"Don't be frightened, my love," she tells me, reaching up to cup my cheek. With a slender thumb she wipes away a tear. Her eyes are soft, unafraid, and filled with something I had not seen in what seemed like an eternity: hope. "Soon it will be over. I am going to the faery country. I will be with the children."

My heart lurches at this. She has not spoken of her faery folk in years. I do not know what to say. I continue stroking her brow, but my hand jerks and trembles and I imagine it does little to soothe her.

"I waited for you," she whispers, coughing. "And now that you are here, I beseech you for your blessing, dearest Thomas."

"You have it," I tell her in urgent tones. "You've always had it."

She closes her eyes. The smile remains.

"Princess!" I cry, cupping her face.

Her eyes flutter open. They are filled with pity. "Let me go, Thomas," she whispers. "Let me go. Please. I am not meant for this world. I never was. You know that."

Despite my urge to dispute this, I find myself nodding. It is true. From the first she seemed to belong to some other place, some intangible realm of existence forbidden to lesser beings.

"What will become of me?" I ask in a small voice, feeling as desperate and despondent as an abandoned child.

She offers a slight laugh. "I don't worry about you," she tells me. "You are a Howard. Howards survive."

She avails herself to a fit of coughing. Blood spews forth, coating the front of her nightdress.

Now, I have seen much in battle. I have been drenched in the blood and gore of my enemies as well as my own, but nothing compares to this. This is my princess. This is not supposed to happen to my princess. . . .

My heart skips in wild fear. "Somebody help her! Somebody help her!" I cry.

Servants flood the room, attending her with gentle hands. But she has no need of it. Her eyes have focused on her faery country; she is gone. I gesture for the servants to cease their ministrations. They depart, heads bowed, some making the sign of the cross.

I gather my princess in my arms. She is limp, heavy. I cradle her head in the crook of my shoulder, watching my tears glisten off her rose-gold hair.

I begin to sway, humming some tuneless song in nervousness.

I am alone. She is the last of my short-lived family.

I am alone.

After her interment, I lie abed at Lambeth, allowing myself the luxury of dwelling on the past. I do not scream or cry or rage against God. I think of my princess, of the first time I saw her at Westminster. I think of our wedding, of our babies. . . . I do not want to think of the losses just yet. I want to imagine them all twirling and laughing in some faery garden. I want to imagine her smile, her sweet soft voice, her gentle touch.

My father comes to me one night, interrupting my musings with more unwanted realities. He sits on the edge of my bed, regarding me with sad brown eyes.

"We both know what it's like to lose," he begins, folding his hands and bowing his head. "What I am about to tell you may sound cold, even cruel but, my son . . . you must move on now."

"Move on? Are you mad? I just buried her!" I cry, sitting up.

My father nods. "Yes. She is gone. Now you must rebuild. You are an earl's firstborn son. Someday everything I have will go to you. And then where? You need a young, sturdy wife and a houseful of children. Your marriage was dead long before your princess—"

It is all I can do to refrain from slapping him outright.

"I have arranged for you to meet with Buckingham's daughters at Shrovetide," he informs me, unaffected by my outraged expression. "You would do yourself credit to make a match with one of them. They are offering a good dowry and it seems the Staffords are of fertile stock." He pauses, then reaches out to pat my leg. His tone is gentle. "We are not a breed who can afford to love. That is left to the peasants; call it their one great extravagance, their compensation for their miserable lot in life." He shakes his head. "But us . . . no, not us. We marry for advantage; we marry so that we might be the founders of dynasties. It is a business, Tom. You were fortunate with your princess if you found some affection. But now you are of an age to put such nonsense away and look toward what is practical. Marry. Assure me a great line of successors."

The anger fades to numbness. I nod, accepting the truth in his words. I am the son of an earl. I cannot leave my inheritance to a sibling or nephew. I have to rebuild.

The princess would understand. She told me I would survive, and part of ensuring that survival is marrying again. It will not be the same. How could it ever be the same?

"A Stafford girl," I say, lying back down and closing my eyes. "I suppose it doesn't matter who she is as long as she's a good breeder."

"Good lad," says my father, patting my leg again. He rises. "Nothing like having your bed warmed again to abate your grief. That's what I did, and Agnes and I have proven quite successful."

"Yes," I say in cool tones. "It is a good business."

No longer will marriage be considered anything else to me.

Elizabeth Stafford, Yuletide 1512

Everything is so wonderful. Father is home safe but has been so preoccupied that Ralph and I have had plenty of time to be alone. He reads me poetry and sings me frivolous little songs. We play with the dogs and take long walks in the snow. My sister Catherine teases me.

"I see roses in winter!" she cries.

"Where?"

"On your cheeks!" She laughs. "Who put them there?"

We dissolve into giggles as I recount Ralph's attributes. Is it his smile I like best or the silkiness of his blond hair, or perhaps his spontaneous laugh? I shiver and giggle for no reason and every reason. Oh, to always remain young and in love and happy!

Ralph decides to ask for my hand at Christmas. It is the perfect arrangement. One of the primary benefits of taking on a ward is ensuring the right of marriage to a member of the guardian's family—in this case, me. How could anyone object? It is probably what they have been planning all along.

While Ralph takes my parents aside in the parlor for a cordial, Catherine and I wait in the dining hall.

"Father loves Ralph," I say, my hands twitching in nervousness. "He must have had plans for him to enter our family from the start, don't you think? Oh, Catherine, it will happen, won't it?"

Catherine offers her gentle laugh. She is a plump and merry girl with deep dimples on either side of her rosy mouth and lively blue eyes. "It will be fine, sweeting. Don't fret so. It was ordained from the start!"

My heart is pounding. My cheeks are hot and my breathing short. My head tingles. I don't know what to do with my hands and keep flexing my fingers.

At last my parents emerge with Ralph. His face is drawn, his eyes are red, and his lips are puffy. He rushes past Catherine and me and I rise, trying to stop him, but am not quick enough. Father reaches me first, seizing my hand.

"I did not tell him no," he informs me in his gentle voice. "But it must wait."

"Why?" I ask, biting my quivering lip.

"We are having a guest," he says slowly.

"What does that matter?" I furrow my brow in frustration.

He reaches out to rub my upper arm. "He is coming to look you girls over and decide which of you he would like to take to wife."

Catherine and I turn to each other. I approach her, taking her hands in mine. We draw near one another.

"Who?" I whisper.

"Lord Thomas Howard."

"Lord Howard!" I cry. "But he's married!"

He shakes his head. "He is a widower newly made."

"How newly?" I demand.

"Lady Anne Plantagenet passed in late November," he replies, bowing his head. "God rest her sweet soul."

"Gracious, he doesn't waste any time!" I cry, furious.

"Elizabeth!" Father's voice is sharp. "Remember yourself! His reasons are not for us to question."

I look to my sister, who at thirteen is already more rounded in figure than I. As uncharitable as it may sound, I hope he chooses her. I shall have speech with her later about endeavoring to make a good impression on him.

My shoulders slump. "He's so much older than we," I find myself saying despite the fact that I wish to make him seem a favorable match to my sister. "He is at least forty," I am compelled to add.

"That may well be, but he is an earl's son and that family is rising in favor every day," Father says, wrapping his arms about both our shoulders.

"And," quips Mother, "you must admit he is in finer form than many men half his age."

I don't care a fig about that. Ralph Neville may not have Lord

Howard's well-turned legs, but he is the sweetest, most beautiful . . . oh, please God. I turn to my sister. She looks as dumb and appealing as any man would want a girl to look. Surely he'll choose her. . . .

Thomas Howard

It seems the sun still shines and the snow still falls. The birds sing and I manage to take in nourishment. I sleep and dream and think and live even without the princess. But the ache, that relentless dull throb filling my chest, encircling my heart like a coiling snake, never abates. It pursues me with the ardor of a new lover.

I divert myself with hunting. I watch the crimson blood of my kill stain the snow and try not to remember the blood of the princess against the stark white of her cheek. It is no use. Sometimes I sink to my knees with my bow amongst the silence of the trees, watching the sun filtering through the canopy of branches above. I watch a chipmunk scamper across the moss. Does he talk to the faeries? Does he know my princess? Can he tell her . . . What would I have him tell her? There is so much, and all left unsaid.

I abandon these strange fancies and at Shrovetide remove to Thornbury, where I must fulfill my obligation to my family and choose a bride.

The pre-Lenten celebrations are in full tilt when I arrive. A feast is laid out in my honor and though food holds little appeal for me now, save for the fact that it is what keeps me alive, I partake of the lamb in mint jelly, peacock, cheese, warm bread, and sweet comfits with feigned enthusiasm.

It is very strange, this choosing of a wife. My first marriage was arranged for me, which was most appropriate for that time in my life. I did not have to fret about a thing. Negotiations were made above our innocent heads and all we had to worry about was pleasing each other. That was easy to do.

But now it is different. Now I am in control of my fate and I must choose a wife, mother, and helpmate. And I have one night to do it.

I assess the girls. They are quite young. I recall the one called Elizabeth from our few encounters at court. Though she is on the thin side, she has grown into a beautiful young lady with her long waves of chestnut hair threaded with auburn tumbling loose down her back. Her blue eyes remain fierce and determined and she has retained that set jawline. Her smile is slow in coming but worth waiting for.

The younger sister Catherine is a beauty as well, though a little too plump for my liking. It is pleasant now, but I imagine once she drops a pup, she will give herself over to resembling the broad side of a ship, which just wouldn't do.

Yet there is a sweet element in Catherine that seems lacking in Elizabeth.

How does one know what is right? We eat and make small talk but they say little. I converse more with the duke, who proudly lists his daughters' talents and virtues, and I listen attentively. Catherine excels at embroidery, but Elizabeth can sing like a bird. Catherine is a beautiful dancer, but Elizabeth is a skilled equestrienne.

I will just have to see how this night goes.

Elizabeth Stafford

Look at him narrowing his black eyes at us as though he is assessing jewels for scrapes and flaws! Oh, I remember him right enough. A well-intended man but an arrogant knight nonetheless. Well, I shan't do a thing to impress him tonight. I will be myself and say and do exactly as I like and if Father is displeased with me, so be it. Let him have Catherine. I love her and I truly don't want to make her a sacrifice, but if it comes down to her or me . . .

"So, Mistress Elizabeth," he begins, leaning forward to look down his long nose at me. "What is your favorite thing to do?"

"I enjoy passing time with young people," I tell him in sharp tones. "Young, merry people."

Mother shoots me a warning glance.

Lord Howard's lips curve into a half smile. "Yes. We all delight in that. And what do you do while passing time with these young merrymakers?"

"We are not all about frivolity, Lord Howard," I tell him. "But as we are of an age, we have much in common to discuss that people of . . . well, a different age would not be able to understand."

He laughs. "Of course. Because people of a different age have never been where you are, is that it? Or have we in our dotage forgotten, perhaps, since it was so very long ago?"

I pause. I do not seem to be the victor in this battle of wits. "Perhaps," I say at last.

Lord Howard rises, extending his elegant hand toward me. "Dance with me, Mistress Elizabeth."

"My sister is the pretty dancer," I tell him. "I do not like to dance."

"Dance with Lord Howard," Mother snaps, then offers a quick smile at the haughty knight.

"You mean to say you, the young merrymaker, do not like to dance?" His tone is mockingly incredulous. "Come now." He takes me in his arms and turns me about the floor.

It is then I recall the first time I danced with Lord Howard, when at twelve years old I felt that strange energy flowing between our joined hands. It is there again. At once my body is not obeying me. It begins to tremble and tingle. A frightening heat surges through my veins.

Lord Howard's face is soft, sort of wistful. I meet his eyes and wonder what it is like to be a man having to start completely over at his age when he should be enjoying his children and maybe even a grandchild or two by now.

I must not pity him. I must not give him any indication of warmth.

Thomas Howard

She's shorter than I, this Elizabeth. The other one looks like she has a few inches in her yet and I definitely do not need a woman who is both tall and fat. This one's drawback is in her slight frame, but from holding her, I have been able to assess her hips with a reasonable amount of discretion and they seem round enough to facilitate childbearing.

And that face! The challenging eyes, the sarcastic little smile . . .

Of course there is absolutely nothing to love in this girl. She will look lovely on my arm, but she does not inspire the madness I once felt for—enough of that. No, if I lost her, I would not be sorry. I could replace her.

But there is something about her face. . . .

After I allow Elizabeth to be seated I dance with the other one. She is a pretty dancer, far exceeding her sister's abilities, and all of Stafford's guests stop to gaze and compliment the fleet little steps.

This one is a bit dull, however. Her face is as docile as a cow's and her eyes lack any real intelligence. I imagine she will be quite fertile, however, and, as I feel her hips, know without doubt that if I choose her, I would beget a veritable empire.

She makes pleasant conversation if one likes to talk about weather and shoes and food, but after a while the shrill little voice begins to grate on me. Perhaps I am being a bit unfair.

I suppose I knew from the moment I saw her again that I would choose Elizabeth.

Elizabeth Stafford

"No!" I cry when Mother tells me the next afternoon that it is I, not Catherine, whom Lord Howard has chosen to wed. "I won't do it. I . . . I am to marry Lord Neville."

"Did he give you a ring?" asks Mother in soft tones as she strokes my hair. "Did you plight your troth to one another?"

"We—we—" I sob, falling against my bed, burying my head in my pillows, knowing it is all useless. Mother leans over to gather me in her arms.

"Darling, I understand how disappointed you are," she tells me. "We have all been in your position." Tears light her gray eyes and I find myself wondering who she gave up for my father. Strange to think one's parents loved and dreamed and hoped with the same passion as oneself. "But this is God's will," she continues in practical tones. "If you were meant to be with young Ralph, the way would have been provided for you. However, it is not to be. You will marry Lord Howard at Easter."

Easter! Why does it all have to happen right now? Why does it have to happen at all? My heart is racing. I want to scream in protest but know it is futile. My father is the premier duke in the realm. What he says is law.

Still, I cannot help but ask, "Why didn't he want Catherine? She's so sweet and agreeable; she's what every man should want."

Mother bows her head. "I'm sorry, Elizabeth. He wants you. It's all settled. Even now they are arranging the dowry."

"Yes, God forbid they wait a moment on that," I say, my tone laced with bitterness. "So that's it, then. I will go to him with however many marks Father sends and you will be rid of me. And what of . . . of Lord Neville?"

"Other plans will be made for him," Mother says, averting her eyes.

"What other plans?"

Mother returns her gaze to me. The gray eyes are hard, impenetrable. "Other plans."

I bury my face in the pillows once more and give way to the release sobbing provides.

Despite the urge to suggest running away to Ralph, I resist. I will not shame my family with such nonsense. There is naught to do but say good-bye.

We stroll in the gardens hand in hand. The air is crisp but the sun is shining, warming my tearstained cheeks.

"Do you believe in the will of God?" I ask him.

He shrugs. "It is what we have been taught."

"It is the easiest explanation," I say. "Easy to say God is responsible for this and that and not us." I swallow the tears in my throat. "Oh, Ralph . . ." I lean my head on his shoulder.

He offers a heavy sigh. "I want you to be happy, Elizabeth," he says at last. "I hope you have many children."

"Please don't speak of it," I tell him. "I can't bear to think of all that just now. Let us be silent and take comfort in each other's company while we can."

Ralph nods. We sit on one of the garden benches. He wraps his arm about my shoulders and draws me near, holding me thus for a long while.

There is no kiss good-bye.

It would not be proper.

It is not the grand ceremony I hoped for. My dress is beautiful enough, yards of soft pink damask inlaid with seed pearls, fitted sleeves, and a five-foot train. But everything else is wrong. It is so rushed. No one, not even my own parents, seems to be in a cele-bratory mood. Lord Howard kneels beside me at the altar, his face drawn with solemnity. I steal glances at him throughout the cere-mony, but his expression does not change. There is no reassuring smile, no squeeze of the hand. Nothing to indicate he is happy with our match.

He slips a tiny gold band about my finger and I hear the words of the bishop pronouncing us man and wife. I hear myself being introduced as Lady Elizabeth Howard.

I turn to my lord. It is over. I have given myself over to the wills of my parents and God and whatever other cruel forces have a role in these decisions, and I am his. He leans over, offering me the briefest of kisses on my cheek.

I begin to tremble with fear. I have just wed a forty-year-old man with experience and I am a fifteen-year-old maiden. I try to still my quivering lip and blink away the tears but find as we quit the chapel, my arm looped through his, that they stream down my cheeks unchecked.

If Lord Howard notices, he says nothing.

Thomas Howard

Well, I did what my father wanted so will hear no complaints from him. I am married. Strange to say it, knowing the wife to which I refer is not the princess I shared seventeen years of my life with.

The girl is a reluctant bride, that much is clear. Her father informed me, with a face flushed in embarrassment, that she had a little infatuation for their ward, Ralph Neville, which explains the boy's stony countenance and brusque manner whenever I tried to converse with him. I am assured, however, that the girl comes to me intact. Whatever childish feelings she holds for the lad will soon subside when distracted with the duties of marriage.

We retire to our bridal chamber. I am pleased to be unaccompanied by the court this time, so I can conduct this business in private. The girl wears a white nightdress of satin trimmed with pink ribbons.

For a while we lie side by side in the darkness. I have not been with many women, but I cannot say I was faithful to the princess. Things happen when a man is at war. She never questioned me; as much as she did not belong in the world, she knew well the ways of it. Our couplings were filled with tenderness, however, and when I was with her, there was no other woman on my mind.

Now, faced with a new bride, I must force the princess from my thoughts.

The girl trembles beside me. She clutches the covers over her shoulders. I do not know how to approach her. I do not know what to say.

At once I decide the best tactic is to just get it over with. With abruptness I draw the covers back and roll on top of her, attempting to raise her nightdress over her hips. She cries out. I cannot rouse my desire looking into those terrified blue eyes, knowing they are not the eyes of my princess, knowing there is no love to be had in them. What am I thinking? I knew well there would be no love in this match when I chose her. I must put aside these infantile fantasies.

I offer a frustrated sigh and roll onto my back.

"I'm sorry," she mutters. "I just didn't expect—"

I grunt and rise. Perhaps it is best if I spend my wedding night in my own chambers. I have the rest of my life to consummate this marriage.

Elizabeth Howard

I lie alone in the big bed, feeling the vacant spot beside me with my leg. I was monstrous. I should not have demonstrated my fear. I rise, fetching my wrap. I am not about to fail in my duties. I cannot dwell on Ralph Neville now. I have married Thomas Howard and I will be his wife.

At last I arrive at my lord's bedchamber. I enter on soft feet. He is lying on his side, back to me, giving no indication that he has heard me. I pad toward the bed, drawing in a breath before turning down the covers and climbing in beside him. For a moment we are still. From the rhythm of his breathing I discern that he is awake.

Trembling, I move closer to him. I wrap my arm about his middle and snuggle in between his shoulder blades, folding my legs against his so we resemble a pair of spoons.

"I did not marry to sleep alone," I tell him in low tones.

He rolls toward me, cupping my cheek with his hand, stroking idly. It moves to the back of my neck, drawing me forward so that he might offer soft little kisses on my cheek, then my jawline, till at last he reaches my mouth. His lips are soft and warm but filled with urgency rather than gentleness. I return the kiss with equal ardor. His other hand explores my body, bringing about sensations I have never experienced before. I tremble when he encounters my bare leg with his fingertips. I dare run my hands over his chest. Through his nightclothes I feel the warmth and strength ebbing through him. I run my hand down his side to his hip, reaching under his gown to feel the strong leg everyone admires. It is now mine. He trembles beneath my touch.

At once he pulls away. He sits up, swinging his legs over the side of the bed. I am so startled I can think of nothing to do but sit up with him. I stare at our feet. His are as well sculpted as his hands. Mine are tiny and delicate. I move one toward him; our ankles entwine.

"Do I displease you?" I whisper.

He shakes his head. The moonlight filtering through the window reveals the tears glistening off his cheeks. My heart stirs.

"It will not be the same," I tell him in soft tones. "But I will try and be a good wife to you."

Lord Howard turns to me, offering a sad little smile.

He wraps his arm about my shoulders.

We sit out our wedding night in companionable silence, watching the sapphire sky through our window give itself over to indigo, then pink as the sun rises and brings with it a new day.

Whatever overtook my lord's ability to carry out his wedding chore is more than compensated for that morning, and half of the day is occupied with the activity. It isn't the worst of ordeals and I imagine I could grow to like it were not my husband's eyes so distracted and my thoughts on Ralph Neville.

It is fruitless torturing myself with these fantasies. They do not serve any purpose. One of us has to be cognizant of the fact that we are married to each other and not to the ones occupying our hearts. And I cannot bear dreaming about Ralph, pretending it is he and not Thomas Howard caressing me. Perhaps if what Lord Howard did could be called caressing, it wouldn't be so difficult, but he is such a rough, urgent lover that I am forced into awareness. It is he and not Ralph who is destined to be my reality for the rest of my life.

So I will be the kind of lover I imagine he wants. I will meet urgency for urgency, passion for passion. I will try to ignore the fact that there seems to be no joy in our couplings but rather a strange frustrated melancholy that leaves one stifling bittersweet tears.

It has to get better. I must remember he was just widowed and Anne Plantagenet would be hard to forget; she was the consummate lady, the epitome of grace and nobility. Not only did he suffer her loss but that of all four—all four!—of his children. One cannot remain unscarred from such tragedy.

I will be patient. In the meantime I will be the best wife I can be. I will not be Lady Anne. I will see that he values me for who I am, and when our first child arrives, it will serve to abate his pain as well. I am not fool enough to believe I can replace his first wife, that our children can replace his first children.

But I can bring him joy, if he will accept it.

*   *   *

Lord Howard occupies himself with the running of his estates, keeping to himself much of the time. He takes day trips, not arriving at Lambeth until long after I am abed. I am always awake when he comes in, eager to fulfill my marital duties, which have become quite pleasant if nothing else has.

We never talk. There is little opportunity and when we do manage a sparse conversation here and there, it is about the most mundane things.

It will take a long time to know his soul, I think.

We are not married a month when my lord learns of his brother's death. Lord Admiral Edward Howard, everyone's favorite little Neddy, was trying to avenge his brother-in-law Thomas Knyvet's death in Brest where the English fleet had been holding off the French navy.

"Not Edward!" Lord Howard cries after shooing the breathless messenger away with a distracted wave of his hand. I send the lad to the kitchens for refreshment, then take to my husband's side.

He shakes his head. "Not Neddy," he says in soft tones, sinking onto the bench in the dining hall. I sit beside him. "He . . . he always defended me." His voice is almost a whisper. He turns his head. After a moment he draws in a breath, lifting his head and squaring his shoulders. "I am lord high admiral now," he tells me.

I think this is a strange way to follow up the lament for his slain brother but say nothing.

"I will have the power to avenge his death," he goes on, his voice so calm it is eerie. His black eyes are burning with the same fire present when making love.

"I'm so sorry about Ned," I tell him, daring to rest a hand on his arm. "He was much loved."

Lord Howard withdraws his arm, rising with such speed he rocks the bench off balance, and only my catching the table behind me with my elbows saves me from falling on the floor.

"Yes, everyone loved Ned," he says, his voice taut. "The king especially. What will he do without his favorite Howard? Rely more on Wolsey and Charles Brandon, I suppose." He draws in a sigh. "But no matter. There are other ways we can retain his favor."

"How can you think of such things and your brother not even buried?" I breathe in awe. "No wonder you worry about retaining the king's favor with deeds—you will not win him with personality!"

Before I can say another word, Lord Howard leaps toward me, pulling me off the bench by the shoulders. "I did not ask for your opinion, madam," he seethes.

"Release me!" I cry, wrenching free, appalled by such barbarous tactics.

His chest is heaving. He is pointing—actually pointing!—at me, his finger inches from my face as though I am a disobedient child. "You cannot understand," he says. "You will not speak of things you do not understand."

Rather than inspiring my silence, this treatment causes a surge of anger to course through me. "I will say as I please!" I cry. "I am your *wife*—"

"That is right!" he returns, drawing back his hand, and before I can dodge or deflect the blow I find I am being struck on the cheek. The slap resounds in my ear with a high-pitched ring; my face tingles with such intensity it seems to hum.

"And what is expected of a Christian wife?" he asks in calm tones that are so incongruous with the violence he just exhibited. "To obey thy husband."

I am far too enraged to think. I respond to the slap with one of my own, enjoying the sound of my palm striking his skin. Lord Howard stands rubbing his cheek in a moment of befuddlement from which he quickly recovers, adopting an expression of impenetrable hardness.

It is an expression I have no trouble matching. I fold my arms across my chest and scowl. "I will obey you, God knows," I say in low tones. "No wife in the realm will be as obedient. I promised to be faithful, to take care of you, and to endure by your side. Endure I shall. But nowhere in the Bible does it say that I cannot speak my heart. Part of being faithful is telling the truth at all costs and, Thomas Howard, I will *always* tell the truth." I close my eyes a moment. My cheek is hot from the slap. I shake my head. "And now the truth we are facing is that your brother, the favored brother, is dead, and you are as angry about his place in the king's heart as you are about his death." I open my eyes to find that my husband's face has traded its ferocity for attentiveness. I dare continue. "If you do not take time to mourn him and sort out your resentment before seeking your revenge, you will be poisoned with it; your judgment will be clouded and you will fail. When going into battle, go in with a cool head. Plan your objective. You want the king's favor? Then you must learn to be what the king loves best: merry, humorous, useful, and intelligent. Above all, indispensable. We already know you are useful in battle, which requires an intelligence of sorts. But there is another kind, a sort of emotional element that you clearly need to improve upon. You have to learn to be in sympathy with the king in the ways he appreciates."

"One would think you to be quite the seasoned adviser," he comments, his tone a mingling of sarcasm and admiration. His black eyes are lit with a kind of approval that I relish.

"You did not marry a fool," I tell him with an annoyed click of the tongue.

He says nothing to this but offers a half smile. "While we are on the subject of truth, do enlighten me with another. Tell me about Ralph Neville."

My heart lurches in my chest. How does he know? I have not seen him since we were wed; I am innocent of anything he could accuse me of, but Lord Howard's expression indicates he does not care whether I am innocent or not.

But I will hold to my creed. I vowed to speak the truth and so I shall. I draw in a breath. "What about him?"

"You loved him," he says.

I nod, meeting his gaze. "Yes."

What is it softening his eyes? Disappointment?

"You did not want to marry me," he states, his voice very quiet.

I shake my head.

He turns toward the window, looking out at the gardens. Spring has arrived. Little green shoots push their bare heads through the soil to greet the sun with the promise of donning their flowery headdresses.

"But I have married you," I tell him, my voice gentle. "And as I said, I will be a good wife. I will be faithful and steadfast as is required of me."

"Yes. As is required." He sighs. He clasps his hands behind his back, turning toward me once more. "Your father warned me of your plight; I do not know why I asked for a recitation. Besides, I was required to marry you as well. Were it expedient, I would have remained in the single estate." He chuckles. "Worry not, my lady. There is no love lost between us. But if you obey me, plan no dalliances, and behave as befitting your station, we shall get on quite well."

I swallow a lump rising in my throat.

He approaches me, reaching out to stroke the cheek still stinging with his slap. "I rather appreciate your honesty," he says offhandedly. "In turn I shall favor you with your own philosophy. I will always tell you the truth, Elizabeth."

He drops his hand. I stare at him in a moment of confusion. Now that we have promised to tell the truth at all times, there are too many to impart and most of them are unwanted. I do not want to know that my lord has a side to him that is dark and cruel. I do not want to know that he is filled with irreparable bitterness. I do not want to know that our marriage has very little chance of being loving.

"And now the truth is I must excuse myself and prepare for my excursion to Plymouth, where I will prepare my fleet," Lord Howard tells me, rubbing my cheek a moment more before quitting the room, leaving me quite alone and wretched.

In all these confrontations with truth, I have neglected to inform him of one that could have changed everything.

I am carrying our child.

Thomas Howard

I sit on my bed and stare at the hand that struck her. I close it into a fist. I hit her. I hit my fifteen-year-old bride.

What would the princess make of this?

It is the grief that made me do it, the grief and the anger about

Neddy. The girl called it. She is not a fool, this Elizabeth, that is certain. I rather like her. But she needs discipline. Regardless of her desire to adhere to her code of truth, she cannot use that as a cloak for disrespect. I am her husband, after all. And she is far more child than woman yet, requiring a bit of reining in. Buckingham must have overindulged her, causing her to become too accustomed to expressing unwanted opinions.

She is almost too clever. I wonder if it would have served me better to marry the dullard. It is too late now.

I sigh. I must make some kind of reparation.

Before setting out to Plymouth, I purchase an aquamarine as clear and eternal as her eyes. The morning I leave, I set it on the pillow beside her, pausing a moment to admire her face, which is set in determination even while asleep. What is she thinking about so hard?

I ponder leaving a note with it but can think of nothing to say, and being that we've spoken a vow of truth, I won't disrespect us both by becoming another composer of courtly nonsense.

On impulse I lean down and brush my lips against her forehead.

I cannot help myself. She looks . . . well, I suppose she looks sort of endearing lying there like that.

Elizabeth Howard

I open my eyes after my husband has quit the room, to admire the aquamarine he has set on the pillow where rested his head the night before. I prop myself up on one elbow and seize the object between thumb and forefinger. It is almost too large to be real, even larger than the knuckle on my thumb. Perhaps I shall have it set in a pendant and wear it on a gold chain about my throat. Or maybe I'll save it for the baby. If it's a girl, she can wear it; and if it's a boy, it can go to his betrothed someday.

I think of trying to catch my lord before he departs but am too tired. I imagine he does not want to see my reaction to his gift anyway; if he did, he would have bestowed it upon me while I was awake.

It is thoughtful, I can say that much, and I am not immune to the charms of a sparkling bauble. But if the only way of obtaining jewels is achieved by bearing the brunt of his hostility, I prefer to remain unadorned.

And so he has left me and prepares to fight in Brittany, where he might prove himself a hero. His enterprises seem to be cursed when it comes to the inconvenience of weather and supply issues and it isn't until June that he can even depart. Meantime, I am three months gone with child and, as I am so small, must add panels to my gowns to hide my condition. I avoid my stepmother-in-law's questioning glances when I take ill in the mornings and rest in the afternoons. I do not want anyone to tell him first. I want to be the one. I blame my nausea on something I ate that day or the heat of summer.

I begin to dream about the baby. This will make my lord so happy, I just know it. Then everything will change. He will soften and I will stop thinking about Ralph Neville. It will not do to dream of a man who isn't the father of the child growing within me. No, I must concentrate on my husband. I focus on all the good I have seen in him, as it is said bad thoughts could be unhealthy for the baby. I dream of Thomas Howard's handsome voice, his intense eyes, his strong and slender hands. I recall dancing with him, how strength and energy flowed from his embrace, filling me up. I think with a fluttering heart of the passion that has brought this child into my womb. My heart is light as I anticipate his reaction. It will rejuvenate his shattered spirit, I know. He will be excited and probably accept anything so long as it survives. Wouldn't anyone after his past?

I do not know what I'll call it. I suppose Edward or Thomas if it is a boy, depending upon what my lord thinks. He may want his brother honored, but then again, considering his mingled love and resentment, he may not. And he may not like the name Thomas either since his firstborn was christened thus. I suppose we could go with Henry, after the king.

If it is a girl I shall name her Catherine for my queen and my sister. I would even go so far as to call her Catalina for the queen's true name but dare not. That would be too Spanish for my family and I'd never hear the end of it.

This is how I wait out the war, sewing a baby's wardrobe and dreaming of names and cradles, of the sweet kissable cheeks of my little one and the tenderness that is sure to descend upon my husband's face when he gazes at the scene.

The Fruits of War

Elizabeth Howard, Summer-Autumn 1513

It seems Lord Howard will have no part in the French campaign after all. He is to stay behind with his father to "play nursemaid to Queen Catherine while the king indulges himself in the sport of war with that churl Wolsey at his side," he had cried in a fury. I told him we should be flattered. Surely the king values the Howards a great deal if he entrusts his wife and kingdom to our keeping, but I am waved off with a grimace of annoyance. Lord Howard takes the assignment as a personal slight.

It is not all in vain when the Scots attack, however. The spark that inflamed the Scots' malice was not only the Barton affair but that their warden of the East Marches, Sir Robert Kerr, was slain by our own John Heron of Ford. Henry VIII refused to surrender Heron to James IV, breaking the treaty of 1502. King Henry also neglected to finish paying his sister Margaret's dowry. So it is easy to understand their ire, and Lord Howard admits that if they were going to attack, now was the perfect time with the king abroad.

As I watch Lord Howard tremble with anticipation, I quake with terror. Bloodlust lights his eyes and as I bid my soldier farewell, I am not in envy of those who will be unfortunate enough to cross swords with him.

After he departs I throw myself upon my bed sobbing. Lady

Agnes rushes to my side with a posset. "Don't upset yourself, girl, for the child's sake."

I sit up, wiping my eyes and sniffling. "You knew, my lady?"

"Of course I knew. I've only spent half my life with child," she says with a wry smile. "I recognize well the signs."

"You haven't said . . . ?" I ask.

She shakes her head. "I would never deprive you of your moment," she tells me, her voice soft. " 'Twill be a happy day for the Howards when your little one arrives. Lord Thomas will certainly cherish you for it."

I rub the swell of my belly. "Oh, I hope so, my lady, so very much!"

And so together we wait for news, united in our anxiety for our husbands, the most illustrious soldiers in the land.

"Victory, my lady!" cries the filthy messenger to my stepmother on a rainy September afternoon. "And a great day it is for King Henry VIII!"

"Lord Surrey and Sir Thomas—they are alive?" I ask, clutching the lad's sleeve.

"Aye," he answers, nodding. He is about to burst with excitement. Blue eyes sparkle from a mud-stained face. "Outnumbered by ten thousand they were, but it mattered not to our brave Englishmen! They took their stand on the hill at Flodden Field and drove the bastards out—even capturing their brass cannon!"

Lady Agnes squeals in delight. "Cowardly Scots!"

"There's more, my lady!" he cries. "And this is by far the most glorious: the Scottish king—he's dead!" he finishes with a laugh. "His body was found near the litter of your good earl."

Lady Agnes presses her palms to her cheeks. "My, such a victory . . ." she breathes. She lowers herself onto one of the chairs in the parlor, her eyes lit with eagerness. "And the Howards secured it. Imagine what this means. . . ." She raises her eyes to the messenger. "Thank you, good lad. Now go feed yourself from our kitchens; we are pleased to share what we have with you."

He bows. "Thank you, my lady!" he cries, rushing off for his dinner, which I imagine he has not seen in a good long while.

Lady Agnes is smiling. "I think we'd best prepare for some changes, Lady Elizabeth," she says. "Big changes!"

At this the baby flutters in my womb. I offer a giggle in delight. Life will be good now; I've no doubt of it. Lord Howard will ride home to the cheers of the countryside. He will be rewarded by his king for keeping the kingdom safe.

But his biggest reward will be from me.

Thomas Howard

According to Queen Catherine, it is God and the leadership of the absent King Henry that won the battle of Flodden, but it is no matter. I suppose she is obligated to say that. Meantime I know the truth and if the look on Queen Catherine's face is any indication when we deliver the bloodied body of King James to her, she knows it, too.

"Dearest Lord Howard," she says in her soft accented voice as she rests a hand on my shoulder. "Well done." She closes her eyes, her face radiating sheer triumph. I cannot help but admire her. This is a woman who rode about in armor to inspire the soldiers at Buckingham before they marched north to Flodden. She is as fierce and proud as a woman can be, but in her these are not grating attributes. She is a queen in every sense of the word.

"Oh, *well done*, my defender and champion!" she cries again in pure joy, taking my hands in hers and squeezing. "Shall we send His Majesty the body, do you think?" she asks with a mischievous glint in her blue eyes.

"It may not be wise," my father intones gently. "King James was his brother-in-law, we must remember. The English would take to that well, Your Grace. But perhaps if we send his coat . . ."

"Yes," she says, righting herself under her canopy of state and offering a bright smile. "See that the coat of the slain king is sent to my husband in France," she orders. "It has been a time of victories for us all, has it not? The king has taken two towns in France and we have Flodden. You will be rewarded for your service," she assures us. "Richly rewarded."

"God bless Your Graces!" my father cries. "God bless and keep you always!"

All I can do is nod and bow. I am struck speechless as my mind speculates on our compensation for keeping England secure.

The queen's promise of rich rewards is made good. For the second time, the dukedom of Norfolk has been awarded to the Howards for our service to a king. My father relishes his new title and I enjoy referring to myself as the newly styled Earl of Surrey.

We will not lose our right this time. Not ever again.

I take to Lambeth where waits my stout stepmother Agnes and a horde of brothers and sisters demanding a recounting of the battle that I am all too happy to provide. It is a long moment before I notice Elizabeth is absent from the welcoming party.

Honestly, I think I forgot I was married.

When I do note she is gone, cold fear slithers through me, creeping up my spine and into my heart, where it rests in an icy knot.

"Where is Lady Elizabeth?" I ask in sustained panic.

"She has taken to her bed," answers my stepmother with a slight smile. Whether it is meant to reassure me I do not know.

"Well, send someone to wake her up," I say with a note of impatience.

"You go, Lord Thomas," says Agnes. "Isn't it a mite more romantic, the gallant warrior returning to his wife's bedside to kiss her awake?"

"Oh, nonsense and drivel!" I say, but it is with a laugh as I commence to our chambers. I do not bother with the door. I enter the room, suppressing the memory of my princess when last I saw her lying on her bed of death, covered in blood. . . . Oh, God, I cannot think of it. It is all right. I am not going to see that. . . .

Elizabeth is in bed but, unlike my princess, is curled up on her side, sleeping. Her cheeks are rosy with life and her dark hair is strewn in waves over her shoulder. Her little hand is curled under her chin. For a moment I just watch her. She is a pretty thing, if nothing else.

I shake her shoulder. "Elizabeth . . ."

She turns her head, her eyes fluttering open. Upon bringing my face into focus, they register a strange sort of joy I did not expect. She sits up, holding out her arms.

"Oh, my lord Howard!" she cries, throwing her arms about my neck and drawing me close in such a swift movement that I fall into bed beside her. "You are home! Home and safe, thank God!"

I find myself smiling.

She sits up and as the covers fall away, I notice something. Her nightgown is clinging to her shape, a much rounder shape than when last I saw her in June.

She rests her hand on her swollen belly and nods. "I wanted to tell you . . ." she says. "But there was no time."

I cannot speak. I am beset with too many conflicting emotions: fear, expectation, fear again. It is a terrible thing, fear. Never on the battlefield have I been this afraid. Against my will, visions of my princess, her belly swollen with my seed, swirl before my mind's eye. Too soon was the fruit of our love plucked from us. Too soon our children went from cradle to casket. To go through it all again, the joy, the pain, the loss, the inevitable loss . . . And having developed a strange fondness for this strong, fiery girl, can I give her up so easily? Should she live, can I bear to see her spirit become as numb and jaded as mine?

"You are happy, aren't you?" she asks, her voice registering the slightest bit of annoyance.

I offer a slow nod.

"It is very lively," she tells me, brightening. "I can barely get any rest, for it's kicking me all the time." She giggles. Her face is so young and dreamy, I want to touch it but cannot seem to will my hand to move. I am immobilized. "I was quite sick in the beginning," Elizabeth goes on. "And I could not hide it from Lady Agnes, but she promised to let it be my news. She's been quite dear. And the queen knows as well. We are thrilled to be with child at the same time."

"Her Grace is expecting?" I manage to say.

"You didn't know?"

I suppose she did look heavier, but I was so caught up in my own triumph that I didn't think much on it.

"Oh! It's kicking now!" She takes my hand, drawing it toward her belly.

I extract it before I can make contact. "No, no," I say quickly. "That will do. I have felt babies kick before."

Elizabeth's face is stricken.

How can I tell her without completely destroying her that my touch will curse it? That it will curse me? To touch it, to feel the life stirring inside . . . yes, I have felt that before. I have felt it and savored it, only to lose it. I cannot do it again. I will not. All I have loved has been lost to me. All I have given has been taken. I am constrained to propagate the Howard line and so I shall. But now, as my father has told me, it is a business, as any breeding business, whether it be horses or falcons or children. Nothing more.

I rise from the bed and avert my head. I cannot look into those eyes anymore, those eyes so lit with hurt that no apologies will ever amend the damage done today.

I quit the room, closing the door on her sobs.

A baby . . . my fifth child. My first with her. How long will this one live? Long enough for me to love it before it is taken away, or will God be kind and reclaim it before I can grow too attached?

There must be another way to survive this. There are many degrees of love. Perhaps I can love this child in a manner different from my first family. If I look at it as though it is a battle that I am directing from a hill . . . yes, from afar.

From safety.

Elizabeth Howard, Winter 1513

I thought he would be happy. I thought this would change everything. After everything he has endured, I thought . . . I hoped. But it has changed nothing. He is as abrupt and distant as he ever was. He does not come to me as my husband. He sleeps in a separate chamber and I refuse to crawl to him, begging for a scrap of affection. I have excelled in my wifely duties only to be repaid by coldness and neglect.

And I will not stoop to forcing anyone to love me.

"You must be patient," Queen Catherine tells me before she retreats to Havering-atte-Bower to meet the king and his French hostages. "You are very young and I appreciate how difficult it must be for you, but you must try and consider the situation from Lord Howard's perspective. You must see that his indifference is a cloak for his fear." She reaches out to stroke my hair with a gentle hand. She has gained a great deal of weight with this pregnancy and her fingers are swollen like sausages. I pity her. There are very few people who can carry off a pregnancy while remaining as attractive as I.

"If only he'd let me help him," I lament. "I want to help him, Your Grace. I want to . . . love him." I bow my head in shame, as though it is a sign of weakness to harbor such an acute desire.

Queen Catherine offers her slow smile. "Of course you do. And I'm convinced he wants to love you, too. Talk to him, Lady Elizabeth. Reassure him that you and your child are here to stay."

"But how can I reassure him if I don't know it's true?" I ask her. "What if . . . what if . . . ?"

The queen crosses herself. "Don't think in what-ifs, Lady Elizabeth. Our Lord does not think in such a fashion. Everything happens for a reason and all for our own good even if we do not understand its meaning at the time." She breaks into a low, melodic laugh and takes my hand. "There, there, child. Do not fret. Your confinement is about to begin. Soon you'll be holding your baby in your arms. I think Lord Howard will soften once he looks at his little one for the first time, don't you?"

"Yes, Your Grace," I reply without conviction as I dip into a curtsy, indicating that for me the conversation is over. I don't know what else to add to it that will not set me into a torrent of tears.

Queen Catherine nods and I am dismissed from her side, praying all the while that she is right and that once this child is born, the happy family life I have always dreamed of can begin.

I cannot say I was much loved as a child; I kept company with my siblings, true, and my parents did not beat us. As the child of a duke, I was ever reminded of my purpose, to glorify Buckingham's name, to make a good alliance. Every piece of instruction ever received was to that end. It is safe to assume Lord Howard's upbringing was similar, if not more harsh.

But our children will be different. I will not delude myself into believing theirs will be an upbringing void of politics, that we will not gain from the alliances made. Our station guarantees certain expectations and sacrifices. But with those will come compassion and, above all, love. Love and friendship. Our children will talk to us, seek our counsel. We will be a close family.

Hope surges through me. I will not allow myself to entertain the possibility that fantasy always eclipses reality. It *will* be as I determine it. It must be.

As I enter my confinement in November I learn that the queen has miscarried. My heart is gripped in mingled compassion and terror. She has known such great pain since arriving in England. The loss of her first husband coupled with the successive losses of the king's children must take a toll.

I do not understand why some are favored with such ill fortune. Yet the queen still smiles. She sends me wishes of good health and a safe delivery during my confinement and claims she cannot wait to see my little one when it arrives.

She has suffered almost as much as my husband, yet retains her kindness and warmth. What strength of character does this queen possess that equips her to grapple with such extensive loss while Lord Howard, my strong soldier, remains broken?

I am shut up in my chambers with the curtains drawn to prevent bad air from entering and upsetting my humors. The deprivation of sunshine and the brisk breeze I so enjoy causes me to quake with sobs. I have hours upon hours to dread the act of childbirth and ponder life's darker aspects. To think I must remain holed up in here for an entire month! I can only read and sew so much before losing my mind, and no one comes to entertain me. The Howards are preoccupied with their own affairs and they will not even let the children visit lest I contract an illness from them. As much as I appreciate their courtesy, the loneliness is unbearable without the shrill laughter and pleasant chatter of my little sisters and brothers-in-law to lighten the mood.

On 6 November, I turn sixteen. To my amazement Lord Howard remembers and spends the whole evening with me. Everything I desire to eat is brought up from the kitchens. We lay out the platters on the bed as though it is a great dining table and sit to our feast in our nightclothes. Lord Howard is so unlike the man I have come to envisage, sitting there with his bare legs crossed in front of him like a child. As I regard him I shiver. He is in fine form, outdoing most men half his age. No wonder he is such an able soldier. If I wasn't so great with child I'd devour much more than the food tonight. . . .

I giggle, shocked and embarrassed over my wild thoughts. "I never thought to see you do something so—spontaneous," I tell my husband.

"I'm not a complete dullard," Lord Howard says, but his voice is gentle and the smallest trace of a smile plays upon his lips. "Besides, I suppose it's time we started trying to make a better go of it."

"Yes," I agree, my voice soft. I bow my head.

Lord Howard averts his face, drawing in a deep breath. He reaches for the platter of cheese, selects a piece, then hands it to me.

I stare at it a moment before taking a bite.

"You are to be the Countess of Surrey," he says with a bright smile, his black eyes gleaming in triumph. "What do you make of that?"

"I like it very much," I tell him in honesty, for who can resist a title?

"And someday you shall be the Duchess of Norfolk," he continues, leaning his elbow on his knee and his chin on his fist, regarding a point just above my head as though he is glimpsing into a future filled with glory.

"That will not be for quite some time," I say in deference to Thomas Howard the Elder.

My lord Howard waves a dismissive hand. "It will be sooner than you think; the man's seventy."

"Lord Howard!" I cry, scandalized. He speaks of his father's future passing with such cool nonchalance, as though he is some foreign dignitary whose tie to him is distant and abstract. He is only as good as his hereditary titles. I shiver.

He shrugs. "I am only doing what you so advocate, speaking the truth."

I am forced to laugh. "My pragmatist."

He offers a decisive nod, then stretches out on his side, propping himself up on an elbow. The expression he regards me with is almost tender.

"You are feeling well?" he asks, his tone almost timid.

I nod, recalling Queen Catherine's advice about reassuring my lord. "I'll bring you a healthy son, Thomas," I say, addressing him by his Christian name for the first time. Familiarity seeps through our guard. I am overcome with the longing for an intimacy that stretches beyond the physical. I reach out my hand. He takes it, stroking my thumb. The fire and energy that accompanies our every touch surges between us. Never have I experienced this, not with Ralph Neville, not with anybody. It is something that frightens and fascinates me at once.

"I—have something for you," he says, rising to remove the trays scattered across the bed and setting them aside before retrieving a gilt box he had set on my bedside table. He sits beside me once more, opening the box to reveal an ornate gold signet ring. He places it in the palm of my hand.

"It's quite heavy," I comment as I admire it.

"Meant to last," says Lord Thomas. "Look." He turns the ring upright. "See the bezel? It is the Howard arms newly acquired in recognition of our victory at Flodden."

On the ring's bezel is a lion ready to pounce. An arrow pierces its tongue through. It is a symbol of the Howards' power. Of Lord Thomas's power.

"We've come full circle, Elizabeth," he tells me, his eyes lit with triumph as he takes my right hand, sliding the ring up on my middle finger. It is weighty and wholly unfeminine, but it embodies all my lord represents. I am determined to treasure it. "We were raised up to be cast down to be raised up again. But now we will stay up. And we will keep going. Up and up and up . . ." He raises his eyes to the heavens, his hand still gripping mine with the urgency I have so come to expect from him.

"What happens when we can go no further, Thomas?" I ask him, scrunching up my shoulders as a strange and inexplicable fear overtakes me.

Lord Thomas shifts his gaze to my face. His eyes are as fierce and proud as the lion on his signet ring. "We are without limit, Elizabeth. You've heard the adage 'We will go as far as we can go'? Well, we will go farther yet."

I do not know how to respond to this. I can only pray he is not as free in his speech around the wrong ears.

There is no giving voice to my thought. Lord Thomas isn't obtuse. So instead I withdraw my hand and make a show of admiring my new gift.

"It's lovely, Thomas," I tell him, leaning forward to kiss his cheek.

"Wear it with pride," he orders. "Remember, you are a Howard."

I begin to tingle as pride courses through me. Never have I been more convinced of another human being's capacity for greatness as I am of my husband's, of my Thomas Howard.

Just as I begin to relish my newfound affection for my husband, he informs me that he will be leaving.

"I have to demobilize the navy," he tells me, standing at the end of my bed, looking into my face without quite meeting my eyes. "And there are repairs that need to be made before winter. Everything must be in order for spring."

"You cannot wait until after the baby is born?" I demand, balling my fists at my sides. "You're to leave me here to have the baby by myself?"

"Babies are born every day. My presence is not required for its arrival." His voice is as hard as his eyes.

I blink back hot tears. "Please don't go." My voice is wavering. I cannot believe I have reduced myself to begging. But he is the father of this child. How dare he even contemplate leaving us at this crucial moment? "Please. It is our first child!"

He purses his lips. "It is not *my* first child." He removes his cap, running a hand through his hair in frustration.

"It is your child nonetheless," I remind him, sitting up to reach out for his hands. It seems confrontation is avoided when we touch. If I can just reach him. . . . If I can hold him, reassure him with my embrace.

But he is too quick for me, evading my outstretched hands and stepping back. He is shaking his head. There is a desperate wildness about his eyes that causes me to shrink away from him.

"God's body, Elizabeth, don't you see?" he breathes. "I can't stay for this. I can't!"

With that he stalks out of the room.

"Go, then!" I cry to his retreating back. "And I don't care if you ever come back!"

When his footfalls can no longer be heard, I lie back against my pillows, too angry to cry. All I can think of are the nasty things I wish I had said to him when he was in the room. It is too late. Too late to be cruel, too late to be kind. He is gone.

I am drawn from my bitter reverie by the creak of the door. Has he returned? I sit up, smiling before I can help myself. I will forgive him, of course. I will throw my arms around him and tell him how happy I am that he has decided to put off his trip till after the baby's birth. . . .

I turn my head. It is not my lord; how naïve of me to assume he would have any regrets. It is my stepmother-in-law, Agnes. She enters with a basket of sweet-smelling herbs, setting them on the window seat before sitting at my bedside.

She expels a heavy sigh. "You know what the problem is?" she asks. Of course I know that she is more than eager to tell me. Agnes can be helpful, but she is nothing if not interfering.

I scowl, waiting for her to enlighten me.

"You cannot just shut your mouth," she says. "You have to learn to let things go. Do you think it is easy living with a Howard man?" She offers a rueful laugh. "Do you think it is easy living with any man? Lady Elizabeth, I urge you to rein in that temper of yours, for Lord knows your husband isn't about to take control of his."

I fold my arms across my chest. My breasts have become so

swollen and tender with the pregnancy that they cannot bear the weight and I drop my arms to my sides, expelling a little cry of pain. I bite my lip.

"It isn't fair," I murmur in despair.

"Life is not fair, Lady Elizabeth, and marriage may well be the greatest injustice of all," Agnes tells me, her voice harsh but her eyes soft with unshed tears. "But it is our lot and we have to make the best of it. Stubborn rebelliousness will get you nowhere." She draws in a breath. "Do you remember Lady Plantagenet, Lord Howard's first wife?"

"I was not an intimate of hers, my lady, but I do remember her," I say, my heart throbbing with unexpected jealousy as an image of the ethereal beauty with the rose-gold hair conjures itself before my mind's eye.

"Lady Plantagenet was fair and fine," says Agnes. "She was strong and at times she could be defiant, but she was subtle. She was endearing."

"I am not Lady Plantagenet! I will never be! I don't want to be!" I cry. "He will appreciate me for who I am or not at all!" Hot tears begin to course sure and steady trails down my cheeks. "After all, I don't expect him to be Ral—" I cut myself short, bowing my head.

Agnes takes my hand. "Don't excite yourself so, my dear. Of course you don't." Her voice is soothing. "And you do not have to be anyone but yourself. But using Lady Plantagenet as a model of wifely submission cannot hurt, hmmm?"

"So it is all up to me?" My tone is laced with bitterness. "I am to amend my ways and repent and submit while he does nothing but break my heart again and again?"

Agnes turns her head away a moment. When her eyes fall upon me at last, they are filled with a sadness as unfathomable as eternity. "Harden your heart, Elizabeth. Harden your heart until it becomes impenetrable, like a fortress. It is the only way to survive."

She leans forward, kissing my forehead before quitting the room, and I am alone again, my heart aching and far from hard.

All I can think about is the life stirring within me and of the father who will miss its entrance into this world.

* * *

Anyone who tries to claim that one forgets the pain of childbirth is either mad or never had children. It is truly the most dreadful thing I can think of, lying abed for hours upon hours, certain I am being ripped in two. My back throbs with a constant ache, my abdomen has been cramping for twenty-seven hours, and my legs are so restless I want to leap out of bed and run about the room.

The midwife Tsura Goodman, deliverer of many Howards, was brought from the country to attend me. She has since been retained as a nurse and knows more about children and childbearing than I would ever want to.

She does her best to soothe my pain with soft words and gypsy songs that transport me to another world, a world beyond the pain and the wretchedness of being a woman.

The queen sent me the Girdle of Our Lady, which is rumored to alleviate the agony of childbed, but it doesn't do a thing and I can hardly be grateful for the thought, so distracted am I by the pain. Even Tsura Goodman's tender ministrations are proving ineffective.

Attending my torture is a small army of servants, Howard women, and Lady Agnes. My father-in-law is even present; he sits in a corner ordering cup after cup of wine till he is slumped over, watching me with rheumy eyes that threaten to close at any given moment. It is terribly embarrassing. I wish they would leave me alone, except Tsura, who is the only one capable of bringing the child forth and the least annoying of the assemblage.

"Come now, darling, it's time to push," Agnes coaxes, propping my pillows up behind me. I want to push her away but am gripped by a pain so fierce that it causes me to reach out to her instead, seizing her hand in urgency. "Come now! Push!"

I do as I am bid only because my body is doing it for me. I am possessed by a force greater than myself as I bear down, grunting and pushing till at last I hear the triumphant cry that the head and shoulder have emerged. As the rest of the child slides forth into Tsura's capable hands, I fall back onto the bed, exhausted.

I do not even think to ask after its sex or its health. I can only close my eyes, panting and sweating and aching to rest.

Tsura's needle mends my torn body and I am called to my senses by the lusty cry of my baby. My eyelids flutter open and my gaze finds Agnes, who is holding a little bundle, her broad face glowing with joy.

"A son?" I ask.

Agnes shakes her head. "A little ally," she tells me as she places the baby atop my chest. I wrap my arms about the warm little creature, stroking its silky dark hair, still slick with birthing fluids. Its face is ruddy and wrinkled and by far the most endearing thing I have ever seen.

"A daughter," I breathe in awe. I plant a kiss on the child's button nose.

The duke rises, crossing the room to sit beside me and rest his hand on his granddaughter's head in blessing. "And what will we call this little angel?" he asks with a smile.

"Catherine," I tell him, hugging my little triumph to me.

"A fine name," says the duke, stroking my baby's smooth cheek. "A fine name for a fine Howard girl."

I never want to let her go. I want to keep her beside me always. Now it doesn't matter if my Thomas comes or goes. He has given me something that will always remain.

Suddenly the ordeal of childbirth has lost its potency.

I am content.

Thomas Howard

The messenger is breathless when he meets up with my fleet, and my throat tightens as he runs up the gangplank, waving his arm, crying, "Admiral Howard! Admiral Howard! News from Lambeth!"

My body tenses. I know the news. Elizabeth and the baby are dead. It will not affect me. I did not see the child and had little enough affection for the mother. I will find another breeder and will not make the same mistake I did with this girl. I do not have need of a clever wife. A dullard like her sister will serve my purposes much better.

When the messenger reaches me, I close my eyes and turn my back, drawing in a deep breath, readying myself.

He bows. "My lord. On six December your good wife, the Countess of Surrey, was delivered of a daughter."

"And?" I ask in a whisper that betrays my sudden panic. It is hard to breathe. My throat is so dry and tight that I keep adjusting my collar in the hopes of allowing myself more air.

"And, my lord?" the messenger asks, screwing up his face in confusion. He shrugs.

"They have survived?" I press, my voice thin with impatience. My heart is racing.

The lad offers a gentle smile and nods. "Yes, Lord Admiral. They have survived."

Relief courses through me as I blink back unexpected tears.

A daughter. A living daughter.

I am a father once more, for whatever that portends.

It is Yuletide before I can bring myself to see them. My business with the navy is all but resolved for the winter and I cannot avoid Lambeth any longer.

Elizabeth must be up and about by now. And the baby . . . I do not know what to think about the baby.

I arrive at night, hoping the household is asleep. I do not have need to confront my siblings or stepmother right now. My presence does not go unnoticed, however, and I am greeted by the servants, who offer their congratulations with nervous smiles.

I enter the nursery first, or at least I try to enter the nursery first. I am stopped short at the door, my heart racing. I do not know what to expect, what to feel. I close my eyes, pushing open the door to find in place of a nurse or rocker my own wife, sitting beside the cradle, holding the baby in her arms. She is dozing, her head tilted against the back of the chair, her hair spilling over her shoulders in moonlit waves. For a moment I can do nothing but stand there staring dumbly, unsure if what I am seeing is beautiful or frightening. It is so reminiscent of before, so reminiscent of my days with my princess. It seems almost a sacrilege to repeat them with anyone else.

I collect myself and stoop down to remove my boots before approaching her. Everything hurts. I don't know when this developed. My joints throb and ache and I have become antagonized by stomach pains. Now is no exception. As I near my wife and baby, my gut twists in knots. My knees are so stiff and achy I am almost hobbling.

I reach the peaceful pair, standing over them. From what I can discern, the baby has a head full of dark hair. I bite my lip, swallowing several times.

Sensing my presence, Elizabeth stirs, then wakens. She raises her eyes to me, a slow smile spreading across her lips. "Thomas . . ."

I force a smile. "Happy Christmas."

She props the baby up against her chest, offering me a better view of its little face. One slender hand cups the back of its head, stroking idly. "And what do you make of your gift?" she asks. I can hear the smile in her voice.

I do not know how to respond. "Very nice," I say at last.

Elizabeth kisses the downy head. "I called her Catherine."

A name . . . oh, God, she gave it a name. My mother said that was when it happened, when the curse began, after you gave it a name, after you've attached to it an identity and your heart. . . .

"So many people we love are named Catherine," Elizabeth is prattling. "The queen, my sister . . . Wasn't your grandmother named Catherine as well?"

I nod.

"We shall call her Cathy. There are enough Kates about," she adds, her tone decisive. "What do you make of that, Mistress Cathy Howard?" Her tone becomes loud with the exaggerated sweetness one often uses when speaking to idiots, dogs, and children. She returns her gaze to me once more. "Here I am being so selfish and you haven't even had the chance to hold her yet."

Before I can protest she rises, placing the baby in my arms. She lights some tapers, illuminating the room with a soft glow, then guides me to the chair, tugging at my elbow till I am compelled to sit.

Once I am situated I begin to acclimate myself to the warm weight of this child in my arms, its head in the crook of my shoulder. I look down into her face. She has opened her eyes, blue as all babies' eyes tend to be. She does not resemble the half siblings that God claimed. She belongs to herself, which makes gazing upon her much easier. She is a sturdy child, near ten pounds at least. Her cheeks are chubby and kissable. I clutch her to me. She is the first of my new dynasty. I must protect her.

"Who is the nurse?" I ask.

Elizabeth's smile broadens. "I am."

Where have I heard this before? And what were the results?

"Abso*lute*ly not," I say, tightening my grip on the baby. She squawks a bit. "Gentlewomen are not capable of nursing healthy children. I allowed my prin—Lady Anne to do so and was rewarded with four graves to visit. No. I see we shall have to regulate our children's upbringing with stricture and discipline. You are to be a countess, not a country maid. We will do things right and proper. These children are not to be mollycoddled and made soft. They are going to survive. They are going to be Howards."

Elizabeth's lips are quivering. I lower my head, pretending to be occupied with my daughter so as to avoid the pain lighting my wife's eyes.

"I will hire a good country girl on the morrow," I tell her.

"No," she whispers. "Please. At least let me do that."

I hesitate. "Very well. But I will have the final say."

"Yes," Elizabeth acquiesces. "Of course you will."

She turns away, leaving me to rock and ponder the great heights my little Cathy will climb to, if God allows.

A Countess's Life

Elizabeth Howard, 1514–1520

A stout country girl is hired to nurse Cathy and she is restrained in swaddling bands to ensure the set of her limbs. I hate seeing her thus. There is nothing I love more than watching my baby kick her chubby legs and reach about to explore her world with dimpled hands. There is no hope for private moments with my daughter. My lord has made certain that my every move is watched, lest I disobey him.

"I suppose we're to get used to it," I say to little Cathy one day as I rock her. At least I am permitted to perform this small act of closeness. "A lifetime of governance."

As I adjust to motherhood, my lord is called to do battle against the French galleys that were responsible for the slayings of his brother-in-law Thomas Knyvet and brother Neddy. He is all too happy to avenge their deaths. He is all too happy to do anything that involves a sword, a ship, and an oath of destruction.

Yet I am proud of him. He is grand, sweeping into Normandy like a force of nature, ravaging the countryside and proving the victor.

When he returns triumphant, we learn that we are to go to France as a family, not in hostility but in peace, for a secret truce has been arranged at the urgings of Thomas Wolsey, the king's rising star. After Catherine of Aragon's father, King Ferdinand of

Spain, deserted Britain in favor of an alliance with the French, King Henry was disposed to offer peace as well, if for no other reason than spiting his father-in-law.

The pawn in the treaty is Henry VIII's beautiful sister Mary, who is to wed King Louis XII of France. The girl is as miserable a bride as I have ever seen, far more than I ever was, and as we witness the proxy ceremony at Greenwich in September, I blink back tears of sympathy. All I can think of is my little Cathy and offer fervent prayers that my husband will be good to her and marry her to someone not only politically expedient but loving as well.

But love matches are too rare. One is as liable to laugh in incredulity at the mention of a love match as at a sighting of the little people.

In October we proceed to France for the actual wedding. As an earl, my husband is allowed fifty-eight attendants. King Louis, a horrid old man rotting from the French disease, dismisses all of poor Princess Mary's court, replacing them with French ladies. He claimed she was being kept from him. Oh, if only someone could keep her from him, the dreadful old cur!

Thomas and I do not think much on them, however. I am too caught up in the dazzling spectacle of a royal wedding, and Thomas is beset with joy at his rise in favor. It is a wonderful trip. We pass our nights practicing all the naughty things the French courtiers educated Thomas about, and our days in feasting and masquing.

By the time we return to England, I am carrying our second child.

My husband is more receptive to this pregnancy. Perhaps it is as I hoped, that the birth of little Cathy has softened him and her show of good health proves to him that more lusty Howards will follow.

He is not solicitous with words, but if his gestures are an accurate testament of his heart I must be treasured indeed. I am showered with jewels and satins, anything that strikes my lord's impeccable fancy. I must say, he does know how to choose a gift. Cloaks lined with fur, kirtles inlaid with pearls and gems without flaw, hoods, pendants, and silk petticoats. And slippers! Never have I known a man to be so absorbed in footwear. He makes certain I have a pair of slippers to match my every gown. All of them are encrusted with the finest gems and pearls, with buckles of silver and gold.

But the reward that outshines any precious stone is his smile. It is rarely given, much anticipated, and treasured beyond what can be estimated. It is a slight curve of the lips, an ironical smile, if not a little lacking in honest joy. But it is his and, to my utmost surprise, I love it.

"It seems we are always with child together," says Queen Catherine to me one day. We have been called to court for Christmas and I am pleased to be in my gentle sovereign's presence again.

"You are feeling well, Your Grace?" I ask her, my shoulders tense with anxiety for the queen's as yet ill-fated pregnancies.

She pats her stomach and smiles. Sorrow has robbed her of her beauty, but her smile retains its sweetness and her eyes their regal strength. "I am very well. So well that the king commissioned for our prince a beautiful cradle."

"All my prayers are with you," I tell her with sincerity. Were I permitted to touch the royal person, I would have seized her hands in mine, but I refrain, adhering to the protocol the queen is so devoted to.

I wonder if she ever desires to break free of it, the rigid boundaries, the formalities, the enforced coldness. Does she ever long to twirl about and run and scream? Does she ever long for the comfort of a friendly embrace?

The king has made no secret of his longing for "comforting embraces" and has dallied with numerous ladies since marrying my lady. He and Charles Brandon even took to sharing a few mistresses, according to court gossip. His Majesty's latest conquest is the beautiful Bessie Blount, a gentlewoman of my age who serves as one of the queen's maids of honor. The affair is conducted under the sheerest veil of discretion; of all the qualities King Henry can boast of, subtlety is not one of them. Bessie Blount is no better, giggling and flirting with His Majesty like a common barmaid. It disgusts me.

The queen, however, tolerates the situation with a grace as habitual as her suffering. We watch the Christmas pageant at Greenwich, a gala of which King Henry stars along with the said Bessie Blount, Elizabeth and Nicholas Carew, Lady Guildford, Lady Fellinger, Charles Brandon, and the Spanish envoy. The ladies are masqued with gold caps covering their hair and lavish blue velvet gowns. The gentlemen are dressed as Portuguese knights who save the ladies from danger. It is a delightful spectacle, one I wish I were participating in, but my condition forces me to watch from the sidelines. It is astounding how much more one sees from this vantage.

The king dances with the curvaceous Bessie Blount, encircling her in his strong arms. She tosses back her blond head, laughing in a tone too familiar, too intimate for the gathering. It would be easy to be swept away by His Majesty. He is so broad and golden, his figure so stunning and fine. But how could one, even in such circumstances, be so carried away as not to remember the woman we as ladies-in-waiting are bound to serve? How could anyone be so brazen in her disrespect? It is a concept foreign to me.

I am not a fool. It is in very few men to be faithful. They seem to have a need to take whatever is in front of them and then some, hoarding it like greedy, gluttonous wolves. My father took on dozens of mistresses. I am blessed that whatever affection my lord has for me prevents him from doing the same.

The queen watches the display, her expression wistful. "He is not only my husband," she tells me in soft tones. "He is a king. We must do good to remember his needs are greater than that of common men."

"Oh, really, Your Grace!" I cry before I can help myself. "And what of your needs? Does not your exalted station as a princess of the blood put you above common women?"

I bite my lip. The face Her Grace turns to me is impassive. I am unsure as to whether or not I will be chastised for my outburst.

Rather than scold me she reaches out, taking my hand. Her smile is sad. "You are very young. You see the world as a child. Good or bad, night or day. One must always remember that there is twilight,

Lady Elizabeth. One cannot see as well in the twilight." Her eyes grow distant. Her grip loosens. "Things we thought to be certain of in the hours of the sun become so much less defined."

There is nothing I hate more than the abstract. I am quick to interject with "But we know how it *should* be defined, Your Grace—"

She does not give me the opportunity to finish but holds up a silencing hand. Her eyes are filled with fierce determination. "We know nothing but what the word of the Lord tells us, which is to be faithful, obedient wives no matter the circumstances. To endure long-suffering and to stand true to God, to ourselves, to our husbands, and to each other, no matter the pain."

But it isn't fair! I want to shout. Why us? Why must we always be the ones to suffer while the men do nothing but profit by it in one way or another?

I do not dare speak against her. Instead I squeeze the hand that still holds mine. "I shall *always* stand true to you, Your Grace," I tell my queen with fervency.

"My loyal maid," says the queen with a gentle smile that reveals very little happiness. She reaches out to stroke my cheek, drawing in a wavering breath. "Loyalty is . . . a very rare and worthy virtue," she adds in a whisper.

She says nothing more, turning her head to watch the pageant that features those exceedingly lacking in that virtue.

The winter is a frenzy of activity. Fra Diego Fernandez, Queen Catherine's confessor and the man my lord husband warned me against as a little girl, is deported to Spain for his amorous and decadent behavior. I am thrilled to see him go. He had never ceased to take me in with his dark Spanish eyes and slow, sensual smile. It made me shiver in discomfort. I truly believe some people are inhibited from performing good works because of excessive handsomeness.

King Louis of France was not one of them. He was neither handsome nor goodly, passing away to be replaced with the dashing and lecherous King Francois. King Henry's sister Mary is left a royal widow and it is up to Charles Brandon, duke of Suffolk, to bring her home to England. Though the king made him promise not to propose marriage, it is no secret that Suffolk had designs on the princess from the beginning. The court is on tenterhooks. Will her last name be Tudor or Brandon upon her return?

Frivolous gossip is overshadowed by the birth of a prince at Greenwich in February. He lives just long enough for his mother to hold him and love him, then bury him in a shroud of her tears. I cradle my own belly with a protective hand upon hearing the news, saddened that Her Grace chooses not to solicit the comfort and society of her ladies during this dark time.

"It would do no good," says my lord Thomas as he holds me in bed one early March evening. He shudders beside me, huddling closer, drawing the blankets over our shoulders and stroking my hair. He kisses my forehead. I relish the demonstration. "Seeing you in your present state would only grieve her more."

I sigh. "I know," I murmur, nuzzling in the crook of his shoulder. "Oh, Thomas, such sadness she has known. May God grant her the delivery of a living prince soon. I fear she may lose her mind if she isn't granted some kind of happiness. Lord knows the king offers little enough."

"Hush now," Thomas says, his voice stern. "It is not for you to criticize His Majesty."

"Oh, not you, too." I roll on my side. The baby has just begun to kick and it swims about in my womb like a little otter. I smile, thanking God for the small pleasures we women are afforded, the kick of a child in the womb, something no man can ever experience or take away.

"Yes, me, too," says Thomas, his voice a little lighter as he leans over me. He is also smiling. "You are too outspoken, Elizabeth. You must hold your tongue now and then. Everyone knows about the king's situation. No one cares to rehearse the said morality of it every waking moment."

"How can you suffer knowing what he does to Her Grace, who is the most Christian of princesses?" I ask, rolling onto my back once more. I reach up, stroking his cheek. "She has always been so kind to you and your father, yet I think if His Majesty asked you to deliver Bessie Blount to him naked across your shield, you'd do so."

"Elizabeth!"

"You know you would," I prompt.

He smirks. "Of course I would—what a sight!" I elbow him in the ribs and he emits a small laugh. "Well, I am his servant first, am I not?" he asks, flopping on his back. "It isn't as though I like bearing witness to his dalliances any more than you do. Her Grace handles it well enough. She knows her place."

"I wouldn't want to be in her place for anything," I say with vehemence.

"That's your mistake, Elizabeth," he tells me, taking me in his arms once more. "You do not realize that it isn't about love and honor. It is about elevation. People do not live the way you think they do. This isn't some French romance you so love having your ladies read you. The only code to adhere to is whatever code the king is endorsing at the moment. The only pleasure is the king's pleasure and whatever we can scrape aside for ourselves. Her Grace knows this. She may not have liked it in her youth, but she isn't fool enough to protest it anymore. She accepts it as the way of the world and adapts herself accordingly, as you must."

"Never," I vow. "Not for anyone, not even the king himself. I adhere to my own code—God's code. And if you want a happiness that is real, you will, too."

Thomas chuckles, squeezing me to him, kissing my cheek again. "Ah, God keep your passionate little ladyship."

"And God keep you," I tell him, wrapping my arms about his neck, pulling him close. "Right beside me."

He returns the embrace, chuckling still.

Somehow it disconcerts me.

The Princess Mary returns to court with the last name Brandon, with the aid of sly Cardinal Wolsey, now lord chancellor of England, who sidled up beside the couple as their ally and convinced King Henry that the marriage should be accepted. Suffolk and his bride are made to pay a large fine and return properties given her for her royal marriage, along with the wardship of Elizabeth Grey,

Viscountess Lisle. They emerge from the scandal no worse for wear, giving the court plenty to talk about.

My husband is not happy about the turn of events. Though I am in confinement, he visits me regularly to update me on the goings-on at court and I am delighted to be sought out.

"This king will listen to anything that churl—excuse me, *Chancellor* Wolsey tells him!" he exclaims one sticky July evening. "Father and I urged him to punish Suffolk for his disobedience, but no! Everything's so bloody romantic and wonderful now we'll be throwing a blooming party to celebrate the match ere long!" he adds, his voice shrill with mockery.

"Wolsey is a devil," I agree, my voice calm. "One wonders what he has that you lack."

"He's the son of a whore and a butcher!" Thomas cries.

I nod. "A man with fortunes newly acquired," I say. "The chancellorship and cardinal's hat in one year. Again, what does he have that you lack?"

"The king's ear, that is certain," says Thomas, sitting on the edge of my bed, scowling.

I nod with a patient smile. "Why?" I challenge him. "Thomas, how do you come across before His Majesty? How does Cardinal Wolsey come across? Observe him. *Why* does the king value him so? I am not advising you to emulate him—of course, far be it from me to advise you of anything, humble woman that I am—" I add for good measure. "But you may take a lesson from him. And from Suffolk as well. If he can marry the king's own sister without permission and earn naught but a slap on the hand, then he, too, possesses qualities worthy of examination."

Thomas is silent a long moment. He turns to me, rubbing my foot through the blanket, offering a distracted smile. "You are a strange creature, Elizabeth," he says at length. I decide to take it as a compliment. "Pretty as a Tudor rose, with a mind and tongue as sharp as a dagger! Ha!" The little laugh is triumphant. I beam. "Anyway, they're married and so be it," Thomas goes on to say in reference to the Suffolks. "We'll endure. Meantime, I shall observe Wolsey and see what can be done with him."

My smile broadens. "You are a soldier, Thomas, the finest of the fine. Approach him as you would a fortress. Even those who seem the most impenetrable have at least one weakness."

He chucks my chin. "And so they do," he says. "So they do."

And so go our visits during my confinement. My lord airs his frustrations and I help him sift through them, trying all the while to appear as though I am not. He knows. I am as lacking in subtlety as Henry VIII, but he does not seem to mind.

He keeps coming back.

Our little heir Edward is born on 31 July. Thomas holds Cathy up to see her new brother and she reaches out a dimpled hand to touch his face.

"Say 'Ned,' " prompts Thomas as he peers into the cradle.

Cathy bounces up and down on her father's lap in excitement. "Ned! Ned! Ned mine!"

"Yes, Ned is your little brother," says Thomas. "You'll look after him, won't you?"

"Ned mine!" cries Cathy again, offering a gap-toothed smile.

I gaze at my dark-haired daughter in adoration, then fix my eyes on the baby, who resembles both sister and father. I wonder if any of our children will take after me. It is no matter. They are so beautiful I am filled with a joy that makes me shiver with fear. Is it a sin to be this proud?

"What is it, Elizabeth?" Thomas's voice is gentle.

I swallow tears, averting my head. "It's just that—well, it's just that they're so beautiful and I'm so very happy."

Thomas leans over, kissing the top of my head. "I am, too," he tells me, his voice husky. "You have done well, my girl."

I reach up, clutching his upper arm. Oh, to hear those words again and again. He is happy.

He is happy and I am the cause.

Thomas Howard

Two children and one a fine son, robust as anything! She is a good girl, this little Elizabeth. For her troubles I order her numerous jewel-encrusted kirtles with gowns to match. The girl has retained her figure, not gaining an inch since before her first pregnancy. She is trim as a willow wand and full of vigor, thus deserving of all the pretty accoutrements.

I must say, I am fraught with eagerness as I anticipate her expression when she receives my gifts. She is aglow with animation, whereas my princess was the picture of reserve. I long for Anne Plantagenet every day, but more and more I find myself subject to a strange sort of excitement when in the presence of my new wife. Oh, she's outspoken and far too opinionated, but now and again her words ring true and it is with a joyous sense of defeat that I feel myself yielding to her advice.

In February of 1516, the queen to whom my wife has become so dedicated is delivered of a healthy princess named Mary.

"If it was a daughter this time, by the grace of God, the sons will follow," His Majesty quips, his cheeks ruddy with pride.

My stepmother and Cardinal Wolsey (a pig in red!) are made godparents. My Elizabeth carries the baby at the christening, flanked by my father and Suffolk. I have been honored with the carrying of the ceremonial taper. It is a grand occasion and the princess seems healthy enough. Perhaps her birth has marked the end of the king and queen's ill fortune and indeed sons will follow. One can only pray.

Celebrations are muted due to the death of Queen Catherine's father, the wily King Ferdinand of Aragon. It is of no matter. In May the king's sister Margaret arrives for a state visit and I am asked to ride in the king's band in the tournaments celebrating her arrival.

"I remember you," Queen Margaret states. She is a beautiful woman with her coppery hair and lively brown eyes. "You escorted me to Edinburgh when I married."

I bow. "Yes, Your Grace."

"You were married to the lady Anne then," she states, as if I would not know this.

"Yes," I say, recalling how my princess dreaded taking our children to Scotland for fear of the winds, for fear of their catching their deaths. . . . I swallow several times.

"Life is so different for all of us now," she says, her tone wistful. "You have founded a new family and I have lost mine. I am a queen without a country, forced into exile by the Duke of Albany, who takes charge over my child, the rightful king, as his regent, leaving me to languish."

I am not sure how to respond to this. "I am very sorry, Your Grace," I say at last, wishing the conversation would end.

"What is there to be done now?" she asks. Knowing there is no answer, she tosses back her lovely head and adds with the robust Tudor laugh, "When the world is collapsing around you, throw a party. So, ride, my dear Lord Surrey. Ride in the lists and champion me, the outcast Queen of Scots."

And so I do, but my joy in the sport is muted by the Queen of Scots's predicament and memories of more innocent times. Indeed, life has changed.

By the end of the month, that rascal Wolsey deprives me of my voice in the council because I dared allow my retinue to be armed at Queen Margaret's reception.

"Well, you knew the law," Elizabeth chides me. We are alone in her chambers at Lambeth. "The king does not want armed guards upsetting his peace. They take too many liberties as it is. You should have known better. Now you have lost what little sway you had—"

I whirl on her. "Elizabeth! It is not for you to say! You are too free in your speech, girl! Far too free!"

Elizabeth scrunches up her face in mockery. "Now it will be harder than ever to retain the favor that one such as Wolsey enjoys," she tells me.

The slap is automatic. I am tired of her high-minded attitude. She is far too precocious, far too presumptuous for her station. She falls against the bed, holding her cheek, her blue eyes wide a moment before narrowing in anger.

"Is this what you want?" I cry, shaking out my hand. "You have too many liberties; you are becoming rebellious and must be taken in hand. God's body, girl, leave politics to me and tend to your duties!"

"I *have* no duties!" Elizabeth's voice is wavering with desperation. "I have an army of servants for the children and a house that isn't even mine. I have no say in anything at all. I hate it, Thomas. When I'm not at court waiting on Her Grace, I would like a home of our own. Now that your presence doesn't seem to be required, for the time being we should assume one of the Howard manors for ourselves. I don't want to live here anymore. This is the duchess's house, your father's house. Don't you see? I want a home that is *mine*."

At once I sit beside her, reaching out to stroke her cheek. God knows I do not want to be cruel, but she must be taught to mind! Yet perhaps we have reached the root of her restlessness. A home of her own would provide her with the challenge she seems to need. The distraction of running a large household may keep her from airing her at times unwelcome opinions and shift her focus to the womanly arts.

I purse my lips. "Of course you want a home," I tell her in gentler tones. I sigh. "Oh, my girl . . ." I bow my head in shame. I do not know why I am so impatient with her. She is so young, after all. It's frightening, this sudden anger that overwhelms and possesses me until there is naught to do but strike out in release, then, spent at last, I return to sanity. It is getting worse and worse. . . . What if one day the sanity does not return? What if my soul becomes imprisoned by this hatred, this rage that consumes and envelops me like the devil's firestorm? I shudder. I will not think of it, not now. Now I will think of what to do for the girl. A home . . . a home of her own.

It must be grand. A palace for a countess and future duchess. A place she can entertain great minds and heads of state, a place she can raise our family. A place where I can hunt and teach little Edward to swim and use his arrows and sword . . .

I have it!

I draw Elizabeth up by the hands, avoiding looking into her face, on which a deep purple bruise has begun to swell. I gather her in my arms, holding her against my chest, rocking to and fro.

"I know just the place," I tell her. "It needs a bit of work but once renovated, it will be a wonderful home for us. You're right. It's far past time that we had our own seat."

"Where is it, Thomas?" she asks in a small voice that causes my eyes to burn with tears.

I stroke her silky hair. "My father's hunting lodge in Kenninghall, Norfolk. It's ideal! But until it is complete we shall remove to the country, to Hunsdon in Hertfordshire."

"Hunsdon . . ." says Elizabeth. "Yes, I should like to go there. When can we leave?"

"Directly, my girl," I tell her, laying her back on the bed and drawing the covers up over her shoulders. I crawl in beside her, taking her in my arms. She is shivering, whether from cold or fear I do not know. I do not want to know.

Elizabeth snuggles against me. Against my cheek I feel her warm, slick tears. "Hunsdon will be the perfect place to have this next baby," she murmurs in husky tones.

At once I am forced to quell an onset of shoulder-shaking sobs. Another baby. This girl is to give me yet another child after I . . . Oh, what have I become?

I will make it up to her. I will build her a palace few can rival and these times between us shall be forgotten.

Yes, everything will be set right at Kenninghall.

On May Day, I am called to assist my father in the quelling of riots stirred up by apprentices who attacked foreign merchants and plotted to kill the lord mayor. By 22 May, after countless arrests and the executions of the central instigators, Queen Catherine begs for the king's mercy on her knees at Westminster Hall.

It is all staged to illustrate the king's grace; even the queen's performance, as backed by devoutness as it is, has a political aim. Order must be kept; the less bloodshed the better.

The king pardons the four hundred gathered before him and they toss their hats up high in joyous relief.

"You've proven yourself worthy," Elizabeth whispers, squeezing my arm. "You have put down something that could very easily have gotten out of control. The king will find you more indispensable than ever, I should think."

I cover her slender hand with my own. Indispensable. Yes, that is what I shall be. To the king and to this country.

But putting down a small rebellion is one thing. Putting down a plague is another.

In the spring of 1517, the sweating sickness comes to London.

The court removes to Richmond while Elizabeth and I take to Hunsdon with the children. It is all I can do to preserve their lives. Our staff is limited; those showing signs of the illness are discharged and kept in isolation.

I cannot count how many perish. The cheery sounds of the farmers in their cottages are silenced. Mass graves are dug; the bodies pile up, tumbling upon one another until they are at last enfolded in the soil, a nameless, unmarked place of horror.

When our little Edward first takes ill, I know I am in Hell.

There is naught to be done for him. Elizabeth and the baby she carries are kept away. It is too great a risk allowing her near. I tend him myself, caring not for my life. It seems my fate to survive anything.

I try my best to keep him awake—they say if the victim is kept awake, he has a greater chance of recovery. The little one shivers with cold, then becomes slick with burning sweat, crying the urgent, desperate sobs of a baby in pain. He is too little to tell me what hurts. I wrap him up tight, rocking him, singing softly until the tune becomes nothing but strangled whimpers in the back of my own throat.

He loses consciousness; his little head lolls against my chest. "Don't go to sleep! Please wake up, Edward!" I demand. "Please!"

It is to no avail.

The child is dead within four hours of the illness's onset.

Elizabeth Howard

Thomas does not tell me of our son's death until after he is buried.

"I didn't want you put at risk," he tells me from across the room.

I am sewing in my chambers, my fingers bleeding from count-less pricks of the needle. There is a strange release to be found in the pain.

I do not even look up. "How could you?" I whisper. "I sent messengers. None would be admitted by you. You couldn't even send word by messenger?"

"They could have exposed you! And if not? Say I did send word through a messenger, what would you have done? Could I have you running to us in your condition? Cathy is still here. She needs a mother." His voice is high pitched with fervor. "Good God, girl, think in reality!"

"Yes," I acquiesce. "Reality. What choice is there?" At last I be-hold him. He stands by the door unshaven, his clothes soiled, his eyes wild. My heart stirs. There is no use continuing in this vein. Reality . . . God, how cruel is reality. "Oh, Thomas . . ." I push my sewing off my lap, turning tear-filled eyes to my husband. "I did not think it would happen to us. I know I may sound ignorant and naïve. Perhaps God is cursing me for my pride. Now little Edward is gone. . . ." I shake my head in anguished bewilderment. "Ed-ward is gone and I cannot begin to understand why."

I rise to move toward him. He holds up a hand, stopping me. "Don't. Please don't. There is nothing we can do. The boy re-ceived a proper burial. When the threat has passed, I will permit you to visit his grave." He bites his lip, closing his eyes, drawing in a deep breath through his nose. "I am leaving for a while," he an-nounces. "I—have business to attend to."

"Thomas!" I cry, sinking to my knees.

He stares at me, his face reflecting my own sense of God's be-trayal.

"Please hold me!" I beg, reaching out my arms.

Thomas shakes his head, tears spilling onto his cheeks. "I must go . . ." he whispers. "I—I must go," he says again.

Long after he departs I remain huddled on the floor in a heap of confusion and despair, my arms reaching out for a man who is not there.

Thomas Howard

There is no business to attend to, only that I must escape Huns-don and Edward's fresh grave and my wife's pitiful grief. It is her first loss, I must remember. I must be patient. Surely God is predictable enough for me to realize that He will assure us more. Elizabeth will no doubt grow as accustomed to habitual grief as I am.

But am I? Oh, God, holding that little baby, knowing I could not save him, just as I could not save any of the others.

There is only one place to go.

I visit the tomb of Lady Anne Plantagenet. My princess.

There, alone beneath a mockingly sunny sky, I kneel, reaching my hand out to caress her cool stone effigy. My tears fall unchecked.

"Princess . . ." I whisper, feeling a proper fool. "I beg you hear me. I am lost. I—should be beside my wife, I know that. But I can't bear it. I feel as though she does not deserve to grieve as I do! And I know that is wrong! Please help me. I do not know how much more I can stand. . . . How much more can I lose before I lose myself?" I shake my head, then lean it against the stone, giving into the need to sob.

It is a fool's hobby, this talking to graves. I rise in anger, cursing my idiotic fancies. Wherever the princess is, it is too far away. She cannot hear me. She cannot help me.

No one can.

There is naught to do but return to Hunsdon and anticipate the birth of yet another child. I almost wish they'd succumb to the sweating sickness in my absence so that I might be prevented from losing them to something else in the future.

It seems my only certainty: transience. Loss.

"She will not eat," Elizabeth's maid informs me upon my return. "The poor child is mad with grief. Her cries are heard the manor throughout."

"Give me something to bring her," I order and upon the delivery of a tray of cheese and warm bread, I draw in a shuddering breath, urging myself to be patient as I approach her chambers.

The girl is curled up in bed, her shoulders shaking in silent sobs.

I set the tray on her breakfast table, then sit beside her, reaching out a hesitant hand to touch her shoulder.

"Come now," I say in gentle tones laced with exhaustion. "This won't do." I do not know what to say by way of comfort. "This won't do at all. What of this next baby? What will happen if you do not eat? It could be our next heir, you know. Its life must be preserved."

"Yes." Elizabeth's voice is bitter as she sits up, rubbing her swollen eyes. "If only for that. Not because it is our child that we are bound to love."

"It is a dangerous thing, you know, getting so wrapped up in them," I tell her, recalling my mother's words upon the birth of my ill-fated sister Alyss. "Their lives are too fragile. I should say the only thing more fragile is our own hearts." I close my eyes, my chest seized with the pain of this most recent loss. My advice, as cold as it is, is practical and Elizabeth is a practical woman if nothing else. After sifting through the emotions females are more prone to, she will make sense of it, I am sure. I continue. "It is best to leave the daily maintenance to the nurses."

Elizabeth stares at me in horror. "Yes, of course. Leave them with the nurses so that they can be the ones to grieve! Heirs and pawns, that's all they are to you, aren't they?"

"That is all they can be," I tell her. "Or else I think we should die of heartbreak."

Elizabeth dissolves into tears, clutching her belly. "Oh, Thomas, why? Why must it be this way?"

There is naught to say to this, so I take her in my arms. "Come now, my girl. Eat. Please eat. This next Howard deserves a fair go of it."

Elizabeth offers a small nod and I fetch the tray. As I do so, I notice the door of her chambers standing ajar, just enough for a little face to be peering through.

Cathy stands, shifting from foot to foot, her large blue eyes filled with tears. How long she was there and how much she heard I have no idea.

"Is my lady mother going to get better?" she asks in her little-girl voice.

Tears clutch my throat. "Of course she is," I tell her. "Come in, little one. Come in and share our meal, won't you?"

Cathy inches forward, reaching out a tentative hand for a piece of bread. She eyes me with caution, then profound sadness. It is then I realize she knows; she heard it all.

She says nothing but sits across from us, the proper lady, taking small bites of bread, shifting her gaze between her mother and me as though we are potential enemies requiring close scrutiny.

So young to be aware of the workings of this world.

Elizabeth Howard

I do not know why I'm so tired. The labor was an easy one; little Henry arrived within ten hours of the onset of the pains. I recover well enough. My figure is as fine as it ever was. But I have no energy. The baby, as beautiful as the others, resembles his father with the long Howard nose and narrow face, but I experience none of the urgent longing for him that I did for little Cathy and Edward.

I do not know if it is my husband's well-intended words of caution that have turned my heart so cold or if it is my own new perspective, altered by this very unwelcome experience. I think of the queen and all her losses. If one loss is as painful as to cause me to lie abed sobbing for hours or to pace the manor without aim, then how must it be for her? How must it be for Thomas? There is no doubt that is what makes him who he is. How much better is my understanding of it all now? No wonder he cautions me to rein in my love.

Yet how can I? How can I not?

Sometimes I think were it not for these children I should take my own life. In this I am different from Thomas and the queen. Thomas is a man; he has all of the occupations of his sex to distract him, a government to participate in, goals and challenges to be met, wars to fight. The queen has a kingdom to be obligated to; she must press on. But a lowly woman with no kingdom and no battle but the daily one of living has nothing. Nothing but her children.

So I must live. I must press on, as Thomas urges. If only for them.

The pain may lessen. Others who have lost say it does. But I cannot imagine how or when or sometimes if I even want it to. To smile at one of Cathy's or Henry's antics grips my heart with agonizing guilt. Should one in mourning feel happiness? Is it tantamount to dismissing the gravity of the event?

I distance myself. It is almost against my will, as though it is something my body and mind are forced to do in order to survive. I watch the children from afar. Cathy handles herself well; she is the perfect little lady. Everything that is expected of her is mastered and performed. She minds her nurses and tutors, is a competent dancer and embroiderer.

"She is just as smart as a girl should be," Thomas always says of our eldest child.

Henry is precocious and bright. He is talking in small sentences at one year and shows himself to be a loving, if not high-minded boy.

"I wonder where he gets that," Thomas teases when the trait is noted.

"Yes, we all know how sweet and docile you are," I remind him with a slight laugh. I am able to laugh a little more now. Perhaps it is because I am with child again and, despite whatever pain seems to pursue me, I love being pregnant.

The queen is great with child as well. The little princess has been betrothed to the dauphin of France, which seems to solidify our at times unstable alliance with that overindulgent lot. With that union secured, it has become the kingdom's foremost obligation to pray for the birth of a healthy prince.

I believe few pray harder than I, save perhaps the queen's dearest friend, Maria de Salinas. What a triumph it would be for Her Grace to give the kingdom its longed-for prince at last!

But no amount of our humble prayers can bring it forth. In November the queen delivers her sixth child, a baby girl who dies before she could even be christened.

"Oh, my poor dear lady!" I lament to Thomas, clutching his hand as I learn the news at Hunsdon. Against my will, selfish thoughts permeate my awareness, fears for the life so new in my own womb.

I curse myself for thinking of myself before the queen but cannot seem to stop. I cup the slight mound of my belly, tears streaming down my cheeks. "Six babes and only one to survive thus far! When does it end?"

My husband pauses. "She has asked us to come to court," he says at last, disengaging his hand and moving toward the window. He stares out at the swans in the pond but does not seem to see them.

"How can I go to her and I with child?" I cry. "It would seem almost cruel, as though I am flaunting my good fortune."

Thomas shrugs. "You are not showing yet; she will not know. You've no need to tell her for quite some time."

I bow my head, rising from my chair to approach him and lean my head on his shoulder, praying for the safe delivery of our child, praying that I can offer some kind of comfort to my beloved queen.

We arrive at court for Christmas and the queen is almost overdemonstrative in greeting. She clasps my lord's hands, offering her sad smile. "How good it is to see you, Lord Surrey," she tells him before turning to me and resting a hand upon my shoulder. "Lady Surrey, dear child, how much we have missed you. How are you?"

I force a smile in return. "Quite well, Your Grace," I tell her as she ushers me away from her entourage. I am not fool enough to ask after her. I cannot begin to fathom the depth of this woman's grief.

"Promenade with us a while, Lady Elizabeth," she tells me, looping her arm through mine.

Though the queen is only twelve years my senior, she emanates an air of motherliness, making those in her presence feel loved and nurtured. No one is more deserving of children than she; the fact that she is consistently denied them confounds me to no end.

"We were much aggrieved upon hearing of the loss of your son," says Her Grace.

"Many thanks," I tell her, painful tears clutching my throat. I cannot allow her to offer her condolences without returning them. "May I offer my sympathy regarding your loss as well?"

The queen bows her head, drawing in a breath. "All we can do is pray for comfort and better times to come. All will transpire as God wills it."

I bite my lip to stifle a sob.

"I try very hard to believe that," she goes on, dropping the royal "we." Allowing me this glimpse of herself as a woman and not a queen is a privilege to match few others. "It is exceedingly difficult. And now I hear Bessie Blount is with child. She is to give my husband, my king, a baby. She, not I, his lawful wife." Her body convulses as she attempts to repress a sob.

I had not heard this latest development. "It is most unfair" is all I can think of to say. Were I in lesser company, I would take to cursing that harlot Bessie Blount with all due fervency, but I refrain, though I am certain it is no less than what Her Grace is thinking already.

The queen's laugh is bitter. "Most." She squares her shoulders, sighing. "But what can I do? Blame an innocent child? It does not ask to enter this world. I must accept the situation with the grace my station requires."

"You are a lady without rival," I tell Queen Catherine with profound sincerity.

Her smiling lips quiver. "And there are other things to look forward to, aren't there? The birth of your baby, for instance?"

"Your Grace!" I cry, covering my belly and bowing my head in shame. "How . . . ?"

"A mother knows," she tells me. "And I would never ask you to hide your condition for fear of offending me. A baby is a blessing to be shared, not hidden as if in shame. I am overjoyed for you and Lord Thomas. After what has been lost, this is nothing less than what you deserve."

On impulse I throw my arms about Her Grace and she hugs me back, offering modest laughter.

"God bless Your Grace always!" I cry, knowing I could not serve a more gracious and honorable queen.

Upon returning home to Hunsdon, I am taken with illness that remains with me for the duration of the pregnancy. I am fraught with misery. Night and day I take to the basin, vomiting wretchedly. I am weak and exhausted and my belly cramps so often that I fear an early labor. I cannot visit Cathy and Henry; it is all I can do to rise from my bed and take nourishment. I spot blood, which causes my heart to lurch in panic. I cannot bear the thought of losing another child.

Thomas does little to comfort me during this time. He maintains a conspicuous distance. No longer does he visit me when my confinement begins. No longer do we engage in the banter that stimulated me during my other pregnancies. Though I make certain the servants communicate my distress, I hear little. He sends gifts; he has always been good about that. But the jewels and bolts of fine fabrics are of little consolation.

I want him. For everything that has passed between us, good and bad, I want him. His mind, his challenging, obstinate spirit, stimulate me. His touch, his kisses, for some unfathomable reason, inflame a passion in me I never dreamed possible. It is not the love I dreamed of as a girl, but I cannot say what I feel is not love just the same, and though our foundation is shaky at best, I yearn for its fortification. But for that, he must be at my side.

He is sent for in June, when my labor begins in earnest. I do not understand why I am in such terrible pain; it is as though this is my first baby. For two days I am assaulted by the tight and terrible cramping of a womb that seems unwilling to part with its tiny inhabitant.

The midwife, a wizened old countrywoman, shakes her head again and again. "I do not understand. Nothing is happening at all." She sits beside me, swabbing my forehead with a cool cloth. "Oh, dear child . . . I fear for you. You've bled overmuch."

I begin to shiver and sweat at once. It is so hard to stay awake. . . .

Thomas Howard

"Lord Surrey, I do not know how long she can go on," the midwife tells me, her crackling tone gentle. "She is so weak . . . you best prepare for the worst. Her strength is gone."

Panic surges through me. Till now I have done my best to avoid Elizabeth. It was not with the intention to neglect; it is just that her sickness repelled me. After all, sickness leads only to one thing and in my vast experience, it is best to be absent for that occurrence. But now I have no choice. And in the face of her prospective loss, my thoughts become muddled. Nothing makes sense, not even in my own head. My heart is racing and skipping, my face is burning.

"And the child?" I demand.

"There is a procedure I could try where one cuts through the belly into the womb, but it is very risky. Few survive it," she says. "It is likely they will both die, Lord Surrey. I'm deeply sorry."

Her dire prediction causes me to shake in anger. No, rage. Searing, burning, and uncontrollable it courses through my veins, a force I cannot deny. "No . . ." I breathe. "No. Not again. Do you hear me? This is not happening again!" My thoughts are racing. I cannot catch up to them. I see my other children; their faces pass before my mind's eye as they appeared during their last moments on earth, in suffering. And for what? God's delight? My limbs are tingling and quivering. I cannot see right. My vision blurs. I proceed into Elizabeth's chambers, pushing past the midwife and servants, making my way to the bed where lies my wife. She is pasty; her eyes are closed.

"Wake up!" I order, sitting on the bed, shaking her shoulders. "Wake up, do you hear me?"

Elizabeth's eyes flutter open. "Thomas . . ." She begins to reach for me.

"It is your wish to leave as well?" I cry. Her arms fall to her sides. She begins to cry, mewing like a sick kitten. "Then go, if it is so easy!" I cannot rein it in any longer. I seize her chin between my fingers, staring her down without being able to focus on her features. She is saying something; I cannot hear her. My other hand reaches out, grasping onto something soft and silky, her hair, I think. I tug at it, pulling her out of bed, dragging her out of her chambers and through the hall to a destination unknown even to myself.

"Come now, let us be off! You must be impatient for the next world!" I cry in a tone that rings with giddiness. "We'll spare you further suffering! I shall do it myself, girl, right quick—ha! I shall beat God at His own game! Beat Him before He can claim Himself the victor!" With this statement comes unexpected laughter. It bubbles up in my throat, releasing itself in a strange cackle that sounds like a dog's painful yelp. I yield to it. It has been a good long time since I laughed.

"Thomas!" Elizabeth's voice permeates the strange fog that has enveloped my mind. "Stop! The baby is coming! You're going to hurt the baby!"

"What baby?" I cry. "There is no baby! What was will never be! You are leaving! You are all leaving!"

"Oh, God, my Thomas! Please stop this!"

"Lord Surrey!" someone cries. Hands seize my shoulders, but I am quicker. My dagger, my reliable dagger, is in my own hand and I wave it at the assemblage. My movements seem slow and exaggerated, like an actor in a staged play.

"Do not interfere with the duties the master of the house must carry out!" I cry. The servants back down, staring at me with blank faces and wide eyes.

I turn to my wife, raising the dagger, bringing it down in one blind and wild gesture, slashing her head from the lock of hair in my hand to the joint in her jaw. A sliver of blood bright as Cardinal Wolsey's hat oozes down her face. Wolsey . . . oh, I hate him.

Somewhere someone is screaming.

At once white light obstructs my vision. I turn. All is silent, save for the pounding of my heart. She stands, shrouded in soft radiance. She is extending her long arm, reaching out her hand. But what is the worst, oh, the very worst, is her face, her ethereal face twisted in agony, her eyes wide in horror as they bear witness to my shame.

The dagger falls to the floor with a clatter and along with it my wife. I reach for the vision. "Princess!"

There is nothing. Nothing but a tapestry and a floor and a screaming pregnant girl bleeding from the head.

I cover my temples with my hands. Bile rises in my throat. I double over.

And run away.

I am in my chambers. At some point, sleep must have found me, for I awaken in my bed. My physician sits beside me, eying me with caution.

"You are well, Lord Surrey?"

I offer a tentative nod that does little to convince either of us. "The girl?" I ask in husky tones, recalling now every horrid detail of the strange encounter. I begin to tremble uncontrollably. The anger, rearing its head in the form of madness . . . oh, the disgust . . .

He nods. "Has been tended to."

"She is all right?" I ask, turning to stare up at my canopy, avoiding the doctor's eyes.

"Yes," he answers. "And you have a healthy daughter."

Tears fill my eyes. I close them.

"The servants are well paid, Lord Surrey?" he asks.

"Yes," I answer.

"Then they won't talk," he goes on in the matter-of-fact tones expected of one of his trade. "And, for modest compensation, I am willing to say the wound was a result of a cut I had to make for the drawing of two teeth. I noted they were missing upon an examination, so it is a solid argument."

I draw in a shuddering breath. "Yes."

"You best take care, Lord Surrey," he advises, his mouth set in a grim line. "These things have a way of getting out."

I say nothing.

He departs, leaving behind a warm sleeping posset of which I drink heartily.

I cannot bear to think on it anymore.

When at last I bring myself to visit my wife, she shrinks away from the sight of me. It is a wonder she will let me touch her again.

I have no idea what to say. There are no words to compensate for this.

"Elizabeth . . ." I begin in soft tones. "I-I . . ." I bow my head. "What did you name the girl?" I ask at last.

"Mary," she whispers, turning her head away.

Tears clutch my throat. "Mary," I repeat, my voice wavering. "For the little princess?"

"Yes," she says in flat tones. "For the little . . . princess." She lowers her eyes.

"I should very much like to see her," I say, forcing my tone to be conversational. I turn to one of the maids. "Fetch the baby, will you?"

The maid drops the linens she was folding and backs out of the room to do my bidding with wide eyes.

I inch toward the bed, then sit beside Elizabeth, reaching into the pocket of my doublet to produce a collar of ruby roses with emerald stems. "For your troubles," I tell her as I hand them to her.

She examines them with disinterest, then holds them out for me to take. "I cannot bear accepting these gifts anymore, Thomas," she tells me in low tones. "They cost too much."

I bite my lip and bow my head. "We'll just lay them aside for now," I say, putting them back in my pocket. "I'm certain a state occasion will soon require their use."

Elizabeth says nothing. We are rescued by the nurse, who brings in the baby. The woman is all smiles.

"Here is your bonny little princess," she tells me as she places the child in my arms.

I gaze down into her face. She is unlike the other children, with her mass of downy golden hair and fair skin. There is something so familiar about her, her etherealness, her delicacy, as though she is not of this . . . no, not this world. *Her* world.

I clutch the baby to my breast. "She's beautiful," I tell her.

"She's your truest Howard if anyone is. If she can survive the ordeal of her birth, I daresay she can survive anything." Elizabeth sighs, rolling onto her side, curling up into a little ball, bringing her hand up to her cheek. Her shoulders begin to convulse. I rise. I cannot speak past the painful lump in my throat. I cannot look at her.

I shift my gaze to my baby, my little Mary, and dare to think of all the things I will do to make her great.

Elizabeth Howard

Is this real? Is the man who attacked me with his own dagger while I labored truly my husband? Now he sits and holds our baby, staring down at her, his face lit with adoration. He converses with me as though nothing happened at all. He dares offer me a gift, whether it is to buy my silence or is some form of an apology he cannot bring himself to utter, I do not know. I am not sure I care at this point.

I am so very tired. My body aches and quivers all over. The wet nurses I used to resent I now thank God for. Baby Mary is well taken care of and is set up in the nursery with her brother and sister. It is painful to look at her. When I see her fair face, I do not see my little girl. I see the nightmare of her birth. I see Thomas, wild-eyed and monstrous, waving his dagger about and next . . . next . . .

I squeeze my eyes shut. I cannot stand the memory; I wish to banish it from my mind but cannot. It rehearses itself again and again like one of King Henry's badly performed masques.

What grieves me almost as much as the wound on my head is the servants' inaction. They did nothing to interfere. It is obvious who they are bound to. I am just a woman, a woman to be treated as any other piece of my lord's property. It matters not that I am a countess, a countess who will become a duchess. Nothing matters but the wishes of my lord. If his wish is my demise, then no one will stand in his way.

I have never been afraid of Thomas. I believed I knew his tempers; after all, I've been on the receiving end of his blows before. And despite the countless warnings from experienced friends and relatives about what to expect from a husband, nothing could have prepared me for this.

I thought I knew him better.

Now I do not know what to expect from minute to minute. Will he be kind? Will he be cruel? In the weeks following Mary's birth, he is nothing but solicitous. But for how long? And what will set him off next?

His greatest fear is loss—a dullard could perceive that—and it seems when confronted with that possibility, he loses all reason. Despite my sympathy for him, I cannot bring myself to justify his treatment. I do not care if he's a man mad with grief or the master of this house and my person. There is no claim he can make great enough to make this right.

I wonder if it shall ever be made right between us again.

When Mary is three weeks old, a smiling Thomas carries her into my chambers and sits beside me. She is snuggled tight against his chest and he makes a show of wrapping and rewrapping the blankets about her, swaddling her up tight as a caterpillar in its cocoon.

He has never attended the other children as he does this one. Perhaps the ordeal of her birth coupled with the knowledge that he almost prevented it prompts him to monitor her progress with more interest.

"We should ask His Majesty to be her godfather," he tells me.

"Whatever you like," I say in bland tones.

He gazes at me a moment, his black eyes wistful. His smile is forced. "Happy news from Blackmore. Elizabeth Blount has given the king a son," he announces. "They call him Henry Fitzroy. You know Fitzroy is a name reserved for royalty. It is most intriguing."

I offer a bitter grunt. "And we are celebrating?"

"The king has acknowledged him," he tells me.

"Openly?" I ask, my tone sharp with shock.

Thomas nods. "He has not legitimized him yet, but if he does not beget an heir . . ." He looks down at Mary, who offers a little gurgle.

"He has an heir, the Princess Mary," I remind him in firm tones, then give way to a sigh. "Oh, Her poor Grace! For him to disrespect her by keeping a mistress is one thing, but to display his bastard before her very eyes!"

Thomas shrugs. "It is not the first time such things have occurred." His tone is absent.

I scowl at him. "And I suppose you support this travesty?"

"I am the king's man, Elizabeth," he returns. "You know that."

I bite my lip in frustration. "Of course. First and last."

"No," he corrects me. "A Howard first and last. When I say the king's man, I mean the Crown's man. Whoever wears the Crown has my loyalty."

I stare at him in mingled bewilderment and horror. He does not indicate whether or not he cares if the Crown is obtained by natural succession or by treachery. If his loyalties can shift so easily and with so little regard for what is right . . . I shudder. I do not want to think of it anymore.

I do not want to think of our codes of honor, codes that more often than not seem at odds.

Though I use my slow recovery from Mary's birth as an excuse to avoid intimacy with Thomas, by the time she reaches three months old, I know I cannot shrink from my duties any longer.

What strikes me as most peculiar is that I miss him. His touch, when gentle, affects me like nothing else in this world. I want that back. I want him back, for whatever he is. I have no choice, anyway. If I have to see this through and honor my commitment, it is best to take what pleasure I can from it.

Meantime I shall pray that his horrific display demonstrated during Mary's birth is his last.

By October I am with child once more.

Thomas is delighted. Perhaps it is because I show no signs of the illness experienced during my last pregnancy, giving no indication that he has to fear for my life. He dotes on me, spoiling me with gifts. I am the owner of more strings of pearls, jewel-encrusted brooches, and collars than I can catalogue. And each are delivered to me in caskets of silver, ivory, or gilt. It is overwhelming.

"You may as well get used to it," he tells me. "You will be a duchess someday and as such you shall be ornamented with only the very best."

"Fitting," I tell him with a slight smile. "As I am your very best ornament."

The smile he offers me in turn is affectionate. "And the most modest."

We are walking arm in arm through the gardens of Hunsdon. They have little to offer, being that it is January, but one can discern from their expansive layout the promise of beauty that spring's arrival will unveil.

"My little niece Mary Boleyn is to marry William Carey this month," Thomas goes on to say. "Not so little anymore from what I hear," he adds with a smirk.

"Indeed not," I say. "From what I'm told, she is old enough to play the harlot the world over. Why, King Francois kept her as his very own mistress! It's amazing a girl of that reputation can land herself one as promising as young Master Carey."

"She had some help," says my husband. He clears his throat. "It seems she has quite a talent for inspiring royal favor. . . ."

"No." My voice is low with annoyance. "You have to be jesting. Does that man have no shame? And Bessie Blount so recently delivered of his bastard!"

Thomas laughs. "It seems the Careys will be given lodgings at court near His Majesty. Very convenient. And the young William is to be compensated for his—tolerance—by being made a gentleman of the privy chamber. Seems the young couple have come a long way." This he says through sputterings of laughter.

"Thomas!" I am too disgusted to be amused. "Aren't you ashamed? This child is your family and she is behaving in a manner unworthy of the Howard name."

"God's body, Elizabeth!" Thomas exclaims, wiping tears from his eyes, his face still ruddy from mirth. "Sometimes I don't understand you at all. Don't you see what this means for us? A satisfied king is a generous one. You must realize how the chalice of his favor will spill over onto all of us. No," he laughs again, "my naughty little niece is a credit to the Howards."

"I have been unfair," I say, my voice fraught with sadness as I

think of my own daughters. "Mary Boleyn is but a ch
a sigh. "And what is easier to manipulate than a child
display of the utmost depravity, Thomas, the king being
nine years old and married and the girl but thirteen."

"We are twenty-five years apart, Elizabeth," Thomas ren
me.

"That was different. We were able to marry and conduct our
selves as Christians should," I tell him. "Now this girl will be forever known as nothing but another of King Henry's whores."

"Not such a bad thing to be known as," he tells me. "You are
wrong, Elizabeth. When serving the king, you serve him body,
heart, and soul, reaping all the rewards for your troubles."

I shake my head but decide not to pursue it anymore. It is fruitless; he will never understand. Instead I say, "And what of Her
Grace, the woman who has shown us nothing but kindness and
love? What will she make of our—no, your—support of your niece's
behavior?"

"She understands the ways of this world well enough to know
it is temporary," he says. "The king's affections are fickle—he'll
tire of the little girl soon enough and she will be replaced. Fortunately, the Howards are of fertile stock—we can keep him well
supplied!"

"Thomas Howard!" I cry. "Have you no sympathy for the queen,
none at all? Doesn't she mean anything to you?"

For a moment his face softens. He averts his head.

We stop walking and turn toward one another. I take his elegant
hands in mine. For a moment I stand captivated by them; how is it
these beautiful hands can be capable of such cruelty? My eyes remove to his face, pondering his mind, a mind I enjoy, a mind that
challenges mine, and a mind I understand no better than his hands.
Why must it all be so complicated?

"I am her maid," I tell Thomas in soft tones. "I have sworn myself to her as you have sworn yourself to the king. You must understand that as such I cannot support this, Thomas."

He sighs. "Your first obligation, as with every subject in England, should be to the king." He runs his hand through his hair in
frustration. "This makes things very difficult for us, constantly

that you are a woman of principle, but
inciple has to be sacrificed now and
he continues. "I don't enjoy it! Do
queen made a fool of? I love her,

though ashamed to admit such in
me with jealousy; I know the love
for Her Grace. She inspires such an in-
that one is rendered helpless by it. But Thomas is
come with any such thing. He is not helplessly devoted to
anything but his own self-interest.

"You wouldn't understand," he says with another dramatic sigh. "Your family has always been great. The Howards have had to fight and crawl and drag themselves up out of the ashes of shame. That is why it is essential to attain and maintain the greatness we are capable of."

"No matter the cost to your soul?"

"Always the soul with you." His voice is thin with impatience.

"Yes, Thomas," I affirm. "*Always* the soul. It is more eternal than anything of this world, even the favor of kings."

"Noble words, Elizabeth, but impractical," Thomas says as we continue our walk.

"For some," I say. "Those who are too afraid of the challenge." I purse my lips. Before he can retort I continue, returning to practicality. "Besides, the Staffords have known their fair share of shame. My grandfather was beheaded, after all."

"You always had a dukedom," Thomas says, his voice tinged with bitterness.

I shake my head in frustration. That's all that matters to him: dukedoms, favor, possessions. I do not abhor such things but I'd like to believe I am not governed by my desire for them, either.

"Anyway, it doesn't matter." Thomas's voice adopts a more conversational tone. "This going round and round is pointless." He squeezes my hand. "There is more news. After Mary Boleyn's wedding, we are to ready ourselves for an extended sojourn."

"A sojourn?" My curiosity is piqued. We never go anywhere and I have been restless. "Where?"

"Ireland."

I screw up my face in confusion. "Ireland? Good God, why would we want to go there?"

Thomas laughs. "I have been appointed lord lieutenant of the rabble. Seems the Earl of Kildare, that damned Gerald Fitzgerald, can't manage a thing and the country is amok with disorder. What's more, Sir Piers Butler has wrongfully claimed the earldom of Ormond since his cousin left no heir, and Kildare doesn't know what to do with him. The Butlers are powerful; there are too many of them, as there are of all those damnable Irish. In any event, Kildare came to London on orders to explain the mismanagement of his island and it was decided someone with a little more experience and wisdom should be given the responsibility of restoring rule to the king."

"Really, Thomas?" I cry. "Ireland? And who was behind this?"

Thomas scowls at me. "It was a decision made by the king and his council."

"And who's on the council?" I cry. "Wolsey? Do you think he may have decided this to exile you from court, where things are really happening? You know how he hates you and your father."

"It isn't exile!" Thomas insists. "The king decided ultimately to favor me with this mission. This is an opportunity to further demonstrate my worth!"

I twist my lips in bitterness. "Well," I acquiesce, "I suppose it is a nobler cause than the whoring out of your niece."

Thomas turns me to face him and wraps his arms about me, drawing me close. "We'll have a lovely house in Dublin with all the amenities for you and the children."

"What of Kenninghall? Now our plans for that will be put off even longer," I say with a girlish pout I am ashamed of.

"Kenninghall will always be there. We will commence with the renovations upon our return," he says. "It will be our palace and there you will be my prin—" He stops himself, casting his eyes to the snow-covered ground. "My little duchess."

"A countess suits me fine for now," I tell him, not wanting to bring about the death of his father by speculating on our inevitable elevation.

But it is easy to warm to my husband's fair words. I put off my fears of removing to the wilds of Ireland, my disgust over the situation with Mary Boleyn, and my frustration with our constant battle of principle as I wrap my arms about Thomas's neck and pull him toward me, planting a firm kiss on his lips.

I shall try to look at this as a good thing, just as Thomas advises.

I will not look at it as Wolsey's strategy for keeping my husband impotent at court. I will be flattered; Thomas must be a great threat to Wolsey for him to send him so far away.

The Isle of Erin

Thomas Howard, 1520–1522

In May, one hundred royal guard accompany my family and me to the island its natives call Erin. It is a beautiful place, this Ireland, a land as green as an emerald and lush as Babylon. If it were not populated with the damnable Irish, it would be ideal. Elizabeth and the children are set up in Dublin. The residence is a mite too modest for our tastes and God knows the girl deserves better, but I remind her to be patient. Someday sooner than later we shall have nothing but the very best.

Elizabeth is proud of my endeavors; she calls me her shining knight. "The great White Howard," she teases, wrapping her arms about me and covering my cheek with kisses.

Her faith inspires me to carry on with my first task, which is to raid Connell O'More's territory southwest of Dublin. It is successful; the churls are put in their place and now the pretended Earl Butler has joined me, bringing with him other lords to support the cause. Once I return to Dublin, I am joined by still more Irish lords, all of whom have personal quarrels with other Irish lords. It is hard to keep track. One thing remains certain; almost everyone's name begins with an *O* or a *Mc*.

With their help I subdue most of the island. I am alive with that tingling thrill that surges through me whenever participating in a battle. I tremble with excitement as the plans are drawn up and executed. This is what I am meant for; more than anything else, I am a fighting man. I am a soldier.

By July, I am optimistic that if things continue in this vein, Ireland might be governable after all. I seek out Elizabeth, who is now in confinement, to report the latest developments.

"It is this lack of money that will undo us," I tell her. "The troops are underpaid and griping louder than fishwives in the market. No matter how I entreat His Majesty, he just doesn't seem to understand that they cannot live on four shillings a day."

"How does he propose you finance this endeavor?" she asks in her low voice. She is lying abed, her dark hair plaited down her shoulders, her alert eyes calculating and keen. I smile ruefully; there is nothing dull about her. She is the picture of cleverness.

"From Irish revenues. But I cannot extricate anything from these bastards without resorting to Kildare's own questionable methods," I tell her as I sit at the end of her bed.

She purses her lips in thought. "What if you sent someone to plead on your behalf? That Wallop gentleman, perhaps. Everyone always says the king cannot resist a personal appeal."

I nod. I could do that. King Henry seems to have a weakness for personal entreaties. Perhaps he will endow me with more funds if I send Sir Wallop to London. No use telling her I may employ the idea; she is far too headstrong as it is. But the idea has merit.

"Thank God you weren't born a man," I say with a light laugh. "Else the house of Howard would really have something to worry about."

"Without a doubt," she assures me with a smile. She rubs her belly, closing her eyes, drawing in a deep breath. "Oh, Thomas . . ."

"Elizabeth?" I reach for her hand. "What is it?"

She opens her eyes; they are wide with fear. "The baby . . . it's time." She withdraws her hand to clutch the covers and begins to shrink away from me, biting her lip. She averts her face.

I stare at her a moment, then begin to back away.

It is better I am not present for this, better for her, better for me.

"I'll—I'll fetch the midwife," I tell her as I quit the room.

* * *

Our son is born on 31 July after ten hours of labor. She did well, my Elizabeth, coming through as vibrant with health as she was before.

"What shall we call this young Howard boy?" I ask her as I hold my little lad.

Elizabeth regards him through tear-filled eyes a moment before fixing her piercing blue gaze on me. Her smile is tentative. "I thought . . . I thought perhaps we could call this one Thomas, for your lordship."

My throat constricts with painful tears as I behold our son, his ruddy face scrunched up as though he is thoroughly annoyed by the whole ordeal of entering this world.

I think of my first namesake, the Thomas born of my princess. He was so full of life . . . so full of promise. . . . Is it a curse to name this child such?

Nonsense and drivel. Whatever is meant to happen will occur whether your name is John or William or Charles. It doesn't matter. There is nothing to a name as long as it is affixed to a great surname. And we can assure him that.

I swallow the lump in my throat.

"That would be fine," I tell her in a husky whisper. I hand her the baby. She clasps him to her chest, returning her fond mother's gaze to his tiny face.

"We do have a beautiful family, Thomas," she says.

I nod.

I cannot speak.

By September, Sir Wallop returns from London with four thousand pounds. But I am told that the king will spare no more; further funds for this campaign will have to be raised on my own. It is his hope that the rents I collect after Christmas will prove sufficient.

The summer triumph is eclipsed by sickness in the Pale, which not only claims the lives of many of my troops but puts morale on the decline. It is not long before they are plotting their escape.

When I catch wind of a plot that eighteen of my men are planning to make off with a boat in order to capture a larger vessel and turn to piracy as an alternative to the honor of soldiering, I am incensed and order their immediate imprisonment.

"I'd hang them all if the damnable lawyers would let me!" I cry to Elizabeth one evening in our parlor. "Damned fools! As if they'd survive anyway! Pirates!"

I pace back and forth before our hearth, running my hand through my hair in frustration.

"It's about discipline, my girl," I explain to her. "If the men do not have that, they are lost. These men need to be made an example of so as not to give any of the others ideas. Mutiny can be more contagious than the plague."

Elizabeth raises her eyes from her embroidery. "If only you had the power over life and death that you hold as admiral at sea."

I stare at her a moment, then offer a half smile before removing to my study to ask my clerk to draft a dispatch.

It's strange how useful this girl has come to be.

Elizabeth Howard

While Thomas busies himself with the rabble both the Irish and his troops are proving to be, I am occupied with the running of my Dublin household. For everything Thomas has against this lot, I must say our Irish staff has been most accommodating. The children adore them and I am grateful their adjustment to this place has not been too taxing.

Through his travels, Thomas is allowed to see the beauty of the island and makes a full report cataloguing its many charms, but as I am tethered to Dublin, I see none of them. I miss Hunsdon and London and the queen. I long for our plans for Kenninghall to be set into motion. I long for our lives to resume at home.

We pass a bleak winter in which the city snow is gray and slushy instead of white and fluffy. Cathy stares down at the street out the window of our parlor and heaves a deep sigh. At eight she is a beautiful girl of slight build, with Thomas's black hair and my blue eyes. Her face is wistful.

"What do you suppose we'd be doing if we were at home?" she asks me.

"We would be at court, most likely," I say. "Passing the winter with the queen."

"That would be lovely," Cathy sighs. She sits beside me, taking up her embroidery. "Do you suppose I shall be made lady-in-waiting to the queen someday?"

My heart swells with pride at her noble desire. She is a good girl; her deportment and carriage is fraught with dignity. She is graceful and gentle, and looking upon her now, I have no doubt that she has the makings of a great lady.

I reach out to caress her cheek. It is smooth and fine as ivory. "You shall. Her Grace will adore you," I tell her.

Cathy rewards me with a smile.

We have grown quite close during our exile. Were she not with me, I do not know how I'd make it through.

It seems sons are destined to lead lives of glory; to them we hand our fortunes and our names and our titles. But the daughters, they are a mother's salvation. To them we hand our hearts.

Traitors and Lovers

Elizabeth Howard

In January, I receive a letter from my sister Catherine. It is the way in which it arrives that sends an uncomfortable chill coursing through me. It is delivered directly into my hands from that of a travel-weary servant, sent from the house of the Earl of Westmorland. Why would Catherine send me a letter through Ralph Neville's servants? My heart skips as I break the seal with a smile.

> *My dearest Elizabeth,*
>
> *I hope that this letter finds you and yours well. So much is happening. I must dispense with frivolous chatter in favor of an entreaty for you and Lord Surrey to beg His Majesty your return home. Our honored father is in danger. He does not seem to understand how much. He speaks freely about his place in the succession since he is descended from Edward III. He believes he is the natural, if not obvious choice, and has even dared say that the king will have no sons. You know how fatal that thinking can be. He has raised troops of considerable number. He says they are for protection while he tours his Welsh estates. I can only pray that is true. The good Lord knows how this could appear to His Majesty and Cardinal Wolsey, who has always hated our honored father.*

I would not write if I did not believe this to be a matter of the utmost gravity. But I shiver, Elizabeth. It is cold under the axe's shadow.

Lastly, I am compelled to tell you before you learn it from another source that, for no reason other than to honor the wishes of His Grace our father, I have married Ralph Neville, the earl of Westmorland. Forgive me. I know you loved him once. I pray you are occupied with the happiness your honored husband provides.

With love,
Catherine Neville
Lady Westmorland

The letter slips from my fingers onto the floor. This is all too much to take in. . . . My father, the premier duke in the land, has allowed himself to be governed by foolish arrogance to the extent that his life is now at risk . . . and my sister . . . my sister. Catherine Neville. It was not Ralph's servant, then. It was hers. He is hers.

I clench my fists in rage. I have no right. I know I have no right. But tears slide down my cheeks in icy rivulets anyway. She has Ralph, my gentle Ralph, who will never lay a hand on her, my sweet Ralph, who will love her and caress her and give her his children, the children I wanted, the life I wanted. . . . How could she? How could he?

I throw myself across the chaise in our parlor and begin to sob brokenly. What am I to do? Ralph was bound to marry; so was Catherine. He was my father's ward. There was no doubt he would marry one of my sisters. But I had put such an effort into blotting him from my mind that I had not anticipated the hurt and sense of betrayal that would accompany this news.

"Elizabeth." Thomas's voice. His footfalls approach. His warm hand rests upon my shoulder. "What is it, my girl?"

Before I can retrieve my letter, Thomas has it and scans it with attentive black eyes.

He throws it to the floor. "We are *not* going home. You know that, don't you? If your father's stupidity proves to be his downfall, then so be it. The farther removed we are from his disgrace, the better. I will not be affiliated with it."

"But, my lord," I beg, "we must go to him. He is your father-in-law, after all. You must intervene. You must use your influence with your father and your other allies to convince the king and Wolsey that my father means no harm. He is an old man—a proud, foolish old man."

"God rot proud, foolish old men," Thomas spits. "No. We will remain here and carry out our obligations. Your father has done this to himself. Whatever happens is his affair."

"Thomas . . ."

"No!" he cries. "Do you hear me? There isn't even a question." He furrows his brow, shaking the letter at me. "I wonder . . . what upsets you more? Your father's idiocy or the marriage of your sister?"

I offer a scowl. "Of course that upsets me!" I cry. "But it's neither here nor there now. He has married Catherine and may God give them many years of harmony and joy, unlike—"

"Unlike us," Thomas finishes for me. His face is stricken.

I am subdued. "I didn't mean it," I say in soft tones. "We have been happy, Thomas."

"Now and again," he says, fixing his eyes on the window behind me. The black orbs become hard again. "There is no more to be said. We will remain here. There are to be no petitions made to the king for our return. I have too much to do here without worrying after your fool of a father."

I rise. "Well, then remain," I tell him. "But I am going. I am taking the children and going. My family needs me. I will not abandon them." As I speak, I realize I have just made the decision at that moment and, having made it, will stand by it no matter the cost.

"You do not seem to understand," Thomas seethes as he approaches me. He grips my shoulders; his face is inches from mine. "We will remain here."

I shake my head. "*You* may remain. I will go. I have an obligation to my family."

"Your first obligation is to me!" he cries. "Why can't you understand that? Before anything! Before your queen and country and children and everything else! I am your *husband*, Elizabeth!"

I shake my head again. "Would you abandon your father in his time of need?"

Thomas narrows his eyes at me but does not answer the question. "Elizabeth, I'm warning you. If you leave me now, you will be making the biggest mistake of your life. There will be no expiation for it."

"That is on my conscience, then," I respond with equal coolness. "If there is nothing more, my lord, I have arrangements to make."

He releases my shoulders. I try to ignore the profound sadness that contorts his expression. It is so brief on his countenance that I tell myself I imagined it.

I curtsy, then brush past him, almost wishing he would grab me and gather me in his arms, wishing he would tell me not to leave because he cannot live without me.

But he can live without me.

There is not a soul on earth whose life and death hinges on the presence of another.

I return to Lambeth with the children and it is only upon my arrival that I realize I can be of no more help to my father here than I was in Ireland. My sister was not appealing for my return; she was asking for my husband. He is the one with the influence. I am just the wife, just the woman.

I pace the house in despair. The duchess, who has grown stout and agitated over the years, is a source of much angst. She criticizes me for leaving Thomas.

"You must redefine your loyalties, Lady Elizabeth," she tells me. "Before you become undone by them. You are married to Lord Surrey first and last. It is to him that you are pledged. You cannot persist in going against his wishes as you do and hope for any chance at happiness."

I say nothing. I cannot argue with everyone. Instead I keep to myself. I take Cathy on little day trips and derive what joy I can in our bond, which seems to run deeper than that of the other children, much to my regret.

"I think you did the right thing," Cathy reassures me in her soft voice.

I offer a sad laugh and clutch my daughter's hand. "Thank you, love."

The rest of the world may turn against me, but she will remain. It is a loyalty I take comfort in.

In April my father is called to Windsor to answer for his outlandish plot to come before the king concealing a knife so that he might slay him. My heart drops in my chest upon hearing the news. How could he be so reckless? Truly, he must have gone mad.

He never makes it to his destination. He is accosted en route and arrested for treason.

My father, like my grandfather before him, now awaits his trial in the worst place a body can.

The dread Tower of London.

I imagine him there, cold and shivering and underfed. Does he regret his dishonor? Will he make his peace with God before his fate is carried out?

My father-in-law heads the committee that tries and sentences my father to his death by beheading. They say the old Duke of Norfolk wept for his friend.

He may have wept, I reflect with bitterness, but it did not stop him from uttering that fateful word. *Guilty*.

And now my father is to die.

"He has disgraced the Stafford name," my stepmother-in-law tells me in somber tones. "And for nothing but pride. It is a dangerous thing, pride. Of all the sins, perhaps it is the worst. It leads us to believe in our own illusions of power and the rightness of our own misguided principles."

I bow my head. I can no longer cry; I am past tears. My father is to die . . . my father is to die. . . . He bounced me on his knee when I was a wee girl. He smiled and joked. I loved him, aloof as he could be. My father is to die. . . .

"I will attend the execution," I say then, my tone just above a whisper.

"You will do no such thing," says Lady Agnes. "You will keep away. You cannot be seen to be offering any support to the fallen duke."

"I am not supporting him," I assure her. "In no way do I support treason. But I will be there for him when the axe falls. I will offer a prayer and my farewells. There is nothing neither you nor anyone else can do to prevent my going."

Lady Agnes's face is wrought with sadness as she regards me. "You are far too willful, Lady Elizabeth." Her tone is wistful.

"I am a Howard," I retort, my tone hard.

The sun shines bright in a cloudless azure sky the day my father is to die. The grass on Tower Green is lush and green-gold; nature is innocent, ignorant of the fates of those who share its realm. The April air is warm; there is even a slight refreshing breeze. I marvel that such evil can take place on this mockingly perfect day.

Gathered about are some members of my family, the court, and the hoard of observers hungry for gory displays, a crowd crude and rough and without compassion. It is good sport witnessing an execution, and the sounds of laughter can be heard ringing out here and there. It is a travesty. No one cares that the greatest duke in the land is dying. They care about the show, the spectacle of a man cut down in his glory.

As he kneels before the block, he raises his head. For the briefest of moments he locks his eyes with mine; they are bewildered blue mirrors that reflect nothing I had envisaged. No regret, no sorrow, no anger. Just shock. Whether it is over his execution or over his failed plot, I will never know. I bite back a sob, trying to convey in my gaze my love and grief and a thousand other emotions that have every and no name.

And then the axe. A swift whir as it cuts through the air, then through my father's neck with lethal exactness. The head rolls onto the waiting straw, its eyes wide in a moment of mingled terror and surprise. Blood pours from his trunk and I stand transfixed by the sight. I cannot scream or cry or rage. I just stare.

"Come, my lady," beckons my gentle servant Molly. "Come away from this terrible thing."

"This . . . terrible thing," I parrot, still held fast by the atrocity before me.

She takes my arm and leads me to my coach, guiding me away from the stench of death and Tower Green.

I pray never to return.

I withdraw into myself after my father's death. No one offers their sympathies. Who would? He was a traitor and few mourn traitors. Even if they did feel some grain of compassion for me, they would not utter it. It would be treasonous.

Charles V blamed Wolsey for my father's death, saying, "A butcher's dog has killed the finest buck in England." I could not agree more.

Ultimately, however, the blame falls upon His Majesty. He signed the warrant. He authorized my father's death, and despite any wrongdoing on my father's part, I cannot help but feel my heart stirring in resentment whenever I think of my king.

"We appreciate how hard this must be for you, Lady Elizabeth," Queen Catherine tells me in her soothing tones one afternoon as I wait upon her at Westminster. "The Duke of Buckingham may have been a traitor to king and country, but to you he was a father. You have every right to mourn him."

I purse my lips, swallowing tears. We are sitting in her apartments sewing shirts for the poor. I cannot concentrate on my work. My fingers fumble and I prick myself with the needle so much that little dots of blood can be seen on the garments.

Queen Catherine reaches out to still one of my trembling hands. "Don't be ashamed of your grief. The Lord tells us to rejoice in our sufferings, for suffering produces perseverance. That is all we can do, Lady Elizabeth: persevere."

I shake my head in bewilderment. "But my lord husband . . . he did nothing to intervene. He did not even send word offering his sympathies. Nothing."

The queen pauses a long moment. She bows her head. When she speaks, her voice is very low. "Your husband could have done nothing without risking his own head. A written message could have been intercepted and interpreted as his not only sympathizing with your father's death but with your father's cause."

Though the logical part of me understands this, I cannot fight the emotions that rage and cry and long for Thomas to reach out to me in some way.

But he does not.

The rest of the year is spent waiting on Her Grace. We pass the days in quiet contemplation, prayer, and charitable works. When I take leave of her, I wait for my husband at Hunsdon in December of 1522. He returns to me, after begging relief from his fruitless chore in Ireland and being afflicted with the dreaded dysentery.

He is a different man, thinner in appearance, sporting a close-cut beard and hair that reaches his shoulders in thick, dark waves. He looks wild and brooding, frightening yet, as always to me, alluring.

For a moment we say nothing. We survey each other as though we are ambassadors about to embark on a diplomatic mission requiring delicate handling. At last Thomas reaches for my hand.

"Hello, Elizabeth," he says in soft, low tones. I had forgotten how handsome his voice is.

Yet my heart stirs with bitterness as I behold the man who did nothing to intervene in the death of my father. I close my eyes against the thought. "Thomas," I say at last, my voice a mingling of longing and sorrow.

He squeezes my hand. Then takes me in his arms.

I yield to his embrace, folding against him, burying my head in his shoulder and allowing myself to cry.

"I missed you so," I weep. "Oh, Thomas, it has been dreadful with Father dying."

He pulls away, cupping my face between his slim hands. I am held captive by his intense black gaze. "You must forget him. He was a traitor, Elizabeth. He disgraced your family and your name. You can thank God you are a Howard now."

I stiffen, furrowing my brow. "*Forget* him? How can you say such a thing? How can I forget my own father? He may have been a traitor, but I was his daughter, bound in loyalty and love! Would you ask your children to forget you?"

"If it were expedient," he says.

"Of course," I say in cool tones. "How can I forget? That is what it is all about, after all. Expedience. Ambition." I pause, choosing my next words with care. "The king granted you and your father some of my father's lands. Why not just throw thirty pieces of silver in with it?"

"What else was I to do? Refuse an offering from the king?" he retorts. "You are a fool, Elizabeth. You live in a world that cannot possibly coexist with mine." His voice is so cool and calm that I shudder. I cannot even think to form a response. Thomas offers a lifeless smile that belongs on a portrait in some cold hall. "I did not come home to discuss such unpleasantness," he tells me. "What is done is done."

"With no help from you," I interpose.

"Yes, with no help from me. What help could I be? Help Buckingham and allow you and the children to watch my own head fly? Yes, that makes sense, Elizabeth," he snaps, dropping his hands from my face. "Now, enough of this. Where are the children? Take me to them."

I swallow my tears and purse my lips. I cannot fight him on this anymore. "They are awaiting you in the nursery, ready for your inspection," I tell him, my tone hard.

Arm in arm and with forced gaiety we make for the nursery where waiting in a little row are our children. Cathy is beautiful at nine years old, her fair head held erect, her long black hair tumbling down her back in a wavy cascade. Next to her stands five-year-old Henry, his face alight with curiosity and unbridled admiration for his soldier-father. Two-year-old Little Thomas stands on one foot, then the other, as if realizing his ability to balance thus is far more important than meeting some stranger he has chanced to encounter in his infancy. Thomas murmurs his greetings and words of approval in jovial tones.

And then his eyes fall upon Mary.

Thomas Howard

Ireland was a terrible ordeal and despite Elizabeth's harangue of complaints regarding her traitor-father's death, I am more than relieved to be home. The only good things to come from my trials are that my brother-in-law Thomas Boleyn will be created Earl of Ormond one day in place of Piers Butler, which will eventually grant him a great deal of property. In addition, Butler's son James will be betrothed to Boleyn's daughter Anne in an effort to secure the peace between the two islands.

But these victories are too small. The king would not allow me to use the force necessary in mollifying the island, hence there was nothing more I could accomplish. So now I am home anticipating new orders with eagerness. I am hungry for another challenge.

My first is acquainting myself with this family, a group of people I cannot seem to relate to at all. It is as though I am looking at them through a window. We are separated by an unbreakable pane of glass, and all that can be done is to hold one's hands up to it in the vain hope of making some kind of connection with the warmth of the human being on the other side.

But all I feel is the cold hard glass.

I distract myself from this dark analogy by surveying the children in the nursery. I think of all the ways they can be useful to me, the alliances they will make. Cathy is bound to be a great lady. She is the perfect embodiment of nobility and grace. Henry is quick-witted and athletic; he will go far, no doubt. It is too early to tell with the baby. He seems a little dull as yet. But they all have the good fortune of being attractive, a trait I credit not only to my own self but to my choice in breeder.

And then . . . my God . . . it is she.

My eyes behold the littlest girl, so different from the others with her honey gold hair, pearly skin, and open, trusting eyes that are as green as Tudor velvet. She raises her face to me, offering up a beatific smile so reminiscent of . . .

I cannot compare them. But it is so strange, this resemblance. It is almost as though she is *her* daughter. . . .

There is a vague blood-tie to the Plantagenets, but I never thought it was enough to yield itself to this kind of family resemblance. Yet what other explanation is there? It is so uncanny. But short of claiming the impossibility of my princess's soul being returned to me in the body of this child, that is the best I can come up with. She is a Plantagenet. That is all. There is nothing cosmic in it.

I scoop my little Mary up in my arms and hold her close, affording myself a better look at her ethereal face. As we walk to the window, she imparts some nonsensical childish chatter to me in a voice melodic as a nightingale and soothing as a summer breeze. Her little arms clasp my neck, and all I can think is I want to hold her forever. I do not care what she says or if she is a dullard and never offers me some grand alliance. I want to seize this moment of perfection and run away.

At once I am terrified by this strange onset of emotions, emotions I can hardly sift through or understand. What spell has she cast on me, this child I have always thought to be from some other world, the world of my princess and her faery folk?

I set her down, shaking my head, bewildered and annoyed by my bizarre fancies.

But as I accustom myself to my homeland, I am drawn to observing her. Through the window of my study I watch the children play in the garden.

Henry chases Mary, tackling her to the ground and forcing her to proclaim him the victor in their childish games. They are quite close, these two, and are often in each other's company, drawing pictures, writing in the dirt with sticks. Henry has become a prolific little writer and student. He tries to instruct Mary on making her letters. She makes a good show of trying; it seems she'll do anything to please her big brother.

Through the window I watch her weave garlands of flowers with her sister, Cathy. Upon their completion they wear them on their heads like circlets. Mary twirls about before her sister as though she is a courtier at a masque. Cathy applauds her antics.

The window affords me a view of her gentle side as she tends to Little Thomas, nurturing him with loving patience. She is a natural.

From my safe vantage, separated by a pane of glass, I watch her play and laugh and turn her smiling face to the sun and God and all those others who cannot resist her.

The window has become obscured.

I turn away, wiping the strange and sudden onslaught of tears away with an impatient hand.

A waste of time this is, staring out windows at children who are, for now, quite useless.

I must press on to more important matters.

Elizabeth Howard

Since Thomas arrived he has been distracted. He locks himself away in his study or broods before the fire, waiting, waiting for orders from his king. He watches the children play through his window, his expression soft and sad and, for once, completely vulnerable.

Seeing him thus softens my own heart. I lay a hand on his shoulder, then lean my head on his upper arm as I take in the sight of the children at play one afternoon.

His eyes are fixed on little Mary, who is laughing at something Henry said.

"She is very beautiful," I comment. "She is not like the rest of us."

"How so? We aren't beautiful?" Thomas returns, his voice bearing the slightest edge of teasing.

My body relaxes at the tone. "Of course we're beautiful!" I cry. "I mean . . . I mean that she is not like us in that she is completely lacking in guile."

Thomas regards her a moment longer before turning to me. His face is sober. "That will have to change," he says. "To be naïve in our world is to be eaten alive."

I shudder at the thought as I think of my father and his naïve attempts at securing power.

He is right. Mary will have to learn as she grows that innocence and court life seldom mix.

And she is destined for court life. Her father will see to that.

* * *

Thomas leaves me again in the summer to raid France. When he returns, it is only to become the lieutenant general of the army against the restless Scots. Alone I wait for him, feeling as though I have spent half my life in waiting: waiting for my husband, waiting for my children, waiting for my life to begin as a wife.

I still have no household of my own. The promise of renovating Kenninghall has been put on hold while Thomas occupies himself with the king's wars. I know he has no choice and I should be honored that the king graces my husband with such heady responsibilities, but nothing can quite chase away the thought that I long for the life of a country lady. I want my husband beside me. I want to be near him, feel his touch, converse with him. . . .

But he is gone and I sleep alone.

I wait upon Her Grace, who is ever patient and pious. She sets an example of perseverance in the face of disrespect and loneliness, which I try my best to emulate.

"It seems young Mary Carey is to give my husband a child," says the queen to me one winter afternoon as we embroider by the fire in her apartments.

"Oh, Your Grace," I say, my tone rich with sympathy. "Are you certain it is not her husband's?"

"She is sequestered in her own apartments, her husband in the privy chamber," the queen tells me. "There would be little opportunity for them to be together. And I know my husband." The face she turns to me is fraught with sadness.

"I am ashamed she is my niece," I say with fervency. "Ashamed of the Howards and of the Boleyns for encouraging her."

Queen Catherine shrugs. Her smile is too sad to be called such. "He tired of the Blount woman after she had a child. Perhaps this marks the end of Mary's favor as well."

I say nothing. The king took up with Mary Carey soon after the delivery of his bastard with Bessie Blount. There is no reason to believe he will not adhere to the same pattern of behavior after the delivery of this child.

"But enough lamentations about things we cannot change," the queen goes on in a voice taut with forced cheer. "Tell me, how goes it with you and yours, Lady Elizabeth? How are your children?"

"I am well," I say. "And the children are fine. Our Cathy shows a great deal of promise. Mayhap I can present her to you someday? She would make a fine maid. She has all the makings of a great lady."

"We should love to meet her," Her Grace says with a little nod.

I expect she is weary of people pursuing her favor regarding placement of their children at court, so I do not persist in the matter.

"And Lord Surrey?" Her Grace's voice takes on a softer note. "How is my champion?"

I laugh. "He is well, I suppose. Off fighting anyone he can. He . . . loves to fight." My voice cracks on the word *fight*.

The queen pauses a moment, as though giving the phrase consideration, then continues in a different vein. "We are sorry to hear of your lord father-in-law's ill health this year. But it is just that he favors your husband with his duties."

"Yes," I say. "But it does keep him busy. I do wish he were home with me. I miss him so."

"You really love him, don't you?" asks Her Grace.

I meet her face. It is softened through the veil of my tears. "Yes," I tell her. "I really love him, for all that he is and isn't. I cannot help it. Sometimes I do not know why I love him. God knows there are times when he doesn't deserve it," I add, shuddering as I recall my Mary's birth. "But yet . . . yet . . . it is as though he is the vine and I am the fruit. He sustains me; even with all the challenges he presents, his life flows into me and sustains me. Without him I would fall to the ground and wither away. And I truly believe without me he would shrivel and dry up just as a vine unattended. I cannot believe that he doesn't need me."

"He does need you," says the queen. "You are a clever girl, sometimes I think a little too clever. But he values you for it, even if he does not know it."

"I hope so," I tell her. "Oh, I hope so. Meantime, all I can do is wait for him."

"That is all we can do," Queen Catherine says. "It is our lot in life, waiting on men."

And so I wait.

Then at Christmas of 1523, my Thomas returns to me merry and in good spirits. We pass a happy celebration at court among family and friends, ushering in a New Year filled with hopes and dreams for our future.

The Duke of Norfolk

Thomas Howard, May 1524

He is dead! My father is dead! Just when I thought the old man was going to live forever, he passes into the next world at Framlingham on 21 May.

I am not completely without heart. I did like him, for what I was allowed to. He was a good man, a good knight, and servant to his kings. But I've no time to grieve. He was in his eighties after all, had lived a fruitful life, and brought the Howards from shame to triumph. For that I owe him a debt of gratitude. But I cannot dwell on any of that. What's done is done. Now I must remove from the wilds of the north to London to organize the funeral and claim my title.

I shudder with delight. I am the Duke of Norfolk now. Me, Thomas Howard! I think of my grandfather, remembering the beatings, the hatred. I was nothing to him, nothing but an undersize child with little hope for a future. He was wrong, oh, how he was wrong!

I am the duke of Norfolk now. I, Thomas Howard!

I am the duke of Norfolk, the wealthiest peer in England.

As I go through my father's papers, I am overwhelmed by the amount of wealth I am inheriting. Though my stepmother retains a bit of property and moneys as the Dowager Duchess, I still will be taking in four thousand pounds per annum.

I think of my son, now the Earl of Surrey, and of the legacy I will pass down to him and his sons and his sons' sons. I will hold this dukedom fast.

I am the Duke of Norfolk!

Elizabeth Howard

"My duchess!" Thomas exclaims as he picks me up and twirls me about like a child.

I cannot laugh. He is too happy about his accession and has not once expressed grief over his father's passing. It seems unnatural to me, inhuman.

He sets me down. "How do you like the sound of that?" he asks breathlessly, his black eyes sparkling.

"It is very fine," I say quietly.

"It does not seem fine," he observes. "What is it?" he demands, his voice threaded with impatience.

I bow my head. "Thomas. Don't you feel anything at all? Your father has *died*."

"It is the order of things," Thomas tells me, screwing up his face in genuine confusion. "Everyone dies, Elizabeth. The living cannot waste their time mourning something they cannot change."

A shiver courses through me and I hug myself to ward off the chill.

"I am to return to the north to settle a matter regarding the Earl of Angus," he goes on.

"Leaving again," I mutter.

"What do you think I am going to do? Retire to the country?" He shakes his head. "Don't you realize what this elevation means?" he asks. "I am the Duke of Norfolk!"

"So you have said," I say. "And I am very proud. But as a duchess, I now require a home of my own. It is far past time."

"Upon my return, my lady, we shall take to renovating Kenninghall," he says, taking my hands and squeezing them. "On my dukedom, I promise."

And he departs.

I watch him go, proud and straight on his black charger. My knight, my husband, my duke.

It is on that day that I cease to think of him as Thomas.

No bridge can cross the chasm between us.

He is not my Thomas anymore.

He is Norfolk.

He does not take to renovating Kenninghall upon his return, for he is immediately called to pursue other matters more pressing to His Majesty. I am alone, waiting, watching the children grow without being able to understand them. Thomas has hired a staff to care for their every need. They adore their nurses and tutors and have very little need of me.

Perhaps it is better. Perhaps it is as Thomas once told me: Leave the maintenance to the nurses, then the brunt of the inevitable heartbreak shall be on their shoulders.

In 1525 we are pleased to attend the elevation ceremony of Henry Fitzroy, who is created Duke of Richmond and Somerset and Earl of Nottingham at six years old. He is a bonny little boy, I must admit, and is his father in miniature. Thomas grumbles about Suffolk being made earl marshal for the ceremony, not necessarily because he relishes the duty held by his father and grandfather before him but because it was denied him by Wolsey. I am just as glad not to have him participate. Though the child is pretty, he is still a bastard, and in truth these elevations are a slap in Her Grace's face, just as his new little half sister, Catherine, by Mary Boleyn is. I attend to support my husband, but my heart churns in sympathy for the open display of recognition by His Majesty.

Richmond is even made admiral of England on 16 July as well as warden general and lord lieutenant of the North Marches. While the boy runs and plays and learns about the world in which he is to enter as a peer, his council performs his responsibilities.

It is a heady thing being the king's natural but not legitimate son. Acknowledged and spoiled but not quite a prince.

I shrug. He is north now. I suppose he matters very little in the grand scheme, save that he is just another pawn for King Henry's use.

At last in 1526 my Thomas returns to me. Wolsey has ousted him at nearly every turn in his political pursuits and my husband is frustrated and exhausted. Pain stalks him daily and he hobbles about on legs that protest being stood upon. I urge him to rest, but he tells me rest leads to death and he is not an invalid. He will get better. He just needs a distraction.

"Then let us renovate Kenninghall," I tell him.

He smiles at me then. "It is long overdue, isn't it?"

I offer a nod.

"Then we shall. We will make a grand palace for ourselves, Duchess Elizabeth," he says.

I soften at his affectionate tone.

And so the renovations begin and I wait, but this time it is in joyous expectation of my first true home.

BOOK THREE

Bess

Mendham, Suffolk

Bess Holland, January 1547

I have been in a daze since the arrest of His Grace. Now he is in the Tower alongside his son, the attainted Lord Surrey, and together they await their fate. I do not know how to feel. Everything has been taken from me: the jewels I tried to hide in the vain effort of securing some kind of life for myself, my lands . . . though I suppose none of it was ever really mine.

All my life I have been given everything without ever really having it.

For the first time, I understand how quickly one can testify against those they love most when the axe is in question.

So I testified along with Mary Fitzroy and the duchess. What choice did we have? We are not complete idiots, as much as His Grace may want to think so. I told them everything they wanted to know. The guard patted my cheek and told me I was a good lady—fancy someone still thinks of me as a lady, let alone a good one—and that my property shall be returned to me.

So I wait. For the first time in my life, I do not wait for the duke. I wait for my property, my things, all that I have in this world, and I think about the new start I will make.

I am overcome with a peculiar emotion most foreign to me these past twenty years. Hope. It surges through me, filling me up, spilling over at last in the form of relieved tears.

I have a future. Poor or rich, I have a future.

What will I do? What will I be?

Suddenly the world does not appear a big and empty place waiting to swallow me up in its vastness. It is a world full of people waiting to meet me, adventures waiting to be had, a world where all that has been lost can be reclaimed. . . .

I have a future.

A Real Live Duke

Bess Holland, Hever Castle, 1526

Oh, it is a wonderful day! Today is my birthday and the future yawns before me vast as the sparkling sea! I am fifteen years old and I am wearing a new gown. It is not really new but a used gown from my mistress, Anne Boleyn. I had to patch it up in a few places and take up the hem as I am so ridiculously short, but I love it anyway. It is pink with a white stomacher and kirtle. The lustrous sleeves hang nearly to the floor in the French style Mistress Anne is so fond of, and I twirl about, feeling as though the breeze shall catch me and I will take to flying about Hever with these grand winged sleeves.

Today is a busy day. Anne's uncle, the Duke of Norfolk. is coming to visit so we are all to be on our best behavior. My brother George says I am not to talk too much and appear my dumb self, lest I repulse the duke with my stupidity.

I allow my white-blond curls to fall down my back under my French hood and apply a little vermillion powder onto my lips, which I think, besides my full breasts, are my loveliest feature. They are like a little bow, full but small. Kissable, I think. Then I apply a little of the powder to bring a blossom to my cheeks. I look into the glass, offering a smile. My round, long-lashed brown eyes stare back at me, filled with anticipation. Oh, I do love birthdays! I hope in the excitement over the duke's visit, no one will forget and I will receive more presents.

When the duke arrives, his entourage of servants and liveried guard take their rest while he sits to a meal provided by his sister and niece. He seems most dark and mysterious with his wild black hair and eyes to match.

"Oh, he's dreadful," Mistress Anne tells me upon her return from dinner. We are in her chambers and I am brushing out the veil of long raven black hair that is her pride. "He's always complaining about his sore legs and eats like a bird. And he's always scheming and conniving! You should hear how he talks about my sister Mary! He's a boor."

"I think he's grand," I breathe, feeling my face flush.

Mistress Anne turns to me, screwing up her pretty face in confusion. "Are you insane? Him? You haven't looked at him up close. He's old, Bess. Fifty-something." She makes a show of shivering. "He's nasty!"

"I think you look like him," I venture.

Mistress Anne's black eyes turn to ice. She scowls.

"In a good way," I say, smiling. "He's handsome. Really. You just don't see it because you're related."

"Oh, Bess, really! You're such a silly little girl!" Mistress Anne cries. "He's . . . he's short and skinny! Have you looked at his legs? There's nothing to him!"

"He has fine legs; they're thin but well formed," I say.

Mistress Anne begins to laugh. It is akin to the tinkling of a thousand chimes. I bow my head, ashamed. I feel a fool to have confessed my admiration of her illustrious uncle to her.

"There's nothing more amusing than a girl infatuated," she quips and I wonder if she is referring to herself as well, since it is well known King Henry has shifted his fancy from her sister to her. "I shall charge you with the task of taking fresh linens and herbs to his rooms. You can have the privilege of dressing his bed," Mistress Anne says with a wink.

I am delighted with the order. "Thank you!"

And with that, I dash off to carry out the chore.

The duke is not in his chambers when I arrive with a basket full of fresh-smelling linens. I set to work, dressing the large canopied bed in which he'll be sleeping during his stay and placing under the mattress sweet lavender, hyssop, and junipers to ward off the bed bugs.

I try to think of something else I can do for him, but there is nothing. My task done, I leave his chambers and head down the hall, so lost in thought that I do not notice the duke himself approaching. He is alone, walking the halls with his cloak thrown over one arm as his eyes scan the doors on the left and right.

I sweep into a deep curtsy. "Your Grace!" I cry, my voice wavering in awe. "Are you lost?"

He smiles. "Yes, actually. Everyone here goes to bed quite early, I must say, and I never thought to inquire as to the location of my rooms."

"I know where they are! I just came from them!" I say, rising and smiling.

He may be a slight man but has the presence of a king and I am trembling before him.

"And what were you doing there?" he asks. I cannot tell if he is pleased or annoyed at my confession.

"I made the bed," I tell him proudly. "And put some herbs under the mattress to chase away the vermin."

He laughs. "Ah, yes. Well, thank you, Mistress . . ."

"Holland," I tell him. "Elizabeth Holland, but everyone calls me Bess or Bessie. I like Bess better, actually. It sounds more grown up but it isn't as formal as Elizabeth. I never felt that name belonged to me; it seems fit for a much grander lady."

Oh, I'm such a fool! I can't believe I'm prattling on this way! He must think me as idiotic as my brother does.

The duke takes my hand. His is warm and fine boned and I stare down at it in wonder as he brings mine to his lips.

"Bess," he says in low tones. I shudder. It seems the heat from his hand has surged through my arm and straight to my heart.

"Your Grace," I whisper, lowering my eyes. "Would . . . would you like me to show you to your rooms?"

"Very much," he says, releasing my hand.

I turn and, trembling, lead the duke to his chambers.

"Good night, Bess," he says with a slight smile as we stand outside his doors.

I curtsy once more. My face is flushing, I am sure of it, and I must appear a grand fool. "Sleep well, lordship," I say, hoping he cannot hear my heart racing.

The door closes.

I shrug and depart for my own quarters, thinking once more about my birthday and hoping my family has not forgotten me.

Oh, my wretched family! No one cares about me at all! George did not wish me so much as a happy birthday, and Father is so distracted with his own household affairs that he has not said two words to me! They are all I have, George and Father. Mother has been dead so long I cannot bring her face to mind, though I do remember her laugh. It was a happy, spontaneous little burst of joy that was so contagious it set the most restrained of people into fits of giggling. She made everyone feel comfortable and nurtured. I know this without having to be told.

But she died of the sweating sickness when I was just a wee lass and now I am left to nothing but these thoughtless men. Most aggravating!

Oh, well. At least Mistress Anne gave me a new gown and I was kissed on the hand by a real live duke.

I suppose the day was not a total loss.

My father has just informed us that he has accepted a position in the duke's household as his treasurer! According to Father it was an unexpected surprise, but it seemed Lord Norfolk was so impressed with him that he could not suffer returning home without him. Oh, I am so proud!

How wonderful it shall be, living in a duke's household. I am told he has four children, one my age who I can keep society with and wait on, and three younger ones who I shall delight in playing with and caring for. George will be occupied in service to the duke as well, so it will be a comfort to know I will be surrounded by these children.

I do hope Her Grace the duchess is kind and that we become

friends. I bet she wears beautiful gowns and is covered throat to foot in gems. It must be overwhelming and wonderful being so wealthy!

I bet there are no forgotten birthdays in their household.

That night I chance to meet the duke again as he heads down the hall to his chambers. I admit I have been lingering, sort of waiting to catch another glimpse of him. He is so grand. . . .

"Well, well, little Mistress Bess," he says. "It seems you shall be coming home with me. What do you think of that?"

"I like it very much," I tell him. "I cannot wait to see Kenning-hall and meet your children. Thank you for giving my father the opportunity to serve Your Grace."

He laughs. "You're most welcome, my girl," he says. "You like children?"

"Oh, yes!" I cry. "I hope to have a dozen of my own someday!"

"Well, being related to Lord Hussey assures you a match among the gentry," he tells me. "Perhaps sooner than later you'll be living in a country manor, rocking your very first baby."

"You paint a lovely picture, Your Grace," I tell him with a smile. "But I am delighted to serve you first. I cannot wait to see your grand home. Is it really shaped like an *H* for *Howard*?"

He laughs as he opens the doors to his rooms. "Indeed, it is."

"How marvelous!" I cry once more, awed by the thought of someone building a house shaped like a letter.

At once the duke grimaces, clutching the door a moment, squeezing his eyes shut. The color drains from his face and he bites his lip.

"Are you ill, Your Grace?" I ask him.

He shakes his head, righting himself. "No, no. Just hounded by this pain. Too long a knight, I fear. It's taking its toll."

"What hurts?" I ask as I imagine him in a suit of armor.

He laughs again. It is a low rumbling sound, like distant thunder. "My back, my shoulders, my legs . . . nothing seems exempt."

"I have a salve," I tell him. "It's lavender and mint oil that cools the skin and helps ease pain. Would you like me to mix some up for you?"

He pauses, considering me a long moment. His eyes affix themselves to my face and I bow my head, flushing. Perhaps I have been too bold.

"That sounds very nice," he tells me. "Let yourself in when you are finished."

I curtsy and scurry to the still room where I make up my little potion, then hasten back to his chambers. He is seated on his bed, a small smile playing on his lips.

"What do you want me to do?" he asks me.

I offer a nervous giggle. "Well, I suppose you should remove your shirt if you are comfortable . . . that way I can apply it. Unless of course you wish to apply it yourself," I add quickly.

"No, methinks I should entrust myself to your skilled hands," he says with a smile, removing the velvet doublet and unlacing his shirt before pulling it up over his head to reveal a slim, well-muscled torso. I turn my head away. My cheeks burn. Somewhere inside I realize he is married and it may not be right, I alone in his rooms, about to rub salve on his body. But I think, really, what could be wrong? I am a servant and I am just helping ease his pain. I'm not making after him. I'll just rub the salve on him and be gone.

"Now?" he asks, his tone very soft.

"Uh . . . lie down on your belly," I tell him.

He laughs, then follows the order, leaning his head on his folded arms. His long hair grazes his shoulders and he appears either a god or the very devil, lying there like that. Most likely a devil—but such a handsome devil! Oh, I must get these thoughts out of my mind!

I sit beside him and dip my hand in the salve, then rub my palms together. They tingle. The smell of lavender and mint assails my nostrils as I dare to massage the oil onto his back. He quivers beneath my touch as I work the knots out of his taut muscles. He begins to relax, heaving a deep sigh of contentment as I rub his shoulders and upper arms.

"Your hands are like velvet," he comments.

"Does it help, Your Grace?" I ask.

"Mmmhmmm," he answers lazily, turning his head so he can see me. "Now if you could only cure my legs . . ."

I shudder. "Would . . . would you like some applied to your legs, too, Your Grace?"

He nods.

I turn away so he can remove his hose and cover himself with the blanket so that only his fine, lean legs are revealed. I am trembling in terror. There is nothing separating me from the nakedness of the greatest peer in the realm but a flimsy blanket. I try to force naughty thoughts away as I begin to rub the salve on his thighs, then his well-defined calves.

"Hallelujah, that's good!" he murmurs with another throaty laugh.

When my ministrations are complete, he rolls onto his back. The blanket still covers him, but I am forced to admire his chest. He brings his hands up to cup my face. They are warm against my cheeks.

"Bess Holland, you have a goddess's touch," he tells me in an urgent voice, and I shudder at the intensity in his black eyes.

"Thank you, Your Grace," I say in breathless tones.

He brings my face toward his and at once I find that our lips have met. Hungrily he devours my mouth and I cannot help but yield to it. Oh, I am a wanton! But he is so handsome! And what if I did say no? I would risk my father's position. And his kisses do feel nice. . . .

"Lie with me, Bess," he whispers, pulling me on top of him and working at the laces of my dress with nimble fingers. "I must have you," he murmurs, kissing my cheek, my jawline, my throat. "I must make you mine."

"Yes, Your Grace," I respond as I wriggle out of my gown and crawl underneath the covers, marveling at the fact that my bare skin is touching that of this great man.

"I must make you mine. . . ." he says again. He cups my face, gazing into it with adoration and lust.

And with that I am made his. Me, a lowly servant girl, is made the lover of a real live duke!

We remove to Kenninghall and it truly is shaped like an *H*! It is the grandest palace I have ever seen. I have never really seen anything but Hever, so I don't have much to compare it to. But perhaps it is because it belongs to His Grace that I love it all the more.

It is the most resplendent place on earth, with its stables, deer park, sprawling gardens, and mews filled with the finest falcons in England. The duke says he will take me hawking one day and that I can ride any horse I want. When he learns my family forgot my fifteenth birthday, he promises me pretty gowns and a different jewel for every day of the week. Never will my birthday be forgotten again.

"I shall cover your fingers with rings," he tells me one evening as he kisses each fingertip. "And your throat will be encircled with diamonds."

"Diamonds!" I cry. "Real diamonds?" Such a thing is beyond my reckoning—me, poor uneducated Bess Holland, wearing actual diamonds!

"You wouldn't expect fake ones, would you?" he asks me, tugging one of my ringlets.

"Oh, Your Grace, you are good to me!" I cry, wrapping my arms about his neck and kissing him on the cheek.

But at Kenninghall the guilt of my secret liaison with the duke assaults me in full as I meet his wife, Duchess Elizabeth.

I had imagined her as sort of homely and haggish, which to me would justify the straying of His Grace to my bed, but to my disappointment, I find her to be of extraordinary youth and beauty, with her chestnut hair and bright blue eyes. Her lips are wide and full and her figure is trim and delicate, whereas mine is full and round. Perhaps that is why the duke likes me; I am her exact opposite. I am blond, she is dark. My breasts are large and hers are average at best.

But it must be more than physical. She must not make him happy anymore. They've been married for years and I'm told men grow weary of their wives after some time.

She assesses me with those keen blue eyes and I tremble before her. She is not dumb at all, that much is plain, and I fear for myself and for her. It is not good to be so perceptive and as she looks at me, I am convinced that she knows what the duke and I have been about.

But she says nothing.

I am introduced to the children. The eldest, Cathy, is two years younger than me and is a haughty little girl, a replica of her mother in carriage and demeanor. But the others are eager for my company and I am delighted to play with Henry and Mary and to hold Little Thomas whenever I get the chance.

Though my age makes it an impossibility for them to be mine, I pretend it is so anyway. I pretend they are mine and the duke's.

Thomas Howard

I did not hire John Holland because I found him to be anything beyond competent. He is not an exceptional human being; nothing about him stands out. Some kind of madness overtook me the moment I set eyes on his daughter, the delectable morsel Bess, and his employment was secured. Ah, but she is beautiful. Sensual yet innocent . . . I admit it is more than mere lust. I've the strange need to protect her, offer her a life she never could have had otherwise.

And how I am rewarded! With her, there are no complications; she is not clever, she is complacent. Willing. So willing . . . Her little button mouth forms all the right answers. "Yes, yes, and yes, Your Grace."

Nor does she haunt my mind in the fashion others do with their strange resemblances. . . . No, I will not think on that.

She is just the distraction I need, so pretty and round and young. What man in his right mind would deny himself a little dalliance with her? And I am no longer just a man. I am a duke with the needs of a duke.

It is wrong, I know, to install her here. I must try to show some restraint and not dangle the girl before Elizabeth. Everything must be kept in separate worlds. If this is done right, everyone can be happy.

Elizabeth Howard

I don't know what kind of fool he takes me for, but I have overestimated my husband in every way possible. Overestimated what little respect I thought he had for me, overestimated his capacity to be an upright, moral Catholic man . . . oh, everything. The knave!

He *is* the king's man in every way and has allowed himself to be influenced by his boundless appetite for things not his to take! Scoundrel!

I will not have it. Others may look the other way and play the willing fool but not me. I have not suffered this long and waited all these years for my family life to begin, to have it all thwarted by a silly, stupid fifteen-year-old girl.

At first I am quiet. I must play this right. I watch and wait for my moment. I take the girl and show her about our home. Together we make candles and weave, and I show her the kitchens, which she exclaims over in wide-eyed awe. She is a pretty little girl—a little *girl!* Oh, how ashamed of my Thomas I am!

She is placed in the nursery as a washer, and I watch her play with my children. Her affection for them seems genuine enough but it does not change a thing. That she can meet my eyes is an endless source of wonder to me.

Thomas comes to me less and less. He avoids my eyes.

And Bess wears quite expensive jewelry for a washerwoman. Where does she get the funds?

Oh, the pain of it, far worse than any beating. I do not know how much of this I can stand.

Bess Holland

I am very wrong. I know I am wrong. I am worse than the Whore of Babylon and I know Jesus must be very disappointed in me. But I cannot say no. I cannot deny him. What's more, I do not want to, and that is by far the most grievous of my increasing sin list.

Duchess Elizabeth watches me with guarded eyes. She knows. Oh, I know she knows! She keeps me at her side and through her silence antagonizes me. Doesn't she know she has won no matter what my relationship with His Grace? She has his ring, his children, and his name. I have but a few nights of his company. Soon he will tire of me, I imagine, and this whole thing will be but a strange, bittersweet memory for us.

At night the duke creeps into my chambers or sometimes invites me to his luxurious apartments. He praises my every move, worships my body, and decorates me with gifts, elegant night shifts, and beautiful day gowns appropriate for my station, which he promises to elevate. He cannot get enough of me nor me of him.

"Will you stay with me all night?" I ask him one evening as he holds me after our lovemaking. "Sleep beside me as though I'm your wife?"

He kisses my cheek. "Fall asleep in my arms if it pleases you," he tells me.

I close my eyes. "Thank you, Thomas," I say, daring to use his Christian name for the first time.

He stiffens.

"You must not call me that," he says in a tone I've not heard him use before. It is hard, icy. Frightening.

"I'm sorry," I say. "I just thought, knowing each other as we do that—I'm sorry. What should I call you?"

He pauses, stroking my bare shoulder. "You may call me Your Grace or simply Norfolk if it pleases you."

It does not please me at all, but what can I do? "Yes, Your Grace," I say because I can't bear to call him the name of a stupid county.

I suppose it is a breach in his strange world of etiquette to call him by his Christian name.

That is another right *she* owns.

Elizabeth Howard

If he will not come to me, then I will go to him. I will remind him of what he has been missing. He has no reason to do this to me. I have been a good wife; I've given him five children and I am a lover without equal. There is no reason, no reason at all. I will drive her from his mind and his bed if it kills me in the process.

I stand outside his apartments, listening to the giggling and playing inside, knowing what is going on, knowing I should make for my own chambers and wait till he is alone. But I am his wife. I have every right to enter his suite and I shall, no matter who he is entertaining.

I will shame him into ending this.

I open the door.

He is there with the girl, fully engaged in his romp. They lie with the bedclothes twisted about their writhing naked forms and I am struck dumb. I did not think I would react this way. I had thought to throw myself atop the girl and pull her from him by the hair. I had thought to be uttering a thousand curses at the illicit couple, curses that would cause their immediate repentance.

But I can do no such thing. I just stare.

It is Bess who sees me first. Her wide brown eyes register shock, then horror, then fill with tears as she wraps her arms about my husband's neck and whispers, "Your Grace," very quietly.

Thomas turns his head.

"Get out," he says in a low voice.

I stand, rendered helpless by sadness and anger and a sense of betrayal that surges through me like a raging fever.

"*Get out!*" he cries, reaching over to throw a little velvet cushion at me. It has very little effect. I am still rooted in place. At last I tear my eyes from them and gaze at the hand that bears his signet ring. The lion with the arrow piercing its tongue. At once I am that lion, my tongue immobilized by the arrow of his infidelity and disrespect.

I pull it off my finger and hurl it at the couple with all my strength.

This gesture gives me the needed strength to quit the room.

I lie alone in my apartments that night staring, staring up at the canopy of my bed, recalling our wedding night, the births of our children, save Mary, and all of our conversations, words that meant so much but now seem so empty.

What happened? is all I can think. Over and over the question torments me. *What happened?*

The door creaks open and I turn to see Thomas standing with a candle in hand. He lingers in the doorway a moment before entering. I do not scream for him to get out. I am mildly interested in what he has to say.

"My lady," he says in soft tones.

"My lord," I answer, my voice breaking.

"You should not have interfered today," he says.

I sit up, my cheeks burning in fury. "I should not have interfered is right! I suppose I ruined your afternoon! My apologies for interrupting!"

"Elizabeth, this is the way of the world," he goes on in his calm voice. "You must accept it. The faster you accept it, the happier we can all be."

"The happier you can be, you mean," I correct him. "Who do you think I am that you can dare treat me this way? Am I not at twenty-seven young and fair enough for you? Have I meant nothing to you all these years?" I add in a voice soft with tears. "I have borne your five children. I have been faithful and devoted—"

"Devoted?" Thomas cries. "Yes, you demonstrated that when you left me in Ireland to run after your traitor-father! Devoted? I think not. You proved to me then that you did not put me first, that you never put me first. Before me comes the Staffords and, of course, Her Grace the queen. And before them, before us all, your mighty principles. I can't compete with that, Elizabeth. I won't even try. So don't blame me for seeking out someone who isn't going to fight me at every turn."

There is nothing I can say to this. I bow my head and try to mute the onset of sobs. I do not want to give him the satisfaction of seeing me reduced to such agony.

"If ever I've fought you, my lord," I say in soft tones, "it is only in the desire to guide you toward right, just as the Lord commands. I have tried to be a good wife to you. I swear by all that is holy that nothing you or that churl's daughter can do will ever stop me from being a Christian wife. I will never, ever cease in trying to steer you toward good. I will not stray from my principles as easily as you can stray from our marriage bed. It is not in me. If this drives a wedge between us, then I am sorry."

"That's it, then," Thomas says. "There's nothing more to say or do. You are there and I am here, as always." He rises. "Good night, my lady."

"My lord," I say.

As he moves to quit the room, I whisper, "Did you ever love me, even a little?"

He stops walking. His shoulders slump. "I don't know," he confesses at last.

"No, I expect not," I say. "I expect you don't love Bess Holland, either. I expect you don't know what it is to love at all."

He turns a stricken face to me a moment, parts his lips to say something, then turns on his heel and leaves me alone, slamming the door behind him.

He is there and I am here.

As always.

Bess Holland

"Oh, I am a bad girl!" I sob in the duke's arms when he returns to me that night. "I should never have come between you and your lady wife!"

His Grace rocks me back and forth, stroking my hair and making little shushing noises. "Drivel, Bess, you've done nothing wrong. Happiness is rarely found and we must seize it when it is made available to us. And you are my happiness. I need you."

He needs me. Does that make it right? But he is a duke, and dukes are much wiser than servant girls. Perhaps I should just listen to him. . . . It would make living with this far easier.

"What of the duchess?" I ask, fearing the woman with the cunning blue eyes.

"The duchess has her own life and will be compensated," he assures me. He pulls away, cupping my face in the fashion I have come to love so well. "Bess. Listen to me. Whatever sin there is in this is on my head, do you see?"

"How can you absolve me?" I ask him. "You're not God."

"Trust me, Bess," he says after a moment's pause, as though he was considering the possibility of having the power of God.

"I trust you, Your Grace," I say at last. "I trust you with my very life."

"Oh, Bess," he murmurs, drawing me against his chest. "Oh, my sweet little Bess . . ."

And he makes it right.

Being with him makes everything right.

The light of day reveals another story, however. Duchess Elizabeth is in a fury and has lost all subtlety.

"You are a churl's daughter, worse than the lowest harlot," she seethes as we pour candle wax into molds. Her voice is so low I have to strain my ears to listen. To see us together, one would think we were the best of friends, our heads close together as we carry out this mundane chore.

"By day you play with my children and tout yourself as the innocent little maid, and by night you seduce my husband," she goes on to say. "Have you no shame? Have you no care for your reputation? You are a young girl; you are marriageable. Don't you want to make a fine match? No one will want to have a duke's leavings."

Tears fill my eyes. I bow my head. I do not know what to say. She is right. . . . I know she is right . . . and I do want to make a marriage someday. It will never be to whom I want, but I know this cannot last my whole life long. Oh, Jesus, what's to become of me!

"I want you to leave my husband alone," she demands. "You hear me? Stay away."

"I can't!" I cry. "How can I keep him away when *he* comes to *me?*" I know I am being disrespectful, but she has gone too far. Claiming I have control where I have none. "It's not my fault, Your Grace—not all of it," I add, knowing I must take some responsibility. "I didn't drive His Grace away—perhaps none of this would have happened if you didn't make him so unhappy!"

This earns me a stinging slap across the face.

"Insolent little fool!" she cries. "How dare you speak to me this way?"

"How dare *you*, my lady?" I cry, holding my burning cheek,

blinking back tears. "I am sorry . . . I should not have spoken so. But you must understand that I have no more power than you."

Duchess Elizabeth turns, covering her face with her hands. "Leave me."

"My lady . . ."

"I said leave me!"

Rising, I run from the room, blinking away tears, marveling at how fast my life has changed and wondering how I will keep up.

Two Ladies

Two years, Bess has been beside me and still they fight over me like she-cats. Flattering as it may be, it still will not do. It is Elizabeth's fault. If she could just accept the situation like a good wife, all these endless battles and dramas could be avoided. Another solution will have to be reached.

But there are more urgent matters requiring my attention. Two other women occupy my mind. One is the steadfast Queen Catherine, whom the king seems to be setting aside in favor of my niece, Thomas Boleyn's girl Anne. She's a raven-haired, sharp-tongued wench who is far too thin to be considered comely in my eyes. If she suits the king, however, I shall extol her virtues to my very best ability. The king is besotted with my black-eyed niece, far more so, it seems, than any woman he has known thus far.

"This must be played out differently," I tell Elizabeth one night. I am beyond knowing what guides me to her—it seems no matter how distracted I am, I always find my way to her apartments. There is no use trying to figure out anything where my wife and I are concerned. As it is, I am here, so I may as well stay a while. "We are after a bigger prize this time."

Elizabeth arches a brow. She is sitting before her fire embroidering. "What prize could be bigger than the king's favor in your eyes?" she asks me in her low voice.

I smile and sit across from her. My limbs are tingling with excitement. "A crown, Elizabeth. A crown for the Howards!"

Elizabeth scowls at me, then shakes her head. "Are you mad to speak this treason?" she whispers. "How could you come here and tell me this, thinking I would support it? What kind of intrigue are you about, Thomas Howard?"

"The king is having an attack of conscience, it seems," I tell her. "He believes he has not been allowed to conceive a healthy male heir with the queen because of consanguinity. He found a passage in Leviticus that states a man shall not 'uncover the nakedness of his brother's widow.' He truly believes he has committed some grievous sin and wishes to solicit a papal dispensation granting an annulment of the marriage so that he might marry our Anne. Can you believe it?"

"No, I can't believe it," Elizabeth snaps. "I can't believe he is willing to even *think* of putting his wonderful wife aside, not to mention the affect it would have on the princess. What will an annulment make her? A bastard no better than Fitzroy or Mary Carey's children? How can he even contemplate such a thing?"

"He's given it a great deal of thought," I tell her. "So much thought that a papal legate is coming from Rome, a fellow by the name of Campeggio, to preside with Wolsey over a trial that will come up with a decision that, once reached, is final. The Pope will not challenge it."

"No." Elizabeth shakes her head in awe. "Thomas, no. What does that Anne girl possibly have that the queen does not?"

"A young, healthy body capable of producing heirs," I say.

"Why would he not just keep her as a mistress if he needs her so badly? He can legitimize Fitzroy if he is so set on a male heir. Why does he have to wreak so much heartbreak?" Her voice is wavering.

"Elizabeth, you must understand civil war could break out if Fitzroy is named heir," I explain. "There is not enough support for his cause as yet. The king wants an heir born of a legitimate bond."

"But a bond with that little slut could not be called legitimate!" she cries, throwing her embroidery off her lap and rising. "There are a million reasons the king shouldn't marry her! What of the precontract she made with the Percy boy that got her sent from court that time? And while we're on the subject of consanguinity, it should be noted that His Majesty had her sister already, and some say he even bedded the mother!"

I laugh at her wild talk. "That may be so, but the king will fashion it all to his advantage; he has a veritable army of people willing to help him do it."

"With you at its head," she seethes.

"With me at its head," I agree. "Elizabeth, I know how you love Catherine, but you must adjust to what is going to happen—if this is played right, we can have it all."

"Now she's just Catherine?" Elizabeth cries. "You do not even have the respect for her to call her by her rightful title?"

I wave a hand in dismissal, then continue to air my thoughts aloud. "I will defer to the queen with the respect she deserves as long as she holds the title," I say. "But it will not be for long, Elizabeth. Mark my words. Anne is in the ascendant." I smile as I think of all the favors that will fall upon the Howards like a summer shower. "Anne will not be his mistress. She will be as upright and Christian as a lady can be. She will drive him wild with the chase—I have made it clear to the girl that in no way should she compromise her virtue and give in until that crown is secured on her little head."

"Do you hear yourself, Thomas?" my wife cries. " 'Upright'? 'Christian'? As if any upright Christian woman in possession of her senses would plot to steal a king from under the nose of his anointed queen! Oh, Thomas, just when I thought you couldn't sink lower—"

I rise, seizing her shoulders. "You will never understand, will you?" I ask her. "You must do everything you can to support your niece and our endeavor. You have no idea the favor that is in store for us if we win this."

Her face is slack with sadness. "No. Never, Thomas. I told you long ago where my loyalty lies. Queen Catherine is a princess of the blood. A queen anointed by God. I will never abandon her."

At once her conviction startles and attracts me. Suddenly, I have never been confronted by a woman more beautiful than my wife. I reach up, tucking a stray tendril of hair, which has escaped from her hood, behind her ear, my hand lingering a moment to trace her jawline.

"Elizabeth," I tell her with the utmost seriousness, "if you give up Catherine, I will give up Bess. I swear to you. I will send her away this very night."

Elizabeth offers a laugh edgy with bitterness. "Oh, that's fair! Offer to give up something you should never have had to begin with! No, Thomas, you cannot tempt me by using your harlot as a bargaining chip," she tells me. "If you were as Catholic as you proclaim, you would see that." She purses her lips and closes her eyes. Her thick, long lashes sparkle with unshed tears. "I cannot give up my queen. I swore myself to her as a little girl. I will not abandon her."

I drop my hand from her cheek and release her shoulder. I shake my head. "We have been called to court. You in your capacity, I in mine. Catherine will be dethroned, Elizabeth. It is inevitable. It may take time, but it will happen. I wish you wouldn't persist in tying yourself to the mast of a sinking ship."

Elizabeth shrugs. It is as if she knows she is defeated and continues in her vein anyway. Somehow this show of strength and defiance touches me. On impulse I gather her in my arms, holding her fast.

"My girl, can't we work together, just once?" I whisper, swaying from side to side. "Think of everything we can gain."

"I have never been as moved by that as you," she tells me. She pulls away, tipping her face up toward mine. "I'm sorry, Thomas."

"I am, too," I say. "Because you are the one who will lose ultimately. You know it. And you stay your course anyway. I don't understand you, Elizabeth. I don't understand you at all."

Elizabeth's lips quiver a moment. She bows her head. "No, I suppose you wouldn't," she says in quiet tones lacking in accusation. It is as though she is just making an observation, a regrettable observation that I cannot understand in any way.

It was futile coming here; I don't know why I bother with her. With one last glance at the woman who forever stands alone, illuminated by the firelight that warms her skin with a golden glow and plays off the auburn threads in her chestnut hair, I shake my head, my heart gripped with inexplicable sadness and frustration. To think of everything that could be had if she'd only work *with* me!

I am done with her. I turn away and quit the room, then head directly to the chambers of the woman I promised just moments ago to give up should my stubborn wife do the same with her queen.

Bess listens to me; there are no arguments or reproaches. When I tell her about my niece's elevation in favor she says, "Oh, how wonderful for you, Your Grace!"

Just what I want to hear.

When at last I make it to my own apartments that night, I am surprised to find my daughter Mary waiting for me outside.

She sits against the door, her night shift drawn over her knees, head bowed, the light of the taper resting beside her dancing off her golden hair, which tumbles down her back in waves. Her arms are folded over her knees and her head is buried in them, and I cannot tell if she has fallen asleep in this strange locale.

"Mary!" I bark. I am wearied by the evening's various exertions, both mental and physical, and cannot imagine why this child would seek me out. I cannot summon to mind two words I've ever said to her consecutively.

The little girl's head snaps up, her wide green-gold eyes meeting mine in a mingling of shyness and fear. "I-I had a terrible dream," she informs me.

"Well, where is the nurse?" I demand.

"I didn't want to wake her," she says, her tone soft with apology. "I went to Bess's room, but I heard her talking to somebody and thought her brother must have been in there. I didn't want to interrupt."

My heart leaps as I thank God that the child didn't walk in to discover what her beloved friend was really about.

"Well, what am I supposed to do about it?" I ask as I open the doors to my apartments, causing her to fall backward.

She catches herself with her hands. "I . . . I don't know, my lord.

It's just that—it's just that it was a terribly frightening dream and I'm afraid the nurse would think me evil if I repeated it."

"Nonsense and drivel," I tell her. "You can't control what you dream."

She stares at me unconvinced, her little button mouth pursed in thought. I avert my eyes, stirred by her beauty and mysterious fancies that are forever reminiscent of another world, another time, when life was so very different from now.

"Where is your mother?"

Mary bows her head, hugging her knees to her chest again. Her little shoulders quiver a moment.

"Well?"

"I-I went to her, Your Grace," she tells me. "I was going to go in her apartments but . . ."

"But what?" I demand, impatient with the child. I want nothing more than to lay head to feathers and not be bothered by this strange little creature.

She raises her head once more. Tears swim in her eyes; they are as bright as emeralds. "She was crying, my lord. So very hard. I-I was afraid to intrude."

I grit my teeth against this news and heave a sigh. "Well, come in, then," I say at last, since there seems to be no possibility of removing her at the present moment.

The little girl scrambles to her feet and slips her hand into mine as we progress inward. The gesture takes me by such surprise that I start. Cathy would never have done that; she is far too proper. And the boys seem to bear the intrinsic knowledge that I am not fond of being handled. But this child reaches up and seizes my hand as though it is the most natural thing in the world. She huddles close against my arm as we take to the settle.

I remove my shoes and sit, then with effort rest my pain-infused legs on the ottoman. My arm is on the back of the settle and Mary scoots in beside me, curling up as close as she can get without having the audacity to climb on my lap. She lays her head in the crook of my shoulder.

I am discomfited by her proximity and stiffen. I do not understand why, and somewhere I am troubled. If she were my little

Maggie born of the princess, I would have sought her out for such moments. But everything is different with this child, this child whose birth sent me into a rage of madness, this child whose very presence causes my heart to lurch and twist in a strange agony I cannot identify or understand.

"Tell me about the dream, Mary," I say in soft tones.

The child shudders against me. "You won't think I'm evil or possessed?"

I laugh. "I will think no such thing," I assure her, for I do not believe in such utter nonsense as possession anyway. People are good or evil of their own accord; they do not need supernatural intervention.

She relaxes a bit. One hand strays to the lace on my doublet and idly fidgets with it as she talks. "Oh, Da." Her voice catches. "There were pretty ladies all dressed fancy," she tells me. "And they were taking turns wearing a beautiful ruby necklace. The first girl put it round her neck and was admiring herself in a pond full of black swans . . . but then . . . Oh, Da, then suddenly the rubies were dripping blood! But the girl didn't see it! Nobody saw it but me! I tried to warn them but no one listened. They just laughed at me! The bright blood dripped into the water, coloring it red, but all the while she kept admiring herself until at last she fainted dead away. Then—then another girl took the necklace and clasped it round her neck. It was just the same as before. At first it was just a collar of rubies, but then—" She is sobbing now, great gulping sobs that make it hard for me to understand her. "She began to twirl and dance until the necklace changed again! Blood began to drip down her neck onto her chest! Oh, Da, it was terrible. At last she, too, fainted and the necklace slipped off her neck onto the grass, just plain rubies once more." Choked by tears, she is rocking back and forth. Not quite knowing how to respond to her hysteria, I reach out and stroke her hair. "And the very worst of it is, Da, is Henry . . ."

"King Henry?" I ask.

"No, *our* Henry! He seized the necklace from the ground and went running with it. I chased after him and tried to stop him, but he just kept saying, 'It's mine! Mine at last!' and then put it on! I tried to unclasp it, but something was holding me back, great invisible hands too powerful for me to fight against. Henry stared at me a long moment till his eyes grew most round. His face turned white as a dove and he clasped his throat—when he removed his hand, it was covered with blood! And then . . . then, oh, my Lord, he fainted, too! He lay beside the pretty ladies and nothing I could do could rouse them. I reached down to touch the necklace, wondering what power this evil thing held, but in my hand it was nothing but a collar of rubies. . . . Oh, Da!" Here she commences to sob with abandon, so much so that she clutches her belly and begins to cough.

"Mary, now that's quite enough," I command, disturbed by her detailed dream and annoyed at myself for asking her to share it. "Stop this crying at once before you make yourself ill." I add in gentler tones, "Come now, it was only a dream. You've heard too many tales in the nursery of strange and terrible things that your little head can't grapple with. It was just a queer dream, that's all."

With effort the little girl tries to modulate her breathing. She wipes her face on my doublet and crawls onto my lap. As annoyed as I am, the childish gesture is endearing. I wrap my arms about her, my throat tight as I try to stay relaxed.

"You won't ever let anything bad happen to Henry, will you, Da?" she asks me, pulling away, her tearstained face solemn.

"Of course not," I vow. "Never ever."

"I knew I was right coming here," she says, burying her head in my neck. "I knew you would make it better—you're the greatest duke in the land, the greatest man who ever lived. You will protect us and keep us safe from all harm."

Her flattering words of innocent adulation touch me and I kiss her silky hair. "Of course I will. You know me well, little Mary. I am the head of the greatest house in England; I am the premier duke in the realm and you must always trust me to know what is best for our family. I will always keep those who are dear to me safe."

"I don't ever want to own rubies, not ever!" she cries with sudden vehemence.

I begin to laugh. "I will make certain that you never shall, my love," I assure her. "I will encircle your pretty little throat with emeralds to match your eyes. And you shall be the most prized girl at court." I pull away, cupping her cheek in one hand, my breath catching in my throat. I am rendered helpless by her innocent beauty. "I will find you a husband who will elevate you to greatness," I say then.

She does not seem to care so much for this vein and nuzzles back against my chest. "Da, will you tell me a story?"

Confounded by the request, I try to summon to mind something that doesn't involve blood and dragons and battles, stories that Henry and Little Thomas would thrive on, but not this delicate girl.

"Tell me about the faery folk," she prompts.

I swallow an immediate onset of tears. I stroke her hair a long moment, then reach over to pull the throw blanket strewn over the arm of the settle atop us. In this little nest I hold her close and commence to tell my tale.

"I met a faery once, you know," I say in husky tones.

"You did?" She tilts her face toward me. "A real live faery?"

"Yes," I confirm. "A real live faery." At once all discomfort at her closeness melts away as I draw her near. I cannot seem to hold her close enough, tight enough. My heart is filled with emotions I cannot wrangle with or understand, but it does not matter. She is the closest thing to Heaven I will ever see. I must hold her while I am allowed.

"She was very beautiful," I begin. "She had hair the color of autumn leaves and her eyes were like the twilit sky on the eve of a storm—a sort of honeyed green. She was very tall and long limbed and I loved her, oh, how I loved her from the very first moment I set eyes on her. . . ."

"What happened to her?" she asks me in her soft, lilting voice.

At once I am drawn from my reverie; for a moment I had forgotten that I was speaking out loud. I clear my throat. "She—danced with me a while. She took me to her gardens and there she showed me how to sing and play and . . . and just be."

"And then?"

"And then . . ." Tears again clutch my throat. "Then she was called back to the faery country, a place mortals cannot go. I watched her disappear behind the mist . . . and I—I could not follow. . . . She was gone."

"D'you think she'll return someday?" Mary asks.

I recall the day of Mary's birth, the blinding light, the vision in the corner of the room. . . . I am transported to another time, another world. My princess stands before me that first day we plight our troth at Westminster. I am sliding the ring on her slim finger. . . . I see her on her deathbed, devastated by the consumption . . . the blood. . . . Oh, God . . . And then this child again, this child in my arms, in my heart, in my blood . . . more blood . . . I do not understand. . . .

"She did return," I tell her, cupping her face between my hands. My voice is taut with urgency. Tears obscure my vision. "She is with me now but, oh, why like this?" I utter in a tortured whisper. "I do not understand! Help me understand! It isn't fair! God, it isn't fair!"

"What isn't fair?" The question assaults me like a whip across the back. I am drawn from my bizarre fancy and can only stare at her, her little head cocked to the side, her eyes wide with bewildered fear.

I drop my hands, rendered helpless and confused and impatient by this whole interlude. "Mary." Yes, this child is Mary. She is just Mary. There is nothing more to her than that. "Mary, you'd best get to bed now," I tell her, collecting myself. My voice is calm, clear, and cool. "You are too old to be fretting over nightmares and far too old for these demonstrations."

Mary regards me a long moment, her face fraught with such profound sadness that I am forced to avert my head. She slides off my lap, backing away from me. "Yes, my lord. Sorry, my lord." She bows her head. "Good night, Your Grace."

I cannot speak.

Long after she departs I sit on the settle, curled under the blanket, dreaming of the faery country and a time long gone.

That spring, Elizabeth and I take to Norfolk House in London to fulfill our duties at court. The children are left behind at Kenninghall because a new outbreak of the dreaded sweating sickness is ravaging the country.

Bess trembles when I leave her.

"Oh, my lord, should one of the children take ill, I shall die! What's to be done should the sickness come to Kenninghall?" she asks me in her little-girl voice.

"All that can be done," I tell her. "We've a competent physician about," I add, then shudder as I recall the "competence" of the physician who bled my other children . . . but they are no more. It does no good to think of them. "There's no use fretting," I go on. "What is meant to be will happen despite any worrying on our part."

Bess blinks back tears. "I'm so frightened, Your Grace. So many have been lost. This dreaded sickness hits anyone . . . oh, Your Grace," she wraps her arms about my middle, burying her head in my chest. "Do take care."

I stroke her abundant curls. "Do not worry, my Bess. Don't worry," I soothe, touched by her concern. I pull away, cupping her face between my hands. Her wide brown eyes are the picture of innocence. "I can survive anything."

Bess leans into my hand and smiles. "I think you can," she says, her little voice registering a sort of awe as she turns her head to kiss my palm.

I draw her forward, bestowing a fierce kiss upon her perfect mouth as though to remind her of who owns her, then turn on my heel and, without looking back, quit her chambers.

It is best not to think of Bess when I am away from her.

Keeping a place for everything, and everything in its place. That is the key.

In London my ability to survive anything is put to the test, for almost immediately upon my arrival I am taken with the sickness. I do not realize it at first. Always riddled with leg pain, I did not think it odd when the pain traveled up my body, assaulting my shoulders, arms, and belly with a churning ache that set me into such a state of nausea, I was constantly swallowing the bitter bile rising in my throat.

Every day, there is news of someone else being taken by the dreaded sweat. Sir Edward Poyntz, my nephew William Carey, and Sir William Compton of the king's privy chamber perish one and all. My niece and current jewel of the family, Anne, took ill with her father, my idiot brother-in-law Thomas Boleyn, but the king's physician, Dr. William Butts, tended them and they recover at Hever.

The little duke of Richmond is sent farther north for his protection while Princess Mary seeks a safe haven at my former residence of Hunsdon.

While this torrent of sickness rains upon us, I think of the offices vacated by the dead that can be filled by able-bodied Howards.

"You are soulless," Elizabeth tells me one night when I am reviewing the options aloud.

"Not soulless, my dear, just practical," I return, annoyed at her summation of my character.

As it is, my plans for arranging the lives of my family members are put on hold. While making my way to my apartments that evening I am seized by a pain so fierce that it takes hold of my body like a great hand, squeezing me till I moan in agony. I am burning, searing hot. My shirt is soaked through with sweat and I cling to a tapestry hanging on the hall, drawing in shuddering breaths, determined to make it to my rooms awake.

I stagger down the hall, leaning on the wall for support. Everything is a blur. My thoughts come to me sluggish and jumbled.

"Your Grace . . ." A voice. Somewhere . . . a voice.

I turn my stiff and aching neck to its source. My stepmother stands before me, her face wrought with concern.

"Your Grace, you are ill. We must get you to your rooms," she says. "Come now." She wraps her arm about my waist. "Lean on me."

"You are my mother?" I ask in a small voice as I allow my weight to fall upon this strong-shouldered woman. She half drags me down the hall to my rooms.

"Now, wouldn't that be a trick, considering I am younger than you are," she laughs as she helps me into bed. "Come!" she is calling to some unknown presence. "Fetch blankets for His Grace! He must sweat this out!"

A darkness is creeping in. I want to yield to it, oh, how I want to!

It is warm and soft there. I do not have to think or plot or plan. I can just sleep.

"Don't you dare go to sleep, Thomas Howard." Another voice. Ah, yes. How could I fail to recognize Elizabeth's uncompromising tone? I feel a slight slap on my cheek. "You stay awake, you hear me? You stay here."

My eyes flutter open and try to fix on my wife's face. I cannot focus. She is a blur obstructed by blazing white light.

"That's it, Lady Elizabeth," my stepmother is saying. "Keep him awake. That is the only way to outlive this thing. If they can stay awake for the first twenty-four hours, they will survive."

"I can survive," I mumble.

"Of course you can," Elizabeth says. "Isn't that the Howard motto? Besides, you are far too stubborn to leave this earth a moment before you are ready. Don't close your eyes, Thomas! Stay awake!"

I start at her voice. The pain is unbearable and the heat, oh, this intolerable heat.

"So many are dying," a gentle male voice is saying. I recognize it to be the king's physician, Dr. Butts, the same man who treated my niece Anne. "And the duke is not a young man."

"I am in finer form than most men half my age!" I cry. I begin to writhe under the oppressive blankets. I want to tear them off me. I am so bloody hot!

"Yes, you are," the doctor agrees with a chuckle. "And God willing it is that fine form that carries you through this."

"God willing," my stepmother chimes in.

The darkness seeps in again. My head lolls to the side and I begin to drift off. Somewhere, there is singing. Is it the faeries? Are they calling me? Princess? Oh, Princess, have you come to take me to your strange country? A form in the mist.

"Is it you?" I murmur, reaching out, hoping to part the mist that forever separates us and feel her slender hand in mine once more.

Elizabeth squeezes my hand. "Stay awake, damn you!" she cries.

"We shall give him some treacle and setwell," my stepmother is saying. "And if he makes it through this first day, I've found it best for the victims to fast sixteen hours and lie abed at least twenty-four. But of course we should not think too far beyond these first crucial hours."

There she is again! She stands in the corner of the room, her arms outstretched, a trace of a smile curving her lips upward. . . . I sit up, throwing the blankets aside. I cannot speak. I reach out. Find me! I am here! Find me!

She approaches, but as she does so becomes smaller and smaller. I draw back, confused.

She is not my princess but my own little girl.

"Mary . . ." I murmur when I find my voice, torn from my throat in a painful rasp.

Elizabeth exchanges a look with my stepmother.

"Who is he asking after?" the Dowager Duchess asks.

Elizabeth is silent a long moment, then offers a shrug. "I haven't the foggiest."

I collapse against the bed. It is no use. Someone is drawing the blankets up over my shoulders. I want to sleep; why won't they just let me sleep? My eyelids are so heavy. . . .

"Stay awake, Thomas," Elizabeth is urging, patting my cheeks again and again.

I force my eyes open and fix my gaze on her face. "Elizabeth," I mutter. "Steadfast Elizabeth."

As the minutes turn into hours, I fight. The poison pours out of my body in the form of the sickening sweat, and the stench of death fills the room. But I will beat death. I will show God that this Howard will choose when to die.

When I reach the twenty-four-hour point in the illness's course, it is decided that I will indeed live.

Strength begins to flow back into me, surging through my limbs like wine. I can move without being gripped by pain. My stomach, churning and empty, is still protesting the thought of food, but I force broth down my throat to keep up my strength.

My stepmother, exercising her rights as mistress of the household, makes certain I am kept abed for a week.

While recovering, I receive a most unusual gift.

"From Her Grace at Waltham," says Elizabeth as she places the wriggling blanket in my arms.

"Why on earth would the queen send me a present?" I demand.

My wife shrugs. "God knows it isn't because of your loyalty to her cause," she says.

"I see you've returned from doting wife to disagreeable self in no time," I observe, and unwrap the blanket to reveal a greyhound pup with a gold collar studded with emeralds, sapphires, and rubies.

Its resemblance to my favorite childhood dog, Rain, the dog that my grandfather slew in a rage, causes my throat to constrict with tears. My lip quivers. I swallow hard. The pup climbs up my chest, wagging its tail, and I find myself stroking its soft scruff and cooing at it like an idiot.

"It comes with this dispatch," Elizabeth tells me as she hands me an unopened letter bearing the queen's seal.

> *To His Grace, the good lord Thomas Howard,*
> *third Duke of Norfolk,*
> *My good lord, it has come to our attention that you*
> *have taken ill with this dread plague that smites England*
> *like the hand of God. Upon learning of your recovery we*
> *fell to our knees, giving thanks to God. You are most*
> *fortunate to have your beloved wife at your side.*
> *Please accept this token of our esteem and appreciation*
> *for all of your services over the years past. We know you to*
> *be a good Catholic man, a faithful servant who adheres to*
> *tradition. We put our trust in your continued services and*
> *constancy and look forward to seeing you at court upon*
> *our return.*
> *God bless and keep you,*
> *Catherine R.*

"Oh, for God's sake," I mutter, tossing the letter aside and turning my head away before Elizabeth can note the tears I am blinking back.

"Good Catholic . . . faithful servant . . . constant," Elizabeth is saying, her voice bitter with sarcasm. "Either Her Grace remains willfully ignorant of your many charms or she has a startling command of sarcasm that I was not aware of. In that case she should be congratulated."

"Don't you have somewhere to go?" I ask her.

Elizabeth smiles; it is as hard as her tone. "But I am your devoted wife, here to tend your every need. Until the court returns, I will remain by your side."

I shake my head. The pup is wriggling about so much that I hand him to her. She softens once the creature is in her arms, smiling upon it as though it is a baby.

"It is sweet of her, Thomas," she says. "She's always thought so highly of you. Even when I was a little girl . . . I remember looking at you once when you were jousting and she asked me to pray for you. She was always thinking of you, wishing you the best."

I bite my lip, touched by my wife's reverie. Trying to keep the conversation from swaying to the queen, I ask, "And what were you thinking the day you saw me at the joust?"

Elizabeth strokes the pup's silky ears. Her eyes mist over. "I-I was thinking of how handsome you were, much more so than the young lads the other maidens were swooning over." She raises her head, meeting my eyes. Tears course down her cheeks as she reaches out to cover my hand with hers. "How did we ever get from there to here?"

I am silent. I do not know how to answer her question, how to explain to her that what has happened was meant to happen. How to explain that I should go mad if I could not keep Bess as a counterweight to Elizabeth and a distraction from something so disturbing that I dare not allow myself to think of it.

I clear my throat, squeezing her hand. "I suppose I should name this little thing. What do you think of Storm?"

"It is a good name," my wife says in quiet tones. "Living in this storm of the court in these uncertain times . . ." She lowers her eyes.

"It's a strong name," I say. "Take him to the nursery. The nieces and nephews should enjoy a turn with him. There's a sweet little girl there just out of swaddling bands—what did my brother Edmund name her? Catherine. How could I forget? Yes, I think they call her Kitty. Show the pup to Kitty; she'll love it."

Were we at home I would have ordered the dog to be taken to our nursery but as it is, it may as well receive attention from the children of Norfolk House.

Elizabeth quits the room, her expression soft and wistful, causing my heart to lurch in unexpected pain. There is nothing to be done. It is best not to think on her overmuch.

When she has departed, I take up the queen's dispatch once more, rereading it, the words *faithful servant* and *constancy* standing out like vicious taunts, racking my conscience and making me wonder how well King Henry has estimated the strength and stubbornness of his wife and adversary, Queen Catherine of Aragon.

With the sweating sickness on the decline, the court returns to London and in October the papal legate Cardinal Campeggio arrives. Anne and the king are more in love than ever, which, while it makes me sick, favors the family with elevations that otherwise would not be achieved. Meantime I have taken to arranging marriages for my children. Thomas is betrothed to my ward, Elizabeth Marney (that was quite the ordeal; I had to solicit her wardship at her father's deathbed, but the end result was worth the pains. The child will bring a great deal of wealth to the family). It is a good match and, from the look of the little girl, should warrant many grandchildren. As for my daughter Cathy, now comely at the age of fifteen, I have found for her a groom in the Earl of Derby, Edward Stanley.

She will be a good wife; she always had the makings of a great lady. Her future will be assured and as a countess she will be secured a place at court. Hopefully, she will soon wait upon her own cousin. I scrunch up my shoulders at the thought. Imagine!

With their futures in order, there is but to think of Henry and Mary.

"The solution for our Henry is simple," says my niece Anne, flashing her black eyes at me as I visit her one evening at Durham

House. We are in the parlor playing dice. "He should wed the Princess Mary. God knows all her other betrothals have fallen through. The Spanish brat is cursed."

My heart lurches at the thought. "I'm not the idiot Buckingham was," I tell her in harsh tones. "I will not be accused of trying to place myself too close to the throne. I like my head where it is, thank you very much. Best not mention that again."

Anne offers her edgy laugh in response. "Oh, but it is a travesty! The Pope told His Majesty that rather than grant an annulment of his marriage, he would grant a special dispensation allowing Princess Mary to wed Fitzroy! Can you believe that? He would rather a *sister* and *brother* marry than allow the king's desired annulment!" She shakes her head. "Sheer madness." She cocks her head, surveying me with a slight smile. "Besides, I have another solution for Fitzroy," she adds in her throaty voice.

I lean in toward her, taken in by the conspiratorial tone.

She covers my hand with hers. I note the little nub of a sixth finger on it and withdraw mine. She grimaces at the empty spot, then covers the hand with her sleeve.

"One of your girls," she says. "Catherine or the little one, what's her name?"

"Mary," I say, my heart catching in my throat at the thought of the ethereal child. "Her name is Mary."

"Whoever," Anne says, waving a hand as though the girls were interchangeable. "No one could accuse you of putting yourself too close to the throne then."

"An intriguing thought," I say. "But Catherine is spoken for. It would have to be Mary."

"Mary, then," Anne says in decisive tones. "I shall bring it to His Majesty's attention."

"Be subtle, Anne," I caution her.

"I know how to handle him, Uncle Thomas," she assures me. "You've taught me well."

With that she rolls the dice. "Ha!" she cries. "I win! See? I win!"

I laugh.

The gaze she fixes on me is cold and hard. "I always win, Uncle Thomas. Remember that."

Something in the certainty of her tone causes me to shudder.

She is an unnerving creature, this Anne Boleyn.

At Christmas, much to Anne's chagrin, the queen presides over all the festivities alongside her husband. Anne makes merry in her apartments, entertaining courtiers who trade piety for vibrancy. She is sought out for favors more than anyone save His Majesty, including Queen Catherine and the hated Wolsey. His decline in favor causes my heart to expand with joy as I wonder what the pompous old fool thinks of the Howards now.

Elizabeth keeps company with Her Grace and I with the king, who puts on lavish entertainments for the papal legate. But despite whatever means of avoidance I employ, I am paired off with the queen during the dancing that follows one of the banquets. The sweet face regarding me is lined with such open misery and anguish, I am forced to avert my eyes.

"You are quite recovered, Your Grace?" she asks me in the Spanish accent I always found disarming.

I nod. "Many thanks for the fine hound," I tell her. "Though I can hardly claim him as mine anymore. He is smitten with my baby niece."

"Your nieces have that affect, it seems," the queen says in wry tones.

I say nothing. The hand that holds the queen's is rigid. My body is tense and achy. My dancing days are over and I want nothing more than to end this farce and go to bed.

The queen's thumb strokes mine a moment and my heart lurches as my eyes seek out hers. The blue gaze is soft with unshed tears.

"My champion," she says with a heavy sigh. "Many years ago you saved my husband's kingdom from the Scots." Her smile reveals a trace of triumph. "And years before that, you rode for my honor in the lists. Would you ride for me again, Your Grace, or do you carry another's banner?"

I force my gaze to hold hers. "I carry the banner my king commands," I tell her.

Her face falls. She seems to age ten years in that moment. "You are a good subject, Your Grace, but you are also His Majesty's friend. As a friend, would your higher obligation to God ever compel you to interfere in a matter of conscience?"

I am growing impatient with the leading nature of her questions and the desperation creeping into her tone. I draw in a deep breath, expelling it slowly. "The king's tender conscience serves as my moral compass," I say in firm tones. "I adhere to his will, which is tantamount to God's on earth."

"Despite whatever divinity courses through the royal veins, he is still a man and influenced by other men, men whose ambitions are far from holy," the queen says. "As his faithful friend, you would not try to guide him if you saw he was headed down a path that could jeopardize his soul?"

What is it with these women and the soul? I want to scream. I doubt my Bess would think twice about such utter nonsense. How I miss her!

"I am not a man of the cloth," I tell her. "Matters of the soul are best left to the theologians. I do not attempt to guide His Majesty; I trust and defer to his judgment."

The queen's lip quivers. My heart stirs.

"Then I am alone," she says, almost to herself. "All alone in a foreign land."

"Your Grace—" I begin but am cut short by my own inability to reassure her.

"Of course," she says with a flash of her blue eyes, "there are a few left whose loyalty I never have to question. Your wife, for instance?"

She is enjoying this, enjoying being caught in the middle, enjoying being one of the main sources of the ever-growing chasm between Elizabeth and me. This good pious woman is enjoying her position and does not seem to know or care what it is costing her friend.

For the first time, I feel sorry for my wife. Frustration heats my cheeks and I clear my throat. Elizabeth decides her own fate; pitying her is a waste of time.

The dance ends. Her Grace curtsies; her smile is twisted in irony.

I bow. The smile curving my own lips is forced.

She returns to her faction and I to mine, wondering which of these two very different ladies will emerge the victor: the Spaniard whose beauty has long since abandoned her or the fresh, new star at her peak?

It is all in the hands of a gouty little cardinal from Rome.

The Palace Shaped Like an *H*

Bess Holland

With His Grace at court, there is nothing to do but carry out my duties as washer and play with the children. Oh, but they are wonderful! I am certain no gift His Grace could bestow upon me would be equal to the joy spending time with these little lords and ladies provide. They get me through the days and help ward off the loneliness. We sing and play all kinds of games, but playacting is our favorite. We put on musicals and masques for the benefit of the staff. Little Henry himself writes many of the plays we perform and takes a great deal of pride in his talent. We go to great lengths to make our shows spectacular, building and painting sets, sewing costumes, and inviting the choir from the chapel to join us.

Even Lady Cathy participates. With her mother away, she has warmed to me. But she knows. What the others have been spared thus far has not escaped her; she is a sharp one, sharp as her mother but with the discretion to keep her opinions to herself. Being the consummate lady, she never accuses, never corrects, never says a word. It is agonizing at times, not knowing what she is thinking, wondering if she truly bears me any love or if I am just something to be tolerated for lack of anything better.

When she learns she is to wed the earl of Derby, she abandons her characteristic self-control in favor of bouncing about the nursery like the child she never was, inspiring the same reaction in the rest of us.

She takes my hands and twirls me about. "I'm to be a wife, Mrs. Holland, can you believe it? I shall keep a home of my own with babies and will hopefully attend the queen at court and . . . oh! I am to be a countess!"

"It's wonderful, Lady Howard!" I cry, squeezing her slim hands while blinking back tears at the travesty His Grace insists I maintain for my dignity, that I must be addressed as Mrs. Holland when Holland is my maiden name and I am as far from being married as is possible.

"Oh, I do hope I get to attend you at your wedding!" Little Mary cries, her green eyes dancing. "Do you think this means I shall be betrothed soon, too, Bess?"

My heart stirs in fondness as I behold the little girl whose very being captures the essence of innocence. It is never Mrs. Holland with her. I am her Bess and she is my Mary most dear.

"Da already said you will marry soon," Henry tells her.

"Oh," Mary says, as though disappointed that she did not bear some knowledge of this. "Am I betrothed, then?"

He shrugs. "Don't think so. He has to finish arranging it."

"It doesn't matter, anyway," says Lady Cathy. "Today is not about Mary." She sits on the window seat, tilting her face toward the sun. "Oh, can you believe it? I'm to be married! I do hope I have a baby right away."

I bite my lip, swallowing the tears that keep threatening to spill onto my cheeks. How much do I long to be in Lady Cathy's place! To be imparting the news of my marriage, to fantasize about the babies I will have . . .

"Will you name one after me?" Mary asks her sister as she sits beside her.

"I shall name one after all of you," Lady Cathy assures in tones smooth as honey, compensating for any previous insult. She reaches out and caresses Mary's creamy cheek. "And you will wait on me. Wouldn't you like that, Mary? Then when I go to court you shall accompany me."

"Oh!" Mary cries, scrunching up her little shoulders, an endearing habit inherited from her father and exhibited whenever she is excited beyond words.

Henry laughs at this. "Nonsense and drivel!" he cries in perfect imitation of His Grace. "Da will never let Mary go."

"Why not?" Mary asks, her tiny mouth quivering as she watches her dreams dissolve in her brother's mocking eyes.

Henry shrugs. "He just won't, is all. He has other plans for you."

"How do you know?" Mary asks, eyes growing round with curiosity. "Did he tell you?"

"I hear things . . ." Henry says. "But I won't tell you unless you give me . . . hmmmm . . ."

"Now, now, Henry, I won't be having you taking your sister's things again," I tell him, knowing poor Mary would give him her beating heart should he request it. "Besides," I add with a laugh. "You don't know anything, anyway."

The boy offers up a disarming smile, caught in his ruse but not the least bit ashamed.

Lady Cathy directs her attention out the window once more. "I wonder how soon I shall go to court. And will I have my own apartments as a countess or will I have to sleep with the other maidens?"

"Listen to you making your plans!" I laugh as I scoot in beside her and Mary. "What a great lady you will be. You will be everything your parents hope for."

"I do hope so," Cathy says. "Oh, I hope so. I want to be a credit to my family."

"You are," Mary says with fervency, taking her sister's hands and squeezing them. "Oh, you are!"

With this we embrace, caught up in the happiness and fantasies of a blushing bride.

"Do you ever think to arrange a match for me?" I ask my father that evening when I call upon him in his chambers.

He is resting before the fire, laying his head back on his chair, dozing with his mouth open and a half-finished cup of beer at his side. When he hears my entreaty, his head snaps up and he laughs.

"A match, Bessie? With whom?" He arches a bushy blond brow. "Or is it that you expect the duke to put aside his wife for you?"

I flush, bowing my head. My shame is no secret at Kenninghall; it has won as many admirers as enemies, but to hear my father call it out into the open causes my heart to wrench with humiliation.

"I . . . I don't know what to expect, Father," I tell him, swallowing the tears rising in my throat. "I suppose that's why I come to you, to ask after my future. Do I have one, sir? I am seventeen now. Perhaps it is time to begin considering prospects."

"Are you mad?" Father shakes his head. "And lose your exalted position?" This he says in a voice steeped in sarcasm. "You're what he wants, Bessie. You hold the fate of this family in the palm of your hand . . . or whatever other body part His Grace prefers," he adds, slapping me on the bum.

I back away from him. Tears pave icy trails down my cheeks. I want to rage and scream but know it would be in vain. He is right. My father is not indispensable. If I angered the duke, he could be dismissed and lose his honor.

Strange to think my father's honor depends on my dishonor.

His Grace sends dressmakers with bolts of the finest fabrics from which Lady Cathy will choose her gown and trousseau for her Shrovetide wedding. Together Lady Cathy, Mary, and I sit surrounded by cloth of silver and gold, damask, taffeta, silk, and fur, a garden of luxury. Lady Cathy is the embodiment of poise and refinement as she selects the material for her gowns. No longer does she exhibit the excitement displayed upon learning of her betrothal; she is composed and collected, the essence of calm.

Mary and I cannot contain our delight, however, and we finger the fabrics and ogle the shoes with wide eyes, trying on hoods and squealing with joy over Lady Cathy's elevation.

As Lady Cathy is fitted for her wedding gown, we are stunned by its grandeur. Embroidered with seed pearls, its sleeves are split to reveal shimmering silver organza with a matching kirtle. The train is five feet long and Mary jumps up and down when she learns she will be one of the ladies attendant, vowing she will make it her solemn duty to carry the train to the very best of her abilities.

We laugh at the passion in the child's tone, then turn to each other.

"Oh, Lady Howard, you are a picture of happiness," I exclaim as I behold her.

Lady Cathy's eyes flutter a moment as she endeavors to hold back tears. "I'm very blessed," she says in husky tones.

His Grace returns with the duchess for the festivities. My heart pounds in fear and excitement as I watch the pair enter the great hall. They are splendid; Lady Elizabeth is wearing a deep blue riding habit, her chestnut hair swept under her hood, her angular face framed by escaping tendrils. She stands so straight, holding her head high and proud, her piercing blue gaze surveying her fine home, imparting to me without saying a word that this is her place. This is her place and I do not belong.

I shudder, averting my head.

His Grace walks with the same brusque steps, surrounded by an aura of pride not to be denied. He has changed a great deal; gone is the shoulder-length hair—it now grazes his jaw line and he is even slimmer than before. But his presence! Oh, his commanding presence! I shudder in mingling excitement and fear at the sight of him.

He and the duchess greet the children arm in arm, and my heart wrenches to see the anticipation on the four faces as they wait for some sign of affection. Mary holds her arms up as her father passes, only to drop them by her sides, hopes for an embrace dashed.

Duchess Elizabeth's greetings are measured with equal coolness. It is something I do not understand. Watching this, I vow that my future children will be showered with all the open adoration they deserve.

That night I am summoned to the duke's apartments. I make certain to perfume my body with the scent of lavender that His Grace adores and don my prettiest gown, brushing out my white-blond curls until they shine.

When I am permitted entrance, he encircles my waist with his arms and twirls me about the room. I emit a giggle, touched at his demonstration. At once my heart is seized by a pang of guilt as I wonder what separates me from his children. Am I stealing their share of his love? If I were gone, would they receive the affection they so need?

His Grace sets me down, cupping my cheek. "What is it, my dear?" he asks in solicitous tones. "Is that a pout I see?"

I shake my head. "You are well, Your Grace?" I ask him, resting a hand on his chest. "When I heard you had been taken ill with the sweat . . ." Tears clutch my throat at the thought. However unsteady my foothold is in his life, the thought of losing him is still unbearable. I swallow, blinking several times.

"I survived," he tells me, leaning in to kiss my forehead. "As I always do. Now. No more fretting. How did you spend your time when I was away? Were you a good girl?"

I nod, wondering what he is implying. If he means faithful, the answer is yes. "The children and I passed a lovely winter. But I missed you so. When you are away I am . . ." I shake my head, searching for the words. "Undefined."

"Undefined?" He screws up his face in confusion. "How so?"

"I don't know," I say, wishing I were more eloquent, like Lady Elizabeth or Lady Cathy. "It's just that, well, I am of an age now when all my friends are becoming betrothed. Watching Lady Cathy prepare for her marriage, well . . . mayhap I am a little jealous."

He pauses. "I can assure you, Bess, marriage is an institution from which happiness cannot be derived. Once you are a little older and the romance of the idea has faded, you will see how unhappy all those giddy maids of yours are and envy them you will not. You will be glad you did not enter into such foolishness."

How long does he plan to keep me in this state? I want to ask but bite my lip, bowing my head lest he read my disappointment, not that I should be fated to endure a lifetime with him but that I should be forced to endure a lifetime of disgrace.

"But they will have children," I venture.

"What are they but little reminders of inevitable heartbreak?" he counters. "Really, Bess, be grateful you are where you are. You have no need of any such drivel. You are mine and I shall make your every dream come true."

The fair words do little to ease the sadness lying heavy in my heart. How can he profess that he has the ability to make all my dreams come true when the two I want most are denied me?

"Anyway, enough of this girlish nonsense," he tells me. "You would like a ring?" he asks in absent tones. "Then I shall give you one." From his little finger he removes a heavy gold signet ring, then, taking my hand, slides it upon my left ring finger. "Here. My coat of arms. Wear it and be reassured that you are mine."

My heart lurches as I stare at the thing; the bezel bears the engraving of an arrow piercing straight through a noble lion's tongue. My eyes widen. I know this ring. It was the ring Duchess Elizabeth threw at us when she found us together that terrible day. . . . It was her ring. What did he say when bestowing it upon her?

"It symbolizes our victory at Flodden," he is telling me, noting my expression and believing it has to do with the lion and not the fact that his gesture is as good as giving me his wife's wedding ring.

"Wh-what else does it symbolize?" I ask in a small voice as I regard the ring. My hand trembles with the weight of it.

"The strength of the Howards, of course," he tells me.

I lower my eyes. "Your Grace . . . I am touched by your generosity, but what should the duchess do if she sees it?"

He shrugs. "It is mine to give. True, it was hers for some time, but she threw it up at me just as she does everything else; she can no longer claim it. Now, now, are you going to accept it or not?"

I blink back tears. "Of course, Your dearest Grace," I tell him, not knowing what else to say. Somewhere, despite his explanation, it seems very wrong accepting this gift. But I mustn't hurt His Grace by insulting him.

"That's a good girl," he tells me, wrapping his arms around me and leaning his forehead against mine. "Now. I have brought you presents."

My heart lifts and I cannot deny the smile that is curving my lips. "Presents?"

"From London," he says as he leads me to a trunk. "You see this? Everything in it is yours."

I open the lid. Before I can gasp, His Grace leans down and retrieves the first object, a cloak lined with fur.

"Do you know what this is?" he asks me as he strokes the soft fur. "Sable."

"Oh, Your Grace, you are so very grand!" I cry as he wraps me up in it. I hug it around myself, brushing my cheek against its softness over and over. The gesture comforts me.

His Grace is kneeling in front of the trunk now. He reaches for my hand and tugs me down beside him. Inside the trunk are bolts of fabric, a collar of fine gems, brooches, and pins shaped like flowers, all encrusted with rubies, emeralds, and sapphires. I have never seen such wealth. Guilt surges through me as I regard the duke. How could I entertain the notion of starting a life with another when he lavishes on me such extravagant gifts? They are not mere baubles or trinkets but symbols of the love this great man bears me. To consider any other position in life is presumptuous and ungrateful. What can I, a mere servant girl, expect? I, who deserves nothing and instead gets everything. There is no hoping for more. I will be happy. I will bask in his adoration and endeavor to show him my gratitude and love in return all the days of my life.

"You will be attended by a dressmaker and fitted for some gowns," he informs me. "With any luck you will be at court soon."

"Court?" I breathe. "Me?"

"If my niece has her way, she will be queen of England," he says with a twist of the lips that seems more sneer than smile.

"How can that be?" I am feeling most ignorant. I know Mistress Anne has stolen the king's heart but did not think she could be any more to him than I am to His Grace.

"Leave the particulars to me," he says, pulling me toward him and covering my cheek with kisses. "You just plan your wardrobe and think about the day you will be attending Her Majesty, Queen Anne Boleyn."

It is a heady thing, I think, being in the arms of this man who has the power to shape a kingdom and my life.

Lady Cathy's is a beautiful wedding, though small, and the festivities last through Shrovetide. She is Lady Derby now and conducts herself with the dignity her title requires. She sheds no tears upon leaving Kenninghall but bestows upon us the briefest of kisses, thanks her parents for supervising her upbringing, and departs.

There are no embraces, save for little Mary, who wraps her arms around her sister's waist and erupts into tears for which she is quickly reprimanded by her father. The child rights herself, sniffling and wiping her eyes, swallowing visibly as she watches Lady Derby embark on her happy venture.

The little boys are delighted, but I imagine it is only because there were so many festivities and they were allowed to stay up late and eat sweets. Their sister's happiness has little to do with it, and when she leaves, they do not feel the void as Mary and I do, a void that for me is made emptier when the duke announces he will be returning to court with Lady Elizabeth.

"Would that you didn't have to go," I lament as I snuggle against his chest the night before he leaves. "Lady Cathy's leaving marks the beginning. Soon they will all be gone and I will be alone."

"You'll always have me," he says, kissing the top of my head. "And I am giving you your own apartments—no more servants' quarters for my Bess. Furnish them however you wish. Make a luxurious little nest for us. Fill them with whatever you like—tapestries, carpets, anything."

I tilt my face up toward him and offer a smile. "Thank you, dear lord," I murmur, kissing his neck. "With my own little world to create, I can divert myself in making it beautiful. Mayhap I will be too busy to be lonely."

The duke says nothing but continues stroking my hair.

I imagine loneliness is not a problem for such as him. When he is not with me, at least he can take comfort in his wife.

The End of an Era

Elizabeth Howard

Thomas dotes on that harlot Bess Holland with the same enthusiasm King Henry demonstrates for Anne Boleyn. They make me sick, the pair of them. Here they are, a king and a duke with everything and both made mad by two lowborn girls, neither of whom can be called great beauties.

After my daughter's wedding we return to court, where I promptly remove to the queen's side while Thomas plots his niece's rise and Wolsey's fall (the latter of which I can't help but support). Queen Catherine is my only refuge now and my heart aches for her as much as it does for my own daughter. Though I am happy to see Cathy secure, I miss her. Our visits to Kenninghall were infrequent, but she was always there, my sanity in a world that had become swallowed up in my husband's lust for another. Now there was no one to rescue me from it, no respite in my Cathy's apartments, that one place at Kenninghall where grace and refinement still existed. Letters are too few and far between and a pitiful replacement for my girl.

And so, with a loneliness more acute than ever before, I throw myself into the service of my queen, who seems my only friend in this world.

Today the queen has requested me alone to sit with her while she embroiders. I sort thread and try not to think of my Cathy, or Thomas and Bess Holland.

The queen is forty-three years old but looks at least ten years older, so aged by her husband's antics has she become. Shadows circle her eyes; her face is puffy. The weight she has gained appears awkward on a frame that is meant to be thin. As I regard her I wonder if I am looking into my own future. Will the misery my Thomas inflicts render my image the same?

"Not a pretty sight, is it?" the queen asks when she notes me scrutinizing her. I bow my head in shame.

"I do not know to what Your Grace refers," I say.

She offers a laugh without joy. "Oh, my dear lady duchess, there is no reason to lie to me. I've known you far too long. It has been a long journey for the two of us, has it not?"

I nod, my throat swollen with tears.

"You have been my faithful little maid since you were twelve years old," she says, reaching out to stroke my cheek. The gentle gesture causes warm tears to spill over; they course down my cheeks unchecked. "And you have been an example of loyalty and devotion. We have suffered much, you and I, at the expense of those who profess to love us. There are times when it would seem most appropriate to yield, to give in—to take the easy path. But God did not walk the easy path, did He?"

I shake my head.

"He likewise did not promise us, as Christians, an easy time of it. However, my dear duchess, it is what is at the end of the path that makes this struggle worthwhile." Her voice is husky with fervency.

I lean into her hand, trying to suppress the sobs that are rising in my chest. "But, Your Grace, do you really think there is something at the end of the path? What if . . . what if there is nothing there?"

"Losing faith, Lady Elizabeth?" she asks me, but her eyes are filled with compassion rather than judgment.

"I do not know," I confess. "Oh, Your Grace, far be it from me to trouble you when you are enduring so much but—" My sobs burst forth, my chest heaves, my shoulders quake. I gasp and gulp like a child. "Forgive me, Your Grace—"

The queen sets her embroidery aside and gathers me in her arms. "Dearest girl," she murmurs, kissing my hair. "What is it? Tell me, please. You are not burdening me. I am your queen and as your anointed queen I am also to be regarded as your loving mother. Tell me, darling, what is it?"

I gaze up into her sweet face, softened by compassion, and attempt to collect myself. "I fear I am suffering a similar situation as Your Grace. My lord husband has been . . . unfaithful and—and I do not know how to accept it."

"You do not have to accept it, Elizabeth," she says in firm tones, abandoning the strict protocol to which she adheres. "But you do have to forgive it, as I forgive His Majesty. It is what our Lord commands."

I fall to my knees before her. "But how?"

"Through God's grace," she tells me, taking my hands in hers. She expels a heavy sigh. "I know that my husband has been led astray by men made wicked by their own ambitions, that he does love me in his good and generous heart, and that, if he can be made to see the error of his ways, he will abandon these blasphemous plans in favor of what is right. Through fervent prayer and study, it is my hope that I can sway my husband from this evil path. You must do the same."

"I do, oh, Your Grace, I do!" I insist. "But it is so different with my lord. Your husband seems to demonstrate some struggle with his conscience on this issue; mine does not. He knows what he is doing and it doesn't matter! He has no care or regard for me at all. He has installed this Bess Holland in our home and has given her fine apartments. He gives her everything her sinful heart could desire and, worst of all, let's her usurp my place in the children's hearts—they're so detached from me now, they are as good as strangers!" The depth of my sorrow has caused my strength to depart. My limbs are quivering. I wipe my eyes. "No . . . that is not quite true," I add in quiet tones. "They were removed from me long before that. My Thomas and I both seem to have trouble—handling the children. I admit after losing my Edward it has been easier to create a sort of barrier between us. But to see Bess take that place, knowing everything else she has stolen from me . . ."

"So it is a matter of pride as well," Her Grace observes.

"It is my greatest sin," I confess.

"Mine as well," she says with a sad smile. "It breeds stubbornness. But it also gives us the will to endure these dark times." She draws in a deep breath, then regards me with a steady gaze. "Elizabeth, as Mistress Anne is a symbol of problems arising long before her entrance into our lives, I believe this Holland woman is the same for you. The real matter lies between you and His Grace. If you can solve that, perhaps your marriage can be made happy once more."

Once more? I think with an edge of desperation. I look down at the embroidery threads and begin to sort through them to bring comfort to my fidgety hands. "We are forever at odds," I tell her. "I do not know how to overcome that. It seems he deliberately believes the exact opposite of me just to spite me."

"He is a determined man, an ambitious man," the queen says. She lowers her eyes. "His position is not an easy one. He is the head of the Howard family. As such, he is witnessing the rise of his niece and feels obligated to support her, as that is what the king believes he needs. Your duke is nothing if not the king's man." She closes her eyes a long moment. "Which brings me to the biggest obstacle between you and Lord Norfolk." She opens her eyes. "Me."

I am silent.

"Please, my lady, you will not insult me by agreeing," she says with a bitter laugh. "It is true." She cups my face. Tears stream unchecked down her cheeks. "Elizabeth, I am your anointed queen. I know you love and support me. But if you need to . . . if you need to abandon me for the sake of preserving your marriage, then you must."

I recall my lord's promise to give up Bess Holland should I abandon the queen. But he is more attached to the curly-haired strumpet than ever. There is no guarantee that, should I cease to serve Her Grace, he would leave Bess now. And then what would I be left with? I would be left with no husband, no children who require me to be anything but a figurehead, and no friend. The notion is unthinkable.

I shake my head. "How could I desert Your Grace? I could not even pretend to do such a thing. I am your servant, always your servant. My loyalties cannot shift as easily as others—they *will* not. It is not a quality I choose in myself but something given."

"But you must think of your husband," the queen tells me in soothing tones. "And your family. You still have three children at home."

I am shaking my head. "No, no. He is not mine. And the children," I lament. "They are his. His and Bess Holland's. I have nothing but my service to you. Please, Your Grace, do not ask me to surrender it."

She removes my hood, smoothing my hair and stroking the tears from my cheeks. "Oh, loyal Elizabeth, God will bless you for your devotion. You have chosen a course most difficult. To serve an anointed queen is a higher calling than that of wife and mother. But you will be rewarded. I promise you. We must remember God's word, which I have told you many a time, that long-suffering produces perseverance. We will persevere, Elizabeth. And someday, we will know happiness for our strife."

"You are very brave, Your Grace," I comment. "I shall pray for your continued strength during your ordeal."

She bows her head. "Yes. My ordeal." She covers her mouth with her hand and grimaces as though in pain. "The trial will begin soon." She lowers her hand, her face hardened with resolve. "God will see us through, Lady Elizabeth. He is on the side of right. And we are right!" Her voice wavers with sustained passion as she draws me into her arms again.

I seek comfort in the embrace of my queen, the woman who has remained the one constant throughout my life, and think if anyone deserves God on their side, it is she.

Thomas Howard

The legatine court at the priory of the Blackfriars in London opens on 31 May. There the fate of the divorce will be decided by two of the most idiotic men ever to wear cardinals' hats. Wolsey is as round as an apple and wheezes all the way to his chair, while gouty old Campeggio hobbles in beside him. They are pathetic and it grates my nerves just looking at them.

The court is called to order. His Majesty enters and takes his place on his throne of state. When the queen comes forth, it is not to sit beside him but to kneel before him.

It is obvious she is in pain for it takes her a moment to lower her trembling self to the floor. My heart is pounding as I regard her. I want to avert my eyes from her shame but cannot.

She raises her tear-streaked face to the king and begins in a voice smooth and soft, "Sire, I beseech you for all the love that has been between us and for the love of God, let me have justice and right. Take on me some pity and compassion, for I am a poor woman and a stranger born out of your domain." She closes her eyes, drawing in a deep breath, expelling it slowly before continuing to address a court silenced by this remarkable demonstration. "I love all those whom you loved only for your sake, whether I had cause or no, whether they were my friends or my enemies." At this her eyes find me. They are lit with profound sadness and I swallow a painful knot of tears. "These twenty years I have been your true wife or more, and by me you have had many children, though it has pleased God to call them from this world, which has been no fault of mine." This she says with sustained vehemence. "And when you had me at the first, I take God to be my judge, I was a true maid." Her voice is soft, reminiscent, as though she is recalling a moment very tender, their wedding night perhaps. She raises her eyes to the king, who is gazing down at her with an expression of mingled shame and impatience. She shakes her head. "I knew no touch of men and whether it be true or no, I put it to your conscience." She blinks several times. "It is a wonder to hear what new inventions are now invented against me, that never intended but honesty," she says almost to herself. Then to the king, "I most humbly require you in the way of charity and for the love of God, who is the last judge, to spare me the extremity of this new court until I may be advertised what way and order my friends in Spain will advise me to take. And if you will not extend to me so much indifferent favor, your pleasure then be fulfilled and to God I commit my cause."

The queen struggles to her feet, then dips into the deepest curtsy before her husband and, leaning on her receiver general's arm, leaves the court to the calls of the crier, who demands her return.

Outside, the cheers of the people can be heard shouting blessings to their anointed queen. I close my ears against their common voices and my eyes to what is now forever committed to memory, a great woman reduced to shame for the love of my black-eyed niece.

But I open my eyes soon enough. What is done is done. Whatever pity I feel for Catherine of Aragon must be put aside for a greater cause.

The king has risen. His face is wrought with sadness. "She has been to me as true, as obedient, and as conformable a wife as I could in my fantasy wish or desire. She has all the virtuous qualities that ought to be in a woman of her dignity or in any other of baser estate."

I force back a twist of the lips as I imagine what my niece will make of this tribute.

His Majesty then proceeds to discuss his scruples. It is a heavy burden he carries, making this painful decision, but for the good of the succession and England, it must be made. His consistent argument remains in the fact that the queen consummated her marriage to Prince Arthur, which voids their union and has them living in a state of sin. It is a condition King Henry's delicate conscience cannot abide.

The Archbishop of Canterbury is nodding in agreement. "You speak true, if it pleases Your Highness," he tells the king. "I don't doubt all my brethren present will affirm the same."

John Fisher, Bishop of Rochester, and perhaps one of the only men wholly devoted to Queen Catherine, interposes with, "No, sir. Not I. You have not my consent thereto."

In a rage the king shakes a paper in the old bishop's face. "Then what is this? Look here! Is this not your hand and seal?"

Bishop Fisher shakes his head. "No, Sire, it is not my hand nor seal."

"You speak true," says the Archbishop to Fisher. "But at the last moment, you were fully persuaded and let me sign for you!"

"Under your correction, my lord, there is no thing more untrue," the bishop scoffs. "The marriage of the king and queen can be dissolved by no power human or divine."

The king shakes his head, his lips twisting with a bitter smile. "No matter," he hisses at the bishop. "You are but one man."

Undaunted, Bishop Fisher meets His Majesty's gaze with eyes that smolder like embers, bearing the promise of the fire to come.

The next few days are spent arguing about Prince Arthur's ability to consummate his marriage to Catherine of Aragon. Forty nobles give evidence as to their own fitness in the sport.

"I was not yet sixteen when I knew my wife," says the Earl of Shrewsbury.

Anthony Willoughby tries to suppress a laugh when he testifies. "Prince Arthur says to me, he says, 'Willoughby, give me a cup of ale, for I have been this night in the midst of Spain.' And then he says, 'Masters, it is a good pastime to have a wife.' " Willoughby sits down with a satisfied smile, made playful by the memory of young men telling tales.

Thomas Boleyn and Lord Fitzwalter waited upon the prince at table, where was repeated the same joke. Lady Fitzwalter recalls seeing the couple in bed together.

And I, when called to bear witness, confess that I knew my wife at age fifteen and was more than capable of performing The Act. This is true only in part, for I did not know my wife till my early twenties, but it is what the king wants to hear, so hear it he shall.

Even when sheets sent to Catherine's mother, Queen Isabella, are displayed, the bishop of Ely confesses that Catherine often told him she never carnally knew Prince Arthur.

I do not know what to believe. While the evidence is compelling, the queen's passionate adherence to her story is just as convincing. I suppose it doesn't matter anyway. Truth is rather a moot point in this world.

On 23 July, Cardinal Campeggio adjourns the case to Rome. Enraged, the king stalks out as the Duke of Suffolk slams his fist on the table and shouts, "By the Mass, it was never merry in England while we had cardinals among us!"

Wolsey regards the duke, his fat face wrought with sorrow. "Of all men in this realm, you have least cause to be offended with cardinals for if I, a simple cardinal, had not been, you should have at present no head upon your shoulders!"

Humbled into silence as Suffolk perhaps recalls Wolsey's intervention for him when he wed the king's sister Mary, his fist unclenches and he bows his head.

I shrug. If the cardinals cannot give us the divorce, we will find another way.

The best thing to come of this, oh, the very best thing, is that no singular event is more worthy of bringing about Wolsey's downfall.

He knows it. As we lock eyes, I find in them an appeal. I offer him a sure and steady smile. Were our situations reversed, there is no doubt he would do the same.

The case against Wolsey is all too easy to procure. The cardinal will be indicted under the Statute of Praemunire, which prohibits interference from Rome in English affairs without royal consent, such as receiving papal bulls. On 17 October, it is with great delight that Suffolk and I strip the corpulent cardinal of his post as lord chancellor by taking the Great Seal from him at Esher.

The king seizes much of the ecclesial property, Wolsey's favorite houses of York Place, the More, Tittenhanger, and Esher. The jewel of them all, however, is Hampton Court, which is a palace in and of itself.

With Wolsey fallen, the post of lord chancellor has opened up. My heart thrills as I ponder the possibility of being chosen, but it is not me but Suffolk—stupid, arse-kissing Suffolk!—the king considers. When I point out that the man is powerful enough, he capitulates and chooses, instead of me, Sir Thomas More, humanist, Lutheran-hating author of the fanciful *Utopia*, which I say I read but didn't and he knows it.

The whole thing is ridiculous! Even I can see that More doesn't want the post! He wants no part in the nullity suit, has no care of anything worldly. His goal in life is to punish Lutherans and himself for whatever unlikely sins he may have indulged in, and spend time with his horde of a family at Chelsea, where he is free to study and ponder and mock his wife in Latin. To think this is the man the king has chosen . . . !

"Ah, but there will never be a chancellor as honest and so thoroughly accomplished as he," says the new imperial ambassador, Eustace Chapuys, in his broken English.

There is nothing but to agree and it is with a reluctant but whole heart that I do so. For More is not like other men. He has something in him that we political-minded lack. The sweet, open-faced man is good, pure of heart and intention.

In reality, I cannot think of a king requiring more than that.

Elizabeth Howard

"All is not lost yet, my dear duchess," Queen Catherine tells me in her chambers while we sew shirts for the poor.

"Your Grace conducted herself with the utmost dignity before the court," I tell her, my voice wavering in awe that she could summon forth words now famous throughout England. "There is so much to be admired in you."

The queen shakes her head. "My motivations are not worldly," she tells me. "I am driven toward a higher purpose. My husband must be made to see . . ." She bites her lip a moment, then shrugs, continuing her sewing. "Meantime I must fight for what is mine."

I nod. "Your Grace, I am compelled to apologize for the behavior of my niece. As a relation, I cannot help but feel responsible."

"Nonsense, Lady Elizabeth," she says with a sad smile. "You've no control over that girl. I daresay she has very little control herself. She is a tool as we all are, a piece of iron meant to be bent and wrought to the designs of others."

"She seems more than willing to be made malleable," I say in a tone edgy with bitterness.

"Perhaps." The queen cocks her head as though in thought. "But that is on her conscience."

Conscience. I am sickened by the misuse of the term. If I have to hear about His Majesty's tender conscience once more, I fear I shall retch.

The queen draws in a breath. "It has been difficult. I will not lie," she tells me then. "Since your niece entered my life, I have not known a day of peace. Never before has anyone been able to sway the king as that woman has. I do not know why and how, except to say that she wields some dark power beyond my understanding."

It would be simple believing raven-haired Anne Boleyn to be a witch. But it is not so and in my heart I know it. She is a concubine and a harlot with French tricks, no different from Bess Holland.

I do not give voice to this, however. I nod and offer a sympathetic sigh.

"Your Grace, the imperial ambassador is here to see you," a servant informs the queen.

Her Grace rises, her face alight with a smile. "Do show him in."

"Perhaps I should leave you?" I ask.

"Please stay, Lady Elizabeth. You bring us much comfort," the queen says, gesturing for me to remain seated at the window.

The ambassador enters and offers a deep bow. An exchange in Spanish rings in my ears melodic as a bubbling brook and I close my eyes a moment, wishing I could speak it, that I might be more intimate with the queen's world. How much more could I understand her if I could speak her language!

"Ambassador, it is my pleasure to introduce to you my dear friend, Her Grace Elizabeth, Duchess of Norfolk," the queen says and I rise from the window seat. "Duchess Elizabeth, this is the imperial ambassador to my nephew, Charles V. Eustace Chapuys."

The ambassador takes my hand, placing upon it a warm kiss as he bows. "My lady."

When he rights himself, I am startled by his handsomeness. He is young, forty years old, I am told, which is only eight years my senior and it shows in his fine form. His liquid brown eyes are alert and engaging, his black hair cascades to his shoulders in glossy curls, and the beard surrounding his full mouth is close-cut. Each feature, from his straight nose to high cheekbones and angled jaw, is sculpted as though from fine marble. His smile is warm and inviting. Regarding him I am reminded of the dashing Fra Diego, dismissed from court so many years ago for his wild ways. I wonder if this man who radiates the same raw sensuality is as amorous, then am ashamed for the thought. My cheeks flush and I bow my head.

"Duchess Elizabeth has remained a dear friend to me throughout my many trials," the queen is telling the ambassador, who, upon hearing her voice, shifts his gaze from me to her. "Besides Maria Willoughby, she is my staunchest supporter in this foreign land."

"No doubt you value her very much," the ambassador says in his broken English. "Good friends can be most useful."

At this I am compelled to fall to my knees before the queen. "Allow me to demonstrate my loyalty to Her Grace and her cause in any way I can," I say, my tone impassioned. "I am her humble servant."

The ambassador takes my hand, helping me to my feet, and I admit to a certain thrill at his touch. He holds my gaze a long moment.

"We are most grateful, Duchess," he says. "Your devotion is admirable. I am certain we will call upon you for assistance in the very near future."

"I am at your command," I say in husky tones.

At that moment no words are truer. It is not only the queen who has rendered me helpless but this man, this imperial ambassador who champions her cause with as much devotion as I, this dark and devastating Eustace Chapuys.

Thomas Howard

The king is far too generous with Wolsey. How that fat man weasels his way into His Majesty's heart I have no idea. In any event, the king allows him to linger too close to court for my comfort. His Majesty has pardoned him—granting him the bishopric of York and his home at Esher once more, not to mention the rings he sends him as tokens of affection. I could tear out my hair at the thought!

I will destroy him.

My dark musings are interrupted by more pleasant diversions. On 8 December, Thomas Boleyn is created Earl of Wiltshire and Ormonde, wresting the title from the Irish Butlers at last. My dashing nephew George is styled as the Viscount Rochford, while Anne and her sister Mary are the ladies Rochford. George is also appointed as a gentleman of the privy chamber, which will keep him close to the king. I admit a certain pride in the boy; he is an accomplished diplomat and consummate courtier, slick and sly as they come. All Howard.

The next day, the king gives a beautiful banquet to celebrate Thomas Boleyn's ennoblement. The court can hardly retain a gasp when they note Queen Catherine's absence. Who sits in Her Grace's chair? None but my black-eyed niece, whose pretty cherry lips curve up in a smug smile that I return when my eyes fall upon her.

Ah, the taste of success!

My wife and stepmother are not as enthusiastic about the seating arrangement, and their blatant scowls reflect it; it is the popular belief that the king's sister Queen Mary should have been seated in Catherine's chair in her absence. But there is naught they can do but grumble, so I leave them to it.

After dinner, there is dancing and I am paired with Anne. "Ah, my little gem," I say with a slight laugh. "How goes it?"

"You have eyes," she quips. "What do they see?"

"An arrogant little girl," I state, "who must be careful. All is not won yet. Queen Catherine has made it clear that she will not yield easily." I pause, then am reminded of another point as I watch the king dance with his sister. "Tell me—you are still being admired from afar?"

She nods. "It isn't easy. He is a persuasive man."

"Don't underestimate your own powers of persuasion," I say. "Remember, keeping your virtue is all that separates you from being another of his dispensable whores. You must not give in till that ring is on your finger—and the crown is on your head."

Anne breaks into a fit of edgy laughter. "Yes, Uncle," she says, squeezing my hand.

We take to whirling and spinning about the floor and I toss back my head, adding my own triumphant laugh to hers.

It is good to be a Howard.

The queen is beside His Majesty as a figurehead for the Christmas festivities, over which my niece throws one of her now famous tantrums, and only the promises of her future station will soothe her. Queen Catherine is packed off to Richmond soon enough, and Anne is reassured of the king's devotion to their cause when he removes with her to York Place.

In January, Thomas Boleyn, for the sheer fortune of being Anne's father, is named Lord Privy Seal and begins to savor his newfound power.

That same month, Elizabeth and I remove to Kenninghall to see the children. I have been appointed governor to the king's son, Henry Fitzroy, who is based at Windsor, and have decided to send my Henry to him as one of his companions. I have also decided to observe the girl Mary to examine her fitness for court. If I find her adequate, she could be a little maid to her cousin Anne and prove useful to me.

As a gift I bring the child a little circlet that I took great care in designing. A subtle piece, it is silver and inlaid with tiny seed pearls, and gazing at it I cannot think of a more appropriate adornment for one such as Mary. When I see the girl, I make a show of placing it upon her golden head and she scrunches up her shoulders in her peculiar display of delight. Gazing at her, her delicacy, fine bone structure, and bewildered green eyes, I realize it is expedient for her to be at my side so that she might be in full view of all. She is eleven years old now, ripe for the plucking. Anne has discussed with the king a possible betrothal between her and Fitzroy. At court she can be seen by the king and approved by him. I have been told by Bess and her tutors that she is an accommodating little girl, a talented embroiderer, musician, dancer, and composer of verse, a skill I find rather useless but one King Henry seems to admire in women.

Elizabeth, predictable as the sunrise, is against the idea of Mary coming to court.

"She isn't like us, Thomas," she tells me in my study. "She never has been. Court is a dangerous place for such as she."

"She'll get used to it right enough," I tell her in impatient tones.

"I don't *want* her to get used to it!" Elizabeth cries. "I don't want her to become hard and cold and accustomed to deceit and betrayal! Don't take her, Thomas! Please!"

I have tired of the constant arguing; she must be taught who her master is. I have been far too lenient thus far.

I take her in hand.

It seems to be the only form of discipline she will understand.

And so, with an Elizabeth made compliant, Mary accompanies us back to court, where she waits upon her cousin and is given explicit instruction to report anything and everything involving Anne and the king to me. I do not worry overmuch about the girl's behavior; should anything untoward come my way, I am not afraid to dole out the fatherly discipline that is my right. But she seems malleable enough and fortunately should not require such stricture.

Meantime I am busy wreaking the final downfall of Wolsey. The former cardinal's secretary, Thomas Cromwell, a lowborn son of a blacksmith with, I must admit, considerable potential in the political arena, has aligned himself with the Howard star and is maneuvering away from his master in order to serve one of more prominence. By March he has begun a polite detachment from Wolsey and acts as messenger. When, uncomfortable with Wolsey's proximity to court at Winchester, I send Cromwell with a message.

"What will he do there?" I demand. "No, let him go to his province of York, where he has received his honor, and there lie the spiritual burden and charge of his conscience. So show him!"

The king sanctions this move and sends Lord Dacre to assist him. But they do not move fast enough! What is that portly priest up to?

"Show him that if he does not remove himself shortly, I will tear at him with my teeth!" I cry to Cromwell, who stares at me with wide eyes. He nods so much that his jowls jiggle. I think he believes me.

In late April, Wolsey remains fifty miles from York, determined to be as close to His Majesty as possible. If I didn't hate him so much, I'd find the display pitiable. But there is no use getting excited about it; he is as far north as I can send him for the time being.

Now it is to the king's divorce. I begin to oversee the collection of opinions from the theologians of English and European universities about the legality of his marriage while trying to sway Pope Clement to see His Majesty's side of the situation.

The Pope issues a bull revoking His Majesty's case. In Rome's eyes, the king is forbidden to remarry.

"The best course is to ignore the bull and do it anyway," I say to Eustace Chapuys.

The handsome ambassador tosses back his head and laughs. "And you are worried about Charles V declaring war? There would be no need, for His Majesty's own subjects would rebel and their king be deemed a heretic!"

I bite my lip in impatience. Something has to be done! How long will this drag on?

In the midst of this I am served a dispatch from a messenger of Derby.

No doubt Cathy has learned her sister has arrived at court before her and is wondering when she, too, will have a place. Impatient with the thought of such trivialities when I am beset with so many other heady tasks, I tear open the seal.

It is no such thing. It is a letter from Derby telling me that Cathy has succumbed to the plague. She is dead.

I am immobilized. Cathy . . . my perfect lady. Born and bred for court life and now . . . now . . .

It was bound to happen. They all die. They all die. . . .

I crumple the dispatch in my hand in a moment of fury as I work my jaw. I try to focus on something to no avail. The carpet is a blur. I close my eyes against the burning tears.

"My lord?" Chapuys takes my elbow. "You are well?"

I nod, pulling away from him. "The duchess . . . I must see the duchess."

She must hear it from me.

She is in her apartments, lying across her chaise before a dying fire, a piece of embroidery abandoned on her lap. Her eyes are closed, her feet are crossed at the ankle, and the contrary expression adopted in her waking hours has exchanged itself for a softer one. For the first time in many years, I wonder how she occupied herself this evening, what she ate, if she enjoyed her day, what she is embroidering. . . . Silly, useless thoughts, these.

I reach down, touching her shoulder.

She stirs, her expression hardening as her gaze fixes itself upon me. Her lips curve into a wry smile. "Why, it's Thomas Howard. Is it a sign of the apocalypse or are you come to see your wife of your own accord?"

For a moment, all I can do is stare at her. I want to speak. Something prevents me. I sit beside her on the chaise, reaching out to touch her cheek. She flinches at my touch. My heart lurches. I swallow hard.

"Elizabeth," I begin. I bow my head. "Elizabeth . . . it's Catherine."

"The queen?" Her eyes are wide.

I shake my head. I wish it were the queen, then am struck by a peculiar surge of guilt.

"Our Catherine," I amend. "She's—she's dead, Elizabeth."

Elizabeth parts her lips. No sound comes forth. She begins to shake her head. Her breathing is rapid. She rests a slim-fingered hand at her breast as she swings her legs over the side of the chaise and doubles over.

"H-how?" she chokes.

"Plague," I tell her. I hand her the dispatch from Derby. She scans it, then lets it fall to the floor as she covers her face with her hands.

"Elizabeth . . ." I wrap my arm about her shoulders and attempt to draw her near.

"No!" she cries, rising, balling her hands into fists. "Don't *touch* me!" She turns toward me, pointing at me. "Do you really think to try and comfort me now when you'd just as soon beat me tomorrow?"

"One has little to do with the other," I say, baffled.

Elizabeth shakes her head, then covers her mouth with her hand. "Oh, Thomas . . ." She sinks to her knees on the carpet. "What have we come to?" She crumples to the floor and begins to rock back and forth, sobbing broken, wretched sobs.

My heart is pounding. Pain is surging through me. I swallow again and again in an attempt to assuage the sensation of my throat closing. Six children gone, three left. How long? How long before the next one goes? I am cursed to outlive them all, I believe.

I kneel beside her and take her in my arms. She does not struggle or offer words of protest. "There now, Elizabeth. 'Tis the natural order of things," I tell her. "Long ago I warned you not to get too wrapped up in them lest it kill you. You know?"

Elizabeth sobs harder. "I wasn't there. She died and I wasn't there. Just like little Edward . . . oh, Thomas, I wasn't there to hold her hand and brush her hair and bathe her face. I couldn't even close her eyes."

I have closed plenty of eyes and held enough dying hands to last my life through. I have no longing for such things and cannot understand it in Elizabeth. Being as far away from Cathy as possible in her dying moments suits me fine.

"It is better like this," I say, almost convincing myself. "This way you can remember her as she was."

Elizabeth turns her face up toward me. "Ah, but she was beautiful, wasn't she, Thomas?"

I nod as I recall the young woman I had given away in marriage such a short time before. "She was a lady," I say. "A great lady."

I hold my wife for a long time that night.

Elizabeth Howard

She is dead. My Cathy is dead and there is nothing I can do about it. She was my light and now that light has been doused by the icy water of reality. Of all my children, it was she with whom I felt the greatest bond. It is unfair and I don't know what separated her from the rest, save her age and our common bond as females. She was like me in a way. Intelligent and well bred, with no other desire but to be a grand lady and servant to Her Grace. That she should be denied that causes my heart to burn in anguish.

When my sister the Countess of Westmorland arrives at court, she is full of sympathy. Seeing her only fills me with irrepressible anger as I think of everything she has: the man I wanted, the life I wanted. . . . It is easy for her to offer sympathy, I should think as I regard the well-dressed, well-loved woman before me.

"Please, sister, understand that I do grieve for you," she entreats me in my apartments.

"I'm certain you do," I say in cold tones. "Tell me, Lady Westmorland, how many children do you and Ral—the earl have now?"

She lowers her eyes. "Nine, my lady."

"And of those nine, how many have you lost?"

"None, my lady," she tells me; then, regarding me with wide blue eyes, she shakes her head. "I have been fortunate. Would you resent me for this? How can I control what God doles out? We land where we fall, Elizabeth! I didn't want to marry Ralph—I knew he was yours. Do you think I *wanted* to infringe on your happiness? But by the time I married him, you were long married to Lord Norfolk. The decision, as well you know, was far beyond my control. So I married Ralph. And since being married, I have known joy and have been blessed with living children—but again it is purely by chance that I should be blessed with everything I could have hoped for. Our situations could have as easily been reversed."

"But they weren't," I say, my tone laced with bitterness.

My sister wrings her hands. "Would you feel better if they were? Would you, as my sister, wish upon me misery? Do you think I revel in yours?" She approaches me, taking me in her arms. I cannot respond to the embrace. I want to. But I can't. "Oh, my dear lady," she continues. "Would that you had found some sort of happiness to cling to that you might endure this grief somehow. If you have not, I am not to blame. I come here to offer my condolences and be a comfort to you, but if my presence only serves to bring you more pain, then I shall excuse myself directly."

I cannot speak. My sister backs away from me. Her eyes are stricken. I want to beg her not to go, but the words will not come forth. I am rooted in pride and anger and disappointment and cannot be moved.

She quits the room and I am alone.

My daughter Mary writes me a letter filled with sweet words and my response is involuntarily curt.

"I curse myself for not being able to see her, but when I think of her I am only reminded of what is lost," I lament to the queen. "Mary is so unlike me. Where Cathy was practical and realistic, Mary is whimsical and governed by fancies. I want to see her; I want to speak with her. But any comfort I would endeavor to offer would be forced and empty and she would feel it. I would feel it. There is no connection. Not with her or any of them, save my Cathy. And she is gone. I do not know what kind of parent this makes me; I daresay I am about as good a mother as Thomas is a father, which puts me in a sorry state of affairs indeed."

The queen, who is so good herself it is impossible for her to conceive of evil in another, holds my hand and shakes her head at me. "Nonsense. I am convinced both you and the duke love your children in your own ways. Sometimes it is very difficult to express. Children are people, Lady Elizabeth, and as with any person, there are going to be qualities that you can approve in some better than others. You must not punish yourself for being unable to be close to your daughter right now. You are a woman struck by grief; you cannot be expected to be all things to all people. Give yourself some time and approach the girl when you are stronger."

"I fear I am losing my strength," I confess. "And Mary is kept so far away from me. Thomas sees to that. When she is not cloistered with my niece and her circle she is with him, sequestered in his apartments. It pains me to admit this, but I believe she is an agent of his."

"Of course she is," the queen says, but her voice bears no malice. "But she is a child. Likely there is nothing she uncovers that he does not already know. And she does not work against me. She keeps him abreast of her cousin's doings." The queen sighs. "Quite a heady task for a child."

"Mary would do anything for him, she and my son Henry both." I cannot withhold the bitterness from my tone. "It is unnatural. She makes sheep's eyes at him like he is . . ." I shake my head. I do not want to say it.

The queen regards me a long moment. "The duke is . . . a bit awe inspiring. And part of awe is fear. Do you not think that Mary and Henry are as afraid of their father as they are admiring and it is that which makes them so acquiescent?"

I bow my head, shamed. "I suppose I'm giving her more control than she has," I say. I offer a heavy sigh. "What hurts most is she is learning all the wrong things and demonstrates a loyalty to all the wrong people."

"It hurts to be betrayed," observes Queen Catherine.

"Cathy would not have been like that, I do not think," I say, my voice catching. "She was so eager to be presented to you so that she might serve you. . . ."

"Best not compare, Lady Elizabeth," the queen cautions. "It pleased God to call her from this world. She serves a being far greater than my humble self."

I bow my head, unable to speak. I am held captive by shattered dreams and do not know how to wrest myself from them.

"As it is, you are here and my good servant," she tells me. She draws in a breath as though she wishes to speak but is restraining herself.

Protocol forbids me to prod her, so I force myself from my wounded reverie to give her my full attention.

"Lady Elizabeth," the queen says in low tones, "I am reluctant to remind you of a promise you made me not one year ago, that you would serve me for the benefit of my cause. Are you able to do so, my lady?"

I blink back tears, touched that she should ask. Rather than being embittered at the thought of being deprived of my grief, I welcome the chance to distract myself with a challenge.

"You know you have but to command me and I shall accommodate," I tell her, my voice wavering with fervency.

The queen rests her fingers beneath my chin, tilting my face toward hers. "I do not want to command you, Elizabeth. I want you to help me because you want to, because you are my friend."

Tears clutch my throat. "I am your friend, Your Grace, always. Tell me what to do, so that I might help you."

The queen hesitates a moment more, then says, "It is very hard being separated from my husband more often than not," she tells me. "It is increasingly difficult to obtain the things I desire." She offers a small laugh. "You know how I adore oranges from my homeland," she tells me with a reminiscent smile. "They will be in season soon, and Eustace Chapuys has promised to send me some, but the king often prevents him from visiting me personally. Were my dear friend to give you a basket of oranges, you would make certain no one received it but me? I would hate for them to become mislaid; I love them so."

I nod in understanding. "Of course, Your Grace," I assure her, squeezing the hand that holds mine. "Nothing would please me more."

With this new charge I am rejuvenated. I will not think of my daughter, the one dead or the one living. I will not think of my Thomas and his Bess. I will not think of anything that brings me pain.

I will think about baskets of oranges.

Thomas Howard

I do not think about my Cathy. To be honest, I didn't give her much thought to begin with after her marriage was secured; she was safe in the country and, I assumed, since she lived to maturity, she would escape the fate of her siblings. She would have children; she would come to court. Her children would come to court. And so on. But she is gone, and gone with her are my hopes for her. It does me no good to dwell.

As it is, another death consumes me, though not with grief. With joy, maddening joy. For Wolsey, that pompous, arrogant fool, is dead! I cannot say it enough. The exiled cardinal collapsed on the way to his execution in London. He was brought up on charges of treason; irrefutable evidence was provided stating that he was corresponding with foreign monarchs and Rome that he might enlist their support for his pathetic cause. Well, perhaps the evidence was not irrefutable. But it was strong enough to obtain the signature on his death warrant. But instead of death at the block, he succumbed to a demise fitting for a butcher's son, twitching in the mud like one of his father's pigs at slaughter. What a delight! Ah, but it would have been nice to see him beheaded, to look into his eyes and convey in my gaze my ultimate victory over he who endeavored to bring my family and me down since his rise to power. Who is brought down now, Cardinal? Oh, excuse me. I had forgotten; gone is your cardinal's hat. Seized it was when you failed.

Thomas More does not share my enthusiasm over his predecessor's passing.

"Corrupt as he was, I think he wanted to do right in the end," he tells me in his soft voice one day when I visit him at his Chelsea home.

"You never liked him," I say gruffly. "You side with him now because he was a churchman, and you are nothing if not the Church's man. Look at you in your quaint choir robe! God's body, my lord chancellor!" I laugh. "A parish clerk! A parish clerk! You dishonor the king and his office!"

More laughs but it contains no humor.

"You cannot tell me you mourn him," I demand.

"Perhaps not as one should," More confesses. "But I am in mourning, Lord Norfolk. We are at the end of something. And I do not know if I am equipped to handle what lies ahead. I fear for the king. If a lion knew his own strength, hard it would be to rule him." He purses his lips, drawing in a breath. "Wolsey knew that and used it to his advantage. Cromwell does not know it. Boleyn does not know it." He turns his gaze to me, his eyes so penetrating, my heart begins to pound. "I do not think you know it, either. Now the lion is unfettered and we all will pay dearly for it." His eyes grow distant. "Yes, my friend, I am in mourning. Wolsey is dead and with him the king's sense of restraint. There is no question as to who is next. Only when. Perhaps I die today and you tomorrow."

I wave a dismissive hand. "Drivel, Thomas," I tell him, hoping to dispel the feeling of dread pooling in my gut. "All we have is now," I say. "We must celebrate our victories." I offer a smile that suddenly seems forced. I bow my head, deciding the best tactic is to completely shift the direction of the conversation. "Your family must prove a distraction. Quite the lot. They are lovely children."

"I am very blessed," he says and seems as relieved as I am. There is a certain respite in useless banter. "As are you. I have seen the girl Mary at court, a beautiful child. So pure."

My heart lurches; all feelings of respite depart. "Mary." I expel a wavering sigh. "Thomas, sometimes when I look at her . . ."

"Yes?" More prompts. "What do you see when you look at her?"

I shake my head in bewilderment. What do I see? The pearly essence of her skin, the wistful face, the golden hair I love to brush . . . "I see the embodiment of someone else. Not just someone else but some*thing* else. The embodiment of another time, another place, a place of innocence . . ."

"Lord Norfolk, she is not someone else," More tells me in firm tones. "She is your daughter. See her as she is. Love her as she is. And, for love of God, do not make her pay for your disillusionment upon the realization that she is just an ordinary girl."

No, I want to scream, *not Mary*. She is far from ordinary. She is some kind of siren, a creature I long to both treasure and protect myself from. It is nothing sordid, as God is my witness. . . . Oh, what is this curse that has befallen me?

I shake my head and clear my throat. This is no conversation for More, the traditional family man. I should have known. Mary is not a topic to be discussed with anyone at any time. There is no one who would understand. I do not understand it myself.

I turn the conversation toward lighter things. Wolsey's death. Yes, think of Wolsey's death, not the children, neither the ones snuggled in their graves nor the one who inspires in me such dark and frightening fancies.

I will think of Wolsey. And I will revel.

Elizabeth Howard

Eustace Chapuys begins sending the baskets to the queen through me with very little trouble. I never look inside. As their communications are in Spanish, I would not be able to understand them anyway and it would do me little good. I am just the messenger and it does my heart good to know I am providing this service to Her Grace, who is pitiably short of friends.

We meet in a secluded area of gardens, where he passes the basket to me with a smile and pleasant exchange. He is never too personal, is always polite, save for those eyes, which are so keen and scrutinizing that they cause me to avert my eyes with the bashfulness of a girl.

One warm summer afternoon he meets me, the basket looped over his arm, and I greet him with a smile. It is a beautiful day. The scents of citrus and roses assault me and I draw in a deep breath.

"A shame to think of anything being conducted within doors on such a day as this," I tell him, expelling my breath. On impulse I give myself over to the childish urge to twirl about. "This must be what paradise smells like."

He laughs. "It is divine," he agrees in his thick accent. "Surrounded by roses." He closes his eyes, sniffing the air. Upon opening them, he smiles at me. "Roses and the beauty of a great lady."

Another typical courtier, I think, as I recall the suave Fra Diego.

"Why the face you put on?" he asks me, his English so broken I am forced to laugh.

"I'm sorry. I was just thinking of an old acquaintance who used fair words to win fair ladies," I say as we take to one of the benches.

"Did he succeed?"

I begin to giggle again. "No! He was sent home in disgrace. He was the queen's own confessor, Fra Diego."

He joins me in laughter. "Well! Imagine a priest with such unholy designs!"

I wipe a tear of mirth from my eye as I laugh harder. By now everyone knows of Cardinal Wolsey's many mistresses and I am certain Chapuys is thinking along the same order as he makes the jest.

"Tell me, are the gardens of Spain as beautiful as this?" I ask him.

"As the Spanish envoy, I am obligated to say, 'No, my lady, they are far more beautiful than this,' " he says. "And while they are pretty, I must tell you that I am not in truth from Spain, so my heart does not think upon it as home. I am from Savoy. You know this place?"

I nod, charmed helpless by his musical accent.

"My first languages were actually French, then Italian when I attended the University of Turin," he tells me. He smiles as though recalling a memory most dear. "And always Spanish, of course, which is now the one I use most. Then there is this English." He shakes his head with a rueful smile. "Well, you can see my English is not so good. English is not, I am thinking, a very pretty language."

"No," I agree. "It is as hard and cold as the English people."

He regards me with soft eyes. "Not all of them," he says quietly. In cheerful tones he adds, "I am most content to speak my romantic languages. For the rest, I have a good translator." He leans forward, resting his elbows on his knees. "Some of the things I need to know are not learned by the spoken word. I observe people, their faces and their ways. A lot can be learned just watching."

I nod. "And what have you learned about me?" I venture, feeling impetuous as a courtier.

He hesitates, regarding me a long moment before saying, "I have learned, Lady Elizabeth, that you are sad."

I bow my head.

"I'm sorry," he says quickly, reaching over to take one of my hands. "I was very bold."

"Very," I say.

We are silent a while and then, reaching into the basket, Chapuys removes an orange. "We were speaking of gardens. Do you know oranges grow on trees, Lady Elizabeth? Beautiful trees. Nothing smells as sweet as an orange orchard. Do you favor this fruit, my lady duchess?"

I swallow hard. "I have never tried one."

"The Spanish queen's maid and you have never tried an orange!" he exclaims. "Well, you must!" He commences to peel it, concealing the peels in a nearby bush. He breaks the fruit in half, then into sections. The juice runs down his elegant hand as he gives me one. "Here. Try, my lady."

I take the orange and pop it into my mouth. Juice squirts out, running down my chin, and I emit a little giggle. A burst of tangy sweetness erupts in my mouth and I offer a purr of delight.

"You like this fruit?" he asks me.

I nod, covering my mouth in embarrassment. I have forgotten my handkerchief, which is tantamount to mortal sin for one of my breeding, and am trying to think of a polite way to wipe my chin.

The ambassador chuckles, then lowers my hand, removing his handkerchief from the pocket of his doublet. Slowly he reaches forward, then dabs my chin with the fine linen. When with his other hand he takes the handkerchief away, one hand remains. Gently it seizes my chin, his thumb running over my lips soft as butterfly wings. I shudder somewhere deep within as our eyes lock.

I do not want to break away.

But I do, averting my head.

The moment is lost.

"Thank you for taking the basket to the queen," he tells me in a whisper. "It means a great deal to us."

"It means a great deal to me as well, my lord," I tell him, rising, taking the basket, and turning away.

"Eustace."

"Eustace," I say slowly.

I walk away, gripping the basket with white knuckles, all the while trying to force away the images that are assaulting me, images that serve me not well at all.

I must stave off thoughts of this dark man. Each time we meet, it is harder to leave him. We do nothing improper; we do not touch.

We talk. He tells me of Europe and the handsome Charles V, of beautiful Turin, and romantic Savoy. He asks me how I feel about things. How do I feel about Anne Boleyn (whom he refers to as The Concubine)? How do I feel about my daughter's passing? How do I feel about Thomas? I tell him. With tears streaming down my cheeks, I tell him of my shame for the Boleyn woman, my involuntary coldness toward my living children, of the deep sense of mourning for Cathy, and of my mingled love and hatred for Thomas. He listens. He does not judge, save to agree with me about Mistress Boleyn. He listens.

It is dangerous to bare one's soul so; I know it. But I do it anyway. The gentle nature and compassionate eyes of this beautiful man make it impossible to do otherwise. It would be so easy to yield to my deepest desires, to follow my husband's example and steal what is not mine. . . .

How ashamed would Her Grace be if she knew of my fancies! The Lord tells us that just to *think* an adulterous thought is tantamount to committing the sin itself. Based on this standard, I have done it a thousand times over.

I am no better than Thomas.

Thomas . . . my lawful husband. We have not been together in so long.

There is naught to do but go to him. If I have to use him as he uses this Bess woman to get the ambassador out of my mind, I will. Far better to give myself to him than sacrifice my honor. Tears constrict my throat as I think of how much I long to abandon integrity and follow my darkest dreams. But that would make me like them, those of this court who have lost all sense of morality and decency. Those who take the easy path.

Perhaps something good will come of it. Perhaps he'll realize . . . no use getting caught up in more useless fantasy.

Eventually, I go to my husband's apartments.

"You were not summoned, my lady," he tells me when I am permitted entrance.

I close my eyes a long moment. "I had thought perhaps to visit you."

Thomas laughs. "What do you want, Elizabeth? Surely you don't desire my company, or is it that you miss our stimulating conversation?"

I swallow my reply and approach him, wrapping my arms about his neck, drawing him close. He is my husband. I must focus on him, for whatever he is. And he is a handsome man, at least to me. Once he was a good man. If I can forget . . .

Thomas is rigid in my embrace. "What's this, girl?" he asks as he encircles me in his arms. He regards me with bewildered black eyes.

"Thomas, I . . ." I do not know how to go about this. It has been so long. I don't want to be a harlot. But I need a distraction.

He breaks away and pours himself a cup of claret from the buffet. "My little niece is a bit peeved with you, I think," he says.

"Who is *she* to be peeved with *me?*" I ask, my face heating in anger that the Boleyn whore should be brought up at a moment I had hoped to make tender.

"Most likely she is your future queen," Thomas tells me. "The sooner you accept that, the sooner you can find some peace. Elizabeth. Stop playing the go-between for the queen and Chapuys."

My heart lurches.

"God's body, girl, you are as transparent as that window," he tells me, gesturing to the pane behind him. "You think I don't know? You don't think it is only a matter of time before the king finds out? I am only playing the innocent to spare you."

"To spare you, you mean," I say in short tones.

"My clever girl," he says, setting the cup down and approaching me once more. "Now, before you and Anne take to fighting like she-cats, I suggest you cease this lunacy and be a good auntie. She is quite useful to us. Because of her . . . influence, the king is considering a match for our little Mary with his son Henry Fitzroy."

"Fitzroy? The bastard?" I cry.

"Besides me, that 'bastard' is the premier duke in the realm," he snaps. "Don't you see how perfect it is, what it would mean for us? Mary would be King Henry's daughter-in-law."

"Oh, there's a privilege! We all know how good he is to his family!" I am scandalized. Tears burn my eyes. "So Mary will wed Fitzroy and then what will become of her? She'll be swallowed up in this world of treachery. She'll learn how to lie and connive and cheat—"

"High-minded till the end," Thomas says, shaking his head in disgust. "I'd rather the girl learn to keep up with the best of them than be trodden down by it. This is how it is, Elizabeth. There's no shame in trying to get the best."

"And this is the best?" I ask, shaking my head at him. "Do you ever once think of her *happiness?* She's our only daughter now, Thomas. Your baby. Don't you want to protect her?"

Thomas's expression changes; it softens with a whimsy rarely seen. His eyes mist over. "I am thinking of her, Elizabeth. I know you don't believe me." His tone is husky. "But, in addition to the obvious benefits the title will hold for us, this marriage will ensure that she will always be beside me."

I screw up my face in confusion as I try to sort out this new line of reasoning.

Reading my puzzlement, he continues. "She'll still be a young girl for quite some time, even after the alliance is made. It won't be consummated right away. I'll make certain she doesn't go to Fitzroy a day before I think she is ready. Till then, she will be mine—er—with us."

My heart drops in my chest. I begin to back away from him.

"What I'm saying is that beside me, she'll be safe. I will make certain of it," he assures me.

"And happy, Thomas? Will she be happy with you?" I ask in soft tones.

"Of course," he answers, as though he cannot conceive of some-one being unhappy with him. "I give the child gifts all the time. She has everything. She has a hundred little friends to play with, a pup she adores, pretty gowns—what more could she desire?"

"You," I tell him. "Are you kind to her, Thomas?"

He grimaces. "What do you mean? Of course I am!"

"But have you ever—have you ever . . ." I don't know how to ask. I don't want to ask.

"Have I taken her in hand?" he finishes. "Only when needed."

"Ah," I say as I sit on one of the plush chairs in his privy chamber. "Hence the gifts." I draw in a wavering breath. "The gifts you give her all the time." The last three words are deliberate, measured.

"I'm her father," he says, as though this answer should satisfy me. "And head of this family. It is not for you to question the discipline that is in my right to administer, girl."

"No," I sigh. Suddenly I am overcome with exhaustion. "I suppose not." I don't want to fight him anymore. I don't want to think about things I can't control. Mary is growing up fast enough in this court; what she does not know, she will learn. Thomas seems an eager teacher. Bile rises in my throat. I swallow hard.

"Now. Returning to the subject at hand. You'll stop serving as Chapuys's messenger, thank you very much," he tells me. Then in thoughtful tones he adds, "And whatever else you do for him. You'll stop that as well."

I rise, anger surging through me as hot as wine. "You will withdraw whatever it is you are implying at once, my lord."

Thomas smiles. "Touchy, lady wife?"

"You know I have been nothing but devoted to you," I cry.

"Oh, you are devoted," he remarks. "But not to me. No, I should say the queen has your devotion before any living being. Her cause and whatever you can do to further it. I must admit I am a little surprised. I did not think you'd reduce yourself to such intrigues. . . ."

"Thomas Howard! You know me better than that!" I cannot stop shaking my head. I cannot believe what I'm hearing. "I'm yours! No matter how ill used, no matter how miserable I have been made in your company, I am yours!"

With this I throw my arms about his neck and do what I had intended to do since arriving in his apartments. Strangely, the anger fuels my passion and I cover his face with kisses, then press my lips firmly against his in a frantic show of possessiveness.

"Yours," I murmur. "Don't you see?" I begin to remove his doublet. "Yours . . ."

Thomas returns the kisses, translating his own sense of desperation. Together we sink to the rush-strewn floor, meeting in a coupling of such intensity that we are left breathless and sobbing. There are no words that can explain or compensate for what is gained and what is lost in each other's company.

As with everything concerning Thomas and me, it is expressed through the physical. Right or wrong, good or bad, that is how it is.

Nothing changes.

In the end, I go to my apartments and he remains in his.

I meet with Chapuys. The smell of the sweet citrus fruit that masks the dispatches between ambassador and queen is also the fragrance of my own betrayal in mind and spirit to my husband and his cause. The honor that remains intact is that of my body, which has committed itself to the marriage vows I was forced to take at fifteen years of age.

I carry out my noble charge, despite warnings from Anne Boleyn herself, who taunts me at every turn. I tell myself that serving this high purpose is worth the pain and disregard of Thomas, that in the end some divine reward must come of it. But my resolve grows weaker with each passing day.

The queen will lose this battle. There is no doubt of it. This world is not meant for the pure and the good. It swallows them up, claiming them as one of their own unless they can escape. And the only escape is death.

It is obvious the queen is dying. Her burden is too heavy; the cup of her deteriorating health spills over onto her poor daughter, so overwrought by the stress and pain of her father's lust for the Boleyn whore that she is tortured by a string of illnesses. This mad king will kill anyone who stands in his way without employ of axe or sword. He will murder them with heartbreak, heaping upon these two pious creatures sorrow after sorrow until, broken, they collapse and yield to the embrace of the angel of death.

And yet this task gives me meaning. I hold fast to it, cherishing it. If I am fighting a losing battle, I will fight nonetheless as I have my life long.

Anne Boleyn, that traitorous slut, has confronted me. No longer satisfied with subtle threats, she comes to my apartments specially to address the matter, all dressed in purple—purple! The color reserved for royals alone! There are no words to capture the hatred that stirs in my breast upon looking at the raven-haired girl whose shrewd, calculating eyes belong to her uncle and whose body belongs to the Whore of Babylon.

Her lips curve up into their courtier's smile as she enters with a great flourish as though to say, "Make way for the queen!"

She dips into the smallest of curtsies before me, as though it is a favor that she should make any deferential show of respect to me at all.

"I come to visit with my auntie Norfolk," she tells me. "How are you, my lady?"

"Quite well," I answer.

"I have had the pleasure of acquainting myself with my cousin, your daughter," she goes on to say in amicable tones as she runs one long-fingered hand along the cherry wood of my breakfast table. "A beautiful little girl," she comments. "She has a great future ahead of her, Lady Norfolk." She drums her elegant nails on the tabletop. "With my help, the king and your husband have arranged things quite nicely. Uncle Thomas loves her quite madly, I should think." She turns, mocking me with her eyes. "Quite madly," she adds deliberately.

"I don't see how that is any of your concern," I say.

"She is my family," Anne counters. "Naturally, she is my concern. And my concern extends to you as her mother and my aunt."

I fix her with a hard stare.

Anne raps her hand on the table. "Lady Norfolk, I know all about my uncle. I know how he waves his mistress under your nose; I know how he's beaten and humiliated you." She lowers her eyes. "I know how he treats poor little Mary."

"I'd have thought he would serve as your inspiration," I say. "Do you really fancy yourself better than Thomas Howard? Than any of them? Are you not just another Bess Holland? How does your treatment of the Princess Mary differ from that of my husband's treatment of our daughter? Who do you think you are to offer me sympathy and counsel? What do you want from me, *Mistress* Anne Boleyn?"

Anne's black eyes flash with anger. "Stop this nonsense with Chapuys! It does not help your case nor that of the queen's. It makes you all look like fools."

"Fools?" I cry. "I look the fool? Who is more foolish? The whore who tries to seduce His Majesty from his faithful wife and holy Church with her heresy and wicked French tricks or the woman who has been nothing but loyal to queen, country, and husband? Fool? Fool indeed!"

"You *are* a fool, Elizabeth Howard!" Anne cries, balling her white hands into fists. "For by supporting that woman, you are throwing away every chance of happiness! You will lose, Lady Norfolk, not I! Your place at court, your husband, your children—everything. And for what? Principle?" Her eyes soften. The pity reflected in them incenses me more than any previous mockery. "I could have been your ally," she says in quiet tones. "I could have been such a help to you. I still could. One word and Uncle Thomas would be forced to rid himself of that harlot girl."

"As if that matters to me!" I cry. "Do you think I want my husband to be *forced* to rid himself of her? He will put her aside for love of me or he won't. I'm certain his"—I choose my words with care—"*conscience* will advise him—like his king."

Anne bows her head. "Very well." To my astonishment her eyes are moist. "Be advised, Lady Norfolk. Your days are numbered."

Anne Boleyn may be many things, but a woman of false word she is not. Moving with the swiftness of a falcon descending on a rabbit, she makes certain word of my transgression reaches the royal ear.

I am banished from court and from the service of my lady.

I knew this was a risk I was taking. I knew it and yet shock courses through me as though I have been thrown against a stone wall. Though a farewell to the ambassador is forbidden, I am permitted one last audience with the queen in her privy chamber, where every endeavor of staying calm is destroyed by her compassionate countenance.

"You have been nothing but a good and faithful servant," she tells me in her soft, low voice. "And God will bless you for it. There are no words to express the sorrow I feel that you should be treated with such disrespect. You are not alone, my lady. Even now the king plots my removal from his presence. It is easier for him, you see," she tells me. "Easier to live with his sin if he is not made to look upon me daily. So I will go. I will be removed."

"Would that I could go with you," I say with fervency, tears sliding in warm trails down my cheeks.

The queen offers her sorrow-filled smile. "It is a journey, this life, and God is our end. I will pray for you, my dear. I am much aggrieved at losing you, Lady Elizabeth."

"You will never lose me," I assure her through tears. "You have my devotion and prayers always. Along with my deepest friendship."

"As do you, my lady," she says.

As I begin to back away, the queen raises a hand. "Fight, Elizabeth. Fight for what is good and right. We shall prevail."

Unable to speak, I dip into another low curtsy. And then take my leave.

"You are a fool, Elizabeth," Thomas rails as he pokes his head inside the curtains of my coach just before I set off for Kenninghall. "Your pride has undone you."

"Not pride, Thomas," I correct him. "Honor. And I'd rather be undone by honor than by the ambition and avarice that consumes you."

Thomas laughs. "I am through with you, Elizabeth. If you think you have a respite in Kenninghall you are wrong; you have no place there. You have no place anywhere. Not even beside your precious queen. You have seen to that. You are alone, Elizabeth, all alone with your honor. Take comfort in it."

With those words he closes the curtains.

I am alone.

Bess Holland

She has returned. The duchess has returned in shame and I am forced to face her every day knowing that I am much elevated in the duke's eyes and she is not. I do not know what kind of madness I have fallen upon. The servants all defer to me as their lady. Some of them are quite nice; everyone makes certain I am cared for. More lilac oil for your bath, Mistress Bess? More hot bricks in your bed, Mistress Bess? More wine, more food? More, more, more.

The duchess is not made merry or comfortable. She is taunted for her disgrace at court. Any and every opportunity is taken to antagonize her, from putting stinging nettles in her bed to more direct confrontations insulting her about the duke's waning affections. No one assists the lady with anything except the most basic tasks. No extra care is to be given her. Most of all, the duchess is not allowed to disrespect me in any way lest she be promptly "corrected" by the staff. Corrected like an errant child or naughty puppy. And all because of me.

For a year it goes on like this. We do not confront each other much, keeping to our own apartments. I try to blot out that I am the cause of her despair. But the knowledge is there. I am a bad girl, no better than a common whore no matter how His Grace dresses me. I am a courtesan. And, if the duke has his way, a courtesan I shall remain. Is it, I wonder, for any affection he bears me or just to spite the duchess for some grievous sin I know nothing of?

My ladies seem to think she is deserving of such treatment.

"She did it to herself, that's what the duke says, so that's what we must believe," says one portly maid called Sarah as we embroider in the parlor. Sarah and her sister were sent by the duke to attend me and take particular pleasure in tormenting the duchess. Brought up with the whip to become tough and coarse, they see nothing wrong with His Grace's form of discipline. "Anyway, His Grace pays us good enough to believe whatever he says, eh?" she adds in her crude accent.

I swallow the rising bile in my throat and bow my head. "I never wanted to be the cause of such sorrow."

"They cause their own sorrow," Sarah tells me. "Bastards, all of them. They have everything in the world and, having it, don't know what else to do but make misery for each other." She offers a bitter laugh. "Besides, she's a haughty enough girl. Does my heart good to see one of them brought down. Now she knows how it feels."

"Aye to that," agrees her sister, a sturdy girl named Becca. "Don't know why you bother feeling so bad about it, my lady. Take what he gives you and be glad of it; few enough get your chance. Be grateful for the lusts of a noble gentleman." She pauses a moment. "Of course, perhaps you shouldn't be thanking His Grace. Thank the duchess." She laughs so much at this that her double chin waddles. "Here!" She raises the mug of small ale she had been sipping at. "To the duchess! To the prideful wench who drove a duke right into Mistress Bess's loving arms!"

"The duchess!" echoes Sarah, raising her glass. They fall together in laughter.

"Yes, to me," a low voice seethes. Lady Elizabeth stands in the doorway, her steely gaze fixed on me. I shudder. I meet her eyes. I cannot behave as though I am devoured by guilt when I am not. Didn't I want the duke as much as he wanted me?

Perhaps the sisters are right; maybe the harshness doled out to the duchess is earned. Was it not her pride and stubbornness that expelled her from court? Was it not her constant disobedience that sabotaged any love the duke had for her?

I tell myself this. I tell myself this to make it right. But nothing makes it right. I keep nursing the belief, however, that I might survive the knowledge that I have caused more misery in another human being than ever I could have conceived.

And it is with all this in mind that I fix my gaze upon the duchess.

She strides in wearing a wry smile. "Drink to me, ladies. Drink to my pain and my humiliation." She stares me down. "Drink to your lover who revels in it, that generous lover who will just as soon turn against you should you displease him. Yes, you've a great deal to celebrate, *Mrs*. Holland."

I start at the farcical misnomer. "You require something of me, my lady?" I ask her.

"Yes, I do," she says, drawing herself to her full height, which is still smaller than me. She stands a delicate sapling struggling to hold her ground amidst the turbulent storm of my treachery. "I require you to leave this place, Bess Holland. For all that is holy, cease the life of a concubine while you still have some chance at redemption. Leave. For God's sake, leave." The plea in her voice is unmistakable and I close my eyes against it.

"I cannot leave, as well you know, my lady," I tell her. "It pleases the duke that I remain."

"Yes, ladyship," Sarah chimes in. "It *pleases* the duke."

"Very much!" adds her sister with a wicked laugh. "Have you heard how much, Sarah? I've heard it. In the hallway, outside His Grace's apartments. He is very pleased indeed!"

"Hold your peace, Becca!" I cry but there is no stopping what is to come, what they have wanted to come since the duchess arrived from court.

Her Grace is trembling in rage. Red faced, she clenches her jaw as she makes for Becca, her hands like claws as she encircles the thick neck.

Becca is too strong, however, and Sarah is even stronger. Together they pin the writhing duchess to the floor. Lady Elizabeth is spitting and cursing, flailing her arms as she attempts without success to defend herself against these oxen of women.

"Stop!" I am crying. "That is quite enough! Stop!"

They do not hear. The duchess is gasping. She has clawed so much at her attackers that her fingertips bleed. She begins to cough.

"Get off her, for love of God!" I cry, running toward them to seize Sarah by her broad shoulders. "Get off her at once!"

A sharp tug of my hair reveals that the duchess is thrilled to have me in what would be a comic display were it being acted out. But it is real and we are all players on a stage in Hell, a stage set and designed by the duke of Norfolk.

When blood begins to spew forth from the duchess's lips, the girls scramble to their feet. They back away. No apologies are uttered. Sarah dares smirk at the prostrate duchess.

"That's from your loving husband," she tells her. "Ye'll not be so quick to disrespect those in his esteem now, will ye?"

Lady Elizabeth lays comatose, blood trailing down her chin in a thin crimson stream. My heart is pounding at the horror of it all.

I look to Becca. "Send for someone to attend her," I order in harsh tones. Then to Sarah I seethe, "How could you? That was unnecessary and cruel and—"

"Don't take offense to it, Mistress Bess. We are on orders. She was rude so we corrected her, just as we were told. We have to do what we're told or we're all out in the street."

"But like this? And—and do you have to *like* it so?" I demand.

She shrugs. "Life is short enough without taking a few small pleasures now and again."

With this she departs.

I stand in bewilderment. Icy fear surges through me. These women do not "correct" the duchess for my sake; they are not my friends. They are paid henchmen who derive perverse satisfaction from the pain and humiliation of another. Lady Elizabeth's words torment me . . . *that generous lover who will just as soon turn against you should you displease him . . .*

How can my duke sanction this? I know he has been cruel, I know he has been wicked, but I cannot believe he would approve this.

Like everything else I am forcing myself to believe, I tell myself he would not, surely he would not. When he learns of this terrible act he will somehow set things right.

The thought is as unsteady as all my other convictions and brings with it little comfort.

For the King's Pleasure

Thomas Howard

It is certain. My niece Anne Boleyn will be queen. It is just a matter of time and stratagems, soon to be sorted out by England's craftiest men, myself among them. Anne reigns in all but name as it is and, upon her creation as Marquess of Pembroke, prepares herself to accompany the king on a state visit to France to be presented before its king.

She is a tiresome little bitch, is Anne, and hard to manage. Her pride and certainty in her impending queenhood gives her a hauteur and insolence that can barely be tolerated. She no longer defers to me as the wise uncle but treats me as she would a dog, hurling insults at me when her bidding is not done. I bite her back; I will not let this tempestuous woman get the best of me.

Her demands increase with each passing day and all of them are met by her doting lover. It is not enough to have the world torn apart for her sake, but she must make life as uncomfortable as possible for everyone around her in the process. Lady Anne is not satisfied with the suite of jewels designed for her visit to France; she wants the queen's—pardon, the Princess Dowager's, as she is now known—state jewels. I am assigned the unpleasant task of retrieving them from the exiled Catherine of Aragon.

With a small retinue I journey north, rehearsing a number of different tactics in which to secure the jewels from this obstinate, pitiable, admirable creature.

She receives me in her presence chamber, sitting under a canopy of state as though still queen and addressed as such by her menial little staff. It's a sight to bring tears to one's eyes, but I blink them away as I approach her, bending into a deep bow.

Her lips curve into an ironic smile. "Rise, Lord Norfolk," she commands. Her accent still plays upon my ears like a wistful melody.

I right myself, daring to look her in the face. She has aged terribly. The exile has caused her to lose the weight she had gained and she sits a wraith on her throne. Her breathing is short and uneven and she furrows her brow as though in pain.

"So," she says, "you have come to visit your old friend."

I swallow hard. "How fares Your Highness?"

She purses her lips. "I am kept separated from my daughter, who is ill and needs a mother's ministrations. I am told I am no longer a queen but a princess dowager. My misled and manipulated husband has put me aside for lust of another and intends to place upon her head my crown. How, Lord Norfolk, do you think I fare?"

I pause. "You look well," I say feebly.

"Please do not disrespect me any more than you already have by lying." She emits a sigh. "Now. Why have you come?"

"I come, Your Highness, to collect the state jewels that are in your possession. The king wishes their return," I tell her in amiable tones.

"The king does not wish it," she corrects me. "You do not argue with this, I see. Your Anne Boleyn wishes it, does she not?"

I nod. "She does. For her visit to France."

Princess Catherine shakes her head. "No. I will not surrender to her the jewels my husband gave me out of love. I will not allow them to adorn a person who is a reproach to Christendom and is bringing scandal and disgrace upon the king through his taking her to such a meeting as this in France."

I heave a sigh of exasperation. "Princess—"

"Queen, Lord Norfolk!" Her voice is sharp. "You are addressing an anointed queen made by God, not man. Leave us!" she cries to her small assemblage of attendants and guards. When we are alone she rises from her throne of state and approaches me. She reaches up, cupping my face between her slim hands. "You have fallen very low, Lord Norfolk," she tells me, her face wrought with sorrow. "And I weep for you." She swipes my hair aside from my forehead and strokes my cheek. Her touch brings hot tears to my eyes. I cannot look away. "You were supposed to be his friend, but ambition and greed have eclipsed even your loyalty to the preserving of the king's soul. Now you risk not only your eternal reward but your sovereign's by pushing your niece to this terrible apex, which will amount to nothing but disaster, I promise you." She pauses, then adds in a small voice. "You were my friend and I loved you well. You saved me from the Scots at Flodden, remember?"

"It was a different time," I say.

She drops her hands to her sides. "A man of the changing times. I imagine it was a different time as well, then, when you treated your wife with the respect due her. You make the duchess suffer as I suffer. I pray if nothing else you will be led to do right by her—"

"Highness, the jewels," I interpose, impatient with her monologue. I've no time for self-examination and guilt. The choices I have made have all been to serve a greater purpose and I owe no one an explanation for them.

She scowls. "Tell my husband that I will not surrender the jewels unless he commands it directly."

"Highness, you make your life very difficult," I tell her.

"You are dismissed from my presence, Lord Norfolk," she tells me. "I will continue to pray for your soul."

I bow once more and turn to leave.

"Thomas!"

I stop short at her call. I turn.

Her blue eyes are luminous with tears. "Why has my champion abandoned me?"

I stride toward her, seizing her hands in mine. I sink to my knees. "Dear lady, I love you well. Had things been different, had he never set eyes on . . . I had no choice. I *am* sorry, Highness. Truly."

She disengages herself from me, shaking her head, her face registering an expression of mingled sadness and horror. "You say you love me. I imagine you believe you love many people. But when you have 'no choice' but to abandon them, you will. Every last one of them, till all that remains is you. All alone. What will you do, Thomas, when there is no one left to abandon? Will you be sorry then, too?"

Fear surges through me as I entertain the thought, then dismiss it with impatience. My God, the audacity of this woman! It is women like her and Elizabeth and Anne that make this world a living hell.

I part my lips to speak, but she lays a hushing finger upon them.

Her voice catches. "Go, do your duty unto your king as your conscience advises," she whispers.

I leave, my mission a failure.

I suppose it does not matter. In the end the king commands her to relinquish the jewels and she has no choice but to obey.

King Henry gets what he wants.

Elizabeth Howard

No one will help me. My children are kept away, save young Thomas, who seeks no one out. He is a quiet, brooding child with little use for anyone. Henry, though married in name to the Earl of Oxford's daughter, Frances de Vere, lives at the French court with the king's bastard, Fitzroy, trying his best to be Thomas incarnate, while Mary remains "safe" at her father's side. Never can any sanctuary be found in their love.

When I write to my brother begging for asylum, he denies me, reminding me of my "willful and sensual" nature, whatever that means. It is probably some reference to my short-lived dream of marrying Ralph Neville. That I am willful is something that cannot be denied. But a woman with less will would have died long ago, either by Thomas's hand or by her own. Of course Bess has considerably less will than I and survives quite well. I ask myself why I cannot be like this soft, round woman everyone adores. I ask myself why I cannot be docile and submissive. The answer is always the same: it is not I, and I will not be broken into being someone else simply because it would be more convenient for Thomas. I am not an actor in a masque. I am myself and will remain true to it.

But at such a cost!

Thomas does not care. When he asks if I would attend the Boleyn whore when the king creates her Marquess of Pembroke, I refuse. Let Mary do it. She has been seduced by the black-eyed witch and loves her with the same devotion I do my queen, even so far as to become a reformist. She considers carrying her train an honor.

The snub earns me a beating, of course. But not by my husband's hand. It is as though it would expel too much of his own precious energy to dole out the necessary discipline, so he contents himself by watching the servants do it. They are more than happy to oblige.

His visits are fleeting, however, and when he is here, he closets himself in Bess's apartments. And Bess, that doe-eyed girl whose sympathetic countenance coupled with her harlotry causes me to retch in anguish, is rendered impotent by fear and stupidity and the same lovesickness that has made us all helpless to Thomas at one time or another, though there is very little about the man to love. I believe, however, that when one is forced to endure another human being for life, one must seek something endearing in the other, else be driven mad. So that is what we have done. We have invented reasons to love this man, for whatever he is, in order to preserve our delicate hold on sanity. Whether it is true or not, knowing there is someone to love makes our pathetic lot easier.

It is a mixed blessing when in 1533 Bess leaves Kenninghall. I take joy in the fact that she will no longer be about to serve as a constant reminder of my husband's treachery but misery that she has left to serve at the court of "Queen" Anne Boleyn, the whore who has torn the world apart for sinful lust of a married man. For this slut, King Henry has abandoned papal authority, named himself head of the Church of England, and invalidated his marriage with Catherine with the help of the Archbishop of Canterbury, thus enabling them to marry at last. Even before their "wedding," her belly was swollen with the supposed prince Henry is so keen on getting, confirming every nasty thought I ever wasted on her. This is the woman to be held above all others; this travesty is to be our sovereign. This "Queen" Anne Boleyn.

As for the true queen, the one and only queen of Henry's England, she languishes in her own hell, exiled to a northern castle, separated from her daughter and all those who love her. My heart yearns to comfort her and in her find comfort for myself.

But Bess is gone, so I shall take comfort in that. To resent her for usurping my rightful place at court is useless. I would not serve Anne Boleyn even if there were never any Bess and my husband were mad with love for me. Nothing can coax me there, not even the news that my daughter Mary will wed the king's bastard, Henry Fitzroy. I cannot abide attending. This was just one more thing orchestrated by Anne Boleyn, and I will not sit there and watch it as though I am giving sanction to anything she does.

I sit out Mary's wedding night sewing shirts for the poor. I pray for her, my Mary, a child as foreign to me as the New World. Regret leaves a bitter taste in my mouth. Had things been different, I would have helped my daughter ready herself for her passage into womanhood. I would have given her counsel on what to expect, what to hope for, and what reality may serve instead. I would have brushed her golden hair and kissed her and praised her beauty in her wedding gown. It could have been as my Cathy's wedding day, filled with promise and joy . . . No. Not Mary. Never her. She is not mine.

From the first day Thomas set eyes on her, she was his, whether out of guilt for the circumstances bringing her into this world, or out of something darker I have no need to explore. She is his, his and some other place, some fey country unattainable to me. The chasm that began at birth has only grown with time, and I fear I may never bridge it. What's more, I fear I may not want to. I blink against the tears that obscure the garment I am stitching. There is nothing to be done. Nothing but to hope she can find some happiness in her marriage and that she will be freed from the influence of her father and that wicked court as soon as possible.

Bess Holland

It is very strange and exciting at this court, a court made so happy by its merry new queen, who presides over us displaying her pregnant belly with pride. Never in my wildest fantasies could I have ever conceived of waiting on a queen, let alone a queen who is Anne Boleyn, the same woman I served as a young girl.

I am not on close terms with her. She has changed. She is hardened, jaded, and the more I observe her, the less merry she appears. There is a frantic edge to her; the joy she radiates is fringed with desperation and I pity as much as admire her.

She has only spoken to me once, to tell me I was most lucky to have found favor with her, for she does not suffer wantons at her court. "It seems you have done well with your duke," she added with a snicker. All I could do was bow.

She has made it clear that I am here because my lord wishes it and since Queen Anne owes much of her crown to his guidance, my presence is a debt paid. I am in the company of many Howards, Mary among them, but she has her own friends now, and despite the love we bear each other and the fact we are in the same place, we have grown in different directions. Mary belongs to an erudite circle. Queen Anne's is a court who reads and writes poetry. I cannot read or write a word, not even my own name, and the duke said it was pointless to spend money engaging a tutor for me. So I am on the fringes of this world. But it is a world I never thought to be a part of to begin with, so I am happy with my lot. I dance and make merry. There are a lot of gentlemen here my age and they are fun to flirt with as long as the duke does not notice. After witnessing the treatment of the duchess, I am careful in all I do.

One of the events I hold most dear in the beginning of Queen Anne's reign is the wedding of my beloved Mary Howard. It signifies so much for so many. For Queen Anne, it is establishing that Fitzroy is no longer a serious contender for the throne. For His Grace, it is the union of his child with that of a king—a most useful alliance. For Mary, it means a chance at happiness, God grant it. And for me, it means hope. Mary's little face radiates it and I absorb its light, knowing if she can forge happiness in this tempest, so can I.

At her wedding feast she dances with her father-in-law, the mightiest man in the world, King Henry VIII, and her husband, whom she is obviously very fond of, the sweet Harry Fitzroy. She dances with her father, and I watch him reach up to touch her hair.

The duke's eyes follow her all evening, enslaved by something I have never understood. It matters not where we are; when Mary is present, my lord has eyes only for her.

When I learn that he will not allow her and Fitzroy to live as man and wife, my gut churns in sympathy.

"Why won't you let her go?" I entreat him. "She would be much happier with her own household to run and ladies to attend her. Why, I could attend her! I would love it! Far more so than here—here it is so lonely and no one bears any love for me—"

His Grace's cheeks flush with a rage I thought to be reserved for anyone but me.

"Yours is an opinion not needed, Bess," he tells me in his calm, even tone. "Best remember your place."

I should never have challenged him. His word, after all, is always the last word. I bow my head, saddened less for Mary than I am over the thought that my opinion is not wanted, let alone needed, by the only man I am allowed to love.

Kenninghall

Elizabeth Howard, March 1534

"Do you think I'm asking for your opinion on this?" Thomas's face is as red as a Tudor rose. His black eyes are narrow. They have developed a permanent squint from his ever-present scowl.

"Of course not!" I cry. "When have you ever asked my opinion on anything?" I add with a bitter laugh. "But as it is, I am giving it and my opinion is no. I will never grant you a divorce, not as long as there's breath in my body."

Thomas hesitates a moment, as though entertaining the possible consequences of moving that process along, then bites his lip, slamming his fist on the desk. "Why? Why do you want to remain in this farce of a marriage?"

I shake my head, keeping my voice very low. "You are the king's man in every way, Thomas. Following his example to the letter. First taking a mistress, then hoping to set your lawful wife aside for her. I have given you five children, along with my tears and suffering. I will not give you Bess as a reward for my pain."

"I'll give you whatever you want," he tells me. "Most of my plate, my jewels, anything. Come now, don't be a fool. What do you expect to gain from our marriage?"

"My soul, a commodity you do not think much on," I tell him.

He flinches. "I may have to die to gain my reward, but it is worth it to watch you writhe. You will not have everything, Thomas. You think because your niece is on the throne and your daughter is married to a king's bastard that you can rule the world, but you have never been able to rule my heart. Never. And that is why you hate me, isn't it? Because you cannot control me like you control Bess and Mary. I will not give you your divorce, Thomas Howard, and make our children illegitimate. You will not have your happy ending, you can count on it, even if I have to appeal to the king himself."

Thomas shakes his head. "Very well, then, Elizabeth. You give me no choice. You may remain my wife but as my obedient wife—being so fond of the Lord's commandments, I imagine you will recall the verse about wifely submission—you are no longer permitted use of Kenninghall or any of my other estates save Redbourne. You will retire there, Lady Norfolk, and cling to the knowledge that you are my wife. Either way, I shall be quite happy, I can assure you. I had just thought to give you this opportunity so you can seek out some happiness of your own—it is clear we have some . . . er, how would you phrase it mildly? Differences of opinion?" He shrugs. "But I should have known you would take the hard road, as always. Such a fool." He reaches out, tracing my jawline. His eyes mist over. He turns away. "Elizabeth, it wasn't that I didn't care for you . . ." He shakes his head violently, then straightens his back, squaring his shoulders. "You need time. I understand. Why should all this be decided today, after all? It is a lot to take in. I feel it only fair that I give you the opportunity to reconsider."

Thomas takes my arm and begins to escort me out of my apartments down the hall toward one of the turrets of Kenninghall, where he throws me into one of the barren chambers with such force I land on the cold stone floor.

"You may think about it in here, where there are no distractions," he tells me. Then, his voice still as calm as if he were planning out the menu for a feast, he calls the servants. "Please remove the duchess's apparel and jewels. I do not want any distractions. She is greatly afflicted in her mind."

Stripped to my shift and humiliated, I draw my knees up to my chest. "You'll be cursed for this, Thomas," I tell him in quiet tones that are fervent with conviction. "God will see that you pay."

Thomas shrugs. "What more can God do to me?" he counters. "Now. I'm leaving you, my dear. I'll let you and God work it out in here. I will give you ample time to make the right decision."

With an exaggerated bow, Thomas quits the room. I hear the turn of the key and at last allow the tears to fall.

If I had not been before, there is no doubt now—I am my husband's prisoner.

But I choose to be. For if I grant him his divorce, no amount of his plate will compensate for the fact that I will be left with nothing. No children, no family to side with me. Nothing. No one.

If I have become vengeful, then so be it. I will not yield to his desires. No matter how ill used I have been, he will not have it all. He will have to kill me first.

And so after a month's imprisonment without straying from my initial decision in regard to his desired divorce, I am removed to Redbourne. Another mixed blessing. No one abuses me here and I am left in peace.

But I am completely isolated. No gentlemen visit me and very few gentlewomen, save whom my lord appoints. Even from afar his hand extends to daily life and I am allowed no true friends.

It is a very lonely life.

Bess Holland

I didn't know one could be so lonely amidst this many people. But with a court who regards me as the previous court regarded Queen Anne, and a duke who has very little time for me, I find more often than not that I am alone, longing for something I cannot identify. I ache and yearn but know not for what. Every need is satisfied. The duke keeps me dressed in the best and I am adorned with the most beautiful jewels one could ever set eyes upon, but still my gut churns with a desire for . . . what?

And then it comes to me, the answer, in the form of a bonny

babe with soft red curls and piercing black eyes. Princess Elizabeth, cherished daughter of Queen Anne and a source of great disappointment to king and country. Her birth changes everything for everyone. It softens Queen Anne's eyes as much as it hardens the king's. It frustrates the duke and causes the kingdom to scoff and curse.

As for myself, it serves as the embodiment of all of my hopes. A child. I long for a child of my own to love.

When I broach the subject with His Grace, he laughs.

"Don't be a fool!" he cries, holding my face in his elegant hands and kissing my nose. "You can play with any number of children if you long for such a thing and have the convenience of returning them to their proper owners afterward. And I will not allow you to have a child out of wedlock."

"But I do everything else out of wedlock!" I cry.

The duke gathers me in his arms. "Now, now, Bess, do not make an issue of this. You do not want to risk my displeasure, do you, sweetheart?" He pulls away, looking into my tear-streaked face and tilting my chin up to face him. "Be a good girl, Bess, as you have always been to me. Be my good, sweet girl."

"Yes, Your Grace," I sob.

From that day on, the duke is very careful about ensuring that I do not become with child.

I am not the only one with that longing. Denied the joy of living as a true wife, Mary Howard Fitzroy seems to grow more wistful with each passing year. And poor Queen Anne, in an effort to bring England a prince, suffers three miscarriages and the waning affections of her husband. He treats her with the same disregard he treated his first wife, taking on mistress after mistress until he has become enamored with one of her ladies-in-waiting, the painfully pious Jane Seymour. My lord hates this development and curses his rival family with vehemence, but he is powerless to stop what happens next.

The king will rid himself of his precious Anne Boleyn, who is now branded a witch and whore. Even her new pregnancy does not stop his pursuit of the meek and mild Lady Jane.

Then in January 1536, the former queen Catherine of Aragon

dies. In a celebratory joust, the king falls from his horse, suffering severe injuries. It is left to His Grace to inform my lady.

Thomas Howard

Damn, damn, damn! All she had to do was have a boy. Is that too much to ask? Heaven and much of earth was moved in order to install this bitch as queen of England and she has proven a constant failure to us all. Since she came to power, England has been thrust into chaos. Thomas More, my sweet friend, adhered to his mighty principles and martyred himself to the axe rather than sign an oath acknowledging her as queen and her children as the true heirs to the throne. It was just as he said—he died first. Maybe I will be next. . . . No. No, I will never be next because I know how to play the game. More did not. He perished along with old Bishop Fisher and several monks, all of them far too good ever to have been thrust into this world to begin with. I suppose death was rather like going home to them.

I sobbed when they died. Stupid men! God curse the high and mighty!

My sweet More is dead and for what? For a barren queen who is a stain on the Howard name and a useless girl-child. Why did King Henry have to have her so badly? Why couldn't he have been satisfied with Queen Catherine? God knows a better queen will not be found, not ever. But I will not think of her. I will not think of her face upon our last meeting, her hand on my cheek, her dignity in the face of such grand scale disrespect. . . . No. It serves me not. Oh, had we but known she would pass this year, he could have remarried and had a baby then! The cruelty of fate!

I am through with Anne. It is clear she has little time left on her throne before the fickle king takes up with the Seymour slut. I must begin my detachment from her. I am not a fool. I know when to stand aside and how to retain favor.

When the king is injured on the tiltyard, it is my unpleasant duty to inform the queen. I storm into her apartments, staring the disappointment in the face.

"The king has been wounded and will most likely die," I tell her.

"No!" she cries. "And I? What will become of me?" Her obsidian eyes make an appeal to me as she rises and strides toward me, taking my hands in hers. "Shall I be regent till the princess attains her majority?"

I offer a bitter laugh. "Are you truly so deluded?" I shake my head. "Think you not on any of that. That is a nightmare unworthy of entertaining at present. No, Your Majesty," I add with a trace of mockery. "You have only one duty, to give us a prince. If you can do that, perhaps there is hope for you yet."

"And if I don't?" she cries.

"Then God save you," I tell her. "For no one else will."

She shakes her head, eyes wide with horror as she doubles over, cradling her swollen belly. "Oh, God, Uncle Thomas!" She offers a groan that causes me to back away in terror. "The baby is coming! Please help me!"

"Fetch a midwife!" I cry and remove myself from her presence.

Despite what I know in my heart, I pray for her. Her destruction, after all, could spell my own.

The delivery of her stillborn monster confirms it. Anne's days are numbered.

The king recovers, sustaining a leg wound but no worse for wear and more determined than ever to be rid of who he now refers to as The Witch. In April, charges are contrived against six men for having criminal knowledge of the queen. One of them is her own brother. Charges are then brought against Anne: witchcraft, plotting to poison Lady Mary, adultery, treason, and incest. The last is needless and horrid. I am sickened.

The task of interrogating and arresting her falls upon me. She does not argue with me for once but carries herself with the dignity of her station, declaring her innocence with cool control and allowing me to escort her to the Tower, her arm looped through mine.

"I have no choice, Anne," I tell her. "Believe me."

"Of course you don't. You are a Howard, after all," she says, her voice laced with irony. I am reminded of my last conversation with Queen Catherine, when I told her I had no choice but to abandon her as well. But I didn't have a choice. Not then and not now.

What can I do but be the king's man, else lose my own head?

Four of the six men arrested are killed, either hung, drawn and eviscerated, or sacrificed to the axe. I preside over the trials. It is my duty to the king, and God knows I do my duty well. At this crucial hour, it is vital I am viewed as nothing but King Henry's loyal servant.

My nephew George was among those killed, my proud handsome nephew who dared read his charges aloud, charges brought against him by his treacherous wife, Jane. I sentence him to death, as is the king's pleasure. All of it is for his pleasure.

Anne is tried as well. I preside and watch my niece carry herself with more dignity than ever before. If she did not live as a queen, she dies as one.

I find her guilty as do the rest of her peers and am forced to sentence her to death by beheading or by burning, again at the king's pleasure.

I weep looking at her. Not only for my lost opportunities but for the baby I once held in my arms so many years ago at her baptism, the baby who challenged me with her steady black gaze so like my own.

There is naught to do but witness her beheading, holding that black gaze till she is blindfolded. I do not look away, not even as the French sword cuts through her swanlike neck and the crimson blood pours onto the straw below, red as rubies.

At once I am reminded of my daughter Mary's childhood dream of a pretty lady wearing a ruby necklace that drips blood. . . . Can it be the child possessed that frightening gift known as the second sight? If so, what horror has she forecast for the house of Howard? I shake my head, closing my eyes against the horrific thought. It was a dream, a horrible dream and a queer coincidence. These reflections do me no good. There is nothing to be done. Anne is dead. Gone. And with her my hope of a Howard sitting the throne of England.

The night after her death I lie stunned in Bess's arms.

"We will remove to Kenninghall," I tell her. "Just for a while. I will think there of what to do."

Bess is wide-eyed and horrified. "Was any of those horrible things they said about Queen Anne true, Your Grace?" she asks in her tiny voice. "Any at all?"

I turn toward her. "It was as she said at the trial. Her one sin was not giving the king the respect due him. She was blameless, Bess."

"And you sentenced her anyway? You said she was guilty, even though you knew she was not?"

"I had to, Bess. To preserve my own life," I tell her.

Bess crawls out of bed and begins to back away from my out-stretched hand. She is shaking her head in terror.

"Don't be afraid, Bess," I tell her. "For God's sake, don't be afraid of me."

"You would let me be killed, too," she whispers in horror. "If you had to, you'd let everyone close to you die. Wouldn't you?"

"Come back to bed, Bess," I order with impatience. "Get these thoughts out of your head."

Bess inches forward, but when she again lies in my arms she is trembling.

I turn away so she cannot see the tears paving hot trails down my cheeks. What is the point of any of this anyway? Why don't I just retire to the country for good?

But I won't do it. I know I won't. I will not lose. I may retreat but I will not go away. I will rise again. I am Thomas Howard and I will survive this as I have survived everything else.

Days after the execution, the king marries Jane Seymour and crowns her queen. Her children will be the only heirs. My little grandniece, the pretty Elizabeth, is now among his growing list of bastards.

That same summer, my son-in-law Henry Fitzroy dies, suppos-edly of consumption but it is my belief that he was poisoned in a plot to remove him from the succession. It is a horrid time to be alive, waiting and wondering who will be struck down next.

I take my little girl to Kenninghall, my precious baby Mary, a widow mad with grief and who must now fight for her inheritance.

There we will think of something. I will regain my favor with the king and come up with a new alliance for Mary. There is hope. She can still be useful to me, and at least with Fitzroy gone, I can keep her with me a little longer yet.

Yes, I will get through this.

I will press on.

The Redbourne Years

Elizabeth Howard

Strange to think they both died in the same year, the true queen and the false one. I am sick with grief for both of them. I expected to mourn for my Catherine, but at least I am assured that she is in Heaven with her Lord and five children. Her suffering has ended at last. No longer do I have to fret over her in her exile, no longer do I have to worry about her failing health, no longer do I have to rail against all those who have shown her such profound disregard. I am at peace with Queen Catherine's death; far better she does not see what her husband has become.

It is what I feel upon learning of Anne's wrongful execution that stirs an unforeseen amount of grief in my aching breast. I think of all the terrible things I called her, all the accusations and confrontations and battles fought in her name. She was not the cause. She was a mere girl, a tool of greed and ambition. Her entire life, forces worked for and against her and all of them so much stronger than she could ever have been. Now at twenty-nine she is dead and a child is motherless.

The injustice of it all is like taking in the sight of a fortress for the first time: awe-inspiring for its sheer magnitude.

My daughter loses the husband she never had that same year and Thomas cloisters her at Kenninghall while Bess is in another one of his manors. I remain here, of course, and am not allowed to comfort my daughter in her time of bereavement, though what consolation I could give, I have no idea. Yet, if I could, I would tell her to be strong, that there is hope. She is a young woman with endless possibilities before her. She could know happiness and love yet if she would persevere. And if there is any of myself in her . . . but there is not. She is of another world altogether, made of some ethereal substance brilliant for its beautiful transience. And though I do not doubt her will and intelligence, I bear the inexplicable knowledge somewhere in the core of my being that Mary will be deprived of any true joy. So long as her father rules her. So long as she allows it. And she will allow it, that much I also know.

I must not think on her overmuch, else I be devoured in regret.

Instead, from the safety and loneliness of Redbourne, I learn of the happenings at court. My husband rises to prominence again when he puts down the Pilgrimage of Grace, a papist revolt against the dissolution of the monasteries and the king's general perversion of the Catholic faith. Our son Henry, Lord Surrey, fights alongside his idol and together they put down their fellow Catholics and are praised as heroes.

Jane Seymour gives birth to the desired heir, Prince Edward, only to die twelve days later. The country is thrust once more into grief and the hunt is on for her replacement.

The king is cursed, I believe. His own actions against his first wife have cursed his subsequent marriages, and no wife of his will ever know a day of happiness.

As these dramas unfold, I write to Thomas Cromwell, a rising star at the court of Henry VIII and a rival of my husband's. Now named Privy Seal, it is Cromwell who has the king's ear above all others, much to my husband's consternation. As such, Cromwell is my only hope for attaining some justice. I do not hope to win my husband from the arms of his harlot. What I need is money. I cannot live on this pathetic amount. I have servants to pay, a manor to run, and food to put on the table. My daily expenses are driving me into debt. If my daughter Mary can be granted a pension for an unconsummated marriage, then I must have some rights to claim.

I send appeal after appeal, pouring out to Cromwell every crime

Thomas has ever committed against me without shame. I will humiliate Thomas into doing right by me. Cromwell's responses are polite and filled with empty promises. Nothing changes. Thomas's letters are filled with threats and remonstrations for my "slander." If I recant and apologize, he will consider granting me a larger annuity.

But I remind him of the vow I spoke to him years ago, that I will speak only the truth, and thus avowed, I cannot recant or apologize for that would be lying.

I never receive a letter from Thomas again.

Thomas Howard, 1540

Cromwell thinks he is crafty and clever, the very right hand of the king, he thinks he is, but he will be brought down and I will be the one to do it. For too long he has been allowed to hover about, whispering in the royal ear, advising and manipulating to suit his desires. Knave and scoundrel! His taunts ring in my ears; he delights in throwing his correspondence with Elizabeth in my face.

"Norfolk, aren't you the happy man," he chuckled when last we met. "Your wife has nothing on you, for if she did, I think she might undo you." How his narrow eyes lit up with that statement, as though he could not wait to help her bring me down! But I will show him. I will show him just as I showed Wolsey. No one fights the Howards and wins.

Cromwell is victorious at the moment, however. His cleverness has secured for the king a Protestant sow from Germany in the hopes of Lutheranizing England. He will not succeed. As it is, Anne of Cleves's German maids will be replaced with good English ladies-in-waiting and I begin to scout out members of my family to secure places at court for as many Howard girls as possible before she arrives.

This task requires a visit to my stepmother's London residence, where I am told resides the daughter of my late brother Edmund. They await me in the parlor, the girl dressed in a gown that verifies my brother's modest estate. Despite this, her beauty is undeniable. Auburn hair cascades down her back in thick waves and her eyes sparkle as blue as the sunlit sea.

I nod to my stepmother and she curtsies, leaving us alone. I sit in one of the Dowager Duchess's hard wooden chairs and shift in discomfort.

The girl offers a clumsy curtsy. For a moment we stare at each other, making assessments. Then, to my shock, she runs toward me and jumps onto my lap, wrapping her arms about my neck and kissing me on the cheek.

"Oh, Uncle, I'm so glad you came to visit me!" she cries in delight. "No one ever comes to see *me!*"

"So you're Catherine," I say at last, resisting the urge to push her off me. She could prove very useful so must be handled with care. I wrap my arms about her tiny waist, assessing with as much subtlety as possible her hips. They are rounded and ready for childbearing. It appears she is blessed with the body of a twenty-year-old, the angelic face of a ten-year-old, and the mind of a complete idiot: a perfect combination for my purposes . . .

"Kitty," she corrects me. "I'm Kitty."

"Ah, Kitty," I say, reaching up to stroke her lustrous hair. It is like silk under my fingertips. "Tell me, Kitty, you must be a very grown up lady. Have you your courses yet?"

She flushes bright crimson. "Yes, for about six months now," she tells me, bowing her head.

"And how old are you?"

"Fourteen," she says, raising her head. It is obvious she is proud of achieving this great age.

"Fourteen!" I cry. "Tut-tut, old girl! It is a sin for a grand lady of fourteen to be shut away at Norfolk House. How would you like to come to court with Uncle Thomas?"

"Court? Me?" she cries in delight. "Oh, Uncle Thomas, but I would!"

"Will you be a good girl and listen to everything I say and follow my every command?" I ask her in severe tones.

Her large blue eyes grow even wider with fear. "Yes, of course I will!" she insists.

"Good Kitty," I say, drawing her close so we are cheek to cheek. "I will make certain you have everything you desire. Gowns and pretty hoods and slippers, jewels even. As long as you are always my good girl."

"I will be, Uncle Thomas!" she cries. "Oh, I will be!" She hugs me tight, kissing me full on the mouth before pulling away. I can barely control the urge to wipe the kiss away. Though there was nothing sexual in it, I am disconcerted and annoyed at being invaded by this little dolt. "Can I go tell my friends now?" she asks.

"Yes," I tell her, forcing patience into my voice. "Go tell your friends that you are leaving them to become the great Kitty Howard."

She offers a smile to light up the darkest night and blows me a kiss. "Dear Uncle Thomas, you've no idea what you're rescuing me from. . . . I love you!"

I wave her off and she skips down the hall, laughing and singing.

She is perfect, I think to myself, a little triumph.

With her I can solve two problems: Cromwell and the resurrection of lost dreams.

A Howard Rose

Thomas Howard

The 1530s proved turbulent for the Howards but we pulled through, ushering in the next decade with renewed purpose. This promises to be our best years yet. Oh, there have been pitfalls. My children have all proven to be disappointments in their own right. Mary refused an advantageous alliance with young Prince Edward's uncle Tom Seymour at her brother Lord Surrey's urgings while the latter grows more impulsive and hotheaded with each passing day, landing himself in confinement more often than not. As for my youngest son, Thomas, he has become an impassioned reformist and I have very little use for him.

Mary is still valuable, however, and serves at the court of Anne of Cleves alongside her pretty cousin, the newest Howard star, my little niece Kitty.

To my utmost satisfaction, the king seems disposed to rid himself of the poor German in record time. She repulses him for some reason, though I don't find her altogether unappealing. It's just as well for my purposes, however, and I take every opportunity to thrust the delicious Kitty in His Majesty's view. Her gowns I take particular interest in, making sure they are designed to accentuate every generous curve to the best advantage, paying attention to the neckline. It must be low enough for the king to appreciate her lovely white bosoms but not too low so as to appear wanton.

Kitty is a natural and, almost without knowing it, plays right into the king's hands. And her protective, doting uncle takes every opportunity to place her in his path. He must see that this beautiful and sensual creature is supervised and cared for, preserved as a prize he will certainly claim as his own.

Kitty is malleable and agreeable to everything I say, so unlike her unfortunate cousin and predecessor Anne. Her lack of wit and basic intelligence, however, is aggravating at times. It isn't as though she is stupid. She is just so young. . . .

And the king is so old. Eighteen years my junior and one would never guess. I have retained my excellent form through discipline and moderation, while excess and decadence has reduced the man once deemed the handsomest prince in Christendom to a grossly overweight pig with a rotting leg oozing with an ulcer that never heals. It turns my stomach to serve him up with this pretty babe. But the end result will make it all worth it. And Kitty is a flighty, superficial thing; she will love the thought of the shiny crown upon her head and will think nothing of putting up with a few minutes of the huffing and puffing king as long as the presents keep coming.

And they do. The king and I keep her well supplied. Kitty loves her gowns and hoods, her slippers and jewels. But of all the things she loves, it surprises me to find that it is her pets that give her the most pleasure. When one day I approach her in the gardens with a little gray kitten, she holds it to her face in delight, rubbing her cheek against its soft fur.

"A kitty for my precious Kitty," I tell her, reaching out to stroke her own lustrous auburn locks. God, she is beautiful.

Tears light her round blue eyes. "Oh, thank you, dearest Uncle. She's so sweet," she coos. "Remember when I was a little girl and you let me play with your dog at Norfolk House?"

I struggle to summon the memory. "Storm?" I ask, recalling the greyhound Queen Catherine sent me upon my recovery from the sweat.

"Yes, do you still have him?" she queries, still rubbing her cheek against the kitten.

I nod. "He's getting old. He's a good dog," I tell her. "I'm certain the sight of you would rejuvenate him."

She giggles in appreciation. She is easily won, a trusting girl. A strange lump swells in my throat at the thought. I swallow hard.

At once we note a procession of the king's guard, followed by His lumbering Majesty as he attempts to take some exercise.

"Norfolk!" he cries, but his beady eyes are on my niece. "How now, dear friend?"

"Quite well, Majesty," I answer, bowing. I elbow Kitty to curtsy. She does so, never taking her eyes away from her treasured kitten.

"And my little kitten," he nearly growls, "how goes it with my precious gem?"

She flushes and smiles. "I'm so happy, Majesty!" she cries, holding out the kitten. "Look what Uncle Thomas gave me."

The king reaches out a fat bejeweled hand to stroke the animal's tummy. Something about the gesture repulses me and I find myself taking Kitty's hand and squeezing.

"You like pets, little Catherine?" he asks her in sweet tones. She nods. "Then I shall make certain you have the entire menagerie at the Tower of London at your disposal!"

"Oh!" She claps her hands. "Will you take me to see them?" she asks.

"Of course I will," he says. "Now run along and play, sweetheart. It pleases me to see you frolic. Later I will set a nice private supper for us with all the entertainments you like."

"Yes, Your Majesty," she answers, dipping into another curtsy, then rising and wrapping her arms about me, kissing my cheek. "Thank you for my kitten. I love you," she tells me as she does every time we greet and part. Never in my life have I been subject to such a harangue of affection. I tolerate it as I must, thinking of the end result and knowing that, unlike my children, there must be something missing in this girl to make her crave male attention so. So I do not push her away. Having her love makes my task much easier. Unlike Anne, there are no quarrels or matches of wits. She is much like my Bess in this manner, full of "Yes, Uncle, no, Uncle." Had she been born years sooner, perhaps we could have avoided the whole Anne debacle altogether, for the court is in agreement: Never before has anyone seen the king so in love with a woman as with this girl, this little Kitty Howard.

When she is out of earshot, the king wraps his heavy arm about my shoulders and we begin to promenade, he leaning on me as though any moment he might fall down. It takes all of my strength to hold him up. Fortunately, carrying eighty pounds of armor on my slim frame for so many years prepares me for this and I walk as though unburdened.

"Ah, Thomas," he tells me. "You have known me since I was born," he comments, his eyes misting over with nostalgia.

"A blessed day, Majesty," I remark.

He smiles at this. "Your first four children were my first cousins and your wife my aunt. You've been my uncle twice over now. What would you say to a third time?"

I smile. "Your Majesty," I say, patting his hand. "Does this mean that you have thought about taking my little niece to wife?"

"Could it mean anything else?" he returns. "Oh, Thomas, but she is so lovely. What is it with you Howards? There is some magic in your blood for you to produce these women. . . ." For a moment his eyes grow stormy and I stiffen, knowing he is thinking of Anne. But the dark look passes, to my relief. I relax as best I can under his weight. "Really, Thomas, with a treasure like Kitty, I can't imagine why you didn't keep her for yourself."

I laugh. "Your Majesty, I have enough women to trouble me," I assure him with a hearty laugh. "One more would likely kill me."

He joins me, adding his robust laughter to my own. "I should say I am the authority on woman trouble!" he declares. "But then," he adds in a soft voice, "this girl is different. Oh, Thomas, she is so innocent and sweet. A rose without a thorn. So far she has warmed to me, to all my gifts and attentions. But I can't imagine her actually loving *me*. Do you think she could love me?"

Bile is rising in my throat. Why does anyone think love has a place in politics? But he is not like other kings. Every marriage, save with the German, has been for one perverse form of love or another.

"Kitty is a vessel of love," I say, thinking of the sweet little girl on my knee, the beautiful child who at every opportunity demonstrates nothing but affection for me and anyone else who bothers to pay even scant attention to her. Oh, what am I doing? God save this little innocent. . . . "I have every reason to believe she loves you a great deal," I finish, clearing away the lump in my throat.

"As a man or as a king?"

What does he want of me? "As a king, of course," I begin, "but more so as a man, a desirable man. Why, she can't say often enough how handsome she thinks you are," I lie. "She is in awe of you."

He enfolds me in a powerful embrace. "Oh, Thomas, my dear Thomas! You have made me a happy man! I will have her! Nothing will stop me. I will have her and crown her my queen and she will carry on the Tudor line. Nothing shall be denied her, not ever." His smile is so bright, it brings tears to my eyes. I don't understand it. This is a man who had my other niece beheaded, let my brother die in the Tower for loving his niece Margaret Douglas, and killed several of my friends. But I pity him. I pity him because he was once great and now he is pathetic, an injured lion that reflects only a semblance of his former glory.

Like my signet ring bearing the lion with its arrow-pierced tongue.

I am unnerved by the thought.

Animals in pain are known to lash out.

Elizabeth Howard

I have lost my one potential ally. Thomas Cromwell, once Earl of Essex and Privy Seal, was stripped of his titles, thrown into the Tower of London, then beheaded for treason because of his orchestration of the unfavorable marriage to Anne of Cleves, which ended in another annulment. He was called a traitor and a heretic, denying the presence of Christ in the Host during communion, or so they say. They will say anything.

I am told Thomas stripped him of his chains of office. I imagine it was difficult for him to refrain from breaking out into a jig at his victory over his hated rival.

Now another Howard sits the throne of England, little Kitty, a mere babe. I cannot summon the same hatred for her that I did for Anne Boleyn. Perhaps it is that I have grown up, perhaps it is because it takes too much effort now. Perhaps it is because I know who is behind it all, who controls the pretty marionette. Oh, God, it sickens me.

There is no hope of escape now. I have even written a letter to my Ralph, a letter my sister could read without feeling threatened, just wishing them well and hoping I can see them and their sixteen children soon. There is no bitterness in the letter nor in my heart. I find myself more often than not thanking God that some have been fortunate enough to find happiness in this world.

My son Henry, Lord Surrey, has four beautiful children I have never seen. I think of them often. I wish I could send them gifts and notes, but Thomas has convinced Surrey to see me as the enemy. I doubt anything I send would get to them.

So I live out my days at Redbourne. I have been ill; suffering as I did at the servants' hands at Kenninghall did me little good. My breastbone sustained serious injury and I often feel a stabbing pain in my chest.

Yet I am some sort of happy. It is a simple life but I keep busy. I tarry in my garden and take pride in its yield. I am proud to say I maintain the finest of figures by brisk walking. I busy myself in the stillroom concocting with the apothecaries all manner of lotions, oils, and possets to keep my skin youthful. I ride and hunt and hawk. I pray for my children and continue to follow my true queen's example of adhering to the Catholic religion, devoting time to charitable works, and focusing on the suffering of others rather than my own.

If my life is a testament of anything, it is one of endurance, which is a triumph in its own right.

Bess Holland, 1541

Queen Catherine has remained childless throughout her marriage to the king, and my duke laments it whenever he visits Kenninghall. He confides in me that he does not believe the man long for this world, hence the necessity of certain "measures" being taken to ensure the begetting of heirs.

"But nothing can be traced back to me," he assures me when noting my frightened expression. "Stupid Jane Boleyn—you'll remember her as the idiot who accused her own husband of incest with his sister Queen Anne." His eyes grow distant a moment, then he shakes his head, his face stony and impenetrable. "She thrives off intrigue like a maggot off dying flesh." He laughs. "She serves as a go-between for the queen and her beautiful golden boy, Thomas Culpepper."

"Oh, Your Grace!" I cry, scandalized and terrified. "But this is so dangerous for the poor child! Hadn't you better warn her?"

"But I don't know a thing, my Bess," he tells me. "Not a thing. And if it is played right, no one will be the wiser, and England will be all the richer. The king is so besotted with his innocent rose that he is rendered blind. They carry on nearly right under his nose!"

"How dreadful for her," I say in genuine sympathy. "Oh, to be so young and married to someone so old and . . . well, he isn't in the finest form these days. It's only natural for one her age to want the companionship of a young, virile gentleman." His Grace's expression does not change at all when I say this, as though he could not even entertain the notion of my statement being a subtle comparison of the queen's situation to my own, though I am far too afraid to be unfaithful to the duke. "She must be very naïve to believe she is not in any danger."

"Don't worry so, Bess," he tells me, pulling me into bed beside him. "Nothing can ever touch us, no matter what happens."

I snuggle against him, taking comfort in his promise. Despite everything, I am glad to have him home. He is as good to me as ever, showering me with gowns and jewels.

I try to tell myself that I can ask for nothing more.

But I was right to worry. It is not long before the whole affair with the queen and her young gentleman is brought to light, thanks to the treachery of a reformist zealot whose sister served in the Dowager Duchess of Norfolk's home, where the little queen was raised. He informed the Archbishop of Canterbury that the queen was precontracted in marriage to a man now employed as her secretary, one Francis Dereham, who confessed under torture to the affair conducted at Norfolk House years before Her little Majesty ever set eyes on the king. It didn't take long for the rest of the story to come to light after that. Culpepper was soon arrested and confessed to his criminal knowledge of the queen, along with a music master who served the girl as a child and tried to tangle with her then. All pay for their crimes with death. It is a sick thing that wrenches my heart, for despite everything, I know the child is innocent. She was unfaithful, of that there is no doubt. But she was a girl, a little girl in a big world, a child-woman who wanted to love a normal man. Why must they make her pay for that?

I hate the king and any man who takes what he wants and cares not who he sacrifices in the process. I pity the girls who are powerless in the face of such destructive desire.

I shall not be powerless. I have waited long enough to take what I want. I know there is little hope of true happiness for me, but I will take what little I can from what is available to me.

I will have my day.

Thomas Howard, 1542

Foolish slut confessed to everything! How is it such stupid people can claim themselves my relations? Yet she is only sixteen. . . . What logic could she possibly possess? Oh, God . . . I will not think of it.

I have retained favor, convincing the king I was in no way aware of the girl's antics, shifting the entirety of the blame onto the bony shoulders of Jane Boleyn (who deserves to die anyway for betraying George and Anne), little Kitty, and her lover. Perhaps as a test of my loyalty, I am given the duty of going to her at Syon Abbey, where she has been removed, that I might read her the Act of Attainder that is also her death sentence.

She is so tiny in her gray gown, this child I used to pet and spoil, this baby queen of England. My gut lurches when I see hope light her tear-filled eyes.

"You came!" she cries. "Oh, you came! I knew you'd help me."

She wipes her nose with her sleeve and stares up at me, as though waiting for a reassurance that will never come. "I didn't mean to be a bad girl, Uncle Thomas. I didn't mean to love Thomas Culpepper, truly. And now the king has had him killed, him and poor Francis—" She chokes on a sob, burying her head in her hands a long moment, her little shoulders quaking. "I did love His Majesty. He was always so good to me. If I could just see him and talk to him, I know I could make him understand—"

I shake my head. "He doesn't want to see you, Kitty," I tell her. "Not ever again. Don't you understand?"

"Will he put me away like he did Anne of Cleves? He was very kind to her. And he was so fond of me, like a father—"

I shake my head again. I cannot believe the girl is this naïve. "He wasn't your father, Kitty. He was your husband. He demanded the respect of a wife, not a daughter. What you did was treason, my . . . girl. You"—I swallow a frustrating onset of tears—"will not escape with your life."

"No!" she cries, stricken.

I avert my head. "Now you come with me. I will be escorting you to the Tower."

The little girl stares at me a moment, then runs toward me as if to offer an embrace. I back away.

"I'm afraid those days are gone," I tell her, not wanting to risk being seen sympathizing with the girl before the guards, who would happily report my actions to the king.

Kitty stares at me openmouthed. Tears stream down her cheeks unchecked. She shakes her head, mystified. "Even you don't love me anymore, Uncle Thomas? Why?" Her voice grows shrill with panic as though the thought of my abandonment is a cross she cannot bear. "Why don't you love me anymore, Uncle Thomas?"

I cannot look at her. I turn on my heel and proceed to the barge while the guards carry the screaming Kitty in their arms. She has to be held down throughout our passage to the Tower.

Still I do not look at her.

I cannot.

Bess Holland

His Grace returns to me, silent and brooding. He did not stay to witness Queen Catherine's execution; I imagine he does not want to watch another of his nieces die and be forced to examine the depth of his own betrayal. For the first few days, he walks Storm, his old greyhound from the first Queen Catherine. They promenade, two lonely figures in the snow, and the duke looks up at the sky as though searching the clouds for some sign of redemption.

The exercise is too much for the retired greyhound and one morning when His Grace fetches him for his walk, the gentle dog does not raise its head to his whistle. It had died in the night.

This seems to send His Grace beyond the edge of reason. He collapses on top of the animal in a fit of sobs. "No!" he cries, gathering the creature in his arms. "No, damn it! Why do they all die?"

I go to him and rest my hands on his shoulders, trying to pull him away from the dog. "Come, love, come . . ."

He raises his tear-streaked face up to me. "She was just a baby . . . she didn't know . . . Anne had all her wits about her; she played the game. She knew the risks. She wanted it badly enough not to care and, in the end, died more a queen than any of them, save perhaps Catherine of Aragon. But this little girl . . . this sweet little babe, she didn't know a damn thing. She just wanted her gowns and her pets and her jewels. . . . She wanted to go to court and play with her friends . . . and we took it away from her. . . . Oh, God!"

Fie on you! I want to scream. I want to curse his self-pity and his regret and compassion, all arriving conveniently too late to save his Anne and his Kitty both. Now they are gone and he is left scrambling to figure out a means to worm his way back into the king's heart, gaining whatever he can in the process. Regret! Yes, now he regrets, now that he has almost lost it all. He won't feel so repentant when he has secured the king's affections again. Then this will all be an unpleasant memory.

Yet I know my duke and have I not avowed to love him despite the dark side of his nature?

So I calm myself. I call for a servant to remove and bury the dog, then guide His Grace to his bed, where we sit side by side. I rub his back and coo soft endearments in his ear.

"My brother and sister-in-law, even my old stepmother, were put in the Tower for a while," he goes on, collecting himself. "The king will stop at nothing till all those who displease him are snuffed out. I cannot be in that number. You may think me evil for what I have had to do, but I will not be made a sacrifice to others' stupidity!"

"Of course not, Your Grace," I say and find myself, in a peculiar way, understanding. "You must not think of these terrible things anymore, my lord," I tell him. "You must think of the future, your great future. Haven't you always been able to rise above the rest?"

He stares straight ahead, determination replacing the tears in his black eyes.

"Now," I tell him, pouring him a large draught of red wine. "You're going to drink some wine and I am going to make you feel better like I always do."

"My sweet Bess," the duke murmurs, pulling me to his chest. Despite everything I know about this man, I wrap my arms about him. He has for years been the only home I have ever known and likely will be for life. Never will I understand why I love him, why in his absence there is relief and yearning, and why, even when I am angriest at him, he can almost justify the vilest of actions. What choice did he really have but to betray those poor girls? He can't die. He is the head of the Howard family and God knows young Surrey is not ready to fulfill that obligation yet. In his situation, would I not be forced to do the same?

After the duke has partaken of his wine, I turn down the covers and pat the vacant spot beside me. He crawls in, pulling me into his arms and covering my face with soft, gentle kisses.

I smile. I have not forgotten the dual purpose of this evening and as I give myself to His Grace, I know I am taking at last what has long been owed me.

Blossom of Hope

Bess Holland

It has worked! I am with child at last! His Grace has not been informed yet, though the baby has long since quickened. To my good fortune, my full figure conceals my pregnancy for the first four months and I do not share the news with a soul, not even Mary Fitzroy, who is too busy entertaining the king's niece Margaret Douglas to notice the changes in me.

But I cannot hide it forever. When my duke notes my weight gain (wrinkling his nose and declaring I shall have to watch myself) I offer my sweetest smile.

"I'm afraid that will have to wait until after your baby is born," I tell him.

He loses all expression, then sits on the bed. He draws in a deep breath, expelling it slowly. "Do you expect me to be happy about this, Bess, after I explicitly told you never to take this course?"

I lay a protective hand on my belly, swallowing hard, trying to choose my words with care. "I know, my lord, and I apologize. I did not mean for it to happen, of course. God meant it to. And now that it has, I am so happy. I do not care that I am unmarried."

"What about the child?" he demands. "Have you thought of it at all? Everyone will know it is my bastard, and the child will be forever branded the son of a whore."

"I will make certain the child grows up surrounded by love," I tell him. "I shall live a quiet life. I—want to live a quiet life, Your Grace."

"I will not acknowledge it," he tells me.

I bow my head.

He holds his hand out to me. I take it. "I shall send you to the manor in Lincolnshire I gave you last year, for the rest of your confinement. The child, of course, once it is born, will be installed at Norfolk House and raised with a proper family."

My heart begins to pound. My cheeks are hot and tingling. I cannot breathe. "What? No! For love of Jesus, why?"

"Because, Bess, it isn't right! The child needs a mother and father!" he shouts. "Keeping you as my mistress is one thing, but I'm not about to let you pop out a string of bastards for me to support! I did not choose you to be my breeder—I did not choose you to share yourself with anyone else! I wanted you for myself," he adds in softer tones. Tears stand bright in his obsidian eyes. "You do not know, you cannot know how painful bringing a child into this world is, Bess. In my life I have had nine children between both wives, and three survived. Three. Bess," he pleads, taking my hands in his. "Can't you see I'm trying to spare you?"

I sit beside him and take him in my arms. "Whatever heartbreak that God has set aside for me, I am ready to bear. But if it pains you too much, then you must not acknowledge it," I murmur, touched by his attempt at thoughtfulness. "Take it on as a ward."

He pulls away, rising with abruptness. Laughing a grating, shrill sound that makes me cringe in horror, he says, "A ward! One only takes on a ward if there is something to be gained from it! What could I gain from your child?" He turns away. "God, Bess, why did you do this to me?"

"To you? Why did I do this—to *you?*" I scream, all previous pity lost in the face of my fury that is at last unleashed as I behold the man who has controlled my every move since I was fifteen years old. "I suppose I have never given you any reason to believe that everything I have done has not been for or about you, Your Grace. So it may come as a shock that I have held fast to dreams of my own these past years." I swallow the painful lump rising in my throat, continuing in soft tones. "The only dream that ever seemed possible of making a reality is that of having a child of my own to love. It won't need a father if that is a role you cannot play. I will love it enough for both of us."

He turns, shaking his head. "No, Bess. No. I will not allow it. With time, you will understand why and thank me for it. The child will be installed at Norfolk House." He furrows his brow, scowling. "Stop looking at me that way!"

My eyes are wide with saddened bewilderment. "How could I be so wrong? I thought . . . I thought that because of the love you bore me, it would be natural for you to cherish our child. I know how difficult it has been for you with the duchess and your other children. But I thought—I hoped with us it would be different."

His Grace's face softens. He rests his hand on my shoulder, seizing my chin between thumb and forefinger and tilting my face toward his. "It is not as though I am turning it out into the street. It will be well provided for. I will see to its every need and secure for it as good a future as its station permits. So you must see how I care. But it cannot be how you envision; you must have known that. However, you may visit as often as you like as its auntie. Now. This subject is closed."

"Marry me off!" I seethe in desperation. His eyes widen. "Select a husband. You are powerful enough to find someone to take me, even in my condition. Marry me off and the child will have a proper set of parents."

"Are you daft?" he asks. "You would leave all this?"

All this? I want to scream. Can he be serious? What is it he has given me that really matters? Will any of it accompany me to Heaven, should I ever be fortunate to be allowed within its gates? I say none of these things, however. Instead I glower at him, saying in low tones, "I shall run away."

"And where would you go?" he asks, all gentleness replaced with his celebrated sarcasm as he mocks me with his sardonic smile. "How would you support yourself? You know everything I have given you would remain here. Who would help you? My daughter? Surely not. She would not risk my displeasure. Your father and brother? Do you think they would assist you in any way? They would be disgusted. You are nothing to them but a commodity;

once you have lost your worth, you are completely dispensable and they would dispense with you to keep my favor, have no doubt. Haven't they already? No, Bess Holland, there is no place for you to run. No place where you would not be known as Norfolk's cast-off whore. So what choice would you have but to become what you are best at? Working the streets of London and the like—"

"Shame on you!" I cry, hurling myself at him once more and clawing at his chest. "I have loved you all these years without asking for a thing in return and you would talk to me this way, you would do these terrible things to me? You are vile, Lord Norfolk. You are worse than the king. At least His Majesty kills those he claims to love; he does not curse them to linger in various states of misery and despair as you have allowed the duchess, Mary, and I to do!"

He disentangles himself from me. "Calm yourself at once, Bess, and apologize. You forget your place."

My place. Yes, I have forgotten my place.

I sit on the bed, exhausted. I bow my head. I know he is right. I cannot run away. I have done wrong. He told me years ago he wanted none of my children and I disobeyed him. No, there is no running away. My child deserves a better life than what I alone could provide.

But to give in . . . surely there is another way. . . .

I raise my head, beholding the duke again. Despite his fine form, he is old. He will not live forever. I shall bide my time, play auntie to my own child until he leaves this world and I can take back what is mine. There is no other way to play this game. After watching the duchess, I know too well what the duke is capable of and will risk neither my life nor that of this innocent child. So I will be sweet, acquiescent Bess. Obedient Bess. Till my blessed release from this man's insane translation of love.

"I'm sorry, Your Grace," I say, forcing sincerity into my tone. "I was very wrong."

He cups my cheek. "Good girl." He pauses a moment. "And if I said anything unkind, it was to remind you of the reality of your circumstances and illustrate how *others* would perceive you. Not me. Never me. You know that, don't you, sweetheart?"

"Yes," I lie. "Of course I do."

"Now," he tells me. "Let me hold you. You've always been my sensible girl. We'll sort this problem out together and you'll feel better in time."

This problem. His child is *this problem*. But in the deepest recess of my heart, how could I expect him to view it as anything other than an inconvenience, an annoyance? Oh, what have I done? Why have I allowed myself to be tangled in this web of hopelessness? Why didn't I run away years ago, when I was young and comely and could have had my pick of men? Now I am older, my hair is dull, and I am far too sturdy to be called shapely. And he is right about my family. They would be no help to me at all if it meant losing favor with their sacred employer. I would have nothing, no money, no family. No friends, for every friend I've ever had was bought and paid for by the duke. Every hope I have lies with this man. There is nothing to be done. Tears pave slick, cool trails down my cheeks as I yield to the helplessness enveloping me like a shroud.

In this state I allow myself to be enfolded in his arms, Norfolk's good girl to the end.

I am sent to Lincolnshire to spend the rest of my confinement. To His Grace's credit, he could not have chosen a better family to foster my child, nor could he have chosen a more capable midwife. Tsura Goodman has been bringing Howards into the world for almost fifty years; indeed, she delivered some of my lord's children, and knowing this creates an instant bond, for I never forget his children are the siblings of the little one stirring within me.

She is a marvel, this Gypsy woman. One would never think someone as wizened and weathered as she could still bring children into this world. To look at the dark, frail creature who squints so hard her eyes have become little slits in her head and to watch her hobble about with her cane, one would not consider her capable of doing much of anything at all. But never do I doubt her abilities. She is so reassuring; she does not judge me or ask unkind questions. She is full of energy, waking before the sun and falling asleep long after the rest of the household. It is as though she is the Great Mother keeping watch over everyone, making certain we are all quite tucked in and safe before she lets herself rest. To know her is to instantly love her. We pass many hours sitting by the fire and talking of this and that. I can cry with her. I can laugh with her. She is the mother and grandmother I never had.

Her grandson Alec Goodman is having a child due about the same time as mine and they have left their posts at Norfolk House to attend me. His young bride, Jenny, will serve as foster mother to my child; from her breast it will receive nourishment, from her lips it will receive comfort. . . . Oh, God, it kills me to think of it.

Yet they are kind people and if I cannot be there to raise my child, I cannot think of anyone more appropriate. They are excited about the prospect. Jenny understands; while she does not act overeager to take my child from my arms, she demonstrates a sincere wish to care for it as she would her own. I try to tell myself I can do this. I have to; he has given me no other choice. At least I am reassured that my child will be in loving, capable hands.

"I read his palm once, your duke," old Tsura tells me one evening as I sew baby clothes by the fire. "Quite against his will," she adds with a laugh. "All I saw in it was the power, that terrible power of his." She shudders. "It will undo him. Take care not to let it undo you."

"But it has undone me," I tell her brokenly.

Tsura shakes her head. "No, Bess," she says. "You are not undone. You are a clever one, far more so than you give yourself credit for. You will know at the crucial moment when to rely on that cleverness; he will not get the best of you, Bess Holland. I promise you that."

Hope stirs in my breast. I lay a hand on my belly. The baby kicks against my palm as if on cue and I emit a soft laugh. This is something His Grace can never take away from me, this feeling of a babe in my womb, the life he gave me, a gift that far surpasses any jewel he ever could bestow.

"Do you see this in a vision, my lady?" I ask her.

Tsura only smiles.

Somehow it is enough. This bit of power she has given me, this power of a promise, gives me hope that I will be happy. Someday . . .

*   *   *

Jane Elizabeth Goodman is born in the spring of 1543 when the king takes Catherine Parr to wife. His latest marriage has little affect on me when I hold my tiny girl in my arms, this small black-haired imp who gazes at me with her father's eyes. She is the image of him and thus her cousin Anne Boleyn as well. It is a startling resemblance that no one can mistake. She is Norfolk's daughter. Norfolk's and mine. This gives me a strange satisfaction and I question it. Is it that I love him still? How can I not love the father of my child? Is this what Duchess Elizabeth feels; is this why she could never divorce him, because of the bond she feels with the father of her children? Yet the father of our children is His Grace, this cruel, brutal man who loves nothing more than his own self. We are fools to feel anything for him. Yet we have been bound to him since childhood; he is all of love we have ever known. He is our past, our present, and, through these children, our future. There is naught to do but love him, if only for that.

His Grace does not come to see our girl, though he is made aware of her existence. I am allowed to tarry for a month, a blissful month of nursing and caring for my little lamb. I take pleasure in everything, every midnight feeding, every bath, every smile and gurgle. Every tear is kissed away. How creamy and smooth is her baby skin! How tiny are her hands and feet! I count her fingers, kissing each one; I kiss the soles of her silky baby feet. I sleep with her on my chest; she does not leave my side. For this one month she is mine, all mine, and I do not relinquish her for one moment.

"I am Bess Holland," I tell her, propping her up on my knees in bed and staring her hard in her earnest little face. She regards me with somber black eyes as though she is an active participant in the conversation. "I am Bess Holland and I am your mother. Always remember it, Jane. Always remember that I am your mother who loves you, and the great duke of Norfolk is your father."

Over and over I tell her this, hoping against hope that it ingrains itself in her young head. I tell her this until at last the great duke of Norfolk orders me home.

I kiss my babe and hold her close, sobbing great quaking sobs until at last I turn her over to Jenny.

"Take care of her," I urge the young woman, who only two months before was delivered of a lusty son. "Take care of my daughter. She is my heart."

"Oh, my lady!" cries Jenny with tears in her blue eyes.

I nod. "My treasure," I say again. "For where our treasure is, there our hearts will be also."

Jenny embraces me, the babe snug between our breasts, these breasts that will give her life and preserve my greatest love.

My treasure . . .

When I return home to His Grace, I sob violent tears against his chest. My breasts have dried yet they still ache for my child. I long for her warm weight in my arms, for her cry, for her smile.

"Better to lose her like this," His Grace tells me one night. He is leaving shortly for France to go to war and though a part of me will always love him, I cannot help nursing the hope . . . oh, God, it is a terrible hope. "Better to lose her like this," he says again, stroking my hair, "than to lose her as I lost mine. You distance yourself, Bess. It is better that way. Then when something happens, you can bear it. It's the only way to bear it. Bess." His voice catches. "Bess, I can't watch you become what I have become. I can't risk it."

I pull away, staring His Grace in the face. He is utterly broken. His onyx eyes are liquid with tears. I reach up and caress his cheek. He has warned me before that this is why he keeps Jane and me apart, in an effort to spare me any future pain. He is so afraid of the heartbreak her loss would cause both of us that he cannot suffer her presence. Neither can he let me go. In a strange way this renews my love for him.

"I understand," I tell him. And I do. I do not accept the situation any better. But I understand. I take his hands, squeezing them. "Oh, my lord, I have loved you since I was a child. All of my innocence has been given to you—everything I am has been given to you and now it seems I give you my suffering as well."

It is a suffering I shall bear. I look into his tearstained face. It is an old face. And as much compassion as I feel for this countenance, I know that it is mortal and I have but to wait. My suffering will end soon. My patience will be rewarded.

As I take His Grace in my arms, I think of his impending journey to France and of all the time it will allow me to spend with my daughter, my sweet little Jane.

Thomas Howard

Bess can think me as cruel as she pleases, but I did it for her. I did it for us. She will understand someday. She always understands. And even if the child were acknowledged, it would be raised much the same way.

Meantime I am on the king's business, but before I make war on France in His Majesty's illustrious name, I remove to Norfolk House to see the child. Perhaps I am getting soft in my dotage, but for some reason I cannot abide the thought of dying in the field without seeing my tenth child, this little bairn Bess and I created together.

Ah, but she is pretty, with skin like alabaster and hair as black as pitch. The keen eyes that stare back at me are black as onyx—my eyes, Anne Boleyn's eyes. I shudder a moment as I take her in my arms. I smile. She has the Howard nose, poor lass! But she has Bess's little bow of a mouth and tiny ears.

I will see that she is looked after. I will make certain to honor my promise to Bess. She will have a happy life and make a good marriage. She will be taught all things courtly and be a great lady. And I will set aside some things for her. Things to remind her of who she is. Though not my legitimate daughter, she is a Howard nonetheless and will someday be proud of the fact.

I hold her close, kissing the downy hair. Perhaps I was wrong to keep her from Bess. I will see how long the child lives; if she lives past five, I will allow Bess active participation in her life as her mother. There is a better chance of survival after that age. Meantime we must wait. We must not get too attached.

Yet that night I unlace my shirt and hold her against my bare chest, feeling her little heart beat against mine. I fall asleep with her in my arms.

So much can happen in five years.

BOOK FOUR

The Howard Legacy

Fall from Grace

It has all come to nothing. The plots and the plans, all ended, all over. The king's last pathetic campaign to recapture lost holdings in France was a miserable failure. The reformist queen Catherine Parr still sits the throne despite all efforts to oust her.

My daughter, my beautiful Mary, was given a chance to sit under the canopy of state, but her histrionics in the face of that suggestion were enough to thwart the whole stratagem. It is a night forever emblazoned on my mind, the night Mary refused to be queen. How she carried on, vowing to slit her own throat rather than take part in the villainy of my plot. Then somewhere between the screaming and the struggling, in the midst of our shared insanity I glimpsed her again, shining out of the eyes of my daughter, my princess. In that moment I knew it did not matter that Mary would not become queen, that my dreams had all come to naught. In that moment everything was forgotten between us, all the hate and the confusion. There were no words. For once we did not need words. It was all there, communicated in one pained gaze and betrayed by a parting kiss. For that instant our souls fled their confining bodies, rising and curling and merging like smoke from the flames of our agonizing connection, unable to be viewed as separate beings. But they returned, imprisoned once more. The moment was gone. And then she was gone, back to Kenninghall, back to life, and I was alone just as I have always been alone.

Yet I am consoled. Mary made the right choice; her wild demonstrations saved her from the king. And from me.

I pressed on—I am a Howard; isn't that what Howards do? I schemed and connived because that is what I was bred for. I conspired against the queen. I would have the Protestant bitch brought down, but even convincing charges of heresy against her were dropped in the end. She has a hold on Henry VIII, does this Catherine.

And so I decided if I am failed I'd best join the powers that be. I planned a triple alliance. Two of my son Lord Surrey's daughters were to marry two sons of the prince's uncle Edward Seymour, Lord Hertfords. My Mary was to wed the rakish Tom Seymour. Though she had once refused him, she was eager for the union now. She wanted it, I think. And it would have been a comfort to me to see her married at last. She could have the children she had longed for her entire life . . . but in the end her hotheaded brother confronted her in the Long Gallery at court. He'd have none of his family mixed with the upstart Seymour clan, he cried, and suggested she become the king's mistress should she yearn for such power. No brain in his head, that stupid boy! How could I have sired such an idiot! He made fools of us all and no matches were made nor will ever be made. It is done, all done.

Surrey, my brilliant poet-soldier, my beautiful boy, proved to be the ruin of us all. For all the time I was plotting, he was plotting, and all for the good of the Howards, or so he thought. But Surrey was never as clever as I. Not even close. He was all whimsy, all heart—a bloody romantic fool. I will never be able to comprehend it. Why he quartered his arms with that of Edward the Confessor, a right that is reserved only for kings, why he would risk thinking about kidnapping the little prince, why he would boast so openly about what the Howards would do once we had control of him. . . . If any of those things had even been possible before, they are not now. For my part, a part I did not even play, I am arrested and stripped of all my titles. How thrilled were my peers when they took away my staffs of office and Garter chain! When I declared my allegiance and faithfulness to the king from the barge on the way to the Tower, their lips twitched in suppressed laughter. They did not believe me, I who always served the king before anyone and anything, before my own family! God, and for what? For a cold, damp cell in the Tower.

I have failed. I have failed my father, I have failed my children, I have failed myself. Now, like he once was, I am a prisoner along with my son, who would have succeeded me as fourth duke of Norfolk but who is now condemned to die.

Surrey is to die today and all for being impulsive and foolish. Surrey is to die and I am betrayed. Elizabeth was happy to testify against me, of that there was never a doubt, and for her part I can hardly blame her. But Bess . . . my Bess . . . What did I ever do to her but give her everything she could have wanted? Yes, I took the baby. But I was protecting her! Why couldn't she see that? She said she understood! She never complained or protested, not in three years! She visited the child as much as she wanted; it could not have been a better arrangement, and after while I planned to restore her the child. But she nursed her pain and her hatred, nursed it like the babe I denied her till it grew into a force greater than all of us. How long must she have been waiting for this moment! When asked to recall any statements I may have made against king and country, she remembered. Ah, what clarity of mind did my Bess possess when she relayed my treasonous prediction of the king's impending death! Yes, that and every other offensive statement I ever could have uttered in confidence. And so she betrayed me, betrayed me for a child who is likely to die anyway and leave her with a heartbreak more agonizing than anything I could ever inflict. She will learn that for herself; my protection is no longer hers even if I wanted it to be.

And then there was my Mary . . . foolish little Mary who never knew from one minute to the next what to do. She implicated her brother and tried to save me by pleading my ignorance of his plots. True enough. I was ignorant of his schemes, but if it means saving my life, I will confess to knowing everything. I'll do anything to survive.

Surrey will not. Surrey, who even dared an unsuccessful escape from the Tower, will not survive. He will die for his unswerving pride.

By the window I watch. Below me my son stands in front of the throng, who jeers him and taunts him; Mary is there with his wife, Frances de Vere. The latter's head is buried in my daughter's delicate shoulder.

Surrey kneels before the block . . . oh, God . . . he spreads his arms like angel wings, commending his soul to the Lord. He is just a boy, a foolish twenty-nine-year-old boy-child. I think back to my twenty-ninth year—what did I really know then? Surrey places his head on the block. . . . Five children he is leaving behind, three girls and two boys, two beautiful boys with curly hair. . . . Tears stream down my face as I curl my hands about the painfully freezing grid of bars that are my window. A flash of memory recalls to mind him playing in the gardens with Mary as children. He is placing a garland upon her golden head. . . .

The axe cuts through the air with mortal precision.

I watch my son, my son who once was the baby I held in my arms; I watch his head tumble into the straw. I watch the endless stream of blood flow from the twitching torso, red   ruby necklace he coveted in Mary's childhood nightma   e that foretold our family's doom with brutal accu

Thunderous cannon announces the dea bedridden king. My body convulses with s must Elizabeth be thinking right now? Tha Thank God she has removed to Kenninghal terrible thing!

And Mary, what is my Mary doing? She stands e her brother's lifeless form. She is holding his sobbing   she does not cry; she does nothing.

Oh, God, let the girl cry . . . please let her cry!

She does not. She turns Frances away from the gruesome scene and together they quit the green.

The crowd disperses and the ravens surround my boy. . . .

The room is spinning. Bile is rising in my throat.

So this is where it has all led me.

I cannot stand. I sink onto the bed and lie back before my consciousness is stolen from me along with everything else.

How did I get it all so wrong?

Cannon. Bells. What is happening? I go to the window. Another execution? Footfalls in the hall. My guard bursts in.

"The king is dead—on 28 January, His Majesty passed! Long live King Edward VI!" cries Lieutenant of the Tower Sir John Markham.

I fall to my knees, stretching my arms toward Heaven. "Long live the king!" I cry in turn. I scramble to my feet at once. "Is there any news on my attainder?"

"You remain attainted and thus imprisoned," says Markham, but he is smiling. "But you are no longer to be executed. His Majesty did not sign your death warrant. It appears he would not."

"Then he did love me! In the face of everything—" I cut myself short; this is not a discussion for Markham. "So the Seymours will not release me. Ha! I'm that much of a threat, am I?" I laugh. "I imagine Lord Hertford, the boy king's uncle, is regent?"

"Yes," says Markham. "He has been created lord protector of England and is now the Duke of Somerset."

"God," I say with a smirk. "Well. Fortunes shift all the time, it seems, and mine will, too. In time."

Markham regards me, his expression a mingling of surprise and pity. I turn away from him.

"Thank you, Sir John, for informing me," I tell him as I wave him away, taking comfort in what little power I still retain. "You are dismissed."

With a slight laugh that raises the hairs on my neck, Markham quits the cell.

I sit on the bed and think about the late King Henry, Henry my nephew, Henry my friend. Henry my enemy. Everything I did was to keep his favor; indeed, I would have risked the flames of Hell for him. Had he been a little stronger, would he have had me released?

I'd like to think so.

Bess Holland, Mendham, Suffolk

How strange it should end this way. Just when I believed there was no hope for the duke, he is spared. I am glad. Though I testified against him, my conscience could not have borne his death. Now he resides in the Tower and I am freed from his suffocating love at last.

And yet I am sad. Sad for never saying good-bye, sad for the twenty years given to him that I can never get back, sad for loving him despite everything he was. Sad because he knows my evidence is what sealed his fate. Sad because of the daughter I am denied.

Joy permeates despair, however, and hope prevails over sorrow.

I am to be married. Me, Bessie Holland, Norfolk's whore, is to be married! Someone wants me, someone will still take me!

My brother hastily arranged the match. This summer I shall wed Henry Reppes, an East Anglian justice of the peace. Because of my cooperation in testifying against the duke, I have been granted my lands at Mendham, Suffolk, and all of my jewels have been returned to me, so I will come into this marriage as a *femme sole*. An independent woman of means.

Henry is a fine man close to my age. He is endearingly shy and when he presented me with a dainty gold band to plight our troth, his thick hands trembled. He is a big man, tall and strong with long, well-turned legs. I would not think him to be a JP but rather a hard-working farmer. His blue eyes reflect nothing but kindness, his smile is easy and sweet, and his speech is soft.

There is not a man on this earth more opposite of the duke of Norfolk than this Henry Reppes, and the fact makes me want to skip with joy.

"I hope you are happy with me, Miss Holland," he tells me the night he plights his troth. "I cannot give you much; I am not a wealthy man. But you will always have what you need." He offers a gentle smile. "And you will always have my respect and devotion."

Oh, such fair words! Can I believe them? Has His Grace ever spoken such sweetness? Yes. But it always seemed empty, as though it was just to placate me. I must stop thinking of him. . . .

I am still not quite over the fact that Henry addressed me as Miss Holland. No longer am I called the inaccurate and humiliating Mrs. I am a miss and for once am not ashamed.

"I am most pleased with the match," I tell him, reaching out to squeeze his large hand. "And I will be a loving and faithful wife to you."

His lip quivers. Tears light his blue eyes; they shine brilliant topaz. He leans across the table and takes me in his arms, placing the gentlest of kisses on my mouth. I wrap my arms about his neck, shocked to feel so much affection for a virtual stranger.

We remain locked in that embrace for a long time and I begin to plan for the future I never thought I'd have. We will have a family, Henry and I. And after the wedding I will tell him about Jane, and he will help me retrieve her from Norfolk House.

It seems God in His mercy is giving me a second chance at first love.

Thomas Howard

After a month of imprisonment, I am allowed a visitor. That it should be my Mary seems most appropriate, though our reunion is far from joyous. Surrey's death envelops us in grief; there is no escaping it. How much have I to say to this girl! But the words stick in my throat. They are fool's words anyway, sentiments that would change nothing after all we have endured. There is no point.

So Mary leaves, taking with her all the beauty and light I am permitted to see. It is after her visit that the full impact of my imprisonment hits me like a lance to the chest. I ache all the time. I lie in my bed. I pace the small room on restless legs. Screams from the tortured assault me and I am reminded of past residents of this Tower. They visit me every night, taking turns keeping vigil by my bedside. My nieces Anne and Kitty stand there. Anne's black eyes reflect a mingling of accusation and amusement at my plight. Kitty's blue eyes reflect nothing but her bewildered sense of betrayal. My father stands there sometimes, shaking his head in grave disappointment. My brother Thomas, who wasted away here for the crime of loving the king's niece Margaret Douglas, also appears now and then. His young face registers a sustained anger that chills me to the core.

The two princes are here as well, my little murdered brothers-in-law. Yes, they are here, forever children, and they look up at me, their eyes pleading. *Why?* they ask me. Why do the innocent perish while evil reigns supreme?

Because, children, there are people like me in this world, and as long as there are, the innocent will expire. There is no room for innocence, no room for the pure. God calls the good to His bosom and leaves existence to the rest of us.

My princess comes. She stands at the foot of my bed, her face wrought with sadness. Her eyes assault me with questions. *What happened to you?*

You died, I answer. You died and left me alone! Any chance of redemption resides somewhere in the faery country, never to be reclaimed.

I reach out to touch her, but as with all these specters, she fades away and I am grasping air.

I lie back in bed, throwing my arm over my eyes to blot out the images. Tears wet my sleeve. Someone is screaming from the dungeons below.

Surely I am in Hell.

In March I am granted a better "suite" of rooms with servants to attend me, clothing befitting my station, and more freedom. I can now take brief walks with the lieutenant. I am even permitted a visit from my wife. I had not seen her in years and find myself struck by her beauty. Her figure is as trim as a girl's; her dark hair is lustrous without a streak of gray, her skin is so smooth. . . . My God, did I never see it? How is it a woman her age can be so beautiful and well preserved? Though she betrayed me, a fact I will never forget, I am glad to see her. Our exchange is full of the same biting wit and I am rejuvenated.

We do not spend much time discussing Surrey; it is a topic far too painful for both of us. Instead she is thrilled to inform me of Bess's impending wedding. I hide my shock behind an impervious mask and let Elizabeth revel in her triumph. But when she leaves, I sink onto the bed and stare at the wall, allowing icy tears to slither down my cheeks. Bess has not waited even six months to secure a match. How could I have not perceived the depth of her hatred?

Elizabeth was right to mock me. What a laughingstock I have become.

She returns now and again, sometimes with my Mary, sometimes without. I cannot help it. My heart races when she enters the room. When she arrives one autumn afternoon with an armful of books, I must refrain from running to her.

She stands smart in her russet gown, looking at least ten years younger than her fifty years. Her blue eyes sparkle with mischief and mockery.

"For your pleasure, my lord," she tells me, handing me the books. "I was told you said you couldn't sleep the past dozen years without reading. Surely you do not count the Scriptures among your repertoire?"

I laugh. "I memorized enough verse to instill guilt in the children. It does not suit me to delve further."

She graces me with a smile and I am reminded of the little girl I danced with so many years ago. "No, I suppose it would be rather hypocritical," she says.

"So," I begin. "It seems all I own has been plundered by the Seymours and their vultures. My lands, my jewels, everything."

"Yes," she replies. "What doesn't belong to the Crown has been divided among Somerset and his cronies. It's a sad day for the Howards." Her face registers genuine pity. "But I have done fair enough and have a little to sustain me. Bess was compensated as well for her troubles," she is compelled to add.

I stifle a scathing retort. With the lieutenant never far away, I am not able to be as free in my speech as I could have been were we alone.

"Everyone profits from another's demise," I comment.

"You certainly did," she says. "For many years."

"I suppose I did," I agree.

"You know, you're still handsome as the very Devil," she says in low tones. She approaches me and takes my hands. A lump swells in my throat. I swallow several times. "All those years of cavorting with him has done you some good," she adds as she leans forward to kiss me. I return it. Her lips are soft and familiar, filled with that old fire and passion. I find myself wrapping my arms about her slim frame and pulling her close. I want her. Suddenly, there is no one on earth I want more than this woman, my wife.

We clasp each other a long moment. There is a tap at the door. Her visit is at an end.

She draws back, offering that same mocking smile before turning away. As she reaches the door, I am compelled to say, "Elizabeth . . . do you remember when you were but a girl and we were celebrating the birth of poor Catherine of Aragon's little prince?" She pauses, her back still turned to me. "The crowds turned wild and stole our clothes. Thomas Knyvet was bare-arsed by the end of that affair."

She offers a slight laugh, turning to face me. Her blue eyes are soft with tears. "Those old crones were stealing my sleeves when you rescued me. I thought you were a hero then."

I bow my head. I cannot bear looking at her. "Elizabeth . . ."

"Yes, Thomas?" she asks in a small voice. If I closed my eyes, I'd believe she was the little twelve-year-old I rescued all those years ago.

What is there to say? Sorry? Am I sorry? If I had the chance to do it all again, wouldn't I do everything the same way? There is no going back, no righting wrongs. There are no second chances.

"Take care, Elizabeth," I tell her.

She turns her head and nods before quitting the room, leaving me alone again.

Bess Holland Reppes

I am married! I am a bride and a happier bride cannot be found. The world is full of beauty and hope and my husband's gentle love. I am thirty-seven years old but run with the love madness of a girl. Within six months of marriage, my womb has quickened with his child and we await the birth of our baby with joy. The midwife—how I wish it were Tsura Goodman—is a woman ten years my junior, but she is capable and kind. I tell my husband—oh, the pleasure of saying that word, *husband*—I will have no wet nurses about. I will care for my own child, and all the children who follow, myself. He does not fight me on a thing. How strange to have such an agreeable partner!

I have not forgotten the duke or his family. Henry is teaching me to read and write, and Mary Fitzroy and I keep correspondence. She is very patient with my poor spelling and worse handwriting! She tells me she has been awarded custody of her late brother's five children and has removed to Reigate to raise and educate them. There she has found respite with her aunt and uncle and is enjoying a friendship with the children's tutor, John Foxe. She is most happy with the religious reforms King Edward VI's government is making. Always a devout girl, Mary is finally allowed the freedom of practicing the Protestant faith. She has found peace at last, and my heart surges with happiness for my dear friend.

I have not made many new friends yet. My husband and I have been far too involved with each other to socialize, which suits me well. There will be plenty enough time for that later.

This pregnancy is too hard on me to entertain as it is. Often I have the queer sensation that the baby is going to fall out of me. It sits so low in my belly that I am fraught with discomfort. Unlike my easy confinement with Jane, I am ill most of the time with bad bile and cannot take in much nourishment. My husband dotes on me, feeding me broth with his own hand and swabbing my burning forehead with cool cloths whenever I take a fever.

I thank God on my knees every day that He has been so forgiving, that, despite my past sins with the duke, I am still allowed to know this great love.

"You are happy, Mrs. Reppes?" my husband likes to ask as he rubs my swollen belly.

I look up into his gentle blue eyes, eyes that do not know how to deceive, eyes that cannot conceive of cruelty, and tell him, "Yes, Mr. Reppes—there is no woman on earth so happy as me."

And there isn't.

Elizabeth Howard

Antagonizing Thomas in the Tower assuages my grief for Surrey; indeed it is about as close to Heaven as I have ever gotten. I cannot help it. I thrive on our visits. Knowing he is a prisoner as I was for so many years fills me with a sweet sense of satisfaction that I know is unholy. Despite this I cannot deny myself the immense pleasure I derive from his misery.

And yet when I see him, my breath catches in my throat. I kiss him, I embrace him, we fire back our timeless witticisms and insults and I know that whatever has been between us, I am relieved he has not been killed. I am glad he is safe and made to reflect upon his many sins. I pray he will receive forgiveness. As time passes I realize that I do not wish any more ill will on Thomas Howard.

When not with Thomas, I enjoy the freedom I have not known these past thirteen years. I visit my sisters and their families. I have even called upon Catherine and Ralph. No more does my heart race for the earl of Westmorland. I am at peace.

In the spring of 1548 I receive a most unusual dispatch from a breathless messenger of one JP called Henry Reppes. The name rings familiar. Reppes. Yes, of course. Bess Holland's husband. What on earth could they want with me?

I take the dispatch with trembling hands.

> *Lady Norfolk,*
> *I do not write well and my hand is very poor but I*
> *knew I must find some way to reach you. I have taken ill*
> *unto death. I have no right to ask anything of you but I*
> *pray God works forgiveness in your heart and you will see*
> *me. Please come straight away. There is much to say and*
> *little time.*
> *Your obedient servant,*
> *Elizabeth Reppes*

Bess is ill—gravely ill. I repeat this to myself several times. My rival of twenty years, the woman who put me out of house and home, the woman who claimed my husband's heart almost above all others and drove him to distraction, wants to see me. Why? Does she seek absolution for her many grievous sins? What gives me the authority to grant it?

And yet if I do not go to her, what kind of Christian am I? Does not the Lord command us to forgive in order to be forgiven? What kind of courage must Bess possess to seek me out and make peace?

But do I forgive her? I want to be a good Christian. Catherine of Aragon forgave Anne Boleyn and the king even as she rallied against their ill-fated liaison. Have I not always striven to follow my long-suffering queen's example? Is this not what she would want me—no, *command* me—to do?

I am not going to her of my own will. As I call for my cloak and coach, I realize a force much stronger than I is drawing me to the deathbed of Elizabeth Holland Reppes.

I go in secret, taking only my most faithful servant to attend me. I do not know what my family and friends would make of the visit so decide discretion is the best course. I laugh at the irony. For years I did the unthinkable, railing against a cherished system and airing my grievances to God and the king and anyone who would listen. And now I choose secrecy. Now my purpose is veiled in anonymity. But it is as it should be. God knows I am here, after all, and His is the only opinion that matters.

When I arrive at Mendham, I am led to Bess's bedchamber. She lies there, white-blond hair matted to her forehead with sweat, eyelids fluttering as she mutters something incoherent to the nurse who swabs her forehead. Her agonized husband sits beside her, gripping her hand, tears streaming down his handsome face.

"Oh, Bess, Bess, Bess," he murmurs over and over. "Don't leave me, please don't leave me. . . ."

"The Duchess of Norfolk," announces a servant as I am shown into the room.

Henry Reppes rises and offers a bow.

I curtsy. "Dear sir, how sorry I am to meet you under these circumstances."

"There are no words to express my gratitude that you have chosen to come," he tells me. "Bess has been calling for you these past three days." His voice catches. "It has been a terrible time, my lady."

"It is childbed fever." It is not a question.

He nods as he dissolves into sobs.

"The baby?" I ask.

"Our son was born dead," he informs me, burying his face in his hands.

I rush toward him, enfolding the poor man in my arms. "Oh, my dear, trust that God has taken him to His bosom," I tell him, stroking his blond hair. "And understand from one who has lost much that you will know happiness and peace again. That you can get through this."

He draws back, regarding me with bewildered blue eyes.

"Now go rest and take in some nourishment. I will keep company with Bess and send for you should her condition change," I tell him.

In a haze the man allows himself to be escorted from the room by a doting steward.

I relieve the nurse, taking the cool cloth from her hand and swabbing Bess's forehead. Never in my wildest fantasies would I ever have seen myself in this place. And now that I am here, I derive no satisfaction from it, no perverse pleasure in my rival's suffering. I look upon her, this wronged girl, and see nothing but a woman who reached out for happiness. To my surprise I thank God that she found it, if only for a little while.

"Bess," I say in soft tones. "Bess, it is the duchess of Norfolk. Can you hear me?"

Bess flinches at the word *Norfolk* and stirs, forcing her eyes open. The brown orbs are glazed over; the whites are yellow. She stares at me a long moment, drawing me into focus, then offers a timid smile.

"My lady . . . you came," she murmurs.

I take her hand, nodding. She offers a faint squeeze.

"I did many bad things to you," she tells me.

"Yes," I agree. I will not lie but neither will I treat her with a malice I no longer feel.

"But the very worst thing was that . . . I never stood up," she says. "I never stood up . . . instead I stood by. I stood by while the duke tortured and imprisoned you. I stood by while he ruined my own life, a life I turned over to him for the sake of a girlish infatuation that turned cold all too quickly and ended in hate."

"It's all right now," I tell her. "The duke cannot hurt anyone anymore."

"My lady." Her voice is very weak; it is pulled forth in a raspy whisper. "My lady, I have lost my son and I have lost my daughter."

"Your daughter?" I tilt a brow in confusion. Is she yielding to delusions?

"Oh, my lady, yes . . . the very worst thing. I stole from the duke a daughter. She was born in forty-three. Her name is Jane Goodman and she resides at Norfolk House." Bess takes in a deep breath. "I never got to say good-bye. Will you see her for me? Will you tell her . . . ?" She gasps. Her eyes are wild with fear as she grapples with the reality of leaving this world.

"I'll tell her," I say in urgency. I stroke her burning cheek. "You must not worry, Bess. I'll take care of everything."

"I'll not ask your forgiveness," Bess goes on. She raises her hand and removes from her finger a heavy signet ring bearing a lion with an arrow piercing its tongue. I recognize it in an instant as the ring my duke bestowed upon each of us at different times in his turbulent life. "But I will give you back another thing I stole. Please take it. It belonged to you first and belongs to you last."

I take the ring but do not put it on. Instead I tuck it into the pocket of my gown.

I rise. "I shall send for your husband now, darling. He will want to be beside you."

She smiles. "Oh, yes. My husband . . . my dear, sweet husband . . . how I love to say that word. . . ."

In that instant I realize that for years Bess was as much a prisoner as I. Charity and compassion surge through me as I seize her hand in mine and press it to my lips.

"Bess, you do not have to ask for my forgiveness," I tell her. "Because you have it. Always."

Tears stream down Bess's cheeks unchecked. Her hand relaxes in mine. She closes her eyes. Her head lolls to one side.

I kiss her hand once more, then lay it at her side.

Quietly, I quit the room as her husband brushes past me screaming, "Bess, no! Oh, Bess, no!"

My steps quicken as I make my retreat. I reach in my pocket. The signet ring is warm in my hand. Hot tears stream down my cheeks for Thomas's former mistress, tears I never thought I'd shed.

Oh, God, take her home. Put to rest the sweet soul of Bess Holland Reppes.

Gratia Dei, Sum Quod Sum!

Thomas Howard

When Mary imparted the news of my Bess's death I cried. I did not think I would cry. After my daughter left, however, and I was quite alone, I found the tears that fell for my betrayer would not stop. Now she is dead. I cannot even restore her our daughter. It is too late. Like all my life, too late.

I had loved the girl in my way. She was pretty and sweet. She gave me a semblance of joy for many years. I cannot say I did the same for her. Her betrayal made it clear that things were otherwise.

It is just another wrong I cannot right.

The years put themselves between her death and me, and I live out my imprisonment taking pleasure in the few visitors I am allowed to see: Mary, Elizabeth, and my son Thomas, who, though we never had much use for each other, treats me with a begrudging respect nonetheless.

And then in 1553 my godson, King Edward VI, dies of consumption. The bells toll and London erupts into chaos as another resident joins me in the Tower. Her name is Jane Grey, so-called queen of England. Edward had named her his successor and for nine days she rules with her husband, Guildford Dudley—of course she does no such thing. Her ambitious father-in-law, John Dudley, Duke of Northumberland, rules through her.

It is short-lived. Mary Tudor takes London by storm and the Tower that little Jane Grey was to celebrate her coronation in now serves as her prison. The daughter of Henry VIII and Catherine of Aragon conquers with the spirit of her royal parents, and one of the first things she does as queen is release a group of prestigious prisoners from the Tower.

I am among them.

The day of 4 August dawns bright and sunny. As I kneel at the Tower gates beside old friend and fellow inmate Bishop Gardiner, Queen Mary, the image of her Spanish mother, leans down and places a gentle kiss on my forehead. I look up at her. My liberator is obscured by the sun.

She holds my face in her hands. "Rise, Duke of Norfolk. You are free and you will be restored to our council. You will serve as our earl marshal and lord high steward as well."

"God bless and keep Your Majesty," I say automatically as I immediately begin to make plans for the grand coronation banquet I will throw her. I will prove indispensable to her; she will never regret freeing me.

It is almost too much to digest. After six and a half long years, I am free! Free! With effort my aching legs permit me to rise and I stand straight and proud as I survey the crowd of cheering onlookers. I search out the faces of my Mary and my Elizabeth, who wait for me in the throng.

When we find each other, Mary embraces me fast and I hug her in turn.

"*Gratia Dei, sum quod sum!*" I cry. "By the grace of God, I am what I am!"

Mary pulls away, her face alight with a radiant smile. The cloak of her beauty envelops me, warming my soul, and all I can do is stare into her face. Oh, Mary . . . my dearest girl. At last I force myself to turn away and face my longtime adversary.

Elizabeth stands composed and calm, her smile filled with the same mockery that has sustained me through my years of imprisonment.

"I have been called to wait upon Her Majesty," she tells me.

"I am glad of it," I tell her with sincerity as I reach out to squeeze her hands. It is quite a relief to have my wife in favor with the Crown once more.

I turn about a moment, invigorated and rejuvenated. I have survived. I have survived!

I begin to laugh.

Of course I have survived, I think to myself. I am Thomas Howard.

Elizabeth Howard

Thomas has swept in with his usual confidence and commences with as much speed as possible to prove himself the same cold-hearted bastard I love to hate. One of the first things he is called to do is oversee the trial of the Duke of Northumberland, whom he is happy to condemn to death for his part in the Jane Grey fiasco.

Thomas did not forget Northumberland's part in securing his imprisonment, nor did he forget the lands he stole from him afterward. For these crimes more than anything else, Thomas ordered a traitor's death for the poor duke.

After the demise of Northumberland, Thomas decided that the education our Mary was giving his grandchildren was inadequate and radical, removing them from her care. The heartbroken girl delivered them herself and Thomas set to making plans for his heir, Surrey's son Thomas, by placing him in Lord Chancellor Gardiner's household as a page.

He is at the top of his form.

Together, Thomas and I attend Her Majesty at her coronation banquet, an exquisite affair my lord arranged for her pleasure.

At one point in the evening, the queen seeks me out and embraces me. "I want to thank you, Lady Norfolk," she tells me as she pulls away. Tears are streaming down her cheeks.

"Your Majesty!" I exclaim. "Please don't cry. 'Tis such a happy day."

She bows her head. "If only my mother had lived to see her dream come true at last. I have been rightfully restored and I triumphed over her enemies. I will never forget your faithfulness to my mother, Lady Norfolk. Know that in turn you will always have my gratitude and protection."

"I thank Your gracious Majesty," I say as I dip into a deep curtsy. I send up a prayer to my queen Catherine that her daughter may rule with the same grace and conviction that she did.

In early 1554, Queen Mary sends my husband to quell Thomas Wyatt's rebellion against her impending marriage to Philip of Spain along with the plot to reinstate Jane Grey as queen of England. He is unsuccessful in his military engagement, but the rebellion is squashed after his retreat and he is celebrated as a hero nonetheless.

Queen Mary comes down on the rebels with the mercilessness of her ruthless father, condemning Thomas Wyatt to death, imprisoning her sister Princess Elizabeth in the Tower for her suspected participation, and even ordering the deaths of poor little Jane Grey, her father, and her husband. Jane Grey and Guildford Dudley had been residing in the Tower since the beginning of her reign and it was thought by all they would be released and pardoned. It is an unjustifiable tragedy. All knew the girl was completely innocent and perished only because of her father's ambitious plotting. The parallels between him and my Thomas cause me to shudder in revulsion.

I begin to fear this queen. She does not demonstrate her mother's understanding or forgiving nature. The years spent under her father's cruel shadow took their toll, and the queen who has emerged from the abused girl is a terrifying one.

But I am loyal to her nonetheless. She is my Catherine's daughter and I must try and guide her with as much subtlety as I can.

Thomas takes ill after the failed rebellion and we retire to Kenninghall for the summer.

"I'll return to court when I am better," he tells me.

"Of course," I say, but as I lock eyes with those hard black orbs, I know he is lying. And he knows it, too.

"Elizabeth . . ." Thomas sits on his bed and holds his arm out. I sit beside him and allow him to enfold me to his chest. "Will you do something for me?"

I nod, swallowing an unexpected onset of tears.

"Will you send for my Mary?" he asks.

Mary. Mary, who has been so wronged by this man, Mary who just now had to sacrifice the children she loved more than her own soul to Thomas's desires, Mary, who I have never allowed myself to love . . . Yes, of course he would want to see his Mary.

"Yes, my lord," I tell him. "I shall send for her directly."

The girl is mortally ill, that much is certain. She arrives hunched over in a Tudor green gown her father had made for her years ago, gripping a stomach that curses her with endless pain. Upon seeing me, she tries to right herself before dipping into a curtsy.

I seize her hands, pulling her toward me into an embrace. "Oh, Mary . . ." I say as I hold her close. "How much I have missed you . . . how much do I long to love you as I should have so many years ago."

She pulls away, reaching up to stroke my face. Her sweet little countenance is surrounded by a halo of golden hair. Her green eyes shine like emeralds.

"How much do I share that longing, lady Mother," she tells me in her tiny voice.

"Then you will stay with me," I say, pulling her to me once more. "You will stay with me and let me take care of you. Let me be the mother I never was."

"It is my greatest desire," says the girl as she buries her head in the crook of my shoulder.

I stroke the honey blond hair and sway from side to side. "Your father wishes to see you."

She pulls away, blinking rapidly. "My father . . . my Norfolk." She bows her head.

I shudder and pretend not to have heard the agony in the last words as I guide her to his bedchamber.

When Mary emerges hours later, she clutches a little silver circlet in her trembling hands. Tears stream down her cheeks unchecked and she turns toward me, green eyes lit with helpless despair.

"How will I live without him?" she asks me.

"You will," I tell her firmly. "You will because you *can*. At last, Mary, you will be allowed to truly *live*."

Mary is distracted and averts her head, shaking it as though she cannot comprehend the thought of life without her Norfolk.

It is a life I have spent many an hour dreaming of and yet now that it is so near, I find myself in mourning.

When I am reassured that Mary is being cared for, I enter Thomas's apartments and close the doors, taking my place at his bedside and busying my fidgety hands by mending a shirt long since cast aside.

"I don't know why you're bothering," he says. "I'm not wearing it again."

I sigh. "Then someone else will," I tell him. "It's a fine shirt."

He offers a slight laugh, then to my astonishment reaches out to still my wrist, keeping his fingers encircled about it. I wait for the pain but none comes. His touch is light. His eyes are grave.

"Mary . . ." he begins. "I fear for her."

"I am disappointed. Such a break in tradition is almost unworthy of you," I say with a slight sneer. It is too late to regret the words.

"She's—she's—"

"She's dying," I finish, keeping my voice hard and myself harder so that I might bear it.

His face is stricken. "You will take care of her?"

I offer a frenzied nod. "You would ask me to take charge of her now, after denying us a connection almost since her birth." I cannot go on. I bow my head.

"What's done is done," he says in gruff tones. "She is the best of us," he adds then, his voice softer. His head sinks back onto the pillows. He closes his eyes a long moment, expelling a heavy sigh. "The very best."

"Yes."

"Which leaves us." His tone is all business once more. "Why do you stay, Elizabeth?" he asks as he opens his eyes, revealing the impenetrable black orbs I know so well. I smile at the sight.

"I am just one of many circling vultures, my lord," I say.

"You're not getting a thing," he says, and though his voice rings with the slightest humor, there is no doubt of his seriousness. He has not forgotten my betrayal. It does not matter. I have not forgotten his. In any event, I am well taken care of.

"Believe me, there is nothing of yours that I want," I return, my cool voice tinged with amusement. "Nothing that I don't already have: the children and grandchildren."

He searches my face. "Elizabeth . . ." He averts his eyes, drawing in a wavering breath.

Something in his tone evokes a peculiar gentleness in me. I find my hand entwining his. In the fading light, it is difficult to tell whose fingers are whose. He reaches up and with a trembling hand strokes my cheek.

"If I could have been the man I was before things—happened," he begins slowly, "or someone else altogether, someone common . . ." He drops his hand. "Everything was wrong."

I cannot speak past the sudden lump in my throat.

"We were cursed from the beginning," he goes on.

"No," I tell him. "No one was cursed; there is no shifting responsibility for our miseries onto some divine fancy. We made our own hells and any chance at happiness we could have had, we drove away like beggars from a feast. We had everything, Thomas. Wealth, children . . . at one time even love." I lower my eyes. "But that wasn't enough." I return my gaze to him. His face is void of its usual indifference; he appears wistfully engaged. "It was never enough. Before your love for any living being came your ambition. It ruled over you with more stricture than God and king alike and proved your ultimate undoing. You wanted favor. You wanted power. If you couldn't have that, you would exert your control over anyone you considered less than yourself: Bess—poor Bess, whom you used as a distraction from your clever wife and beloved daughter—me, your nieces, the poor dead queens." I pause. "And Mary, of course."

I draw in another breath. "And all the while, even as I hated you I loved you, Thomas, God knows how much." I shake my head. "I followed you everywhere you allowed me to go; I'd have gone to the very depths of Hell with you." I offer a rueful smile. "I believe I did on one or two occasions." The smile fades. "But you made it irrefutably clear that I was not your chosen accompaniment. So I found another way. If I couldn't have you, I would have my revenge—in denying you your divorce, I would keep you from the person I thought you wanted most." I offer a bitter laugh. "But it was the wrong person. For all your love of her, for all the desire that had you running mad, it was never Bess who could claim your heart. No, in that, God was truly cruel. Your greatest love was delivered in forbidden form—your 'princess' reborn in your own daughter Mary."

Thomas is silent a long moment. At last he draws in a wavering breath. "You knew it, too." His voice is just above a whisper.

"I've known since you were ill with the sweat, when you called her name above all others." I look away, unable to bear the tears that are now streaming down his craggy cheeks.

"It was not unholy." His voice is so thick with sadness that my eyes are once again riveted to him. "It was not . . . I would never—"

"Oh, Thomas, I know that," I tell him in soft tones. I draw in a breath. "It is a strange thing, the human heart, this chaotic heart that lusts and yearns and envies. It is immune to logic. There is no sense of right or wrong. It keeps its own counsel; the paths it travels are secret, sometimes even to the mind that claims dominion over it. It goes where it will and we can only rein it in with the commandments set by God and the laws put down by men." I gaze at him pointedly. "We put the limits on one another. We draw the boundaries. But those boundaries and limits serve to protect only what is physical. Nothing can curb the emotions; nothing can stop the raging torment in the soul. And that torment raged in all of us. How we suffered for it . . . but, Thomas, I think you suffered most of all."

"Oh, Elizabeth," Thomas whispers, sitting up and placing his hand on my cheek. I look into his face and cannot find in it the savage old man of so many years past. He is the knight who won the day at the joust, the man whose power and energy surged through my twelve-year-old hand and into my woman's heart when he danced with me. He is the father of my children, the man I am fated to spend my eternity with because I would be nowhere else. For all that he was, for all that he is, for all that he can never be, he is mine. I am glad he is mine.

"Do you know why you were hardest to love?" he asks me then. I shake my head.

"Because you were me," he whispers.

"That's strange," I tell him, touching his face in turn. "Because that was the very reason I loved you."

"Always at odds," he says.

"Always."

He draws me to him, pressing his lips to mine, and I yield, wrapping my arms about his neck, tracing his strong shoulders, stroking his thick silvery hair. For a long moment we cling to each other thus, lost in the passion that has always served as our catalyst for destruction and delight.

When at last we part, I rise and dip into a curtsy. "Good-bye, Thomas Howard," I tell him.

"Good-bye, my lady wife," he says. Then, to my retreating back he says, "Elizabeth."

I turn.

His face is filled with the words; it is all there, naked, assailable, raw. He parts his lips. My heart catches in my throat, racing in anticipation. Still he does not say it.

"I know," I whisper at last.

And I leave him.

He does not die in my arms but leaves this world clinging to the hand of his steward, George Holland, Bess's brother. I am told only a single word left his lips as he succumbed to his mortality: *Princess.*

When the will is read and I am predictably excluded, I do not protest. Mary is provided for and thanked for her appeals in trying to secure his release from the Tower, and the grandchildren are provided for. And little Jane Goodman is awarded one hundred pounds for her upbringing and marriage.

He did not have to leave me anything. He knew well his death would afford me my life to live as my own at last. I can ask for nothing more.

At his interment, I stand by the grand effigy that lies upon his sarcophagus. I run my hand along the collar of medallions that graces its neck where is carved Thomas's motto, *"Gratia Dei, sum quod sum!"*

By the Grace of God, I am what I am.

He was just that.

Norfolk House

Jane Goodman, Winter 1555

A great lady is coming to see me today, the Dowager Duchess of Norfolk. I am beside myself with curiosity and excitement. Could it be I am being called to attend her? I am told to be on my best behavior. My foster brother William warns me I must not betray my stupidity. I hope I succeed—I am a hopelessly stupid girl and cannot bear the thought of disgracing myself.

I wear my best gown, a sumptuous pink damask affair trimmed with ivory lace; it was from my good aunt Bess Holland, who left me everything after she died. How much do I miss her! I did not know her well. I was but five when she passed. But I remember her laugh—her beautiful, rippling laugh. And her softness. I loved to sit on her lap and cuddle with her.

At fourteen, I do not fill out the gown as I imagine my curvaceous aunt must have. I am diminutive in stature and slim as a willow wand. My black hair cascades down my back in thick waves. I stare down my reflection in the glass. I wish I didn't have such deep black eyes. Obsidian, William calls them. Colorless, I call them—I always wanted blue eyes or green. I shrug. I suppose I am pretty enough. Many say I will be a stunning beauty when I am older, so I take comfort in that.

I enter the parlor to meet the duchess, who is seated before the fire. She is a woman of extraordinary beauty and grace, and as I dip into my practiced curtsy, I begin to tremble.

All color drains from her face when her gaze falls upon me. She closes her eyes and draws in a deep breath. "Sit, Jane," she tells me in low tones.

I obey, arranging my gown about my feet and hoping I do not appear a grand fool.

"Do you know who I am?" she asks me.

"Yes," I say. "You are the Dowager Duchess of Norfolk."

"Indeed," she says. "Now. Do you know who you are?"

The question confounds me. "God's body, of course I know who I am!" I cry, unable to contain my annoyance. "I am Jane Goodman!" I am stunned by my bold response and clamp a hand over my mouth. "Meaning no disrespect, my lady," I say, hoping to redeem myself. "It's just that I do not understand."

She laughs and shakes her head. She reaches into the pocket of her red velvet gown and holds out a signet ring that bears a mighty lion with its tongue pierced through by an arrow. "Do you know who owned this ring?"

I shake my head.

"This ring belonged to your father," she tells me.

"Oh, no," I say, admiring it. "He could never own a ring so fine."

"The duke of Norfolk loved fine things," she informs me.

It takes me a long moment to digest what she is telling me. When the duchess sees that I comprehend her implication, she goes on.

"But one of the finest by far was your mother, Bess Holland," she says. Tears light her penetrating blue eyes. For a moment she averts her head.

"My lady . . ." I murmur, unsure of what to say, what to do, what to feel.

I knew I was a fosterling. I accepted the story the Goodmans told me about my parents dying of plague when I was a wee girl. Yet did I? As I sift through my racing emotions, I begin to realize I did not. That somewhere, in a deep place I never acknowledged, I had always known I belonged to the Howards in a way that could not be explained. I have no logic to support the thought. A memory stirs, ancient, a woman holding me, telling me in a tiny voice, "I am Bess Holland . . . I am your mother, and the great duke of Norfolk is your father. . . ." These words could never have been spoken, not really. It is some wild fantasy I have convinced myself of as reality. And yet it is true. It has always been true. And I knew it.

The duchess faces me once more. Her strong countenance reveals a woman who has learned to endure and prevail over the greatest obstacles. Admiration surges through me as I regard her.

"You will tell me of them?" I ask her as tears begin to warm my eyes. I allow them to fall unchecked down my cheeks. I slide from my chair to the floor and sit at her feet.

She smiles. "Yes," she says. "I will tell you of them. I will tell you of them and of your cunning cousin, Anne Boleyn. I will tell you of your other cousin, the beautiful Kitty Howard, and of your sweet sister Mary. I will tell you of the kings and queens from whom you descend." She reaches out and takes my hand, then slides the signet ring upon my middle finger. It is weighty with history. "Today, Jane, you will know all. Some of it is far from pleasant, but I have avowed to always speak the truth. Can you appreciate that?"

"With all my heart," I tell her with fervency.

And so she begins.

Further Reading

Elton, G. R. *England Under the Tudors*, Third Edition. London: Routledge, 1991.

Elton, G. R. *The Tudor Constitution: Documents and Commentary*, Second Edition. Cambridge University Press, 1995.

Hackett, Francis. *Henry the Eighth*. Garden City, NY: Garden City Publishing Co., 1931.

Head, David M. *The Ebbs and Flows of Fortune: The Life of Thomas Howard, Third Duke of Norfolk*. Athens, GA: University of Georgia Press, 1995.

Hutchinson, Robert. *The Last Days of Henry VIII: Conspiracy, Treason, and Heresy at the Court of the Dying Tyrant*. New York: William Morrow, 2005.

Loades, David M. *Two Tudor Conspiracies*, Second Edition. Bangor, Wales: Headstart History Publishing, 1992.

Nott, George Frederick, D.D., F.S.A. *The Works of Henry Howard, Earl of Surrey, and of Sir Thomas Wyatt the Elder*, 2 vols. New York: AMS Press Inc., 1965.

Warnicke, Retha M. *The Rise and Fall of Anne Boleyn: Family Politics at the Court*. Cambridge University Press, 2004.

Weir, Alison. *Henry VIII: The King and His Court*. New York: Ballantine Books, 2001.

RIVALS IN
THE TUDOR COURT

D. L. Bogdan

ABOUT THIS GUIDE

The suggested questions are included to
enhance your group's reading of D. L. Bogdan's
Rivals in the Tudor Court.

DISCUSSION QUESTIONS

1. Explain Thomas Howard's descent of character. What were the key factors in his life that contributed to his moral and spiritual decline? Did he ever redeem himself?

2. Is there anything in this novel that supports the theory of nature vs. nurture? Was Thomas's nature predetermined genetically or was he solely a product of his environment?

3. Elizabeth, as a sufferer of domestic violence, was ahead of her time in that she reached out to several sources for help, including Privy Seal Cromwell. Was she a heroine or a victim? Did she have any real allies in her life?

4. Catherine of Aragon seemed to be a consistent source of contention in Thomas and Elizabeth's marriage. Compare and contrast Elizabeth's and Thomas's relationships with this formidable woman.

5. Throughout the story, Thomas and Elizabeth's relationship undergoes many changes. Note the turning points in their marriage. Did they love each other?

6. Compare and contrast Thomas's attitude before and after he attained the title duke of Norfolk.

7. Bess Holland's position as mistress and servant is not an unusual one for the times. Why did she stay? Did she love Thomas?

8. Bess also undergoes changes in character throughout the novel. Did she become stronger or weaker?

9. Compare and contrast Thomas's relationships with Anne Boleyn and Catherine Howard. Did he love either of his nieces?

10. Did the women in this story, Bess, Elizabeth, and Mary Howard, do the right thing by testifying against Thomas at his trial?

11. The novel focuses on some mystical elements, touching on reincarnation in the subplot involving Princess Anne Plantagenet and Norfolk's daughter Mary Howard. Do you believe in reincarnation? Why do you think the author chose to portray this subplot this way?

12. Compare and contrast Thomas's relationship with his first wife and family as opposed to his second.

13. Did Thomas love Henry VIII or was the king simply a channel for his ambition?

14. Did Thomas's time in the Tower change him in any fundamental ways?

15. Did Thomas and Elizabeth find forgiveness for each other by the novel's end or was it merely a deathbed truce?

16. What is the relevance of Thomas's signet ring for him, Elizabeth, and Bess?